WE ARE
ALL LIARS

Carys Jones is a thriller writer based in Shropshire where she lives with her husband, daughter and dog. When she's not writing she can often be found indulging two of her greatest passions: either walking round the local woodland or catching up on all things Disney-related.

www.carys-jones.com

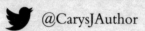 @CarysJAuthor

WE ARE
ALL LIARS

Carys Jones

ORION

First published in Great Britain in 2021 by Orion Fiction,
an imprint of The Orion Publishing Group Ltd,
Carmelite House, 50 Victoria Embankment
London EC4Y 0DZ

An Hachette UK Company

1 3 5 7 9 10 8 6 4 2

A CIP catalogue record for this book is
available from the British Library.

ISBN (Paperback) 978 1 4091 9601 3
ISBN (eBook) 978 1 4091 9602 0

Typeset by Born Group
Printed and bound in Great Britain by Clays Ltd, Elcograf S.p.A.

www.orionbooks.co.uk

To R.G.

'The companions of our childhood always possess a certain power over our minds which hardly any later friend can obtain.'

Mary Shelley, *Frankenstein*

Prologue

'A dreamer, an adventurer, a seductress, a princess and a rebel.' Stephanie Hayworth drank in every moment of her time in front of the camera as she spoke with the overly made-up reporter.

'You knew them well?'

'They were . . . perfect.' There really was no other word for it. Stephanie pushed back her shoulders and pulled her thin lips into a self-satisfied smile. She imagined the people at home, sitting on their sagging sofas, gazing at their grotesquely large television screens, eyes widening and slack jaws dropping even lower when they saw her face. Her name. She was on *the news*. She'd made it.

She'd need to call her mother. Her sister. Even her dope of an ex-husband. Everybody needed to bear witness to her moment of glory. She was on *television* talking about *them*. Finally some attention, some chance to bask in their reflected glow.

Because they *were* perfect, the Fierce Five. They were the girls everyone wanted to be at school, a walking shampoo advert. They always wore the right shoes, went to the best parties. But theirs was a club of extremely elitist member-ship – there was only room for five.

Stephanie had spent so many hours of her life watching them through her thick glasses, studying their every move. Coveting them.

Did they even know she existed? Did it even matter now?

'They were perfect?' the reporter pouted her ruby-red lips and arched a militantly plucked eyebrow at Stephanie. The quaffed hair and cloud of Chanel No. 5 was a testament to the reporter's own pursuit of perfection.

'Perfect.' Stephanie felt a warm glow flicker along her pale skin. Talking about them always made her feel this way. Proximity to greatness. And now everyone would know that she knew them. That she regarded them as friends. That when the BBC showed up in their sleepy nowhere town, Stephanie's decision to stay there and push out three kids had been worth it. If she hadn't been in Tesco that morning then the reporter wouldn't have approached her and asked the question on everyone's lips:

'So what do you think happened up on that mountain?' The reporter leaned in, a lion focusing on a gazelle. 'Reports are still unclear at this point; all we know is that—'

'I desperately wanted to be like them,' Stephanie dreamily interrupted her. 'To be one of them. Can you imagine how wonderful it is to be one of the Fierce Five?'

Transcript of interview between Officer Fields and Person of Interest regarding incident 3605 and ongoing investigation.

Officer: So tell me, in your own words, what happened?

POI: I feel like all I've done is talk.

Officer: We need to go over everything, for the record.

POI: So this interview is being recorded?

Officer: Yes.

POI: To be used as evidence?

Officer: Quite possibly. Can you clearly state your account of events from the dates in question, from the beginning?

POI: We all met up at the cabin.

Officer: You travelled there together?

POI: No. We didn't.

Officer: Why not?

POI: Because of course we didn't travel up there together, that would be too easy, wouldn't it?

Officer: But you were all friends. Best friends. Don't best friends do things like travel together?

POI: Maybe we used to. In the past.

Officer: But not anymore?

POI: No. Not anymore. Things changed over the years.

Officer: Then why meet up at all?

POI: Because some things stay the same.

Officer: Okay. So once you were at the cabin, what happened?

POI: Patience, Officer Fields. We have to get there first.

One

Allie opened her stainless-steel fridge and reached in for a half-empty bottle of milk. As she did, she clocked the invitation held up with Scrabble magnets and closed the door with unnecessary force. The plastic milk bottle was still in her hands, icing her palms as she stared at the invite.

It had been peering at her from its position on the fridge door for the past six weeks, ever since it landed on her doormat with a heart-sinking thump. An invite for Gail's thirty-fifth birthday party: a girly weekend in her Scottish cabin.

The invite promised *wine, giggles and the creation of cherished memories.* In gold embossed lettering. When Allie had tacked the invitation to the fridge she'd felt the weight of the smooth cream card. It felt expensive.

She imagined Gail driving her rust-clad Land Rover down into the nearest town and trotting along the cobbled streets in her mud-speckled Hunter wellingtons, hair askew from the fierce mountain winds she'd been traipsing through all morning. So much care had been taken in the production of the invitation. Had Gail painstakingly pored over different styles of font, textures of card as she stood in a little printing shop, her clipped Midlands accent in stark contrast to the hearty Scottish ones around her? The level of planning, the intense thought process involved in creating the invites alone was more Emily than Gail, as was the premature expediency with which they had been

5

sent out.

Six weeks. That was how long it now took the 'Fierce Five' to assemble. Leave from work had to be scheduled, childcare arranged. They were not the free-spirited girls they had once been, able to act on a whim. Every gathering had to be arranged with military precision, each detail scrutinised as though they were planning a royal wedding rather than a friendly reunion.

Where had her friends been when their invites arrived? Was Emily buried beneath her soft-skinned twins as hers was carefully dropped into the mailbox of her luxury Manchester house? Stacie was probably out on yet another date when hers landed flatly on the doorstep of her flat, or maybe she hadn't even returned home from another wild night out. And Diana . . .

Allie's lips curled in contemplation. She didn't even know where Diana lived. Diana, who seemed always to petulantly forget to include Allie in any invitation to a flat-warming or night out.

'She's seeing a musician,' Emily had noted softly when Allie had last taken the train up to Manchester with the earnest intention of spending time with her. But her flaxen friend had become a package deal and where she went the twins followed, enabling them only to chance snippets of fragmented conversation between bouts of crying heralding the arrival of the terrible twos.

'A musician?' Allie tried to keep her voice level, devoid of too much curiosity, even though it was Emily she was addressing, not Diana. To show too much enthusiasm felt like rewarding Diana's pointed absence from her life.

'Hmm, a struggling one at least. Oh, damn.' Emily was scooping forward, muslin in hand to wipe spittle from the side of one of her twins' mouths.

'I don't even know where she lives at the moment.'

Emily did a good job of sounding surprised by this. 'You don't? But she's in London too. You should call her.'

But Diana wouldn't answer her phone, wouldn't reply to a text. She never did anymore. These last few years she'd somehow managed to graduate from distant to non-existent.

Allie stared into her cup of coffee, trying to anchor herself back in the moment. Her kitchen felt hollow. The stainless steel that coated the counter tops, the cooker and the fridge, seemed cold and unfeeling. She remembered a time when it had felt glamorous, inviting. She crinkled her nose at the thought and shoved the milk back into the fridge, refusing to lock eyes with the embossed invitation a second time.

Her entire flat felt unpleasantly cavernous lately. It felt like the aftermath of a bomb exploding – walls had been torn down, precious items destroyed and tension lingered in the air, clotting and choking.

Nursing her coffee in her favourite red mug, she strode through the open-plan living space and dropped onto her sofa. It barely sagged beneath her. It was still so sturdy, so new. Sometimes the newness of it all was able to creep above the oppressive stench of loss and for brief moments the flat actually seemed homely. Then the walls would come crashing down all over again when Allie remembered the emptiness that was slowly consuming everything around it, including her.

Reaching for the remote, she flicked on the television. Before the screen came to life, its glassy black surface showed Allie her reflection. She looked so small. Golden hair cropped short, hazel eyes cast in shadow. Her joggers and hoody hung off her frame. She'd lost a lot of weight in the last few weeks as she'd barely been able to eat. But at least her hair was different. A week after Gail's invite had arrived, she'd chopped most of it off, letting it fall straight to her ear lobes, no further. A thick fringe hung above her eyes. She thought it looked edgy. Modern.

'Dramatic,' her father had said when she'd met him for dinner, his bushy silver eyebrows disappearing up his forehead as he took in his daughter's new style.

'It's a . . . statement,' her stepmother had offered more carefully. They both hid poorly disguised looks of concern behind their comments.

The television came to life. An episode of *Westworld* continued from the point it had been paused the night before. Allie watched with dead eyes, struggling to engage with something she usually loved. Even coffee tasted different now. More bitter.

Something rang.

The sound was so sudden and shrill that Allie physically jumped. Her phone rarely ever rang. People texted her. Emailed. These days no one ever actually wanted to talk, and that suited her just fine. But the phone kept ringing. With a reluctant sigh, Allie pulled herself up and went over to the small table, on which sat an old-fashioned red telephone complete with a rotary number pad which she'd picked out from an antique store in Bath. Grabbing the receiver Allie pushed back memories of the phone's purchase. She didn't need to dwell.

'Allie,' a sweet, sing-song voice greeted her through the phone.

'Stacie.' Allie would know her voice anywhere.

'So, are we all set for later?'

Allie frowned and glanced towards her front door. Leaning against the door on the very mat on which Gail's invitation had landed were a designer holdall, a pull-along and a backpack, all bulging at the seams.

'Yeah, we agreed to meet at the station at ten, right?'

'I'm just checking,' Stacie sung sweetly, 'and I figured I'd call to check since, you know, you rarely answer texts anymore.' Her voice abruptly lost its melody.

'I answer texts.'

'Rarely,' Stacie countered with an overly dramatic sigh. 'You've become more of a hermit than usual since, well—'

'I'll be there at ten.' Allie was ready to hang up. It was hard enough to face her flat every day that mocked her with its emptiness. She didn't want to endure the same judgement from her friends.

'Ten it is.' The song had returned to Stacie's voice. 'Be there or be square, Allie Bear.'

'It's an ugly word, isn't it?' Stacie, still with a youthful glow in her cheeks even in her late twenties, drew her eyebrows together as she studied the half-eaten sandwich on her plate.

'What is?' Allie mumbled around a mouthful of tuna melt.

'Divorce.'

Swallowing, Allie wiped her mouth and straightened, hiding how the movement made her wince. 'It's not so bad.'

'Isn't it?' Stacie's eyes were wide. Wild. 'I'm in my twenties, Allie. Twenty . . .' she lowered her voice conspiratorially '. . . seven. What will people think?'

'Who cares?' Shrugging, Allie grabbed what remained of her lunch. Beyond the windows of the small café, the sun was shining, bathing the pavement in glorious golden light. It was a summer's day which should have burned, but Allie had yet to shrug off her cardigan, keeping it tightly drawn even as she'd sat on the tube, wedged between sweating commuters. These days there was a chill which never left her.

'Allie—' Stacie was already shaking her head. Allie knew

what was coming, her friend was about to lament about how not everyone could hide within the four walls of their flat, could live their life behind a computer screen. It was the same speech Gail gave whenever Allie seemed a little too eager to shun the outside world.

Dropping her sandwich, she raised a hand in defiance. 'Stace, it doesn't matter what people think. What matters is that you're happy.'

A wry smile elegantly widened across Stacie's face. 'Allie Bear, I was going to say that I knew you'd be okay with it. That you wouldn't see the ugliness. Not like . . .' She crinkled her nose. 'You just know that Emily is going to have a problem with it. Is going to remind me that I made a vow. A number of them, actually.'

'She's just a romantic. But romance doesn't work in the real world.'

'It doesn't?' Stacie narrowed her eyes shrewdly.

'I mean, come on.' Allie desperately reached for her mug of coffee, needing something to steady the tremor in her hands. 'Life isn't just some Disney movie, we're not princesses waiting to be saved by princes.'

Beneath the table Stacie gently kicked Allie's feet. 'I've missed you, you know. You shouldn't disappear as often as you do.'

'I'm—'

'Working on your book, I know.' Stacie raised her hands apologetically. 'But I feel like I need to remind Lucas of the terms of your marriage. He doesn't have sole custody of you, it's shared. I feel like we barely see you these days.'

'Stace, you're going to be okay. Divorced at twenty-seven isn't a big deal. Hell, it makes you sound interesting.'

'You think so?'

'I know so.'

'Do you feel like splitting a cupcake?' Stacie asked mischievously.

'Definitely.'

Two

It was frenzied at Euston Station. Voices bounced off the high rafters and people stood like lemmings before the digital announcement boards, waiting to be told which direction they needed to run in.

'Allie Bear.' Stacie found her within minutes, abandoning her Ted Baker suitcases to wrap her arms around Allie. 'It's so good to see you.' Stepping back, Stacie cocked her head and pursed her lips. The scent of her vanilla perfume hung to Allie's parka jacket and jeans. 'Your hair . . .' Stacie's lips quirked into a smile. 'You've changed it. It looks good on you.'

Stacie's hair was pulled back in a fishtail plait casually slung over her shoulder, ruby red. Her big blue eyes glistened brightly as she took in Allie's new look.

'I wanted something different.' Allie nervously fingered the blunt ends of her hair. She'd never been comfortable being scrutinised, even by her friends.

'Different is . . . good,' Stacie said finally and turned to peer up at the announcement board. 'How long is this train journey again?'

'Seven hours. Give or take.'

'Jesus.' Stacie stroked her fingertips across her forehead, revealing white lacquered nails. 'That's longer than a really long movie. That's longer than like . . . *Titanic*.'

Allie laughed. 'True.'

'Or *Gone with the Wind*.'

'Also true.'

'At least we have each other.' Stacie looped an arm around her friend's shoulders. 'And we have a *lot* of catching up to do.'

'It's your turn to pick.' Lucas had said it so seriously, as though there were more on the line than just their film choice for the evening. Since getting married he'd become more intense, or perhaps just more committed, Allie struggled to tell the difference. She turned to him as they passed through the doors into their building, the wind playfully tugging on her long hair and letting it dance in her line of vision.

'If it's my turn then you can't complain.'

'I'm not making any promises that I can't keep.' The ends of his mouth lifted with mirth as he strode towards the lift.

'Either you let me pick and be done with it or you just pick.' Allie knew she was taunting him but she was enjoying this game they'd adopted as newlyweds – where they'd banter and berate one another over the most trivial of things. Mirroring his grin her fingers strayed to the golden band gracing her left hand, which shone with optimistic newness.

'And your choice is?' The doors to the lift parted and he bustled inside, arms laden with plastic shopping bags out of which protruded a long breadstick and several sticks of celery.

Allie waited until she was beside him, close enough to smell the bread in the bag and the slight musk of sweat on his skin. She watched the lobby disappear as the doors closed and then they were alone.

'I'm thinking The Virgin Suicides,*' she revealed.*

His smile promptly died, replaced by a wounded expression. 'Again? Seriously, Allie? That film is so . . . maudlin.'

'First of all – it's not maudlin, it's evocative. And secondly, this is my choice, so keep your opinions to yourself.'

'But really, that film?'

'That or Ghost. Beyond those I refuse to budge.'

'Bloody hell.' The plastic in his grip rustled as his body prickled with agitation. 'You've placed me between a rock and a hard place, babe.'

'Deal with it.'

They reached their floor and the lift chimed joyously to alert them to their arrival. With a grinding shudder the doors parted and Allie stepped out. Only he wasn't keeping pace with her, he was lingering back, teeth clenched over his lower lip. 'Are you coming?'

'Just . . .' A stiff sigh and he was vacating the lift, joining her in the communal corridor. 'Tell me why you like it so much.'

'The film?'

'Uh huh.'

'Which one?'

'You know which one.'

Allie felt her shoulders rise and fall. 'I don't know. I guess it . . . appeals to me.'

'Like you understand it?' he tried to clarify dubiously.

'I don't . . .' They were at their door and Allie was reaching for her keys, wrestling with the lower section of her handbag. Her hands scraped against her purse, lip gloss, a battered paperback copy of Rebecca. 'Lucas, I can't really explain it. I guess maybe because I see my friends like sisters.'

'But in the film the sisters . . .' he massaged his throat as though summoning up the right words '. . . they all commit suicide, Allie. Like I said, maudlin.'

'Lucas, it's representative of their bond, of—' Allie exhaled sharply, felt heat rising in her cheeks. Why was she suddenly on trial for her selection of film for the evening? 'I guess it reminds me of my friends, our bond, that's all.'

'What bond?' Lucas wondered sharply, the question hanging between them for several long seconds. 'You've not seen them since

13

New Year's. And even before that, it was sporadic. You're not close anymore, not like you were when we first met.'

Allie found the key and shoved it hard into the lock, blinking furiously. 'I thought this was about my film choice, not an interrogation about my friendships.'

'It is.' He followed her inside, keenly offloading the bags upon the kitchen countertop. 'I'm just . . . Allie, I'm only trying to understand why you like something so depressing, that's all.'

'Maybe stop analysing me and accept my choices!' She felt the heat of her words on her tongue, in her cheeks.

'Allie, I just—' He was raising his hands defensively.

'Fine, damn it, we'll watch something else!'

'Look, I—'

'I don't challenge your decisions like this.' She was storming through their flat, heading for the bathroom, needing to place both a lock and a door between herself and the conversation.

His final plea was soft, as though spoken only to himself, but Allie caught it as she thrust open the bathroom door and looked at the little white suite.

'Sorry, Allie, I'm just trying to get to know you better, that's all.'

Three

Through Allie's train window there was greenery. Endless fields stretched towards little lonely white farmhouses and solitary trees standing barren and stripped, their copper leaves stolen by roguish winds. It was early December. Christmas carols were playing in the shops and every other advert on television was about the festive season and all the wonderment it held. Allie was actually glad for the seclusion of Gail's cabin. It was up in the Scottish highlands, away from the internet, away from mobile phone signal. Away from the rest of the world. It would be a complete escape. Except for the four other members of her group.

'So how are you holding up?'

Stacie drummed her long nails against the plastic table between her and Allie. She'd been delicately sipping her gingerbread latte since they'd left Euston and peering over at her friend, seemingly trying to find the right moment to begin her line of questioning.

Allie shook her head and frowned. 'I'd rather not talk about it.' She looked down at her own cardboard cup of coffee. Raising it to her lips she took a long sip, savouring the bitterness.

'Okay, then we won't talk about it. We can talk about my favourite subject instead.'

'Which is?'

'Me.' Stacie laughed.

'Okay.' Allie discreetly rolled her eyes. 'How are you?'

'Well, as you know I'm between husbands right now,' Stacie shrugged casually. 'But' – she pointed a long nail at Allie – 'I'm tired of the casual side of dating, I'm in the market for husband number three and things are looking up in that department. The American guy I'm working for, Roger Ernestine, is really something of a silver fox and I've caught him eyeing me up a few times.'

Allie noticed the way Stacie's gaze didn't quite meet hers when she spoke.

'Your boss, Stacie, really?' She tried not to sound too judgemental. Men had always been a hobby for Stacie. She collected men like she collected shoes and handbags, citing that life was too short to settle on any one thing for too long.

'She'll outgrow it,' Gail would insist whenever Allie vocalised her concerns over her friend's worrying trend of treating partners like accessories.

'Will she?'

'Of course.' Gail was always so confident when it came to the behaviour of others. 'One day she'll realise she isn't getting any younger and snap out of it.'

'When? By the third marriage? The fourth? She's becoming a caricature.'

'Don't be cruel, Allie.' Gail could never tolerate cruelty. 'Stacie will settle down when she's good and ready.'

'Maybe she'll never be ready.'

Allie expected another snapped retort but Gail was silently shaking her head, lips pulled tight in a flat line. 'She just needs to let go,' Gail said, at last, her hand clasped to her throat, fingertips grazing her chin. 'And you know how hard it is to let go, don't you, Allie?'

'So how did Lucas propose?' Stacie peered at Allie over the handbag she was currently scrutinising. She ceased smoothing her hands against its leather exterior to stare intently at her friend and at the ring newly adorning her finger.

'He . . .' Allie drifted deeper into the store. Someone sprayed perfume close by and she was almost choked by a vanilla cloud. Coughing, she took refuge beside a display stand crammed full of designer purses.

'Was it insanely romantic?' Like a shadow Stacie followed, eyes wide and hungry for details.

A shrug. 'I guess. I mean, it was in a bookshop.'

'Oh?' A pristinely plucked eyebrow lifted in interest. 'Sounds a bit dry for a proposal,' Stacie added dubiously.

'Well, we met in a bookshop.' Allie grabbed the nearest purse to her and began turning it over, pretending to be captivated by it.

'Ah . . .' The item was quickly snatched from her grasp and returned to its shelf. Stacie was cradling her hands, applying gentle pressure as she grinned excitedly. 'So it was très romantique! I knew it would be. Lucas strikes me as the type to go with a grand gesture, he's the typical modern alpha male after all.'

'Uh huh.' Allie was trying to discreetly struggle free from her friend's grip. She knew that she was going to be pushed to divulge additional details and she'd already said as much as she wanted to.

'Have you set a date? How are you feeling? What sort of dress are you thinking?' Stacie rattled off her questions with machine-gun speed. Allie smiled wanly at her.

'We should get married as soon as we can,' Lucas had insisted as he kissed her in the Gothic Fiction section. 'You and me, Allie, we're going to do this. We're going to build a life together, a family.'

'I don't know, maybe this summer.'

'This summer?' Stacie's smile widened but her eyebrows flattened into a hard line. 'Really? Why the rush? It's not like you're' – she tilted her head in a pitying manner – 'you know.'

'It's just talk at this point, nothing more.'

'I remember my first proposal.' Stacie linked arms with Allie and began guiding her towards the shoe department. 'Aiden pulled out all the stops. We were at that little restaurant near your old flat and when we came out, he'd set up a flash mob to sing "I Will Always Love You". It was just . . ." Sighing deeply Stacie clasped her free hand against her throat.

'Perfect,' Allie concluded for her.

'Yes . . . perfect.' Stacie unlinked their arms and began drifting towards a pair of black patent court shoes. 'Like these shoes,' she quipped, picking one up.

'Stace—'

'A perfect proposal doesn't equal a perfect marriage.' Stacie slammed the shoe down with undue force. 'I'm happy for you, Allie. So happy. You deserve perfection. Have you told the others?'

A cloud entered their sunny autumnal day. Allie shivered beneath the shadow it cast. 'I . . . not yet.' Her fingers drifted to the place a modest faux diamond ring was sitting.

'Once this latest script sells, I'll buy you a better ring, a really decent one that's quirky, just like you. Maybe a black pearl, what do you think?' Lucas was holding her chin in his hands in a way that made her feel small yet safe.

'You should tell them.' Stacie was reaching for a biker boot in a steel grey. 'Emily and Gail will be just thrilled for you.'

'And Diana?'

Stacie pursed her lips and studied the boot in her hands with sudden intensity. 'Do you reckon they have these in my size?' She was striding off to locate a sales assistant when Allie reached for her shoulder.

18

'Just because your first marriage didn't stick doesn't mean this one won't. You're happy now.'

'Yes.' Stacie grinned and a vein in her neck throbbed. 'So happy. How lucky we both are to have found the men of our dreams.'

Four

The train thundered over a rough section of track.

'He's loaded.' Stacie beamed.

'He's still your boss.'

'True.' Stacie's gaze drifted towards the window and Allie could feel the distance beginning to stretch out between them, the plastic table becoming more of a metaphoric barrier than a physical. 'Hey.' She was relieved when Stacie clicked her fingers, staring right at her, this time allowing her blue eyes to connect with Allie's hazel. 'It's a shame Diana didn't want to ride up with us.'

'I think she was busy with work or something,' Allie muttered, keen to keep focusing on the rolling countryside outside rather than Stacie's now piercing stare.

'Always has to be different that one,' Stacie said with an exaggerated roll of her eyes. 'I don't even know what she can possibly be rebelling about these days. I mean, a bit of conformity never hurt anyone, but she always acts as though she'd literally catch on fire if she were to do something normal like get married or sign a long-term lease on a flat. What does she even do anyway? She's always so damn vague about her job.'

'Maybe she values her privacy.'

'Maybe she's ashamed.' Stacie leaned forward and lowered her voice. 'I mean she tells us barely anything about her job, even less than you do.' She shrugged flippantly.

'And she's been living with that guitarist Peter . . . Paul . . . something. Yet we've never met him. I parade all of my boyfriends in front of you guys.'

'Yet they still don't stick.'

Now Allie was sounding like Diana, too quick with her judgement and harsh pragmatism. Biting down on her tongue, she fought to keep her emotions in check.

'You spoken to her lately?' Stacie leaned back, eyes narrowing and lips curling down.

'Umm . . .' Allie picked at the chipped red paint on her nails and bowed her head. She was stalling. It still felt shameful to admit how little contact she had with Diana these days when once they'd been so close. Diana had been the one to pierce her ears, to assure her that the man behind the *Scream* mask didn't exist when Allie failed to sleep from fear for four nights straight.

'Have you seen that garish pink streak through her hair?' Stacie snapped the question across the table and Allie blinked, fighting against the sluggish droop of her eyes which reminded her how little sleep she'd been getting lately. How easy it would be to just drift off and let the rattle of the train against the tracks rock her towards absolution, at least briefly.

'Uh huh.' Her response stuck in her throat. Allie yawned to loosen her jaw. 'On like, her posts and stuff.'

'Talk about regression.' Stacie gave a haughty sigh. 'Diana thinks she's still fifteen while the rest of us have to live in the real world.'

'Mmm,' Allie made a non-committal sound.

'And all those tattoos. The woman is becoming a bloody tapestry. And did you see that table she bought for her flat, the strange black one?' Stacie must have registered the sad slant of Allie's eyes as she quickly coughed and straightened. 'I mean, she barely has anyone over.'

21

A lie. Allie was sure of it. The others had all seen Diana's flat, had gone with her to cramped pubs that smelt of sweat and stale beer to listen to Peter, Paul, whatever the hell his name was, play with his ramshackle band. Stacie was probably lying about having never met him.

'Are we still meeting Emily at Edinburgh Airport?'

Allie nodded, grateful for the conversation to be steered in a new direction but still she braced herself for the ensuing flow of vitriol. It was in her companion's nature to grind down the people she was supposed to love as though it were a sport.

'Hot air and lipstick,' was how Diana had once labelled Stacie.

'Urgh she's *flying* up from Manchester, right?' Stacie groaned and shook her head with dramatic dismay. 'She couldn't just meet us on the train. Oh no, too delicate for that.' Stacie was sucking in her cheeks and scowling. 'We could have flown up too, you know. Done Gatwick to Edinburgh.'

'You said it was too expensive, remember?' Allie gently reminded her.

Stacie's scowl deepened. 'It was. Some of us *can* afford two flights though. I'm sure Emily didn't flinch at the price, oh no.'

Allie tried to smooth the folds out of their conversation.

'I think travelling really tires her out, so flying was her best option.'

'She's diabetic, not dying.' Stacie frowned petulantly, clacking the tips of her nails against the table top. 'I mean . . .' The hard line of her eyebrows softened '. . . don't you think she gets exhausted pretending to be so perfect all the time ?'

'Life is far from perfect for her. She had that pump fitted

last year. She really suffers at times.' Allie's hands wanted to fumble for the base of her spine at the mention of suffering but instead she reached forward and locked them around her cooling cup of coffee.

'Things look pretty perfect in all her pictures.' Stacie's shoulders sagged and her gaze dropped to the tips of her nails, still drumming against the table top. Her lips might have puckered with jealousy but Allie couldn't be sure. Stacie had become too adept at hiding her true emotions over the years, ever the wannabe actress even in her daily life.

'My feed is just full of images of her, Adam and the twins, always smiling like they just won the bloody lottery or something. And you know, I find the twins kind of . . . creepy.'

'The twins aren't creepy.' Allie was instantly on the defensive, though she knew that she and Stacie were just rehashing an old dance routine. Stacie had always loved to play up to the caricature she'd created for herself as the one who could be cruel and cutting about others, even friends. It was as though she enjoyed the negative attention her outbursts could bring like she relished pushing other people's buttons. Attention. Stacie craved it, thrived on it. But Allie knew it was just a front, another face her friend put on when addressing the rest of the world.

'They are *identical*.' Stacie's eyebrows shot up, a pair of crimson arches against the waxy white canvas of her forehead as she further committed to her performance. 'Like, straight up complete carbon copies of each other. There isn't even a birth mark or a dimple to separate them.'

'So what?' Allie's patience for the theatrics was beginning to get worn down.

'Ever seen *The Shining*?'

The train slowed as it reached a new station, brakes hissing.

'Twins are creepy,' Stacie continued, leaning back in her seat, 'even Stephen King thinks so and isn't he like a God to you?'

'I mean I admire his work and—'

'He tweeted you right? Last year?'

'Yeah.'

'About your book?'

'Uh huh.'

A few weary-looking passengers came and settled in their carriage. Allie flicked her gaze over them while Stacie paid them no attention.

'I'm surprised Emily is coming, to be honest.' Stacie was now rummaging around in her Marc Jacobs handbag. It looked new, its sapphire sides completely unblemished. It was probably a gift from her boss or an impulse purchase she couldn't afford. Allie felt inclined to believe it was the latter.

'You are?'

'Like how can she *bear* to be away from Adam? According to all their status updates the two of them have become one entity that exists on sickly comments.'

'Hmmm,' said Allie, non-committal.

During the nights that had felt the longest and the darkest Allie had sat in her bed, iPad in hand, and scrolled through her friends' social media feeds. They all seemed to be living such wonderful lives. In every picture, they smiled and those smiles shone. Emily took countless pictures of her cherub-faced twins, she and her husband of eight years, Adam, each holding one. Each grinning so much their cheeks were in danger of bursting open and splattering scarlet blood all over the camera.

Allie wondered if that's what happiness looked like. She

wouldn't know. Her social media feed was stark, empty. A string of book tour updates and signing schedules. Nothing personal. Nothing wholesome. No images so filled with love that they almost melted the digital screen with their saccharine sweetness.

'It's downright sickly.' Stacie almost choked on her words. 'Her entire cardboard reality makes me nauseous. None of it is real, it's all for show.'

'Maybe they are just really, really happy. It can happen.' Allie refrained from highlighting the irony of Stacie's comment. Her friend was the ultimate show-woman of the group, perhaps that's what irked her about Emily – that she feared she was somehow being upstaged.

Stacie waved a dismissive hand in front of her and resumed rummaging through her handbag. 'I mean' – she pulled free a large leather cream purse and gazed at Allie – 'both of us have been married and it didn't make either of us very happy, did it?'

Allie froze. It was still a secret tucked up against her heart; a needle that pierced her with every beat. To talk about it would be to breathe life into it, to let the truth infect more than just her small flat.

'Another coffee?' Stacie was getting up, her voice lilting in soft song, a cheery smile on her face.

'Uh, sure,' Allie mumbled as she reached for her phone feeling hopeless in the compulsion to see if he had bothered to message her.

Inbox: empty

Missed calls: none

With a weighted sigh, Allie turned to look out the window as the train began to pick up speed. She remembered evenings sitting on the staircase in her parents' old home clutching the hallway telephone against her ear, its spiral cord spread across the plush beige carpet. There she'd sit and talk to her friends until her back went numb. They'd chat through the events of the previous day with urgent dedication, debating everything from people's lunch choices to strange looks passed around the classroom like contraband notes. There was numbness now in her back, but it was different. This lack of sensation wasn't a result of something good, something uniting. It was the complete opposite.

Stacie returned in a cloud of designer perfume and cheap coffee. She handed Allie a fresh cup and then shuffled back into her seat, tossing her fishtail plait over her shoulder as she did so.

'Drink up,' she instructed brightly. 'We're going to need all our energy when we reach the cabin. I've no doubt Emily will be keen to start singing a rendition of "When will Stacie have children" followed by a rousing chorus of "You need to settle down and make it stick". Emily thinks just because she's married with babies, we all need to be married. With babies. Like having a baby is a fix-all. Shit!'

Allie flinched at the sudden expletive.

'Crap, Allie Bear.' Stacie was staring right at her, piercing her with her blue eyes that had dipped at the corners with sadness. It was a look that Allie loathed. Had her face momentarily betrayed her, is that what had prompted this reaction? Because she thought she'd just been nonchalantly listening to Stacie prattle on. 'I'm . . . I'm sorry. I know she won't bombard you with the baby crap and I'm not trying to—'

'Emily is only looking out for you.' Allie tried to pull her features into a smile filled with kindness but it was proving a great effort. 'Don't . . . don't even think about me.'

26

'Allie—'

Her phone. She grabbed it and fired off a message to Gail, needing a distraction.

Hope you're having a good birthday. We'll be there soon xx

As she hit send, the train bounced along a section of rough track, causing Allie's coffee to spill.

It was a December that promised snow and yet had failed to deliver. Allie, dwarfed within the long wool coat Lucas had given her for her thirty-fourth birthday the previous month, shivered on the station platform, gift bag in hand. She'd chosen to travel up to Manchester alone, it was easier that way. Soon enough she'd be crammed into a pew beside her friends and then later a cosy restaurant where they'd all eat a roast dinner and pretend that everything was fine.

She wasn't waiting for a train. She'd already reached her destination. Allie should have been calling for a taxi or an Uber, but instead, she was procrastinating. Stalling. Already she could hear the questions which would be flung at her the moment she arrived at the church . . .

'Travelled up alone? But where is Lucas? Didn't he want to come?'

Of course, he'd have wanted to come. That was why Allie had needed to be discreet. When the invitation to the twins' christening arrived via post the previous month, she'd been careful to keep it in an unassuming drawer in the kitchen, out of sight. Her husband of just eight weeks thought this was just a standard excursion up north for Allie to visit Emily.

Her fingertips were growing numb. She couldn't linger on the platform forever. Filling her lungs with icy winter air, Allie headed away from the station.

'Finally.' Stacie's greeting was blunt as Allie scurried up the winding gravel path which led to the little church.

'My train was Delayed.' Allie breathed out her lie in a fogged breath.

'Oh.' Disbelief settled between Stacie's brows in a deep furrow. 'We could have travelled up together you know.'

'I didn't want to trouble you.'

'Ha.' The laugh cracked like a whip through the frigid air between them. 'You mean you thought I'd be travelling up with Diana.'

Allie felt her muscles steel beneath her skin. She glanced at the few guests milling around them, all stamping their feet and rubbing their hands together against the bitter chill. A hand slapped at her upper arm.

'Don't worry.' Stacie beamed a smile that was brightened by the thick layer of scarlet lipstick she was wearing. 'She's already inside, she didn't hear me. I know you've not spoken since your wedding, but you can't avoid her forever.'

'I'm not, I'm—'

'At least it hasn't snowed yet.' Gail was striding over to the pair, cutting a distinguished figure in the flattering navy trousers and fitted jacket she was wearing. Her dark hair was swept back in a loose bun and she moved with an ease Allie envied, unencumbered by anything boring into her broad shoulders. 'Allie, you're here.' She embraced her small friend briefly and then stepped back, openly assessing her. 'Well, aren't you coming inside?'

'We're waiting until the last minute for fear of bursting into flames once we enter,' Stacie deadpanned.

Gail ignored the comment and continued to focus solely on Allie. 'Where's Lucas? Did he not want to come?'

'He . . .' Allie had prepared for this moment on the train. Over and over she'd told herself what she needed to say. 'He's sick. Flu. Well, man flu.'

Gail arched an eyebrow in Stacie's direction.

'Urgh, man flu.' Stacie linked arms with Allie and began to edge her towards the stone steps which led up into the little church.

28

'I've heard it can be lethal, you know. So men say.'

Gail was on godmother duty. 'She's just so together, it made her the natural choice,' Emily had explained several months ago, hands neatly clasped in her lap. Allie was about to open her mouth to question if that meant she was less than 'together' when the baby monitor on the mantle shone red and Emily jumped to her feet as though she'd been skewered by a hot poker. By the time she returned to the lounge, cheeks flushed and apologies rolling off her tongue it was time for Allie to return home, taking any lingering questions with her.

So at the christening, Gail didn't sit in the assigned pew for the friendship group, she got to gather with the parents around the font. Emily waved enthusiastically when she clocked Allie before one of her plump little twins was returned to her arms. Both babies were cherubic perfection in white lace, rosy cheeks glowing. Allie felt the walls of her throat growing coarser. Coughing, she shifted in the stiff pew. Stacie was beside her and beyond her was Diana who had remained stone still since the others joined her.

'Really, we should have travelled up together,' Stacie had to whisper as a hush had settled over the assembled well-wishers and worshippers. The service was about to begin. 'Especially if you were coming up alone.'

'Honestly, I . . .' Allie could feel herself stumbling over her excuses. 'It's fine, really.'

'Well at least smile,' Stacie suggested. 'Christenings are supposed to be happy occasions, you look like you're at a funeral.'

Two hours later and Diana had still failed to approach her. Allie kept seeking her out, trying to catch her eye, but between departing the church and sharing a taxi with Stacie to the restaurant she'd failed to get near her fourth friend. Now that dinner had been eaten, all that was left was to eat the piece of christening cake on her plate before politely standing up from the table, heading over to Emily to hug her and saying goodbye. It was nearly over. Allie was nearly free.

'I should really go and give the twins a squeeze.' Stacie was pushing her chair back from their table and getting up. 'I've been putting it off forever for fear of ruining this dress.' She gestured at the smart Ted Baker floral skater dress she had on and her eyes shone, but not with pride.

'Stace, are you—'

'Just a quick cuddle, I'll tell Emily. Don't want to risk her little darlings getting too attached to their Auntie Stacie now, do we?' And then she was darting away, leaving only the cloying scent of her perfume behind. Allie exhaled and picked at her cake. She just needed to run out the clock. Soon she'd be back on the train, her worries being rocked away by the steady, rhythmic motion of it. Then once home she'd—

'No Lucas then?' Diana had appeared in Stacie's vacated seat, dark eyes narrowed in shrewd observation.

Allie was instantly flustered. 'What, oh, um, no. He's—'

'I'd have thought this would have been his thing,' Diana cut in. 'I mean, after what he said at your wedding, I'm surprised he's not—'

'Sick!' Allie struggled not to choke on the word as she thrust it out. 'He's sick, Diana.'

'Right.' Diana leaned back, but the fire of interrogation didn't leave her gaze. She wore a grey shirt dress and a stern expression. She too had come alone and Allie wasn't questioning that. In fact, they had all arrived without partners in tow. Only Emily had her husband on hand, as they gleefully passed the twins between them.

'Sick, sure.' Diana shook her head, letting her hair rustle against her dress. 'Whatever, Allie.'

'Look, he's . . .'

'Ooh, is there a turf war for my chair?' Stacie enquired mockingly as she returned.

'Not at all.' Diana abruptly stood up, looking beyond Allie towards Emily and the twins further down the large table. 'I was just leaving.'

'I should really be making tracks too.' Allie was gathering up her bag, reaching for her coat. Her cake remained on her plate, barely touched.

'I'll come with you.' Stacie began shadowing her movements. 'We'll be getting the same train after all.'

'No, no, you stay, have fun. Don't hurry off on my account.'

'It's fine.' Stacie had one arm stuffed into her coat. 'I've more than shown my face enough anyway, I'm good to go.'

'Are you leaving?' Emily hurried round the table, one comatose twin clutched to her chest. Her blue gaze flicked between Allie and Stacie as the corners of her mouth dipped down. 'You've barely been here a few hours. Stay, come back to mine for a while.'

'I need to get back to Lucas, he's sick. Man flu,' Allie added apologetically.

'Oh right, yes, of course.' Emily had lost some of her sparkle as she briefly hugged each of her friends.

'But it's been so great seeing you,' Allie said as she reached in for an additional embrace and Emily gripped her tight, the slumbering baby wedged between their chests. 'I know today can't have been easy.'

Emily stepped back, her smile faltering once more. 'You'll be back for New Year's though, right?' she enquired hopefully as she followed Allie and Stacie towards the entrance to the restaurant.

'Wouldn't miss it for the world,' Stacie gushed over-enthusiastically as she grabbed Allie's elbow and ushered her out into the cold with sudden haste. 'What did you mean?' she hissed as they crossed the car park and Allie realised with a sinking sensation that she'd yet to book a taxi to the station.

'Huh?'

'About today not being easy for Emily. I heard you. What did you mean?'

'Stace, it was just—'

31

'What did you mean?' There was a sudden wildness in Stacie's eyes and Allie could clearly smell the vodka on her friend's breath.

'I meant that she has twins, two babies to take care of, and that can't be easy.' Allie shook herself free of Stacie's grip and began reaching into her handbag for her phone. 'I need to call a cab.' She was facing the restaurant, chin dipped against her chest. 'Shit, we didn't say goodbye to Diana.'

'After you,' Stacie gestured grandly. Allie didn't move. 'That's what I thought.'

Five

It was dark by the time Allie carried her luggage from the taxi to the glass entrance doors of Edinburgh Airport's departures. A biting cold chewed at her bare cheeks and hands. She bowed her head against the chill and focused on hauling herself and her holdall through the doors and into the airport's welcoming warmth.

Stacie was several feet behind her, loudly panting and moaning as she dragged her suitcase along, its wheels rumbling nosily against the ground like an approaching storm.

Within the airport, Allie paused to shake off some of the traveller's fatigue that clung to her. The journey had been long and it wasn't over yet.

'God.' Stacie burst through the glass doors, her suitcase boisterously rattling along behind her. 'Is it me or is it taking us forever to reach Gail's bloody cabin? First the never-ending train ride, then the leery taxi driver and now a flight up into the Scottish wilderness. We could have got on a long haul flight the time it's taken us to get here. We could be somewhere exotic by now. On a *beach*. Sipping cocktails.' Stacie sighed wistfully at the fantasy she'd concocted for herself.

'Maybe you and your boss can have a beach holiday together after Christmas,' Allie remarked with a hint of sarcasm as she looked at the display boards, searching for their flight details.

'It'd definitely need to be *after* Christmas.' Stacie was holding a compact mirror up to her face, having seemingly thought Allie's comment sincere and frowning as she surveyed the damage the long day had done to her make-up. 'He spends the holidays with his family.'

'Has a big family does he?'

'Couple of kids I think.'

'And if you got together with him it wouldn't bother you that you'd broken them up?'

'I wouldn't lose any sleep over it.' Stacie snapped her compact shut and returned it to her handbag. 'All's fair in love and war,' she added with a flirtatious wink. It was a caricature remark accompanied by a similarly unnatural gesture. Over the years Stacie had over-invested in what people perceived her to be; flirtatious and fickle. Now she wore those traits as more than just a badge of honour; but a disguise.

'There you guys are.'

Allie turned and saw Emily walking towards them. Although walking undersold the way she moved. She seemed to glide wherever she went with effortless grace: the epitome of an elegant waif.

'Emily.' Allie dropped her bags to her feet and stepped forward to embrace her. Emily hugged her tight, she smelt of wet wipes and oranges. 'It's so good to see you.'

Emily made travelling seem effortless. There wasn't a single crease in her outfit, nor a kink in her hair. Her eyes were bright and there was a flush to her cheeks. She had a Berkin bag draped over one arm and wore pale skinny jeans and a silk blouse and sweater-set beneath a trench coat.

'Don't touch me.' Stacie outstretched her hands as Emily approached her. 'I reek of train carriages. Those things are just sweat houses on wheels. I feel hideous.'

34

'Well you *look* great.' Emily's glossed lips lifted into a smile. 'And your hair . . .' Reaching out she let her fingertips graze the blunt edges of Allie's new style. 'It makes you look so sophisticated.'

'I'll just be glad to get this over with,' Stacie interjected as she tossed her plait over her shoulder and grinned primly at her friends. 'I am sick to the back teeth of travelling.'

'Diana didn't come up with you two?' Emily fell in step with them as they approached the check-in desk.

'No . . . she's making her own way up here,' Allie explained, feeling the poker heat of shame prickle across her skin. She sensed that she alone was the reason for Diana's decision to travel up solo and that everyone else already knew that. Though why her friend felt that way Allie didn't understand, it was like being told half a secret, forever striving to learn the rest and finally get some closure.

'And how are you?' Emily asked as Allie slid her passport over to the airline clerk.

'I'm . . .'

Fine.

That was the practised line: *I'm fine.* Allie had been repeating it to her agent and editor for weeks. And they bought it. Her friends were different. They were four mirrors that reflected her truest self right back at her. But Allie wasn't ready to inject such candour into her life. Not yet.

'I'm fine.' She finished the remark with a half-hearted shrug.

'You're so strong.' Emily placed a hand on her smaller friend's shoulder. 'If it'd happened to me, I'd be a wreck. I'd—'

'Not everyone lists having a man up there with oxygen as a priority for survival,' Stacie snapped, shouldering her way between Emily and Allie and slapping her passport down on the counter.

'I really wasn't—'

'How long is this damn flight?' Stacie directed her question at the smartly uniformed clerk with forced politeness. 'I'm severely in need of a lie-down in a decent bed.'

Last New Year's Eve. That was the last time the five of them were all together, almost an entire year ago. They had all gathered in Manchester, where Emily lived. The twins were almost eight months old, able to sit up and shove anything they could grab with their podgy hands into their toothless mouths.

As midnight arrived the friends counted the new year in together beneath the small glass chandelier in Emily's living room. Jools Holland was on the television.

Diana and Stacie had wanted to go out. Gail and Allie suggested staying in, since the twins were still so young. Emily struggled to be in a separate room from her newborns let alone a different location entirely.

'Ten . . . nine . . .'

Allie looked around at the faces which were as familiar to her as her own was. She was a newlywed. Emily a new mother. Stacie had just enjoyed her second wedding anniversary to her second husband. Wasn't this the perfect life they had dreamed of? That they had talked about in pillow forts during childhood sleepovers?

'Eight . . . seven . . .'

It had been six months since they'd last been together, at the christening. There used to be a time when they wouldn't go a day without seeing one another. Looking at her friends made Allie feel a strange ache in her chest.

'Six . . . five . . .'

She wanted to tell them about the start of a black hole she thought she'd found in her flat. The cold that had crept into her marital bed.

36

'Four . . . three . . .'

But there was never the time. Their reunions were always rushed, frantic. They'd barely hugged in greeting when the day had slipped away and they were waving goodbye. Where were the hour-long chats? The endless streams-of-consciousness they'd permit one another to babble into the small hours when they should have been sleeping?

'Two . . . one!'

The room erupted with whoops and cheers. They hugged. They toasted champagne glasses. Emily hurried out to check on the twins. Allie drank from her flute, the bubbles bitter as they slid down the back of her throat.

'Here's to next year,' Stacie gushed as she pulled Allie close. 'And we'll definitely see more of each other. Absolutely.'

Another false promise. Allie was growing tired of them.

Six

Officer: How long did it take you to reach the cabin?

POI: Long enough.

Officer: And during your journey up there how were you feeling?

POI: Tired. I was feeling tired. Travelling is draining.

Officer: Were you excited to be reunited with your friends?

POI: I was excited to reach my destination and finally get to relax.

Officer: And your thoughts about seeing all your friends?

POI: Maybe I was excited then, I don't know. So much has changed.

Officer: Have your feelings towards them changed?

POI: No. Yes. Maybe. Christ, I don't know. I'm tired, so do we really need to keep going over this?

Officer: I'm afraid so, yes. There's still an awful lot of unanswered questions which I need you to clear up.

Seven

The sky was red. Allie leaned against the wooden railing and let the wind tangle itself in her hair. She could smell the heady aroma of the pines, the sharpness of the earth beneath them which remained damp despite the heat of the day, always cast in shadow. She wanted to savour this moment – her debut novel had been released into the world, she was up at Gail's cabin being celebrated. She was twenty-seven, she had everything she'd ever wanted, didn't she? And yet the ache in her back was growing ever-persistent, a clock ticking down to doomsday.

'I'm proud of you.' Gail drew up beside her, long fingers curled around a glass of champagne. She was in her swimsuit, beads of water still clinging to her skin.

'Thanks.' Allie twisted to glance back at the hot tub, at the three women still gathered amongst its bubbles. 'At least one of you is.'

'Don't be like that.' Gail prodded her sharply in the lower arm. 'We're all proud of you, Allie. Some of us are just better at showing it than others.'

'I just . . .' Allie breathed in deeply, letting the gentle coolness of the evening fill her lungs. 'You liked it, really?'

'Truly.' Gail sipped from her glass and shuddered against the evaporating warmth of what had been an unseasonably hot day. 'It's a great book, Allie. So . . . so personal.'

'Too personal?'

Gail kept drinking.

Allie let her gaze stray along the treetops, down the mountainside which was a sea of green. 'I really appreciate you letting us come here to celebrate its release.'

'Of course.' Glass now empty, Gail placed it upon the railing and gazed out towards the horizon. 'What's the point of living in a beautiful cabin if you can't have your friends come up to stay with you now and then?'

'You're enjoying working up here?'

'I love it.' Gail gave her answer so simply, so wholly, that Allie envied her. 'I like the solitude, the quiet. Being with the animals.'

'It's a perfect fit.' Allie nodded in agreement.

'Like you with writing.'

'Oh?'

'You've always been prone to live in your own head, Allie. Getting what you feel down into words that's . . . that's powerful. And important.'

'Sure, but Diana—'

'Remember my rule,' Gail cut her off. 'When we come together like this, we make the most of it. We don't dwell on the past.'

'I wouldn't say it's always the past it's just—'

'She wouldn't be here if she didn't love you.' Gail's voice was as firm as the mountain the cabin stood upon. 'None of us would,' she added more quietly. 'Take comfort in that, Allie.'

'I know, but—'

'The greatest loves are always complicated.' Gail took her by the elbow and began guiding her back towards the hot tub, towards Emily, Diana and Stacie who were shoulder deep in bubbles and laughing heartily together. 'Don't ever lose sight of that,' Gail urged in a whispered breath as Allie stepped forward to dip her toe back in the warm water.

*

Forty minutes. That's how long their flight would take. But before that, they had to wait around the airport in the departure lounge. Travelling involved so much waiting. Waiting for the train, waiting at stations, waiting for a taxi, waiting for a flight. Allie was exhausted from waiting around.

'I need to go to the toilet.' Emily was finally released from the spell her phone had been holding her under as she stood up and glanced at Allie, who put down her book and scrambled to her feet. She knew to respect the code. Women were like wolves when it came to using public restrooms; they operated as a pack.

It was relatively quiet at their gate. A few lone travellers were scattered about, heads bent over phones and newspapers, but the airport felt like it was slowly releasing its final breath of the day, preparing to close down for the next few hours. In the distance there was the hum of an industrial vacuum cleaner, reminding Allie of the times she'd leave school late from a club – or worse, detention – only to hear the cleaning staff taking possession of the long corridors with their hoovers and mops.

'Do you need the loo?' Allie looked down at Stacie who was intently focused on filing her nails.

'I'm fine.' Stacie waggled her fingertips in her friends' direction. 'You two go. I'll watch the luggage.' As she spoke, Stacie's blue eyes didn't leave the diamond encrusted glass file she was using. Allie doubted how keenly she'd watch their luggage. But she had seen Stacie's gaze occasionally stray over to Emily when she was fervently engaged with her phone.

'Adam message you a lot?' she'd enquired coolly.

'Oh, all the time,' Emily had immediately gushed and something had danced over Stacie's features. It was there for barely a moment, but Allie had seen it, clocked its

41

unmistakable presence. Despair. For a second it had twisted Stacie from fiery to fallen. A look Allie saw every morning when she peered at her own reflection in the little mirror hanging above her bathroom sink. A lump was forming in her throat, words travelling around it to reach her lips.

Stace, is everything all right? Is something bothering you?

But they were never released. Heading towards the toilets, they left Stacie alone with her demons.

'You sure you're doing okay?' Emily asked. Her tone was soft but piqued with concern. She glanced warily over her shoulder at Stacie who was still diligently filing away at her nails.

'I really am, yeah.' And then Allie asked the one question which she knew would distract Emily from prying further. 'How are Adam and the twins?'

'Amazing!'

Of course.

'Ana and Erin are just starting to walk. It's so cute watching them stumble around together. They truly are so wonderful and to think that I *made* them,' Emily gushed, resting both hands against her chest. When she talked about her children she lit up in a way that Allie couldn't help but envy. She seemed so complete, so happy. 'And Adam is just great with them. He was made to be a dad.'

'Uh huh.'

'I miss them already.'

'When did you leave them?'

Emily turned her wrist and checked her watch. Its smooth rose-gold face shone in the garish lights of the women's bathroom. 'About four hours ago.'

It was quiet in the restrooms. Just like the entire airport was quiet. Their flight was one of the last scheduled to leave that day. Allie lingered by the wall lined with mirrors as

Emily disappeared into a cubicle. There were deeper shadows beneath her eyes, accentuated by her thick fringe and the bright strip lights above. She wanted to believe that they were a result of her long day but she knew that her countless nights lying awake in her double bed had created them. She'd stare into the darkness and listen to the cars outside, the voices that would occasionally float up to her window and burst like bubbles as someone walked by. She envied their focus. They had somewhere to be. Somewhere to go.

'And we were talking about going vegan.'

Allie spun round, briefly disorientated as Emily strode out of her cubicle. She realised that her friend had been chatting away to her the entire time.

'Vegan?'

'Uh huh, me, Adam and the twins.' Emily started washing her hands, something she was always fastidiously thorough about.

'Would that be wise with your diabetes?'

'Not really,' Emily sighed as she reached for some paper towels but brightened in an instant. 'I mean it would bring extra restrictions on my diet. And yes, it could be tricky. But think of the benefits.'

'Ethically,' Allie stated bluntly.

'Huh?'

'I mean there are ethical benefits, for sure. But for you, I mean, with your problems isn't it wise to *not* overly restrict your diet?'

'Ah.' Emily bristled as though she'd just stepped on a thorn. Allie's gaze dropped to the tiled floor, searching for the culprit of her friend's sudden pain. 'He was vegan, wasn't he?' A hand rested on Allie's shoulder, alabaster smooth. 'I'm so insensitive for bringing it up. Consider the topic dropped.'

'But it's not about—'

'Flight 903 is now boarding.' A crisp female voice boomed over the loudspeaker.

'Ooh, that's us,' Emily gave a light squeal of delight. 'We're almost there, Allie Bear. Soon we'll all be at Gail's and the Fierce Five will be reunited! I can't wait!'

Stacie's temple throbbed. She reached for the glass of water resting beside her on the large table, raised it to her lips and drank greedily from it. When she placed it down there was a red lipstick smudge across the rim.

'Been a hot summer.' The lawyer, flabby in the jawline and stomach, but still smart in a suit, smiled at her from where he was sitting across the table, sausage fingers rifling through a pile of papers.

'Uh huh,' Stacie managed to respond, wishing she hadn't guzzled champagne so greedily the previous night. But she was celebrating, wasn't she? That was what she had insisted to Diana when she turned up on her doorstep just shy of ten o' clock, the streets of London already a labyrinth of shadows. 'Tomorrow I will officially be single again,' she had declared grandly, even throwing in a graceful bow. 'I want to celebrate my glorious return to the dating scene by going out and getting completely shit-faced.'

Diana scowled. But then she always did. With a bit more convincing she threw on a fresh T-shirt, applied more eyeliner than was required and out they went. Stacie remembered bottles with labels like Moet and Veuve Cliquot, things she really couldn't afford to be drinking.

'So I'll just need your signature here, here and here.' Her lawyer was sliding papers across to her, their journey smooth against the polished wood of the table.

'And that's it?' Stacie asked, voice hoarse, throat still as dry as it had been when she awoke on a sagging couch, Diana looming

over her to curtly inform her that she was about to be late for her own divorce proceedings. Stacie glanced down at the shirt dress she was wearing, noting all the crumples, the splash of red wine near the hem that she already knew would never come out.

'That's it,' her lawyer echoed, scrunching his faded blue eyes to study her with sudden intensity. 'As much as I'm keen to have loyal clients, in my line of work we rarely get repeat business from people.'

'Uh huh.' Stacie was picking up the fountain pen laid out near where her glass of water was perched, preparing to sign her married name for the last time.

'Thirty-two and twice-divorced,' her lawyer continued.

Stacie signed once. 'Well yeah, at twenty-one it was all marry in haste crap. And they were right. Took me until I was twenty-six to realise the mistake I'd made.'

She signed twice. 'Didn't learn. Married again at thirty and . . .' she looked down at the papers before her. She signed thrice. 'Well, here I am, divorced again at thirty-two. Throw me a fucking parade.'

'No one sticks?' her lawyer wondered openly, reclaiming the freshly signed documents as Stacie pushed them across the polished table.

'No,' she agreed tightly. 'No one sticks.'

Only that wasn't true. And that was the problem. Gathering up her bag, trying in vain to smooth out the creases in her dress, Stacie muttered her goodbyes and left the blissful air-conditioning of the legal offices in Shoreditch. She stepped out into the baking summer sun, thinking all the while of the boy she had first loved, and the old adage her grandmother would lament in her rare lucid moments: 'First love, last love, worst love of all.' Stacie reached into her bag for oversized sunglasses and hastily put them on, keen to hide both her hangover and her despair from the rest of the world.

Eight

Allie gazed at her reflection in the window. Edinburgh was beneath them as the plane lifted higher, soaring above the clouds. But looking out Allie saw mostly darkness and deep within it the distant twinkle of lights far, far below.

Flights on aeroplanes were supposed to feel liberating, glamorous. Allie used to like to close her eyes and dream up exotic locations she could be headed to, even on her honeymoon to New York. As Lucas sat watching back-to-back movies beside her, occasionally nudging her to scorn some sloppy dialogue he'd just had to endure, Allie fantasised about all the places in the world she wanted to visit. New York had always been on her wish list. Their time there had been frenzied and exhilarating, with hours spent prowling second-hand bookstores and museums and evenings spent enjoying Broadway shows. It had been perfect.

Her stomach dipped as the plane pitched ever higher. A soft chime rang out and the seat belt sign turned off. Now she could move around the suspended tin can if she so wished. And she wished. Snapping her window visor closed, Allie quickly unbuckled her belt and straightened. In less than three steps she was traversing the aisle, walking amid strangers as she tried to create some distance between her and her thoughts.

'I say we get this party started a little early.' When she returned to her seat Stacie was clutching two small bottles of white wine, arms outstretched across the aisle towards her in offering. Allie grabbed at the nearest one and sat back down.

'Oh.' Emily pursed her lips and shook her head. 'I really shouldn't. You know I can only have one drink.'

'And here's your one,' Stacie replied smoothly.

'But Gail will want to toast her birthday when we arrive,' Emily protested.

Stacie scoffed loudly. 'Lara Croft won't want to toast anything. She'll have us all out hiking at dawn tomorrow if the weather permits it.'

The lust for adventure; it was within Gail's genetic code. Whenever Allie called, she was always outside, struggling to hear anything over the whip of the wind roaring against the phone. Even after Melissa left, Gail kept hiking across rugged highlands with just a compass for guidance. She continued as though everything was fine.

Allie had checked in once or twice, asking how Gail was holding up. The response was always brisk, 'I'm okay, don't worry.'

But Allie trusted the honesty within it. Gail was a survivor. She tackled life like one never-ending exped- ition, always being prepared for the worst before it could actually happen. Maybe if she'd been there that day, out on the bridge, then—

'I wouldn't be surprised if Gail has plotted an entire route for us along those bloody mountains she lives on,' Stacie prattled on indignantly.

'You think?' Allie drifted back into the moment and thought about the clothes she'd hurriedly packed into her holdall. There were jumpers, scarves, jeans. A pair of Timberland boots, but no shoes that she felt were particularly well suited for hiking in the Scottish Highlands.

Didn't you need professional footwear for something like that? Wouldn't Gail have specifically mentioned if she had hiking on the agenda for the weekend? She'd know that the others lacked her militant sense of preparedness and would need guidance if certain items were required to traverse the mountainside.

Six weeks. There had been ample time to pack. Yet Allie had procrastinated. Up until the last minute, she'd told herself she wouldn't, shouldn't go.

There'll be too many questions.

But loyalty was a hard habit to break.

'Gail lives for the outdoors.' Stacie rolled her eyes and leaned back in her chair. 'This *cabin* is actually a hunting lodge she bought just outside her laird's estate, remember?'

'Hunting?' Emily looked frantic. She glanced between the bottle of wine she'd been handed and Stacie, unsure which was more dangerous.

'Selective memory,' Stacie hissed under her breath, then raising her voice, 'Well her job is all about hunting, isn't it?'

'Stace—' Allie tried to stop what was coming but her friend powered over her interruption.

'She's the *grounds keeper*, Emily. Up in the highlands that doesn't involve mowing a lawn and pruning some hedges like it does in Manchester.'

'Then what does it entail?' Emily wondered aloud.

'Culling.' Stacie's lips twitched up into a cruel smile.

'Stace.' Allie threw her friend a warning look which went ignored.

'It's not all sunshine and rainbows at the cabin,' Stacie continued, 'or in the rest of the world. I know that *you* like to act as though nothing bad has ever happened but some of us don't enjoy living in the land of denial and—'

'Let's just keep things upbeat, okay?' Allie snapped, smiling so hard her cheeks ached with the pressure of the pretence.

'I'm not a child,' Emily muttered darkly, focused on her phone on which there was a picture of her beloved twins giving gum-filled grins. 'Don't treat me like one.'

'Em, I just . . .' Allie felt her cheeks starting to burn.

'Let Stacie carry on.' There was a challenge in Emily's voice, in the hard set of her shoulders, as she raised her gaze to meet Stacie's. 'I want to know more about how she thinks I act.'

'Shall we talk about you or the hunting lodge?' Stacie's eyes bored into Emily's.

'I know what Gail does up at the cabin.' Putting down her phone Emily raised a hand to massage the space between her eyes, as though waving a white flag. 'She doesn't hunt, she herself would point out the distinction between hunting and culling to you. I'm not as sheltered as you like to believe.'

'Hey, come on, this trip is meant to be fun!' Allie's face continued to ache with the effort of smiling so brightly. Stacie wore a stony pout as she flicked her hair over her shoulder but at least she was remaining silent. But in the ensuing silence, Allie's thoughts found her, turbulent and unsettled.

Was Diana now anxiously making her way up to the cabin just as they were? Would there be any joy at all to soften her expression when she locked eyes with Allie, or would she look the way she always did – guarded and resentful.

It should be me not you, Allie wanted to scream at her surly friend, the mutinous thought tightening her muscles.

'As if she's anything other than bloody sheltered,' Stacie muttered as her nails tapped a fast beat against her pull-down tray table. 'She lives in a fucking fairy tale. She acts like the past never even happened, all she cares about is preserving her happiness ever after.'

'What are you guys talking about?' Emily leaned forward, curious.

'Nothing,' Allie answered quickly as she dragged up the visor beside her and pointed at the window. Outside there was only darkness. It blanketed the small aeroplane like a dense, impenetrable fog. Looking out into its depths it seemed impossible to imagine that light had ever existed in the world. 'Why don't you keep a lookout for lights? We should see the landing strip for the airport soon.'

'You think?' Emily turned to peer through the porthole-sized window.

'Yeah, any minute now.'

Stacie clicked her fingers together. 'Hand me that.' She was staring at the small bottle of wine resting on the arm of Emily's seat, abandoned. 'If she's not going to drink it then I will.'

'Here.' Allie sent the bottle back across the aisle.

'I so need this.' Stacie unscrewed the cap and tipped the contents of the bottle into her plastic cup.

'Stace, take it easy. This isn't a race.'

'Isn't it?' Stacie wondered darkly as the flight attendant announced that they would soon be landing.

The walls of the small university halls room were bare. Where once there had been images of leather-clad rock bands there was now just the smooth grey paint that had now outlived their time in halls. Allie leaned against the doorframe and peered in, watching dust motes dance in a sliver of sunlight as Diana zipped up the last of her bags.

'You all done packing?' She asked the question lazily, as was fitting with the subdued tone of the afternoon. Final exams were

finished, dissertations had been handed in. All that was left to do was pack up three years of memories and move on.

'What?' Diana dropped the faded black T-shirt she was holding and instantly straightened. Eyes thickly covered in kohl liner narrowed, she raised a hand to tuck a loose strand of neon pink hair behind her ear.

'Packing.' Allie nodded at the bags strewn about the floor. 'Are you all finished?' Crossing her arms, she held them tight to her chest and remained on the threshold to the little room.

'I'm . . . yeah . . . pretty much.' Diana spun in a circle, eyeing the now vacant corners of her room. 'Gail asked you to check in on me?'

'Sure did.' Allie nodded stiffly. 'Wants to know when you're ready to go out for pizza.'

'Pizza,' Diana echoed with a heavy sigh. 'Right, yeah, of course. Gail couldn't let us all just bloody pack up and leave, that would be too easy, wouldn't it?'

'Do you want to just leave?'

'What?' Diana's voice was briefly shrill as she locked eyes with Allie. 'Fine, fuck it, pizza, whatever. It's just a few more hours of my life, what do I care?'

'Don't come if you don't want to.'

'And risk Gail's wrath?' Diana shook her head and resumed packing. 'I don't think so.'

'Where are you rushing off to anyway?'

'The rest of my life, Allie. Maybe now I'm done with university I can actually start living it.' Stretching forward she plucked a lace thong off the floor and the sleeve of her jumper rolled up to reveal the curved base of a fresh tattoo.

'When did you get that?' Allie leaned forward but didn't step inside.

'Oh.' Diana hastily shoved her sleeve back down. 'Last week to, you know, commemorate graduating.'

51

'It's an . . . anchor?'

'Points for perception,' Diana deadpanned.

'Into sailing now, are we?'

'Actually . . .' Wrapping her fingers around the etched mark in question Diana turned her body fully towards the door. Allie shivered as a slice of cool air blew in through the partly open window behind them. 'The anchor doesn't represent sailing.'

'So what does it represent?'

Diana chewed on the inside of her cheek before replying. 'Being held in place by something.'

'Ah.' Allie dropped her arms to her sides. 'I see.'

'But it can't hold you forever.' Diana crouched down to zip up the last of her bags. 'That's the point of an anchor, it can be raised.'

Hands clasped Allie's shoulders. 'How are we doing in here?' Gail was all brightness and enthusiasm, a general rousing her troops. 'Nearly done?'

'I'm pretty much there.' Straightening up, Diana dusted her hands together, her latest tattoo now hidden away by her long sleeves.

'Awesome.' Gail gave Allie's shoulders a squeeze. 'So how about we all head out for pizza to Marco's for the last time?'

'Actually . . .' Allie slid away from the threshold, from Gail's grip, and began moving back towards her own vacant room. 'I'm really not all that hungry.'

'But, Allie . . .' Gail stepped towards her, arms outstretched like a bridge. 'We're all going, it's the last thing we're going to do before we finally leave.'

'She's not hungry,' Diana snapped. 'And in all honesty, neither am I.'

'Oh, come on.' Gail's angry gaze flitted back and forth along the corridor, taking in her pair of friends. 'This is tradition, this is—'

'I think it's time to start some new traditions.' Allie's hand had found her door handle and she was pushing it down, hearing the now-familiar squeak of old hinges.

'Allie Bear.' Gail hurried after her, sending anxious glances over her shoulder. 'Did she say something?' Lowering her voice she entered Allie's room uninvited. 'Because if she did—'

'No, it's fine. Really. Today should be about new beginnings, not past traditions, that's all.'

'She's just lashing out because her dad's bail hearing was this week,' Gail revealed, taking care to close the door. 'Please, Allie, don't exclude yourself from dinner. You really don't need to.'

'Honestly, I'm fine.' Her words were slightly shaky, but in time she'd come to perfect the lie. Unsatisfied, Gail's lips and eyebrows plateaued into heavy set lines.

'Allie—'

'I still need to finish packing.'

The room around them was stripped bare.

'Her bark is worse than her bite, you know that.'

'Maybe I'm tired of being barked at.'

'Allie—'

'Don't make me an anchor, Gail. Please.'

'But you're—'

The door was thrust open and Stacie stared at them both, hair pulled back in a severe ponytail. 'Christ, are we going out to eat or not? I swear if I don't get some pizza in me soon I'm going to waste away.'

Gail stepped into the corridor and held out her hand to Allie. 'So, are you ready?'

Allie didn't take it. But she closed the door to her empty room and turned the lock.

Nine

An hour later and they were traversing the final part of their journey.

Nausea greeted Allie at every turn as the taxi rumbled its way along winding roads, navigating through snow that fell like stardust from the black sky and gathered in drifts beyond the glare of the headlights.

We can't let go.

The thought vibrated through her like a poorly struck chord. And it wouldn't leave. With each bounce in the road, her mind kept tormenting her. Glancing at Stacie she saw that she clearly wasn't the only one haunted by her thoughts. Stacie was staring fixedly into the oncoming snow as though she'd just seen a ghost standing beneath its confetti-like veil.

'Stace, you okay?'

Stacie remained frozen, the question seemingly unheard.

Allie had checked her phone before leaving the airport. No new messages, no missed calls. And as the taxi inched ever higher up the mountainside road her signal ebbed away. Did it even matter? No one was calling her.

Had Diana already arrived at the cabin? Were she and Gail laughing merrily together over glasses of wine? Laughter which would die on Diana's lips the second Allie arrived.

With a jolt the car came to a standstill out in the snowy wilderness. 'This is as far as I can go.' The driver turned to look at the three women bundled in the back of his taxi.

'But we're not at the cabin yet.' Stacie looked through her window, at the darkness which was closing in on them from all sides.

'It's just at the top of this path. Snow's too deep for the car to get up there.'

Allie leaned forward from her position wedged between her two friends. She looked beyond the windscreen, following the line of the driver's pointed finger where he was gesturing into the black beyond. It looked as though they'd literally stopped in the middle of nowhere. For a moment she thought she was peering into the black hole which had grown beyond her heart, her flat, and was now taking over her entire life. Her hands started to shake just as she blinked herself back into reality.

In the glow of the headlights, she saw the snow. It glistened like a thousand tightly packed diamonds. Way up in the distance she saw a yellow light; a sagging star in the night sky. She swallowed against the knot in her throat. The yellow light was the cabin. It had to be.

'I guess we've got to walk then.' Allie nudged Stacie to get out.

'Walk!' Stacie's voice was fierce with protest but she was tightening the scarf around her neck and pulling up the faux-fur-lined hood of her coat. Allie flexed her hands in her fingerless gloves. Inside the taxi it was warm. The heating was turned all the way up and the car hummed as it fought to keep out the cold.

'You girls take care climbing up there,' the driver instructed as they began to pile out of the car. Allie thrust a twenty-pound note towards him as she heard the boot pop open behind her. She quietly groaned at the thought of lugging all the bags up towards the cabin. 'Thanks.' The driver stuffed the note into his coat pocket. Allie was about to climb out when he tugged her back by the hem of her parka. 'Radio says there's a big storm blowing in. Make sure you've got lots of supplies up in that cabin of yours.'

'Thanks, I'm sure my friend who lives up there is fully prepared.' Allie smiled courteously, knowing they wouldn't be short of supplies. Gail was a planner. She'd have made lists of what she needed to buy, prepared all the bedrooms for her guests and shovelled away as much snow as she could. But clearly not enough of it. It crunched underfoot as Allie rounded the taxi, joining Stacie and Emily in the beam of the headlights where they'd dragged their luggage through the snow.

Emily hugged her arms against herself, already shivering despite the added layer of a bright pink gilet she'd put on since their flight had landed.

Allie had to admit that it was no longer just cold out, it was freezing. The wind carried knives that scratched against her cheeks and numbed her fingertips. 'So, we're just heading up this path.' She looked down and saw only snow. It was perfect. Pristine. Save for . . .

'Ah.' Stacie shone the light from her phone against the ground, focusing on the indentation. A footprint. 'I guess we just follow these up.'

The taxi pulled away, taking its light with it. Stacie's phone was the only thing keeping the shadows at bay. The snow seemed almost blue within its limited glow.

'It shouldn't be that far . . .' Allie shouldered her holdall, already regretting having packed so much. But she was a worrier, always preparing for the worst. In her experience, it paid to.

'Are you all right with that?' Emily shot Allie a concerned look as she angled her own case behind her, ready for the climb.

'It's fine.' Allie smiled a little too brightly. The truth was that on her back, where there should have been pain there was often numbness. A reminder to Allie that not all that is lost is eventually found again.

'Let's do this.' Stacie took a determined step forward, juggling her suitcase handle in one hand and her phone in the other. 'I'm going to tell Gail to pop something expensive when we get up there.'

'It's a steep path.' Emily sounded a little breathless.

'I remember the cabin being isolated,' Allie recalled.

'Mmm,' Emily mumbled in agreement.

'But last time we came it was summer and everywhere was green.'

'What did we . . .' Emily grunted as she forced her suit-cases over a bump in the path, hidden beneath the snow which continued to loudly crunch underfoot, 'come for?'

'My thirtieth.' The wind stole away some of Allie's voice, carrying her words up the mountain.

On her thirtieth birthday, there had been sunshine and cocktails. They'd sat out on the decking behind the cabin and looked at the majestic Scottish landscape. When the sun set and turned the sky pink they gathered in the hot tub, their merriment carrying across the steep mountains. Her friends had toasted the success of her first book.

'To Allie,' they had chimed as they clinked glasses. But one voice was absent from the congratulatory chorus.

'Dammit.' Stacie stopped walking which meant that the others had to too. The light from her phone lingered on her booted feet as she stared at the screen, her expression shrouded in shadow.

'What's wrong? Is your battery running out?' Allie was already dipping her fingers into her coat pocket, grazing the smooth surface of her phone. 'Shall I grab mine and—'

'There's no signal!' Stacie sounded like she was telling them that they only had minutes left to live. 'None at all. Not even one single bloody bar.'

'Oh.' Allie abandoned her phone and readjusted her holdall against her back.

'No signal,' Stacie squeaked, her voice rising so high that soon only dogs would be able to hear her. 'I mean, what are we supposed to do with *no signal*?'

'Maybe Gail has a signal booster in the cabin,' Emily offered hopefully. 'Adam bought one for the house and it works really well.'

'You know most people don't need a signal booster in their home' – Stacie was once again lighting the way, allowing them to carry on – 'because most people live in houses, not McMansions.'

It rarely snowed in London. Allie couldn't remember the last time she'd seen the streets tightly packed with it. But back home, back in the embrace of the north, winters were often white.

When Allie was twelve the snow had fallen so thick and so deep that it came over the top of her wellies when she went outside.

'Snow day!' Stacie had screamed down the phone just after eight that morning. 'We're all going to Emily's since she has the biggest garden.'

And she did. Emily's garden swept away from her detached stone-washed house and included a grand oak tree which now stood stark and bare, its branches stripped of all their greenery.

Diana and Gail were already committed to building a snowman when Allie arrived. Together they were rolling large snowballs around the garden.

'Allie Bear!' Emily greeted her as she always did, with a hug. 'Can you believe how beautiful everywhere looks? I stayed up all night watching the snow fall.'

'Yeah, it's . . .' Allie glanced around. The entire world was blanched and muffled, glittering and serene. And the day stretched ahead of them all, potentially endless and joyous. 'I love the snow,' Allie admitted with a shy smile.

'My mum says you're too pensive,' Stacie stated, mouth full of caramel from the chocolate bar she'd been chewing. 'She said it's not good for little girls to be so serious.'

'Be serious,' Diana had interjected. 'In fact, never stop being serious. It's what I like best about you.'

Diana wore her troubles behind a permanent scowl and dramatically short hair, the ends of which now stuck out beneath her frayed woollen hat. If there had been a row in her home the previous night she wasn't showing direct signs of it. If anything, that morning in the snow, she seemed uncharacteristically content, the crease in the centre of her forehead slightly softer than usual.

'He's like a summer storm,' she'd explained one night as they lay on the floor at the base of the fort they'd made in Allie's bedroom. The other three girls were downstairs making batches of microwave popcorn for the Dawson's Creek marathon they were about to embark upon. A pile of VHS videos were already stacked up beside the portable television, which Allie's dad had kindly carried up to her room earlier that day.

'How?' Allie wondered. Talking about Diana's father made her uneasy. She couldn't imagine her own dad getting angry, striking out at the people he was supposed to love.

'Like, you know you hear the thunder going away and think it's okay again?'

'Yeah.'

'And then suddenly it cracks above you so loud you think you might go deaf as it's back right overhead, on top of your house.'

'I know what you mean.'

'My dad is like that. He thunders away and just when you think it's quiet, think it's safe, he's back again, shaking the walls with his fists.'

The world was white and dazzling in the early morning sunlight and amidst a wealth of freshly fallen snow even Allie failed to be serious. She scooped up a ball of snow in her gloved hand and fired it directly at Diana. It connected squarely with the side of her head, leaving a white imprint.

The fun of it all throbbed within Allie's veins. She felt almost delirious with delight. When Emily's father ordered them all inside to warm up, they didn't object. They collected around the fire and nursed mugs of fresh hot chocolate provided by Emily's mother, who fretted over them like a nervous hen. Drinking in the sweet contents of her warm drink, Allie felt more than content – she felt happy. Her body held that desirable kind of ache that promised a deep night's sleep. She wished there was some way to capture the moment, to store it along with the taste of cocoa and marsh-mallows upon her tongue. Only of course there wasn't. But if Allie had known what was coming, she might have tried harder.

Ten

The cabin smelt just as Allie remembered it: pine and vanilla with a slight undercurrent of mothballs. The trio burst in through the front door, Stacie refusing to knock. Allie's body instantly began shuddering with delight as the warmth of the room wrapped around her.

A fire was burning in the hearth, crackling and spitting as it ate its way through an assortment of logs.

There was an open-plan living and kitchen area, bordered by six doors which led off to four bedrooms and two bathrooms. A narrow staircase in the right-hand corner of the room led up to the final set of bedrooms which were both en suite and the most highly sought-after in the property. Everywhere was covered in smooth pine wood from the floor to the walls. Even the epic dining table, wedged like a barrier between the kitchen and the living space was made of pure pine.

Three large blue sofas were nestled around the fire and Diana was curled up in the corner of one, a cup of tea in her hands. But Gail was standing, coming over to her friends, an untainted look of joy softening her features.

'You guys, you're here.'

Gail was like Wonder Woman. She wasn't just adventurous; she also looked like the iconic character, even in a white cable-knit jumper and dark jeans. Hair so brown it was almost black was gathered at the nape of her neck in a messy bun. And she was tall, the tallest of them all, bordering on six feet. But she wasn't willowy and slight, like Emily and Diana. She was muscular, powerful. At school, she always got picked first for netball teams. She was faster than anyone else. And fiercely competitive.

'Yes we're here, just about.' Stacie dramatically wiped a hand across her forehead and wilted against her luggage. 'That's one hell of a walk-up.'

The wind slapped against the side of the cabin. It sounded like an enormous party cracker being pulled. Allie jumped.

'It's blowing up a real gale out there, huh?' The light didn't leave Gail's eyes as she came over to embrace each of her friends, enjoying her own joke.

'Is there a storm setting in?' Allie wondered uneasily as Gail pulled her in close and gave her a squeeze, pressing her against the softness of her jumper. 'The driver mentioned something about a storm and—'

'It's December. It's Scotland. There are going to be storms.' Diana had got up. She lingered on the periphery of the group, red lips set in a hard line.

Diana didn't like being thirteen. She didn't like the way her chest kept getting larger, her legs longer. She didn't like the cramps which now came every month.

'You're becoming a woman,' her mother had told her sourly, 'you'll learn to realise what a burden that is.'

She'd told Gail first about getting her period, correctly predicting that her most mature friend would offer practical advice.

'Hot-water bottles,' she'd curtly told Diana, 'but not too hot.'

Allie had seemed almost in awe. Little Allie, who was always behind with any physical development, the runt of their litter. At thirteen Allie was still in a training bra, not that she even needed that.

Secondary school had been a shock to the system for all of them. The days longer, the teachers stricter than they had been at their comfortable primary. Diana lived for the weekends and the almost obligatory sleepovers that came with them. The location switched between Allie's and Emily's houses since theirs were the largest and that suited Diana just fine, the last thing she needed was to give her friends a front-row seat to the drama going on at home.

'My dad is working late a lot,' Allie confided during one such sleepover when she and Diana were alone in her large kitchen, standing beside oak countertops on popcorn duty. 'Even later than my mum does.'

'At least he comes home,' Diana said flatly.

'Your dad doesn't come home?' Allie asked, eyes growing large.

Kernels popped. In the nearby lounge, the sound of laughter carried through the closed doors.

Diana looked at her smallest friend, always eager like a small, stray dog that just needed a home and to be told it was good. Diana wanted to grab her slim shoulders, shake her and tell her that she had everything anyone could ever want; a big house, two nice cars in the driveway, a bedroom filled with a double bed and her own television. But there was a sadness inside Allie, a loneliness, which Diana had always been drawn to. Had understood. So instead she sighed, shifted her weight onto her other foot, one arm resting on the kitchen counter.

'Most nights he doesn't come home, no.'

'Where is he?'

Diana gave a brief shrug. 'Drunk in some pub, I guess. Spending the night on a mate's couch, a park bench. Who knows? I hear him and my mum shouting about it all the time.'

'That can't be good,' Allie noted sadly.

'No,' Diana agreed. 'It's not.'

The microwave pinged to alert them that the popcorn had finished popping but neither girl moved, knowing that the instructions called for a solid minute to pass before the bag could be opened and the sweet contents tumbled into a large bowl.

'You know, if things at home are stressful, you can always come and sleep over here more, like in the week and stuff,' Allie offered with a tentative smile.

'Thanks.' Diana breathed in the now buttery air of the kitchen. 'But home hasn't felt like home for a long time, I'm kind of used to it being that way.'

'That sucks.'

'Yep.'

The minute was almost over. The laughter in the next room had died down.

'The invitation to stay here, it doesn't have, you know, a limit or anything. Because we're family. We'll always be family.'

Diana scratched at her lower arms. She could see that Allie truly believed in what she was saying and she pitied her for that. Diana knew first-hand that even family didn't stick around forever. All relationships had an expiration date. A part of her wanted to point that out, harden the hopeful optimism in Allie's eyes into her own jaded stare. Instead she pointed to the microwave. 'Let's empty that out, shall we?' She managed to smile somewhat convincingly. 'I'm starving.'

Eleven

Sometimes, Allie thought that her friend's tattoos and dyed hair were a warning system, like a brightly coloured bug, poisonous to consume. But now most of those tattoos were covered under an oversized sweater dress and thick black tights as Diana peered over at the newcomers, still clutching her Cath Kidston mug. There was a wobble in her hands, a slant to her posture, which hinted that she'd been drinking something much stronger than tea before their arrival.

'Oh, Diana' – Stacie tossed her plait over her shoulder and boldly strode over to her surly friend – 'almost didn't expect to see you here since you declined our offer to travel up together.'

Allie cringed, keen to keep tiptoeing around one another in the dance of denial which they had all perfected over the years. This weekend was not the time to start ripping open old wounds.

'I flew in from Heathrow,' Diana replied flatly. 'I didn't have the time to waste being stuck on a train all day.'

'Too busy colouring in your hair with crayons?' Stacie glared, one hand wedged against her waist. Her eyes burned with the challenge of confrontation, but she was merely a bull snorting with no intention to charge.

'I like how my hair looks.' Diana raised a single eyebrow.

'It makes you look about fifteen.'

'Okay, ladies.' Gail moved to stand between them, a hand on each of their shoulders. The only thing she was missing was a referee's whistle. 'Let's not squabble. Let's remember the real reason we are up here for the next three days – *me*.'

'On that note.' Emily wrestled a large bottle of champagne out of her suitcase. 'Let's get this party started. It's Gail's big day, happy birthday, lovely, here's to the next thirty-five.'

After echoes of celebratory comments had flickered around the room Stacie pressed a hand to her stomach and loudly declared that she was starving.

'I've not had a decent meal all day.'

Even Allie had to admit that now the nausea from the taxi drive up the mountain had passed she felt an emptiness in her stomach that the drinks she'd downed during the day couldn't fill as they sloshed around together. And she was growing nervous. The desire to bite down on something, anything, was almost compulsive. For the moment she had to contend with nibbling on the end of her thumbnail as Gail explained what their dinner for the night would be.

'Pizza all round,' she said – words which surely filled them all with a sense of nostalgia. 'And don't worry, I made sure to pick up enough varieties to keep everyone happy.'

That final admission, that she wanted to *keep everyone happy* pricked at Allie like an exposed needle. Even though it was her birthday, Gail was still inhabiting the role of mother, doing her best to care for the group. She wanted to tell Gail that she should have been putting herself and her needs first for a change, but if she did that, what would become of the rest of them?

'Your thirty-fifth birthday and you're eating *pizza*.' Stacie's lips dipped with disdain, but the way she followed Gail towards the small cooker nestled within the built-in kitchen hinted that she was more excited by the prospect of the modest culinary delights on offer than she wanted to let on. Her negative response to everything was almost a tick.

'Pizza is uni food,' she noted quietly.

'Be grateful that you're being fed at all.' Diana stretched her arms along the back of the sofa, scowling. 'Gail is already putting us up for the weekend. She's not a bloody bed and breakfast you know.'

'I know.' Stacie snapped as she spun round, returning Diana's hard stare with one equally as iron-clad before exhaling sharply through her nose and turning back to Gail. Wordlessly she helped the birthday girl unbox their dinner and load various varieties of pizza into the warmed cooker.

'There isn't all that much fresh food in the local store this time of year,' Gail explained apologetically as she straightened and dusted her hands against her jeans.

'Couldn't you have just gone outside and got us something fresh?' Stacie smirked devilishly as she looked across the room, locking eyes with Emily. 'I quite fancy some venison.'

'Pizza is great,' Allie quickly interjected as she too sought Emily, who had strayed over to the fire and was watching the dancing flames with interest, raising her palms to it as she absorbed some of the heat. 'We've all always loved pizza.'

'Rare for us all to agree on something,' Diana muttered from where she remained positioned on the sofa, legs curled up beneath her in a feline pose. The pink in her hair didn't suit her, Allie thought.

'That's why I chose pizza.' Gail divided her grin between each of her gathered friends. 'Because it's something we all like.'

The smell of melting cheese began to curdle with wood smoke. It was a strangely alluring combination, comforting in its starchy thickness. Emily remained close to the fire, still offering her palms to it in reverence.

'Sometimes Adam and I make pizza with the twins.' She smiled into the twisting flames as she spoke.

Stacie's eyes instantly rolled. 'Course you do. I can just picture Adam busily kneading the dough, dressed in his apron and—'

'Help me set the plates out for dinner.' Gail was already grabbing Stacie's elbow, guiding her back to the table.

'Because it's such a daunting task.' Again, Stacie's mouth seemed to be working separately from the rest of her body as she began gathering plates and neatly setting them out. 'I mean, how many forks will we each need?' She paused to snigger at her own joke.

'There goes the bucket list for thirty,' Stacie had scoffed as she entered the third decade of her life, eyes bloodshot from the numerous glasses of champagne she'd downed at the exclusive Mayfair club they had all gathered in. 'I was supposed to have made my West End debut by now. Fuck it.' She'd grabbed a fresh glass and began chugging down its bubbling contents.

'You've still got time.' Allie wanted to believe this was true, didn't want to see her friend sink down into the depths of regret that seemed to have claimed so many of their parents and peers over the years. Allie saw the shadow of sadness that hung beneath her own mother's eyes, felt the ache in so many words left unsaid at each stagnant family meal. Divorced at sixty, she knew that her mother felt like she'd been put back on the highest shelf – one where she'd never be reached or seen again.

'And to not become a grandmother . . .' The words had tumbled out after one too many sweet sherries. 'Even that chance

at joy has been stolen from me.' Somehow Allie had kept her face calm despite the verbal slap she'd just been given.

We can't let go.

How far did the ripples of that day extend? Were more than just her friends tainted by what had happened? Had Allie's parents been damaged too?

'You wrote your book.' Stacie grabbed at the air as though reaching for something invisible. Her shoulders dropped in a sad slump and she released a long sigh, blowing at the fiery ribbons of her hair that had strayed across her face. 'That was your dream and you achieved it.' Her hand reached for Allie, grabbing at her little friend's cold wrist. 'But at such a cost.' Stacie's blue eyes were awash with developing tears. 'Do you ever wonder when you'll stop paying for it all? And if it was worth it?'

Allie couldn't answer. Diana had drifted over, hair cobalt blue, and wedged herself between the birthday girl and the writer, her back turned towards Allie.

'You should be dancing.' Diana was leading Stacie away, returning her to the centre of the dance floor where the others were swaying to the music, their movements shaky from too much drink. Only Emily still stood up straight, but her eyes were on Allie, blonde eyebrows drawing together. Her lips parted as though she were about to speak, but anything she said would go unheard, the music was too loud, too powerful. Allie knew she should join them out on the dance floor, should spin Stacie around until her friend was on the verge of throwing up, but she needed distance. Her legs began carrying her away, towards the restroom, before her mind even knew what she was doing.

Twelve

Allie floated amongst her friends as dinner cooked, never settling in any one position for more than a few moments. The warmth of the cabin caressed her but brought no comfort. She felt restless though she had no idea why. Already her muscles were throbbing from the long day spent travelling the length of the country. She should have been settling down on the sofa, savouring the heat of the fire. Instead, she paced the room like a nervous cat.

Fifteen minutes passed with the crackling of fire and clattering of plates and glasses as Gail and Stacie hovered around the table while Emily and Diana lingered by the fire. It was only Allie who drifted.

'Dinner's ready,' Gail announced with a smile. 'Bon appetit.'

A modest meal of pizza and salad was covering the large pine table. In turn, each of the friends gathered around it, lowering themselves into stiff wooden chairs while breathing in the welcoming aroma of freshly cooked food. As Allie bit down on a slice laden with pepperoni she couldn't help but be escorted back to the days when she'd lived alongside her friends in a single corridor during their time at university. Back then pizza and pasta were the staples of their diet, the girls taking it in turns to cook dinner each night.

The spicy meat deliciously singed her tongue. Allie reached for another slice.

'So have you had a good birthday?' Emily asked politely as she took bird-like bites of her slice of vegetable pizza. Several minutes had already slipped by during which no one spoke, they just ate. Allie wondered if the others were chewing in contemplative silence as she was, allowing the melted cheese and stodgy base to stir up memories of the past?

'Mmm.' Gail nodded, her mouth too full to speak.

'Have you just been up here all day?' Stacie wondered as she reached for a new serving of the spiciest pizza in the centre of the table – it was topped with beef and jalapenos.

'I arrived earlier.' – Diana was wiping crumbs from her mouth – 'so she's not been alone all day if that's what you're asking.'

'That wasn't what I was asking.' Stacie's tone was flat, but her eyes sparkled with a challenge.

Again, Allie found herself wondering what had transpired at the cabin before her arrival. Had Gail and Diana settled around the fire and enjoyed glasses of wine as they caught up with one another, maybe even reminisced? Had Diana smiled, laughed? Allie couldn't recall the last time her friend had smiled around her. The thought made the pizza catch in her throat.

'It is as beautiful as I remember up here. But so remote.' Emily was continuing with her polite line of conversation.

Gail swallowed and nodded primly. 'I like it. Some days it's just me and the mountain and I don't see a single living soul.'

'Sounds lonely,' Stacie noted, fingers tightening against the slice of pizza she was holding.

'Sounds perfect.' Allie couldn't conceal the longing in her voice. What she wouldn't give to be able to seclude herself somewhere so remote, somewhere so far removed from pitying glances and the endless treadmill of hospital appointments and check-ups. And him. If she were up here, alone, she wouldn't see him in every corner of her home, in the back of every tall, slim stranger on the street. Twice that week alone her heart had all but stopped as she prepared to descend into the tube station and thought she saw him several paces ahead, blending into the crowd. On both occasions, Allie had scurried back to her flat like a frightened rabbit returning to the safety of its warren. She wasn't ready to face him, to put on an act in public and pretend that everything was fine.

But you are fine.

That's what she kept telling everyone. And if she said it enough, she might even start to believe it herself.

No one responded to Allie's comment. They'd know why Allie longed for solitude, why she shunned the world as much as she did.

'I admire you for sticking it out up here like you do,' Diana commended Gail as she plucked up the last piece of spicy pizza, blatantly ignoring Stacie's glare of alarm that she'd beaten her to it.

Stacie leaned back in her chair, openly seething, mouth set in a tight line. For a moment Allie ceased chewing, waiting for the display of fireworks to begin.

'Let her attack them like she does,' Gail would say. 'It's her way of coping. Better she behaves like this than to reopen those old wounds, don't you think?'

'You make living up here look easy.' Emily smiled kindly across the table.

'It's not so bad.' Gail raised her shoulders in a modest shrug. 'You get used to the weather, the isolation. Plus, I love working with nature. With the deer.'

'But don't you ever feel bad about what you have to do to the deer?' Emily had ceased eating, her attention now solely on the birthday girl.

Allie loudly cleared her throat in an attempt to provide a distraction.

'I . . .' Gail leaned back in her chair in contemplation. Looking around the table her dark eyes found each of her friends as she gently drummed her fingertips against the pine of the table. 'Not really, no,' she admitted honestly. 'I mean, it's hard, yes, to kill something, but at the same time, it has to be done for the good of the herd. You kill the one to protect the many.'

'I couldn't do it,' Emily whispered softly. 'I couldn't kill something that was alive.'

'Well you can't very well kill something that's dead,' Stacie jested.

A chair grated against the floor as Diana stood up. She moved away from the table and plucked a bottle of champagne out of the fridge. 'I think it's time we move on to the drinking stage of the night. What do you think?'

As everyone else either nodded or mumbled in the affirmative Allie noticed that she'd eaten the entire pepperoni pizza that was out. There hadn't been the chance for anyone else to grab a slice as she'd wolfed it down, not through hunger, but from nerves. Back during her first date with Lucas at a little independent cinema in Shoreditch, she'd ordered a large bag of popcorn and subsequently eaten the entire thing before the trailers had even finished. Now her nerves were eating themselves rabid once again, the butterflies in her stomach still dancing despite the carb-heavy dinner that had just descended on them.

The champagne was opened with a loud pop. Diana had expertly relieved the bottle of its cork and was now lining up flute glasses on the kitchen counter. Already the lingering smell of pizza had been overridden by the woody aroma of the blazing fire.

'We should do a toast,' Emily suggested as she aided her friend in distributing the glasses around the room.

'We should just bloody drink!' Stacie remarked before taking a long sip from her own drink. 'Who wants to toast getting *old*?'

'We're not old.' Allie said the words but knew it was a lie. Maybe they weren't old yet but they were certainly *older*. Considerably so. But Allie still saw the traces of the girls they had once been. Gail was still brave, Emily serene and elegant, Stacie dramatic and Diana distant. If anything, time had exacerbated their core traits.

And Allie, what did her friends see when they looked at her?

She sipped on champagne and looked around the room. Stacie was laughing gregariously as she stood over by the stereo and Diana was leaning against the fireplace, staring into the flames. Gail and Emily were side by side on the sofa each taking tentative sips from their drinks.

On the surface, it looked like a party. Allie downed some more of her drink, savouring the sensation of the champagne bubbles popping as they slid against the back of her throat.

'Everyone having a good time?' Gail stood up and put her back to the fire, chin raised as though she were about to give a speech. 'Allie, how are things?'

Allie knew that Gail wanted to hear the words, wanted her small friend to crack open and spill the contents of her heart across the wooden floor of the cabin.

'I'm fine, Gail, really.'

'We've been worried about you.' Gail couldn't seem to

74

help but press the issue, perhaps hoping that one of the others would back her up.

'God, enough with the therapy session,' Diana spat. 'This is meant to be a party, remember?' She strode over to the stereo and turned up the volume. Stacie whooped in approval.

'When were we last even together?' Raising her voice over the boom of the music Gail thoughtfully let her fingertip circle the rim of her glass. 'Was it . . .?'

'Last New Year's Eve,' Diana deadpanned loudly.

Allie had already known the answer, but she still felt her breath catch in her throat as she listened to Gail's response; 'Wow. That's almost a whole year ago. How did we go so long without seeing one another?'

'I thought that was the norm.' Allie's head was still bowed as she studied her chipped red nail polish. 'It seems so often we just go months without seeing each other with no real explanation as to why.' All eyes were now on her, studying her, not quite daring to draw too much meaning from her words.

Emily released a nervous laugh like the soft ringing of silver bells.

'It's Gail's birthday party,' Diana stated tersely. 'Stop being so bloody morose.'

'Fine, let's dance,' Allie hurriedly clamoured towards Emily and dragged her up onto her feet. 'If *Diana* wants a party we'll give her a party.'

A tree branch slapped against a nearby window sounding almost like applause. Or condemnation. Allie was now twisting up the volume on the stereo, inching it ever higher, the frown on her face made sterner by the blunt line of her new fringe.

The music pounded in her ears, her veins. She wanted to turn it up ever louder until her eardrums popped and she was plunged into blissful, solitary silence. The others were close by dancing and laughing together, all too easily slipping into the old shoes of their regulation roles within the group. Allie glanced at Emily who was humming softly to herself at her side.

Where did you go?

The question risked infecting the moment, so Allie swallowed it down unspoken, along with a fresh sip of champagne.

Music. She needed to hide in the music. Allie closed her eyes and forced herself to focus only on the song, the frantic melody of an almost forgotten 90s hit.

Sound pulsated through the cabin as though the stereo had become the beating heart of the building. Allie let the vibrations dance through her bones, reminding her of how her old university room used to shake whenever Stacie or Diana turned up the volume on their CD players. Back then The Killers would fight with My Chemical Romance for dominance over the airwaves of their halls. And the walls were so paper-thin.

It was better to hear music, because, without it, Allie often heard voices. She'd be at her desk, hunched over her laptop trying to finish her latest essay for her English Literature class when she'd hear words like scratches behind the posters of Leonardo DiCaprio and Johnny Depp which lined her walls.

'How long are we going to keep doing this?'

'Keep doing what?'

'This. Always the five of us.'

The conversation seemed to be on a loop. To Allie, the decision for them all to attend the same university had been organic.

'It just makes sense,' Gail had stated stoically.

'You know most normal, functioning people move away from their childhood friends as they grow up to try and gather some semblance of . . . well . . . *self.*'

Allie knew that Diana's muffled words should hurt but they didn't. Instead, they struck a chord. For some reason, the group kept clinging to one another, even as they were draining the life out of each other. And now resentment had moved into their halls. All because of Allie. All because of one day that none of them could ever take back.

'It's about taking care of you and Emily.' That had been the line Gail fed her when she'd taken it upon herself to organise all their UCAS applications. 'You need us.'

There should have been an objection on Allie's tongue, but she'd felt numb for so long. Too long. And if she stayed around her friends, she'd be safe. Wouldn't she?

A Backstreet Boys song started up and Stacie swiftly skipped past it on the play list, jabbing a long-nailed finger against the iPod's screen with undue force.

'No one wants to hear that shit,' she scolded the stereo with venom. Allie glanced and saw the look of hurt briefly bloom across Emily's face. But then she blinked and it was gone. They'd been her favourite band once, they all knew that. Just as they knew each other's discography like a road map they had ardently followed throughout their lives.

Allie picked at the tips of her fingers as the next song started.

'Dance, come on, *dance.*' Stacie shimmied over as the up-tempo Fat Boy Slim song boomed across the room. She was smiling brightly, cheeks flushed. 'Come on, Allie, move a bit.'

Stacie threw her arms up and twisted as though she were in a packed Las Vegas night club instead of a remote Scottish cabin. But there was something in her eyes, an almost feral desperation.

She's not okay.

Allie knew it about her friend as much as she knew it about herself. Because she recognised the act, the way Stacie's face fell, for barely a second, and then her mask of confidence would slip back into place and the world would level out on its axis.

'I'll never let it in,' Stacie had once remarked after trying absinthe for the first time.

'Let what in?' So often Allie felt like she was playing catch-up with her friends.

'Him. It. The whole fucking thing.'

Allie felt her heart beating in time with the music as she regarded Stacie with a serious stare, remembering how distant she had seemed during the taxi ride up to the cabin. How her mask had fleetingly fallen enough to reveal someone truly troubled, truly lost.

'Stace, you having fun?'

For a moment Stacie frowned and then smiled brightly as the mood upon her face switched from night to day, the way it so often did. Allie imagined her practising these forced expressions before a mirror until they almost looked natural. Almost. 'Hey, of course, don't worry about me. It's Gail's birthday, she's the one you should be policing about participation.'

'I know but . . .'

'We're here.' Stacie tugged sharply on Allie's arm, drawing her back into the conversation. 'We're *all here*, Allie Bear. That's an achievement in itself. Be happy about that.'

'I am.'

'Then look it,' Stacie strictly advised. 'Because right now you look bloody miserable.'

Allie's mouth opened with an objection, but the music suddenly rose in volume, drowning out anything she was

78

about to say. She glanced over and saw Emily at the stereo, smiling sweetly as she turned it up and started dancing with Diana, grabbing her friend's slender hand and spinning her around. Everyone had shifted positions; Gail was now at the fridge topping up her drink and Stacie stood with Allie behind the sofa, the stereo claimed by Emily.

TLC's 'Waterfalls' was playing. Allie instantly recognised the soulful opening chords. She sipped some more of her champagne and felt herself beginning to relax, the drink working its magic. Then she glanced at Stacie and saw the look in her eyes. Her latest sip of champagne suddenly tasted bitter.

Time always behaved differently when Allie was intoxi-cated. Stacie had dashed off, muttering something about needing to use her phone, but instinct told Allie that was a lie even more than Stacie's indirect gaze did. But there was little she could do about it, her body was gripped by the beat of the latest song, swaying haphazardly to it like a blade of grass caught up in an updraught.

I can hide here, in the music.

Closing her eyes she kept swaying, kept pretending she was somewhere else. Maybe she was back in London at the little club down the alley near her flat with the navy walls and neon signs. It was the kind of club where you could wear jeans and flats and no one cared. The low-key element worked for Allie. She could slip into the shadows and enjoy vodka and Coke as records from her youth played all around her. And that had once been his favourite place to drink too.

Music bounced off the wooden walls. The howling outside paled against the throbbing melodies of boy bands, Destiny's Child and Lady Gaga. Allie was drunk. She twirled around in the centre of the living space, holding her half-empty glass of champagne. She was drunk and it felt good. She was light of foot, clear of mind. With the alcohol swimming in her system, she could focus on the music, on the fun. Not on the black hole back at home. Not on what he was possibly doing at that very moment—

'You're drunk,' Emily observed with a laugh.

'Am . . . not.'

'You're all drunk.' Emily raised a perfectly shaped eyebrow at her, blue eyes shining sadly. 'Sometimes it sucks being the only sober one.'

Allie looked towards the fire. All of her friends were gathered around it, swaying absently to the music, giggling drunkenly together. All except—

'Stacie went upstairs about twenty minutes ago,' Emily explained. Allie sensed that something in her tone was suggesting she go up and see where their friend was. 'She mentioned she was trying to find some signal. If she finds any, will you let me know?' Emily pulled her phone from her pocket and stared wistfully at the screen saver; her and Adam clutching a twin each and grinning madly at the camera. It looked so posed. So wholesome. So achingly perfect. Allie downed the rest of her drink and nodded.

'I'll . . . um . . . I will.'

'I'd love to check in on Ad and the twins.'

'Uh huh.'

The stairs creaked as Allie climbed them. Her footing felt as uneasy as it had out on the snowy path and she was forced to clutch the bannister for support. When she reached the small landing she was confronted by two pine doors. She opened the closest one and stepped into a darkened room. A king-sized bed sat beneath a vaulted wooden ceiling. The open curtains against the grandwindow revealed a snowy wilderness that sparkled even in the depths of night. Allie's feet guided her to the window. Trees wilted beneath the weight of snow. Everywhere looked so beautiful, so serene. She felt like she'd just stepped through the wardrobe into Narnia, right when the fantastical world was under siege by the Snow Queen's dominion.

'Allie?' a voice croaked her name.

Startled Allie spun round and saw a shadowy form on the floor, leaning against the bed, looking out at the snowy landscape as she was.

'Stacie?' Allie scrambled to the floor and went to sit beside her friend. Stacie's head was bowed to her chest, tendrils of her red hair had broken free from her plait and were plastered against her forehead. The glow from the snow outside revealed her damp cheeks. 'Is everything okay?'

'They played "Waterfalls",' Stacie sniffed and dragged her hands down her face, taking what remained of her mask of happiness with it.

'"Waterfalls". The TLC song?'

The champagne had filled Allie's mind with an annoying fog. It took her a moment to find her way through it but then she understood. 'Oh, yeah.' She softly hummed the melody of the song.

'I fucking hate hearing that song,' Stacie grumbled heatedly.

'It's not so bad.'

'It was *our* song.'

Realisation pierced Allie like a blade. It blew away the fog and snapped her almost completely into the moment. 'Oh, shit, yeah. Are you . . . you okay?' Memories of a summer better off forgotten began to seep into the room.

'I'm . . .' Stacie's voice trailed off. She clearly wasn't as comfortable with the *I'm fine* lie as Allie was. Was she thinking about all that had happened? Was her heart aching with regret or something deeper than that, something more akin to loss? Allie knew that some things, once you lost them, never came back.

'Gail just didn't think,' Allie deduced pragmatically. 'It must have been on some playlist and it coming on was an oversight. You know what a planner she is and—'

'Emily turned it up.'

'Em?' Allie frowned. 'I guess . . . she forgot too. Stace, it happens. No one would have meant anything by it.'

'When I hear that damn song it's 1995 again and I'm fifteen, with him, and everything is perfect.'

'Stacie, don't torture yourself.'

Or me, Allie almost added. Where Stacie was going, Allie didn't want to follow.

'At fifteen the future is supposed to loom ahead of you, this empty canvas you've yet to completely fuck up.'

'Stace . . .' Allie leaned her head against her friend's shoulder and sighed. Her stomach churned in the unpleasant way it always did whenever she thought of that summer. Allie feared that her pizza might be looking to make a return appearance. She smiled thinly and tried to force down more than just her meal. There was a rising tide of emotion within her which had the potential to drown her if she let it. 'Come on, let's just try and enjoy this weekend.'

'You must get it. That year was pretty fucked up for you too.'

On cue, Allie's back ached. She squirmed against the bed, trying to ignore it.

'But it's been twenty years, Stace. We have to let go at some point.'

'Do we?' Stacie's voice was as cold as the snow outside. She leaned her shoulders against the bed and sighed deeply, the sound seeming to ripple up from the base of her very soul. 'I want to let go, truly I do.' She let her fingertips dance around where a golden ring had once resided. 'But I can't. Can you?'

The wind lashed against the window as snow continued to fall. Tiny flakes tumbled down from the darkened heavens in a dizzying scramble towards the ground and the already overloaded fir trees.

We can't let go.

'Stace, I'm fine. You should be too, it's been such a long time.'

Allie knew she was lying, singing a tune she wasn't committed to. But what choice did she have?

'Whenever I hear that damn song my heart breaks all over again. Like literally gets torn in two.' Stacie's hand was now against her chest, head bowed. Allie wished she'd put her mask back on, go back to pretending that she was fine. It made everything easier to deal with.

An image flashed through Allie's mind, brief and brilliant. She was eight and she'd gone to visit her old Aunt Doris who had been shuffled between various nursing homes and was now holed up in Sunnymead, a single-storey structure a half-hour's drive from Allie's house. It had rained the entire journey there which reflected Allie's mood perfectly. She hadn't wanted to visit some old relative, she'd wanted to spend her weekend how she always did – with her friends.

But both parents had been insistent.

'Aunt Doris gets lonely,' they'd said. So Allie had gone. Besides, at eight, there was little she could do to go against her mum and dad's wishes.

When they found Doris she was in her little private room, the television playing a rerun of some dated game show. Her legs were stretched out before her, broad like tree trunks and clad in white bandages which Allie thought were just thick white tights. And it was easier to think of her aunt's legs like that. Thinking of the bandages as tights meant that Allie didn't need to dwell on what they actually covered. But that day, with the rain lashing at the window, they'd misjudged their timing and it coincided with a visit from the nurse.

'We should leave,' Allie's mother was saying but Doris shook her thick neck and bulbous chin.

'No, no, stay. This won't take long.'

And it didn't. The nurse had come in, smiled softly at Doris's guests and then began un-swaddling the layers of bandages covering the old woman's legs. The more layers she removed the more the colour changed, turning from white to crimson. Allie began to feel sick.

'Really, we can just wait in—'

But Allie's mother wasn't quick enough. The bandages were off and Doris's cellulitis was exposed for her guests to see. Her legs were ulcerated and bloodied. Where there should have been peachy skin there were savage red welts. It almost looked as though her flesh had been burned away completely revealing the tender tissue of her muscles beneath.

Was that what their friendship had become? Allie needed Stacie to put her mask back on, to let her pretend that the bandages were something they weren't.

'That sucks,' she offered gently, referring to her friend's pain. It felt like the grossest of understatements, something a fifteen-year-old Allie would have been uttering, not a grown, intelligent woman capable of more profound empathy. The memories which were trying to entwine themselves around her like ribbons of bloodied gauze were changing the dynamic in the room. Allie desperately wanted to leave.

'Have you ever done something . . .' Stacie's voice began to strain, 'something so terrible that you know you can't take back, but you wish you hadn't done it?'

'Wait.' Allie frowned at her, stomach clenching with the promise of a purge. She had anticipated fielding questions about *him* not about the more distant past, not about that which they all knew better than to disturb. She revealed her indignation in her tone. 'Is this about the accident, because I've made my peace with it and—'

'No, not that.'

'You regret not stopping him that night?' Allie's voice softened as the wind outside lifted in fervour. If Stacie wasn't referring to the accident, she must have been talking about the other tragedy which befell the group that summer.

'I—'

'Because there was nothing you could have done, Stace. I'm sorry if hearing the song is painful but it wasn't your fault. It never was.'

'You stand by her so solemnly.'

'Who?' Allie wished her system wasn't so flooded with alcohol because her mind was once again sluggish. If she were beside the warming embrace of a fire she could easily curl up, close her eyes and drift away to another place. A happier place. 'What are you talking about?' Allie was growing concerned about the unnatural tilt of the room. She really needed to lie down.

'Nothing.' With a shake of her head Stacie rested her hands on her knees and exhaled slowly. 'I'm talking about nothing at all, just drunken ramblings.'

'Oh, okay.'

'Thanks for coming to check in on me.'

Despair was still working like gravity, pulling down the corners of Stacie's eyes and mouth but Allie couldn't linger there any longer. She needed to get out.

'Anytime,' she whispered hastily as she scrambled to her feet and drunkenly made her way to the door.

Thirteen

Stacie was finding being sixteen less than sweet, it was more like unbearably sour. She couldn't contemplate going to school the next day. Going back to normality.

'It'll be good for you,' her mum had insisted, 'might bring you out of this slump.'

Slump. The word made a mockery of Stacie's grief. Legs hanging over the brick wall of the bridge, Stacie looked down at the rippling reflection of the moon on the water. It shone so brightly against the blackness of the river. In her hands, she held a half-empty bottle of store-brand vodka. Lifting it to her lips she titled her head back and drank, the clear fluid no longer burning as it travelled down her throat, sending a pleasant warmth through her entire body.

For the past month, this had been her routine. Her mum would go up to bed at eleven, following several hours staring glassy-eyed at the small television screen in their lounge while she drank warm white wine from a plastic glass. She'd creak open the door to Stacie's room and check her daughter was there, safely tucked in bed, sleeping. Stacie would keep her breath low, listen for the tell-tale click which meant her mum was now in her own room, soon to be asleep. She'd throw off her duvet, open her window and climb out onto the small partition roof and then shimmy down the drainpipe before running to the overgrown hedge at the back of their small garden in which she concealed the vodka she'd convinced Diana to buy for her using her fake ID.

The temptation to just wander the streets was strong. For the first couple of nights, Stacie had done just that. But by the third night, she could feel she was being drawn to the river and the stone bridge which crossed it. It was for pedestrians only, not big or strong enough to carry the weight of a car, which meant that come night-time it was completely empty. No other souls sat upon it, swinging their legs and peering down at oblivion.

It was the water that lured her. Stacie looked at it, at its velvety richness, wondering how deep it was, how strong its hidden currents were. She knew the answer. A body had been washed up a few miles south of where she was sitting just a few months ago. If the fall from the bridge didn't take her then the strong waters definitely would.

She drank more vodka, feeling herself tipping towards that point of drunkenness where her emotions became mountains she knew she would never overcome. The first time Ollie told her he loved her they'd been in the back of his car, one of his hands on her knee, the other cupping her face, and he'd looked at her, really looked at her, deep into her eyes and she knew, right there and then, that he saw her for who she truly was. That their love was the kind which people wrote songs and poems about. That it was a love that would last forever. Only . . .

Stacie kept drinking, needing to push past this point. She kicked her feet against the wall, growing restless. If she jumped, she would be with him. She wouldn't be alone, in pain. She'd be . . . free. Stacie looked at the water – the moon's reflection seemed to be swirling, as though someone had pulled the plug on the river. She blinked and it was still once more.

'Fuck,' she muttered, wiping a hand across her mouth. Even sitting there, she could tell she was extremely drunk. If she stood up she'd sway, scarcely be able to walk in a straight line and surely in an hour or two she'd be vomiting up her efforts from the night.

88

Just jump.

She kept staring at the calm, still water. Where would it carry her? Would the sound of her falling in alert someone? What if they were able to save her? There'd be so many questions, maybe hospitals too. Stacie opened her mouth to draw in deep breaths of the cool, evening air, not quite ready for her thoughts to be completely derailed by the vodka in her system.

The papers said Ollie was high when he died. Was that why he'd done it? Had it been all too easy to lose control of his car when the whole world was warping beyond his windscreen?

Stacie knew he would never knowingly leave her. He loved her. There had to be something. Or someone. A push from an outside force.

'Whoever took you,' she was telling the moon's reflection, imagining Ollie somewhere in a great unknown in the universe beyond it, 'whoever made you . . . made you leave me. I'll find out, I promise. And . . . I'll . . .' Talking was becoming a struggle, her tongue feeling too large for her mouth. 'Pay, I'll make them pay.'

As her resolve strengthened it pushed back the worst of her drunkenness. In an ungainly manner she swung her legs back over the wall, back to safety, planting her feet on the ground and wobbling as though she'd forgotten how to use them. She tossed the almost empty bottle of vodka down into the river and staggered away along the path, wearing her grief like a stain which would never come out.

Fourteen

Officer: The storm was setting in.

POI: Apparently.

Officer: But you weren't aware of it?

POI: We were distracted.

Officer: None of you thought to keep an eye on the weather reports?

POI: No one anticipated it getting as bad as it did. It was just suddenly upon us.

Officer: The news had stated it was to be one of the worst snowstorms in years.

POI: Weather reports can be wrong.

Officer: Not in this instance.

POI: No. But that's not the point. We just didn't view the storm as a threat.

Officer: When did that change?

POI: I guess . . . when other things started getting bad.

Officer: Like what?

POI: To answer that I'll need to carry on with what happened that first night.

Officer: How did it feel seeing all your friends again that night?

POI: Strange.

Officer: Strange?

POI: I don't know, different. Odd.

Officer: Most people find comfort in their shared memories; it's what keeps them close in later life.

POI: And what if there's no comfort to be found in the memories? Only pain?

Officer: Are you saying that memories of your friends are painful?

POI: Things that happened in the past can't be changed.

Officer: Whatever connected you girls in the first place must still be there, else why keep meeting up?

POI: Maybe old habits die hard.

Officer: Do you think that's what you were all doing – meeting up out of habit?

POI: No. We wanted to be there. I just . . . I think people undervalue how motivating a factor guilt can be.

Officer: What were you feeling guilty about?

POI: No.

Officer: No?

POI: You wanted a timeline. To ask me about my guilt would be to go back much further than that weekend and we're not doing that here, we're going forwards. So may I continue with what happened that night?

Officer: Fine. Yes. Do.

Fifteen

The evening stretched into a dark night, not that the blackness outside allowed for the passage of time to be marked. Allie's back ached, telling the story of a long day spent travelling the length of the country. She needed sleep. Yet instead she staggered down the stairs, blinking to try and sharpen her senses. She needed to focus.

'Go, go.' Stacie had ushered her away as she sat, glassy-eyed and focused on the falling snow. Allie stumbled across the room, needing space to clear her head.

'I'll be back in a few minutes.' Was Allie slurring her words? She couldn't tell.

'I'll come down in a moment. I just need to gather my thoughts. Okay?'

'Okay.'

Downstairs the music was still playing. It drowned out the wailing drone of the wind. Diana and Gail were over by the iPod, clutching their glasses of champagne and swaying back and forth as they sang along to the current track.

Emily was waiting at the base of the stairs, peering up at Allie and biting the tips of her pink nails.

'Is she okay?' Her eyes flitted past Allie to the top of the stairs where the small landing was bare.

Allie went over to the kitchen area and Emily followed, watching her intently as she poured herself a tall glass of water.

'She's . . . upset.' The truth seemed unavoidable. When Stacie returned to the party with red-rimmed eyes and blotchy cheeks everyone would know she had been on the verge of crying. Although Allie imagined that now alone, she was letting her grief fall freely from her blue eyes, no longer needing to pretend that she was stronger than she was.

'What upset her?'

Allie gulped down her water. It was so cold, but its icy temperature made it even more refreshing. She finished the entire glass and then poured herself another.

'Some song came on that brought back some bad memories I guess.'

'Huh.' Something flashed across Emily's face. What, Allie couldn't tell.

'I guess Gail didn't put all that much thought into the playlist,' she added.

'I . . . um.' Emily looked down at her feet as her cheeks turned crimson. She studied the pink tips of her nails before releasing an awkward sigh and forcing herself to look Allie directly in the eye. 'I did the music. Gail asked me to help out, so I sent over some of my playlists from home. I thought it would be . . . nostalgic.' Her gaze lifted up and above Allie, settling on the wooden ceiling, at the beams of wood that ran across it in perfectly precise lines.

'I really didn't think it would upset her. I thought she'd like hearing some old stuff. Thinking back to when we were young. After all, it was you who went through all that crap back then. Not them.'

'Yeah . . . true.' Allie bristled.

'I really miss the twins.' Emily's shoulders sagged. 'Should I not have left them? I mean, am I a bad mother for going away?' Concern crinkled at the corner of her eyes and her lower lip quivered.

'What – no.' Allie was instantly reassuring her friend, placing down her glass of water to briefly hug Emily, breathing in the lingering scent of baby powder that clung to her. 'You are an awesome mum, truly. You adore the twins, and Adam, everyone can see that. But, you know, sometimes you have to remember to make time for yourself and that's okay. You understand that, right? That it's okay to still be a person as well as being a mum?'

'Right. And you.' Emily was turning Allie's concern back on her. 'You're okay, aren't you, Allie? I know you've been going through a lot and we don't talk as much as we used to. I can get kind of distracted by the twins.'

'I'm fine, really.' Allie rushed her statement, allowing the words to run together unintentionally.

'You never said why.'

'Sorry?'

Emily tilted her head in a pitying way. 'Why he left.'

Allie seethed as she saw the head tilt. It was a look people had been giving her for almost twenty years and she loathed it as much now as she did back when she was fifteen seeing it for the first time.

The music was suddenly turned up even higher. The song pounded through Allie and the cabin like a quickening pulse, bouncing off the walls. She turned to see what had caused the increase in volume. Stacie had resurfaced and she was bouncing and singing with Diana about it being Gail's birthday. Her cheeks weren't even blotchy. Her moment of sorrow had clearly passed, her mask of confidence returned and the party was once again in full swing.

Gail stood poised beside the fireplace, nodding her head in time with the music and smiling. As Allie approached the stereo she tried to catch Stacie's eye, to ensure that there was now just calmness in her gaze, but her friend was too busy putting on a show to look at her directly.

Since coming downstairs Stacie had grabbed Diana and now they were twisting side by side. Gone was the disheartened girl from upstairs, so quickly she had been hidden away.

Too quickly.

They danced. The five of them gathered around the MP3 player, near the crackle of the fire. They bounced, they clapped, they spun each other around, drunk enough to forget about the lines upon the floor, the barriers between them. They were back in the Student Union at Sheffield Hallam. They were back upon the sticky floor of their hometown's singular nightclub, Passions. They were back at the school disco, standing in the gymnasium which forever smelt like old socks, forming a line and doing the Macarena.

And then the music died.

The darkness and the ensuing silence were so jarring that Allie almost couldn't breathe. She looked to the fireplace, to its golden glow, which now fought alone to push back the swelling shadows that had penetrated the cabin.

'Holy crap, what happened?' Stacie gasped from where she was standing close by.

'What the hell?' Diana yelled. 'Why did everything just go out?'

'The fire is still on.' Emily scurried towards its halo. 'At least we still have some light.'

'Yes, but we need power!' Stacie cried. 'We need hot water, the TV, music!'

'It'll come back on soon, right?' Allie cautiously angled her question at Gail who was looking beyond her circle of friends, towards the thickening shadows that surrounded them all.

'You can't expect us to cope up here for two more days without it,' Stacie screeched.

'The power must have got knocked out by the storm.' Gail wandered into the firelight, her fingertips pressed to her forehead. There was a hunch to her shoulders. Had it always been there or was Allie only just noticing it? Normally Gail loomed larger than life, but now she looked almost defeated.

'Don't you have like, a generator or something?' Stacie demanded desperately.

'*That's* what must have got knocked out.' The words snapped out of Gail as if they were released from a frayed elastic band.

'So, we're completely out of power?' Diana grunted and threw her hands up in dismay.

'Until this storm passes and it's safe to go outside and fix it, yes.'

'Until it passes?' Stacie wailed. 'When the hell will that be?'

'How are we supposed to know that?' Diana raged. 'We're not bloody weather reporters!'

'I'll check my phone.' Instinctively Allie reached for it, only to see in the top corner the lack of 4G signal. Her stomach sank as she returned it to her pocket. Glancing around she saw her other friends mirroring her actions.

Stacie strutted over to the window. 'It's bad out there,' she declared, peeling back the curtains. 'Really bad.'

'But we're safe in here,' Gail declared with authority. 'We have food, shelter. We can light some fires. We'll be fine. There's no need to panic. The storm will eventually pass.'

Still watching the snow, Stacie's skin seemed paler than usual, almost iridescent, red lips set in a tight line as she shook her head nervously.

'Honestly, we'll be fine.' Gail clicked her fingers to order her friend away from the window and the disturbing vista of the storm. 'We just need to wait this out. It'll be fun, like . . . like our old sleepovers used to be, before we even knew what WiFi was.'

Resigned grumblings rippled through the group.

With the wind knocked out of their sails, the girls collectively dropped onto the sofas and peered at the flames which continued to devour the altar of logs in the hearth. Outside, the storm pressed against the walls, made the wooden timbers creak and the windows tremble.

'I hate storms.' Emily tucked her long legs up underneath her as she knelt close to the fire.

'Me too,' Stacie agreed, tossing a loose strand of hair out of her eye line.

'I like them.' Diana leaned forwards to stare directly into the fire. 'Storms are dangerous.' She rubbed a hand over her forearm where she had one of her latest tattoos; a wolf baring its teeth.

'And you laugh in the face of danger, blah blah blah.' Stacie rolled her eyes. 'We get it – you like to live on the edge. You're so brave, woo bloody hoo. But you and Gail are welcome to your sky dives and bungee jumps. I prefer to engage in activities where the possibility of me dying is *low*.'

'It's about the adrenaline.' Gail didn't sound completely invested in the conversation. She'd stood up and was surveying the darkened corners of the cabin. 'It's about pushing yourself out of your comfort zone, discovering your limits.'

Around the time university was ending Diana had developed an insatiable lust for extreme sports and activities which Gail had claimed to share, but Allie often suspected that she was just going along for the ride, ensuring that Diana wasn't alone in her new pursuit.

Gail lived as though they were at war, the whole 'no one gets left behind' thing. She tried to be there for everyone, all the time. But she wore herself too thin. When Melissa left, Gail claimed to not blame her.

'I was never there for her. Not really.'

And though she didn't say it, Allie understood. Being a part of their five-piece was draining.

The wind slapped against the cabin and the walls shuddered. The snow that was falling must have turned to ice, as it sounded like there were footsteps on the roof, thousands of them. Allie sunk low on the sofa. 'The storm sounds pretty bad.'

'Only because the music has stopped,' Diana replied bluntly.

'I know, but—'

'I'll go and get my radio.' Gail clicked her fingers at the group and then disappeared.

'She wants the music back?' Stacie frowned and picked at a loose thread in her jumper. 'Someone needs to tell the birthday girl that we have more pressing issues. Like where are we all even going to sleep? Everywhere is going to be freezing with no heating.'

'There are fireplaces in the bedrooms.' Allie remembered noticing their shadowy outline when she'd gone looking for Stacie. 'We'll need to light those, get this place as toasty as we can.'

'And Gail must have some candles stashed about the place.' Emily sounded genuinely excited as she jumped up, bright with purpose.

'I am not doing a séance, or a Ouija board.' Stacie held her hands up to the other girls. 'I'm still reeling from that one we did in Gail's uni room. I didn't sleep for weeks after that.'

'You know I was the one moving it, right?' Diana briefly turned away from the fire to eye Stacie.

'Doesn't matter.' Stacie shook her head. 'You might *think* you were moving it, but you were just being a vessel for the spirit controlling it through you.'

'Jesus.' Diana looked back towards the fire.

'Here.' Gail returned clutching an old wind-up radio. 'It's not much, but at least it's a connection to the outside world and should let us know when the storm is due to pass.'

'Great.' Emily clapped her hands together, she was now positively chipper. 'Let's get it set up.'

It was Allie's eighth summer and the sun hadn't shone for three days straight. In the airy conservatory that backed onto Emily's large, manicured lawn she was sitting cross-legged on the cool tile floors, brushing the golden hair of her doll. 'It's like yours,' she noted to Emily as she tilted the doll back, it's glassy eyes instantly closing.

'I suppose it is . . .' Emily paused brushing her own doll to smile. 'But mine is straight.'

'True,' Allie agreed as she tugged her brush through her doll's tight curls. She liked how yellow they were. And how the doll's cheeks blushed pink and how if you gave her water from her bottle and then placed her on her little plastic potty and squeezed her stomach she'd do an actual wee. 'She's amazing,' Allie had exclaimed with glee when she'd opened her doll the previous Christmas morning, her parents watching from the sofa where they nursed their second sweet sherries of the day.

The world beyond the conservatory windows was all shades of grey, the lustre of the lawn, the efforts of the gardener Emily's parents employed, going unenjoyed.

'Maybe we could go to the park,' Allie suggested, thinking that at least it wasn't raining. She'd heard her mother make a remark that morning before she kissed her forehead, leaving behind a smear of lipstick which Allie still hadn't been able to rub off. 'It's dull but not raining, that's something,' her mother had stated across the table to her father who was immersed in reading his morning paper and only grunted a response.

'We can't go to the park.' The corners of Emily's mouth dipped, but her tone remained bright. She moved her doll over to a push-chair near the doors which opened onto the garden. 'Remember, we can only play here. My daddy won't let me go to the park.'

'But it's just on the corner.' Allie wanted to push her doll on the swing, to watch her pretty curls blow in the breeze.

'You know we have to stay here.' Emily's posture grew tight, she snapped the clasp on her pram with undue force. 'We can walk around the garden' – she pointed beyond the glass of the conservatory – 'and we can push them down the slide and go in the playhouse.'

Allie liked the idea of playing on the slide. 'Okay.' She jumped to her feet, clasping her doll to her chest.

'You can borrow my old pram.' Emily was already passing her by. 'I'll just shout for my daddy to get it from the garage.'

'Great!' Allie felt excited. She'd always admired Emily's old doll's pram with its four grand wheels and stiff sides.

'Just think, Allie' – Emily glanced back at her from where she was about to enter the living room which was attached to the conservatory – 'one day we'll be real mummies with real babies.'

'And still best friends?'

Emily smiled and her entire face lit up, almost banishing away the gloom of the August morning. 'And still best friends.'

Allie listened to her friend's footsteps depart and hugged her doll tight, whispering into her curls, 'One day you'll be real and I'll be a mummy. One day I'll be all grown up and everything will be perfect.'

Sixteen

Candlelight flickered through the cabin. Emily had commandeered every available surface so that the living space was bathed in a golden glow, little flames whispering, caught by rogue draughts.

'You're creating one hell of a fire hazard,' Diana had challenged, as Emily darted from wick to wick, lit match in hand. She had sunk low in the sofa, the heat of the flames in the hearth held in her eyes.

'It's too cold to start a fire,' Emily objected.

'You know, this place can still burn to the ground, regardless of how cold it is outside.'

Gail discreetly leaned across the stretch of the sofa between them and pinched Diana's upper arm, scowling at her.

'Emily is helping,' Gail hissed, her voice low and scolding, 'let her help.'

Diana merely rolled her eyes.

The radio wasn't quite as effective as the candles. It took Gail almost twenty minutes to find a station. It seemed that all that was broadcasting was static. Brow furrowed, she kept twirling the controls, refusing to give up. 'Terrible signal up here,' she grumbled repeatedly as she twisted the radio's dial back and forth between AM and FM. The sound of static seemed at odds with the whisper of the candle flame and crackling of logs. It reminded Allie of the blizzard that used to engulf her television screen whenever channels were off-air, dozens of white dots fizzing together, hissing.

Finally, Gail found BBC World Service, smiling in triumph as a clipped RP accent filled the room. And for the last hour, that's all they had listened to. The steady drone of the well-spoken newscaster was strangely reassuring, like being read a bedtime story by John Hurt. Collected around the fire they all sat, heads drooping as the clock crept past ten. Allie watched her friends, wondering who would be the first to fall asleep. It was almost as if she were twelve again, at a sleepover, battling against exhaustion so she didn't risk nodding off before anyone else.

Back then their systems were filled with sugar rather than alcohol which made it easy to stay up past nine, to welcome even ten and eleven with girlish excitement as they watched old movies and snuggled together in their sleeping bags and sheet forts. But midnight was always tricky. Allie would feel a pleasant numbness begin to spread through her limbs which told her that soon she'd be closing her eyes; soon she'd be falling asleep.

Not that her concern about being the first to do so was ever a valid one. Emily always succumbed to slumber before anyone else, pulling her blankets up tight to her chin and curling onto her side.

When the morning came they all woke easily, blinking against the early sunlight. All except Diana. She was notoriously difficult to rouse from sleep. As the others tiptoed around her she'd remain in a ball, eyes tightly closed, chest lazily rising and falling. At sleepovers, she always slept as though she hadn't done so properly in days. Even weeks.

'I feel like we need to do something fun.' Gail stretched and looked expectantly at her friends who were wilted against the numerous sofas, candlelight dancing over their tired faces. 'This is my birthday weekend, remember? So what if we've got no power. We've got food. And each other.'

'And champagne.' Stacie stood up and stumbled into the shadows. Moments later she was loudly rooting around in the fridge. 'Lots of champagne!' she yelled over to the others.

'Then let's do something fun.' Gail's voice was ripe with hope.

'Like what?' Diana countered drolly. 'The drone talking on the radio hardly makes for a good drinking game.'

'Truth or dare!' Emily declared with a soft shriek of excitement. 'Come on, we've always loved that.'

'Yes, that'll be fun!' Gail enthused.

'No, not truth or dare.' Stacie was returning to the halo of the fire with a bottle of champagne in each hand. 'We'll play never have I ever.'

Allie chewed against the inside of her cheek. It was a game she had never favoured. Back when she wasn't as fluent in the ways of dating as her friends were the game had a way of highlighting her inexperience which made her uncomfortable. Not that they'd played it since they'd all sat cross-legged on the floor of their shared kitchen at university. Then they were gulping down cheap vodka and bad wine while giggling drunkenly to themselves as Stacie regaled them all with her latest exploits.

'It'll do.' Diana reached for a bottle of champagne and after popping its cork she tipped its neck to her lips and gulped down several large swigs. 'Beats sitting here in the dark being bored.'

The wind scratched at the walls.

'I'll start.' Stacie sat back down and began to wrestle the other bottle open.

'No, Gail should start,' Emily hurriedly offered. 'She is the birthday girl after all.'

'Okay . . .' Gail extended her empty glass towards Diana who topped her up, bubbles popping softly. She took a sip and then looked around the room, the fire crackling behind her. 'Never have I ever been scared in a cabin.'

Emily drank from the bottle of water she was cradling in her lap. Allie and Stacie sipped down champagne.

'Wimps.' Diana frowned at them.

'Fine.' Stacie scowled. 'Never have I ever had a threesome.'

For a moment no one moved. Then Diana drank. Emily's mouth dropped open in shock as Gail discreetly snapped her fingers at her. Allie was watching her friends, trying to ignore the scrape of ice on wood that was surrounding them all.

'Never have I ever cheated on someone.' Diana was staring at Stacie as she slurred her part of the game.

Stacie drank. She drank deeply from the bottle she was holding and then she smugly wiped her mouth. 'Never have I ever—'

'No.' Gail removed the bottle from her possession and looked over at Emily. 'It's Em's turn.'

'Oh.' Emily looked nervous at the sudden scrutiny. 'You know how bad I am at this game.'

'Just bloody play,' Stacie ordered. 'You're holding up the drinking.'

'Okay.' Emily was smiling sweetly. Gentle Emily who truly was terrible at these kinds of games, worse even than Allie. 'Never have I ever knowingly betrayed a friend.'

There was a shriek outside – the wind as it whipped past, pushing against the walls as though it were trying to do more than just knock them down, as though it wanted to pull them down the mountainside, to uproot the entire cabin.

No one moved. Allie held on to her drink, felt her fingertips pressing too hard, felt the resistance coming back at her from the glass.

'That's your go?' Stacie finally blurted. Allie looked at her, saw how her eyes looked damp in the dull light. Was it just the fumes from the fire smarting her gaze? 'Then fuck it, we should all drink.' Stacie reached for the bottle of champagne, but Gail pulled it back out of reach.

'Let's move on. Allie, it's your turn.'

'No, no.' Stacie was standing up, sounding strident. 'Emily had her go, Emily needs a response.'

'No one drank,' Gail snapped. 'Now sit down and let's keep going.'

'Then we're all fucking liars!' Stacie fumed.

The wind howled and the voice on the radio crackled. Allie looked down at her glass of champagne, at the bubbles which rose up to the surface only to die there. The darkness around them was growing thick, pungent. She inhaled, drawing the scent of the fire deep into her lungs and threw out an olive branch.

'Never have I ever let someone suck my toes.'

Diana spat out the mouthful of champagne she'd just swigged down.

'Allie!' Stacie shouted her name, appalled. 'I told you that in confidence.'

Allie shrugged innocently. 'Drink up, Stace. That story haunted me for weeks.'

Emily was now giggling, the shadow which had briefly darkened her features replaced by her usual sunlight. Stacie snatched the bottle from Diana's grip and swallowed down huge gulps of champagne, she was about to drink some more when Gail reclaimed it, wrapping both hands around its emerald core and tugging it back into her possession.

'Gail?' Diana choked as she looked over at her friend. Gail was now tipping the bottle to her lips and swallowing. 'You dark horse! Who was it? Melissa?'

Gail said nothing, she just kept drinking. Emily's giggle became a full-bellied laugh and it was infectious. Allie laughed along too, laughed at Stacie's continued indignation.

'It wasn't like I enjoyed it,' she implored her friends.

They were all laughing loud enough that for a moment they managed to drown out the growl of the storm outside.

The glow from the fire enveloped them. It was a bubble in which they could co-exist. The game went on, but the combined warmth of the fire and the alcohol was intoxicating. Exhaustion crept up on Allie. It pulled at her feet, encouraging her to lie down on the sofa. Then it tugged on her eyelids, sealing them closed. Her breathing slowed as she relaxed against the plush cushions. The voice on the radio sounded distant, otherworldly. The fire crackled and Allie drifted away.

'You need me to punch him? Jasper?' Stacie asked, cheeks red. 'Because I will. I'll bloody punch him, just say the word. I've always thought he was up himself ever since he didn't turn up for drinks for your twenty-third.'

'I'll do more than punch him,' Diana muttered through gritted teeth.

'You guys have been together for years, how could he do this!'

'No, no one is punching anyone.' Allie was hugging her knees against her chest, dwarfed by the oversized cardigan she was wearing. It felt strange to be back in the front room at her parents' home. So much had changed since she'd last sat on the leather sofas with her friends beneath the wall adorned with family portraits. Over the years the pictures never changed, hanging there gathering dust, one of the few enduring elements within the home.

'He just left you?' Stacie leaned forward, eyes wide with a desperate eagerness. 'Just like that, no reason?'

'He . . .' Allie squirmed, felt the roughness of the wool against her arms. She was beginning to regret meeting her friends here, letting them into a place that had become foreign and familiar to her in equal parts. It was the day before Christmas Eve so Stacie and Diana were back in their hometown too, visiting family, their fledgeling adult lives briefly put on pause. The lights from the tree twinkled on and off, forever fixed on the most jarring setting. Allie could still remember the year she broke the switch and forced her parents to be plunged into darkness and then giddy light over and over.

'It's fine,' her dad had insisted with a tight smile, but an edge had entered his voice the previous summer which had embedded itself like a thorn and now more than just his tone was changing – his gait was more stooped, his hair thinner, his patience more frayed. 'Allie, it's fine.'

'But it's broken.'

'Allie, I said it's fine.'

So the broken lights remained. Allie wished her parents would just admit the fault and change them.

'He had a reason.' Sighing, Allie pushed her chin into her knees and regretted the admission. Across from her Stacie loudly inhaled and Diana was already shaking her head back and forth, the ruby-red accents in her hair briefly flashing within the glow intermittently offered by the tree.

'I knew it,' Diana seethed. 'I fucking knew it. Prick.'

'Allie . . .' Stacie's hand was on her chest, over her heart as though she were protecting it, as though the decaying of Allie's latest relationship could spread across the room and infect her too. 'Did he leave you because of—'

'I . . . I don't want to talk about it.' And she didn't. She'd already thought about it too much – back in London on a loop in my mind and then during the train ride up it had consumed *her thoughts, coating them in a thick tar so that it took her too long to process even the simplest task.*

'Then let's not talk.' Diana was suddenly on her feet, pointing towards the staircase at the back of the room. 'Go and get changed. We're going out.'

'We are?' Allie asked roughly, feeling the way the words grated against her sore throat.

'We are?' Stacie echoed with more glee. 'Ooh, I've not been out in town in forever! But Emily and Gail aren't here.' Her shoulders slumped. 'They're not back this year, remember? We can't go out without them.'

Diana was watching Allie, studying her. 'We can and we will,' she stated, eyes still glued to her small friend who huddled beneath her cardigan like a wounded animal. 'We're going to go out, to Passions, we're going to laugh at how sticky the floor is, how watered down the shots are, and we're going to dance until our feet fucking fall off. Got it?'

Stacie clapped her hands together. 'Yes, oh yes! It's been too long since we went out together!'

'Are you sure?' Allie returned Diana's concerned stare. 'I mean . . .' She didn't want to have to dredge up what she needed to say. There was already too much bile in her stomach, too much dread clenching through her core.

'We're your friends,' Diana declared dutifully. 'It's our job to make you feel better. So get your arse upstairs and get changed.'

At the foot of the stairs, Allie glanced back at her friends, at the blinking tree. The two women bathed in its intermittent glow smiled at her and Allie felt the brutality of time. How one moment they had been just girls, full of potential, full of life and then she'd blinked and they were adults, wearied and held together like fractured rag dolls. Then her thoughts drifted to Jasper, of the belief he'd once had in her when she dared to show him an early draft of what was to become her first book.

'You should submit this to an agent,' he had eagerly suggested to a twenty-three-year-old Allie. He had worked for an independent newspaper and always wore plaid shirts. Allie had met him just after she graduated from university and moved to London to work in a bookstore. 'It's a great story,' he'd added, 'and it explains so much.' She hadn't pushed him to expand on what he meant by that. Looking back she wished that she had.

Seventeen

Allie awoke to the murmur of voices. Deep shadows now filled the room as the candles had burned low. As the fog of sleep ebbed away she noticed her friends in the firelight, gathered upon the sofas. Diana was stretched out, Emily sat upright near her feet. Across from them were Gail and Stacie, both with their legs tucked up beneath them.

'Do you remember him?' Gail was asking through a smile. 'The way he kept calling you Shirley?'

'It was so annoying!' Stacie laughed heartily, eyes bright even in the dimness of the room. 'I was forever correcting him.'

'You'd get so mad at him,' Gail shook her head, laughing.

'Stacie, Mr Gulliver. I'm Stacie, want me to spell it for you?' Stacie recalled, her chest heaving with the hilarity of the memory.

'He was just old.' Gail's smile held. 'I think Stacie's anger at him never quite grasping her name was what made it so funny.'

Diana clicked her fingers. 'And that bowler hat! I don't think I ever saw him without it! Even in the middle of summer.'

'That flat,' Stacie sighed wistfully. 'It was such a shithole with damp in the bathroom and an actual gap in the wall near my bed but it was my first proper place in London.'

Allie remembered it. After university three of them had been drawn to the capital. She was still enduring a trying flatshare when Stacie went and got herself a husband along with a flat they rented as a couple. Stacie had seemed so mature compared to the rest of them – she was freely swimming in the adult world while the others were just trying to tread water. When the marriage ended, Stacie's time at that flat did too. It had been on the eighth floor of a soulless concrete high rise stuck in the eighties. The best thing about it was the view. Allie had liked to look out through the windows at the way the city sprawled out beneath her, watching cars trace a path like ants returning to a nest. It was hypnotic.

'How long ago did you live there?' Gail asked.

'I . . .' Stacie chewed on her lip and squinted thoughtfully. 'I guess over ten years ago. Shit. Now I feel old.'

Diana hurled a cushion at her. 'We are old.'

'Some of us more than others.' Stacie stretched out a leg to playfully kick Gail.

'You realise we've known each other for over thirty years.' Gail looked around at the faces bathed in the light of the fire. 'Now that should make us all feel very old.'

'Thirty years . . .' Diana raised her arms over her head as she stretched. 'You know you get less for murder.'

The wind scratched at the walls. A beast forever trying to get in.

'Allie, you're up.' Stacie was looking over, fingers now tousling through the end of her plait which she'd pulled over her shoulder.

'Mmm.' The lingering warmth felt like a lullaby trying to lure her back into the realm of sleep. Allie's mouth opened wide in a yawn.

'You were flat out,' Gail informed her.

'It's the cold.' Tugging on the ends of her sleeves Allie smiled softly at her friends. She didn't want them to know the truth – that the reassuring rumble of their voices had helped her drift away. It had been nice to be surrounded by people rather than emptiness. 'Sorry for nodding off,' she continued. 'But I'm awake now. What's next, birthday girl? Some shadow puppetry with the candles?'

'Ah.' Stacie shook her finger at Allie. 'She is birthday girl no more. It's quarter past twelve.'

'We should all try to sleep.' Emily's posture was rigid. While the others lolled upon the sofas she was sitting with raised shoulders, kneading her forehead with the tips of her fingers. 'I'm so tired.'

'It has been a long day,' Gail admitted.

Now that Allie's eyes had finally adjusted to the swelling shadows around her, she noticed how Gail's eyes were bloodshot, how Stacie's head kept drooping and how Diana was discreetly yawning behind her hand. It was as though time had been reversed. Gone were the young women who could party until dawn, they were once again at a sleepover struggling to remain up past midnight.

'You know,' Gail began drowsily, 'it has been so nice having you all here.'

They all made sounds of mumbled agreement as Diana rolled onto her side and Stacie plumped up a cushion and then wedged it behind her head.

'Do we have to sleep down here?' Emily's voice was sharp, fingertips still working her forehead.

'It's warm down here,' Gail yawned her response. 'Upstairs the bedrooms will be freezing.'

'Right.'

'I mean it.' Gail pressed the heel of her hands against her eyes and then smiled contentedly. 'Having us all here, together, it means a lot. We don't do it enough anymore.'

Allie was warm. And tired. A pleasant lethargy clung to her limbs making it easy for her to sink down upon her sofa, letting the plump fabric embrace her. In the moment she had to admit that she agreed with Gail; it was nice to all be together again.

It didn't take long for sleep to take her once more. The wind's howl was accompanied by the slowing breathing of her friends and the snapping of logs on the fire. Allie curled up on her side and tried to think of Stacie's old flat, of Mr Gulliver in his bowler hat, but as usual her thoughts strayed to him. Allie wondered where he was. Was he sleeping now too? Was she running through his mind or did she no longer occupy his thoughts? A single tear dampened the cushion beneath her head as Allie crossed the threshold into sleep.

Something rumbled. A deep, guttural sound like thunder. It shook the air. Allie tried to latch on to the sound, but she was falling. The sun was above her, high in a rich blue sky. The rumbling became a deafening hiss and then a squeal. The air filled with the pungent aroma of burning rubber. Allie was still looking at the sky, at the burning sun within it.

And then a great force crashed against her. It met her with such a jarring blow that every scrap of air was punched out of her lungs. Allie was tossed like a rag doll against the tarmac of the road which burned hot beneath her skin. She either heard or felt something snap. She wasn't sure. Hot fluid gushed down her forehead, dripping into her eyes and skewering her vision. It felt thicker than water, more viscous.

She wasn't screaming, but someone was. A pitched, terrible wail. She could hear the horror in their voice. Allie tried to move. Tried to reach out for whoever was screaming, but she was frozen. Oil. It was in the air, she could taste it. Except there was already copper on her tongue. The rumbling had ceased but now she was seized by a fire that burned through her limbs. Was she being torched alive? Every muscle, every nerve, was ablaze. Her mouth dropped open and something seeped out. It slid down her chin, coated her neck, just as warm as whatever had fallen into her eyes.

This is what it feels like to die.

The thought was so clear, so calm. Allie could only stare ahead at the world which lay beyond her on a twisted axis and embrace the inevitable.

'Allie?'

Someone nudged her shoulder, pulling her back into the room. Allie blinked lethargically as the haze of sleep continued to linger around her, blanketing her thoughts.

'Huh?'

'You were twitching in your sleep.' Emily was crouched down beside her. She looked pale in the firelight. Like a ghost. 'I figured you were having a nightmare.'

'Um . . .' Slowly Allie sat up, dragging her fingers through the more unruly parts of her hair. 'I guess I was, yeah.'

'I need your help.'

Allie rubbed at her eyes. The fire had dimmed but still bathed her nearby friends in a warm glow. Diana was curled up at the end of the opposite sofa, asleep. Stacie and Gail were spread out close by, each with their head twisted into a cushion, their eyes closed.

'What time is it?' Allie sounded hoarse. She heard the clipped voice of the BBC World Service newscaster and tried to latch on to it to gain some clarity.

'Just after two,' Emily explained softly.

'Two?' How long had they all been asleep? Allie tried and failed to recall what time the power had gone out. Was it the alcohol or the disorientation of the darkness that was making her memory sluggish?

'I just can't get comfortable down here.' Emily reached a hand out to Allie and helped her stand up. 'I was wondering if you'd help me start a fire in one of the bedrooms so that I could sleep up there.'

'Yeah, no problem.' Allie was too tired to register that she wasn't completely sure how to competently start a fire. That kind of thing required Gail's assistance, or at the very least Diana's. But Emily had called on her specifically, so she felt compelled to at least try to help. Besides, the others were all sleeping so soundly, it felt wrong to disturb them. She took in Emily's usually flawless skin in the dim light and noticed the beads of sweat dotted along her forehead like raindrops. Allie assumed that her friend had curled up too close to the fire in her ongoing effort to get warm.

'I don't have great circulation,' she'd once explained when Allie queried why Emily was always adjusting the thermostat in her family home, bringing the house up to a balmy twenty-two degrees even in the milder spring months.

Emily was already weaving through the shadows so Allie quickly followed. Together they walked through the flickering candlelight and approached the stairs. Even at the foot of them, Allie could feel the chill which gathered above, waiting to greet them like a malevolent house guest. 'How do we even start a fire?' she wondered hesitantly. 'I mean, is there stuff up there?'

'There's a stack of logs and some newspapers and matches. I went up and checked before.'

'Right, okay.' Allie figured that they sounded like all the components needed to start a fire.

'I just wasn't, you know, completely sure how to get it going. I'd have woken Gail; I know this is more her thing, but everyone was sleeping so peacefully. Everyone except you.'

Night terrors. It was the term the doctors at the hospital had used when Allie would wake up in the middle of the night, mouth open in a wretched scream, her heart a jackhammer in her chest.

'It's common in cases like this,' a smooth-voiced paediatrician had told Allie's parents during an appointment ahead of their daughter's discharge. 'It is akin to PTSD but should subside over the coming months.'

And he had been right, in a way. While the screaming abated, the nightmares did not. Allie would still wake, heart in her mouth, while the rest of the world was still. Over and over again she kept crashing against heated tarmac, feeling her bones crack and splinter. Somehow, she'd just learned to stop screaming when it happened.

'I get nightmares a lot.' Allie massaged her neck and began climbing the stairs, keen to hide the blush that crept up her face from her friend. Her night terrors were just another enduring symptom, one she tried to keep a closely guarded secret. People already had more than enough reasons to pity her without her adding to that load.

'I'm not being precious or anything, wanting the bed.' Emily hurried after her. 'I know that Stacie will say that I am being . . . That I'm being high maintenance, but I ache so much since I had the twins. You get how that feels, right?'

'Right.' Allie reached around and needled the base of her spine with her fingertips. She felt nothing. And the pain was good, pain meant that things were working, that nerves and synapses were firing. Numbness was bad. Potentially very bad. Allie sighed as she withdrew her hand and opened the nearest door. She staggered back, briefly stunned. Emily peered around her, eyes wide.

'Jesus Christ,' Emily whispered fearfully.

The storm had grown more savage. No more shadows swelled around the bed or beneath the overhead beams. The large bedroom window had previously offered a peaceful vista over the Scottish mountainside, now there was just a whiteout that glared so brightly it felt like it was the middle of the day. Snow fell so furiously, so densely, that it hid everything else from view. Allie reverently approached the window and tentatively pressed her hand against the icy glass. She saw only snow. There were no trees, no distant white peaks. No rocks. There was just an impenetrable blanket of white.

'Do you think it will pass soon?' Emily was lingering by the fireplace seemingly hesitant to gaze upon the blizzard in its full glory.

'I hope so.'

'And if it doesn't?'

'Then we'd better hope we've got enough firewood and food. Because no one is going anywhere in this.'

Allie felt like they'd just been dropped into the Arctic as they slept, stolen away from civilisation. Now there was nothing to do but wait out the storm.

Eighteen

The snow battered against the window as though it were trying to find a hole, a gap in the seal, some way to sneak inside and extend the blizzard into the cabin. Allie stared at the billowing snow until her vision began to blur. It looked like nothing and everything all at once. A swirling, white vortex of weather. Allie kept watching the snow as her temple throbbed. It felt like staring into oblivion.

'God, I'm exhausted.'

Emily's voice drew Allie away from the window. There was something shaky to her words. Something uncertain. Blinking away the dots that lingered in her vision she looked towards her friend who was now perched on the edge of the bed, her hands gripping the sheets at her sides as though she might topple forwards at any given moment. Her skin was like alabaster, sheened with sweat.

'Em, are you okay?'

'No, I'm not okay.' There was a tempest swirling in Emily's blue eyes where normally there was just an endless calm ocean. She snapped out her words, her entire body shuddering with annoyance.

This was an Emily that Allie rarely saw. A previously docile animal that had once been tender and friendly was now snarling and snapping as though they'd been backed into a dangerous corner. Allie cautiously stepped closer to the bed. 'Em, what is it? Are you feeling all right? You need some sugar or something?'

'I need my medication.' Emily's grip on the sheets beside her became vice-like. Her current demeanour was so at odds with her usual, genial self that for a moment Allie wondered if she was still downstairs laid out on the sofa, still dreaming.

'Dammit.' Emily released the sheets and began to massage her temple as she hunched forward. 'I'm sorry, Allie. I get kind of short-tempered when my blood sugar levels start playing up. I'll be all right once I have my insulin.'

'Okay, well you go get that and I'll start the fire.'

Emily left with quick, jerky steps leaving Allie to attend to the fireplace. She wished that her time spent as a Brownie had been more useful. While the Scouts were learning how to camp and build fires the Brownie Guides were being taught how to make cups of tea and be thrifty.

Diana had made a terrible Brownie. Every week she mocked the pack leader, Brown Owl, a local busybody with too much time on her hands, for all the sexist stereotypes the girls were being forced to comply with. And for a while, her outbursts were tolerated, perhaps because the adults in town gossiped so freely about what was going on between her parents.

'Why aren't we out in the woods making a fire? Why aren't we learning how to defend ourselves from an attacker?' Diana would demand, her cherub features twisting with resentment. 'What good is it to teach us how to make cups of tea and crochet? Are we all supposed to grow up and be someone's bloody secretary?'

It was the use of the word 'bloody' that got Diana kicked out of Brownies. Stacie and Allie quit soon after. But Emily and Gail stayed on to become Girl Guides. Something the others mocked them for relentlessly.

Allie was smiling at the memory of Brown Owl's face paling with shock when Diana swore at her. The former hospital matron's mouth had fallen open and flapped like a fish gasping for breath. No one had ever challenged her in such a way before, not even Diana.

It had taken time, but Allie had managed to bundle an assortment of wood and newspaper into the fireplace and now she struck a match and held it to the edge of one of the sheets of paper. Memory had been her guide. Her Aunt Doris had once had an open fire in the little council terrace she lived in, though she mainly fuelled it with coal. But as coal rose in cost the old woman began to integrate newspapers and scraps of wood into her fire-building regime. Allie used to loathe the open fire, the way it crackled erratically.

'Don't sit too close,' her aunt would warn, despite the presence of a wrought-iron fire guard. 'You wouldn't want the fire to spit and catch in your lovely long hair.'

Just the thought of her hair going up in flames was enough to terrify Allie. She got used to giving the fireplace a wide berth whenever she went to visit her aunt who loved to ply her young relatives with toffees wrapped in crinkly golden paper.

Despite Allie's trepidation, something about Aunt Doris's methods had stuck. Allie knew to build up newspaper between pieces of wood and now, match in hand, she was ready to test her handiwork, though her eyes scanned the nearby hearth nervously for a fire guard. There wasn't one. The flame she tentatively offered to a protruding piece of newspaper quickly caught, causing the page to curl and blacken. After several minutes the fire was crackling as flames in their infancy began to dance across the wood.

Raising her hands towards the fire Allie let the heat settle around her. It blanketed her, filling the bedroom with a comforting halo of light that made the icy glare of the storm feel more distant.

Emily burst back into the room, panting. 'It's gone.' She threw her handbag onto the bed. It was the bag she'd had with her during the flight.

'What's gone?' Flexing her hands, enjoying the looseness she felt now they were warm, Allie turned round.

'My . . . my insulin.' Emily was throwing the contents of her bag all over the bed. A phone. A Ted Baker purse. Several Clinique chubby sticks. A compact. A pack of tissues. A pack of baby wipes. Items kept landing on the duvet as she delved to the bottom of her bag. 'It was in here in my medical travel kit. I always keep it in my hand luggage in case . . . in case.' She stepped back from the bed as though one of her items had suddenly bitten her. With a yelp she clasped her hands over her mouth.

'It will be here.' Allie came and stood beside her and began rummaging through the discarded contents on the bed. There was nothing that resembled the deep purple cosmetic case that Allie knew her friend used for storing her medication. 'And if it's not here . . .' Allie tipped the handbag upside down for good measure. A packet of Tic Tac fell out but nothing else. '. . . then it must be in your suitcase.'

'No, it must be in *here*,' Emily wailed as powerfully as the storm. 'It *has* to be in here. I packed it this morning right after I'd used it to make sure I didn't forget it.'

'Okay, but maybe it's in your suitcase. Maybe in the chaos of sorting the twins before you left, it got moved and you just don't remember. Let's go and check.'

Emily sniffed and nodded as the fire spat at them.

'There's no use getting yourself worked up until we know for sure it's not here.' Allie was busy ignoring the pang of panic in her own chest. Seeing her friend in flux like this, despairing, filled her with dread but also a strong instinct to react, to protect. No one should ever be vulnerable, weakened by something as horrid as—

Allie blinked and for a second she saw the stark hospital room that had been her home for so many months. Then she blinked again and was returned to the bedroom in the cabin. The panic in her chest began to twist into something else; the burning pain that came from abandonment. She looked at her blonde, lithe friend and almost asked the question which she never breathed life into: *Why didn't you come?*

But she knew better than to ask.

'I always know where it is,' Emily noted tearfully as she left the bedroom and Allie followed her back downstairs. 'It's the first thing I pack and—'

'We'll find it.' Allie leaned forward to squeeze her friend's hand and looked down at her with what she hoped was a smile that conveyed confidence.

The suitcases were piled up in the living area, an assortment of black, silver and pink. No one had yet bothered to unpack. Allie pulled Emily's suitcase away from the others, the wheels loudly dragging across the wooden floor, squeaking like frightened mice.

'Hey?' There was movement near the fire. Stacie sat up, wisps of her hair splayed over her face like a russet spider web. Rubbing at her eyes she peered at them as she leaned over the back of the sofa. 'What's with all the noise?'

'We're just looking for Emily's insulin.' Allie dragged the suitcase to where the candlelight was brightest and then began unzipping its sides.

'It should have been in my flight bag.' Emily dropped to her knees and began rifling through her clothes and toiletries.

'What's happening?' Gail had also woken up. The floor-boards creaked beneath her as she padded over to her friends.

'Emily just needs her insulin,' Allie explained as she checked a bag of make-up and shook out a cashmere jumper. The little purple medical kit did not materialise.

'Isn't it normally in your flight bag?' Gail wondered nonchalantly, mouth widening as she yawned.

'Yes, that's where it always is.' Emily's voice was like a crack of thunder that split across the cabin. No one dared speak. The fire sputtered and the wind howled but the women were silent.

Allie kept searching, feeling her heart start to sink as she did so. She was surrounded by small mounds of Emily's clothes; white jumpers and crisp dark jeans. Toiletry bags had been pillaged, their contents spewed out across the floor. Allie clocked a lipstick roll beneath one of the sofas but didn't bother to chase after it. She was searching for something much more precious.

'It's not . . . here.' Emily leaned inside her suitcase and scraped her fingers along its satin-lined interior. She explored every corner, pressed down on every inch in the vain hope that her medication might have slid behind the lining. It hadn't. 'It really isn't here.' She leaned back and drew her fingernails along her scalp, bunching up her golden hair in her hands.

'It has to be here.' Gail sounded so calm. So sure. Allie considered how her most adventurous friend was wasted working up in the Scottish Highlands. She should be out on an Arctic expedition or climbing Everest. Gail never lost her head. She was always calm, always pragmatic. A born survivor. 'We just need to keep looking.'

'I need to . . .' Emily groaned and pinched her eyes shut.

'Go and lie down.' Gail gave her order and then looked at Allie. 'Take a glass of water up to her and make sure the fire is lit in her bedroom. We'll look for her medication.'

'What time is it?' Diana had stirred, her mouth gaped open as she yawned and raised her arms above her head, stretching.

'Time you got up and helped me search for Emily's insulin,' Gail briskly replied.

Allie felt pressure on her shoulders. A shaking sensation. Blinking her eyes open, she was greeted with darkness, solid and alienating.

'You were screaming.' She heard Lucas before she saw him. The sheets rustled around her as he positioned himself at her side. 'You were calling out for her and you sounded so scared I just had to wake you.'

'I was . . .' Allie raised a hand and dragged it across her eyes. Slowly the moonlight creeping in through the window was revealing the room of her London flat to her — the vanity table over by the radiator, the antique wardrobe with its ornate wooden panel doors which had been a steal at a Dorset car boot sale the previous summer.

'The owner doesn't even realise what a gem they've just sold us,' Lucas had declared in triumph as he secured the piece of furniture against the top of his dad's Volvo with lengths of rope. 'Not like me.' He'd winked conspiratorially at her. 'I know something special when I see it.'

'Screaming?' Allie's mouth was full of cotton wool and her skin was clammy on the verge of wet, as though she'd been drowning instead of sleeping. With a gasp, she released the lingering cries that were stored in her chest.

'And shouting for her.'

'For who?' It was bewildering to be awake. Allie was both within the moment and completely detached from it. She kept staring beyond the foot of the bed at her wardrobe, needing something to visually anchor her in reality.

'Diana.' As he said the name, he stroked his fingertips against the soft inside of her arm. His touch was cold, ice against brimstone. Allie flinched.

'No, I . . .' She turned onto her side, offering him only her back and snatching her arm away from his reach. 'It was just a dream.'

'You sounded terrified.'

'A nightmare then.'

'Allie . . .' She felt the mattress shift, knew that he was sitting up, probably adopting the serious expression he wore whenever he was editing a newly completed script. He was scrutinising her, judging her. She longed to delve back into the pool of darkness that had been her dream, no matter how turbulent. Whatever nightmare she'd been having it was gone now, banished by moonlight from the room. 'I'm just concerned. Were you dreaming about the accident?'

No.

Allie clutched her pillow tightly, letting her fingers tingle as they applied too much pressure to the soft cotton of the eggshell-blue case. She wouldn't revisit the past. Not now. This was her marital home, it was supposed to be a place of happiness, a safe place. Had she truly uttered Diana's name or was he manipulating her, trying to induce a reaction? She'd seen him do it before, with his characters, when he tailored their dialogue to reach the desired end. He could be a master storyteller, it was what had drawn her to him all those months ago. She'd so keenly wanted to bask in the glow of his excellence. But now . . . she was no character in a show. She was real, flesh and bone. She wouldn't have called out for Diana. Would she?

'Let's just go back to sleep.' The order was muffled, her body too weary to be stern.

'But is that it, were you dreaming about the accident?'

She pretended to have already left the port on a boat bound for slumber, as his hands grazed her back, trying to ply her into confessing more. 'Tell me, Allie, let me in.'

Of course, she wouldn't. She couldn't. To let him in would be to lose him.

Nineteen

Allie tried not to think about the passing of time. She sat on the bed beside Emily, who was curled up on her side looking so much like the girl who used to drift off to sleep before anyone else at a sleepover. Allie gently stroked her friend's forehead as she released a weary sigh and then turned to watch the fire dancing in the hearth, a part of her still fearful of its capacity to destroy.

Emily had always been diabetic. The first thing she told Allie when they met, three years old in play school, was that she couldn't eat sugar like everybody else could.

'I'm different,' Emily had announced proudly, her plump, rosy cheeks rising with a smile. Allie desperately wished that she was different too, especially if it would make her anything like Emily.

Even at three years old Emily was golden and beautiful.

Emily's condition became an ailment carried by the whole group. They always looked out for her, aligned their diets with hers on group holidays. Gail even administered Emily's insulin the one time she got too drunk to do it herself during a very messy girls' holiday to Ibiza. It was the first and last time Allie saw her drink to excess.

'Foolish girl.' Gail had chastised her worse than her own mother ever could have once Emily's hangover had lifted. 'You can't take risks with yourself like that. You need to be careful.'

'I thought it was fun,' Stacie had coolly countered from where she sat on a nearby lounger, her pale skin turned golden by the sun. 'We all need to let loose sometimes, Gail. Don't be such a stick-in-the-mud.'

'Letting loose is fine unless there are consequences. Emily needs to think about her health. She doesn't want something awful to happen and then lose everything like—' Gail cut off when she saw that Allie was watching them from behind her book.

'Allie?' Emily murmured sleepily and rolled onto her back. But when she looked up at her friend, her blue eyes were bright and alert.

'You okay, Ems? You warm enough? You want some water?' Allie was reaching for the long glass resting on the bedside table.

'I can't even call them,' Emily's voice caught in her throat as her eyelids fluttered closed and released several tears that trickled down her cheeks. Despite the warmth in the room, she remained paler than the snow outside, lips turning to a watery shade of pink.

'The twins? Adam?'

'Uh huh.'

'Well, they'll be sleeping now. I'm sure once the generator is all fixed and—'

'What if it's not here?'

'Gail will find your insulin. Remember that time Stacie lost her phone in town when she got blind drunk and tried to wee on a policeman? Gail went back the next day and searched every side street, every bin, and she found it in that bush outside Passions. Because that's what Gail does. She fixes things. She's Wonder Woman, remember?'

'But if it's not *here*?'

'It will be.' Allie pushed as much certainty as she could into her words.

It has to be.

Discreetly, Allie slid her phone out of her pocket and checked the bars in the top corner. Nothing. There was still no signal, no way of contacting the outside world.

Twenty

There was a gentle knock at the bedroom door and Gail walked in. Her head was bowed, her lips pulled into a tight line. Allie reached for Emily and hugged her.

'We turned the place upside down.' Gail squared her shoulders and managed to keep her voice level.

'And?' Emily peered up at her friend, eyes widening with hope.

'And you're right. It's not here. We can't find your insulin.'

The wind united with Emily as they both howled. Allie held her tight, pressing her against her chest and letting her cry.

'No. It can't be gone! What will I do?'

'Just . . . let's just stay calm and think.' Gail raised both hands as the fire hissed and spat behind her. 'Your insulin isn't here so we need to contact someone to bring some to us. Allie' – she clicked her fingers – 'I need you to check every square inch of this place for signal. Rope the others in, too. Even one bar is enough to call down to the village and the doctor there. Let me know if you find some.'

'I'm on it.' Allie moved to scramble away from Emily, but her friend's fingers closed around her own, drawing her back.

'I'm scared.' The admission was a whisper.

'Don't be,' Allie reassured her. 'We're all here for you, we'll fix this.'

★

'There is no signal.' Stacie was standing on a dining-room chair in the far corner of the main living area, phone held loftily above her. 'There's no signal anywhere!'

'Keep looking,' Allie ordered as she paced across the room, arm outstretched as she clasped her own phone and stared fixedly at the top right corner which remained absent of any bars.

'You know this is pointless, right?' Diana was by the fire, her back to the others. 'There's no signal up here. Our best chance at calling for help is to fix the generator and restore some power.'

'She's right.' Gail came down the stairs, cheeks flushed and phone in hand. 'I've checked all over upstairs and there's no signal anywhere. We need to use the satellite phone and to do that I'll need to get the generator up and running.'

'And how long will that take?' Stacie asked as she remained in the corner, wafting her phone back and forth above her head, straining on her tiptoes to make herself as tall as possible.

'I don't know. First I need to assess the damage.'

'But it'll take a while though, right?' Diana left the fire to pace over to the nearest window. Drawing back the curtains she tapped against the glass with a single finger. 'And you see this? We're getting bloody snowed in up here! If you manage to call for help how is anyone even going to get to us?'

Gail drummed her fingers against her temple, frowning. 'Look, just . . .' She withdrew her hand to raise the palm in Diana's direction. 'Let's not panic, okay. What we need right now is to keep level heads.'

'We're not doing survival at a Girl Guides camp now,' Stacie muttered.

'What?' Gail whipped her question in her direction.

'Nothing.'

'Thought so.' Gail's hands were now on her hips. 'Generator,' she declared decisively. 'Let's see where we're at with it. Maybe it's not in that bad shape. Allie?'

Hearing her name, Allie abandoned her search for a signal to glance at the window and the flurries of snowflakes that peppered the glass. Diana was right. Even if they got through to someone, they were isolated. 'Who can reach us here?' The question echoed the bleakness outside. 'Surely we need to go down, find help.'

'Not happening.' Gail stared her down, hands remaining on hips. 'In this weather, in her declining condition, it's too risky.'

'*Declining condition?*' There was a squeak as Stacie dropped from her perch. 'What do you mean?'

'I mean what I just said.'

'But . . .' Stacie was waving her phone around as she spoke. 'That can't be the case. Emily is going to be okay, right? She's just forgotten her meds, it's no big issue. Right?'

Gail was silent.

'She should have packed some extra fucking insulin. Who doesn't bring spare medication with them? Christ!'

'Stay. Calm.' Diana stalked back over to the flames of the fire. 'The last thing we need right now is your hysterics.'

'*Hysterics?*'

'Even bickering,' Gail barked like the exhausted mother the group had a habit of making her feel like.

'How long does she have, exactly?' Stacie folded her arms against her chest and looked between her friends,

133

biting her lip, voice softening. 'Because you're all rushing around like she doesn't have long at all.'

'She doesn't.' Gail's voice was hard. 'I'm not completely up on how her pump works, but back when she was injecting, she needed insulin several times a day. Without it, she risks going hypoglycaemic.'

'So has the pump stopped working?'

'The pump is now empty,' Allie noted quietly.

'Empty?' Stacie squeaked.

'That's what her supplies in her flight bag were for. To restock her pump so that it keeps working.' Gail massaged her temple and looked up at the ceiling.

'Won't just a chocolate bar work? We've got loads of food in the cupboards and—'

'No.' Gail and Allie snapped their reply in unison.

'It was just a suggestion,' said Stacie, defensively raising her hands up at them.

Allie rested a hand on Stacie's arm. 'She needs insulin.'

'Did she say when she last topped up her pump?' Gail levelled her gaze at Allie who paused for a moment to think.

'Yesterday morning, ahead of her flight.' She was certain of her response, though she added for extra clarity, 'Before she left for the airport.'

'Right, okay.' Gail started to pace around the back of the sofas in quick, frantic steps. 'Less than twenty-four hours ago. So we have a few hours at least. If only she'd remembered to pack her damn meds instead of being too distracted about leaving the twins. We just need a plan of action.' Biting her lip, she clenched her hands into fists of frustration.

'We're helpless up here.' Diana stared at the flames in the fire.

'Signal,' Gail ordered, pointing first at Stacie and then at Diana. 'Keep checking for signal while I go and check out the generator.' She raised her chin and looked across the room. 'And, Allie?'

'Yes?'

'Come with me. I'm going to need someone to hold the torch.'

The snow burned. It was just a short distance from the back door of the cabin to the shed beside it which housed the generator, but it may as well have been on a different mountain. Allie remained close to Gail as they trod a path through the whiteout, hands groping ahead to guide them.

The shed door was reluctant to open. Gail grunted as she pulled on it with her full force. Allie was stepping forward to assist just as the hinges gave way with a sharp whine and then they were moving inside, enjoying a slight respite from the battering of the weather. Allie guided the beam of the torch around the small space and instantly highlighted the problem.

Part of the roof to the shed had completely caved in. A tree had crashed down, overladen with snow, and now its branches gnarled and scratched against the generator which stood silent as flakes gently settled upon it.

'Shit.' Gail was swearing before she'd even reached the tree. 'Shit,' she repeated as she tried to remove it with gloved hands. It remained rigidly in place, offering a soft cascade of snow for her efforts, which dusted her arms. 'The damn thing has knocked out the generator completely.' She kicked at the tree and then turned back to Allie. 'Give me some light.'

Raising the torch Allie shone it against the display panel for the generator. A red light was on in warning.

'Without this, there's no satellite phone.' Gail was studying the panel. 'I mean, maybe I can get it up and running again' – she looked back at Allie – 'but Emily doesn't have very long.' The light from the torch cast long shadows upon her friend's face. Allie nodded in grim understanding.

'Okay, so we need to think of another way to help her.'

'I can fix this. I mean I'm pretty sure I can. I'm just worried how long it'll take.'

'And if it takes too long?'

Gail hung her head.

'We have to help her,' Allie implored.

'That's what we're trying to do, Allie.'

They both stared at the broken generator, feeling helpless.

'It's like you're never there.'

Gail folded her arms to her chest as she prepared for the verbal assault Melissa was about to fire at her. Melissa with her waves of chestnut hair and dimple in only her left cheek.

'I'm here,' Gail told her calmly, the sunlight beaming in through the cabin window and casting golden rectangles upon the wooden floor. 'I'm always here.'

'No,' Melissa instantly retaliated, hazel eyes ablaze with anger, 'you're not. You're always checking your phone, jumping every time it rings. And when one of them does call, it's like I don't exist.'

'That's not true.'

'They say jump and you ask how high.' Melissa withdrew from the arena of their disagreement, moving to the window, one hand clasped to her forehead.

Gail internally sighed. They were locked in a déjà vu of this same argument. Over and over they had it in different incarnations. Gail always desperate for Melissa to see, to understand that her friends were family to her, and for that reason, she'd always need to be there for them.

'I hate to see it,' Melissa noted, voice suddenly soft. 'How they use you.' She pressed her palm to the window and gazed out at the emerald trees on the mountainside.

'They don't use me.' Gail felt her cheeks growing hot at the mere suggestion.

'The worst part is you don't even see it,' Melissa continued sadly. 'You give them so much. You call, you text, you send birthday cards, presents. All this effort. This energy. And it's not reciprocated. Not even a little bit.'

'Look, that's not fair, it—'

'When we got engaged' — Melissa spun back round to face her — 'where were they? They weren't falling over themselves to congratulate you.'

'They just . . .' Gail breathed in the pine-laced air of the cabin. 'Mel, can we stop having this same argument. Please.'

'I'd ask you to choose.' Melissa blinked, her eyes glistening. 'But I know it wouldn't be me.'

Gail stepped forward but Melissa raised a hand, halting her in place. 'I'm tired of playing second fiddle to a group of friends who don't even care about you, or each other,' she explained.

'Please,' Gail begged her, 'if you could just try to understand. Things with my friends . . . it's . . . it's complicated.'

'Complicated how?' Melissa demanded.

Defeated, Gail sighed. The web between her and her friends was so tangled, so dense, how could she ever hope to explain it to somebody. They were broken, each of them, each of her Fierce Five. Like a tattered blanket, Gail was the one strong piece of thread holding them all together, preventing them from becoming rags. They needed her. And as she looked at Melissa, at the single tear falling down her perfect cheek, Gail knew that for her, feeling needed was everything. It gave her purpose. Made her feel strong when others around her were weak. Her friends were for life. Love . . . it was fleeting. The others had shown *her that. Partners came and went. But thanks to Gail the Fierce Five stayed together.*

'I won't cut them out,' Gail told Melissa, who nodded, already expecting the answer.

'I just wish you could see how they are. How they truly are. I love you, Gail. But I'm tired of sharing you.'

Gail waited until after Melissa's bags were packed and her Audi A3 had pulled away from the cabin, down the steep mountain road before she allowed herself to cry. Once the sobs subsided, she called Emily, keen to hear a familiar voice, to unburden herself. But it rang straight to voicemail.

Twenty-One

Officer: You couldn't call for help?

POI: No. We were cut off. There was no phone signal and we couldn't use the satellite phone with the generator down.

Officer: And there was no way of repairing the generator?

POI: Gail was concerned about the extent of the damage done by the storm. She wasn't sure if it was salvageable.

Officer: And you believed her?

POI: Of course. She had no reason to lie.

Officer: But without the generator and your phones there was no way to call down for help. You were completely stranded.

POI: Yes, I'm painfully aware of the situation we were in.

Officer: So what did you do?

POI: What could I do? I was trapped. We all were.

Twenty-Two

'I'm feeling really rough.' Emily had balled herself into the foetal position and Allie was at her side, rubbing her back. Her brief stint outside still clung to her, the cold having settled in her bones.

'It's okay, we'll get you your meds.'

'How?' Emily sniffed. 'How are you going to call anyone?'

Allie drew her mouth into a tight line, not wanting to reveal the true extent of their isolation. 'Diana and Stacie are looking for some phone signal,' she finally offered in a hopeful tone, 'and Gail is going to fix the generator.'

'And if she can't fix it?' Emily countered sharply, sweat gathering on porcelain cheeks like droplets of rain.

Allie looked over Emily at Gail who was standing at the foot of the bed, arms folded against her chest. She turned away from the conversation. 'She will,' Allie offered sternly.

'It's a mess,' Gail exhaled, looking down at her feet. 'A real fucking mess. A tree has come through and busted up the main panel and I . . .' Turning back she raised her head, met Emily's watery gaze. 'It's going to take quite some time to fix.'

'Quite some time,' Emily repeated with a tremor in her words. 'Time that I don't have?'

Gail's jaw clenched.

'Diana and Stacie might still find some signal.' Allie tried in vain to raise her friend's spirits.

'And if they don't.' Emily shuddered beneath Allie's hand. 'This is serious, Allie. I could . . . I could . . .'

'I'll go and find help.' Allie was surprised to find that the words had come from her own mouth.

'It's a full-on blizzard out there,' Gail stated factually, pointing a long finger towards the whiteout just a few feet away beyond the large window. 'No one is going anywhere in this. Let me fix the generator. I'll go and start on it now and—'

'Emily needs help!' Allie interrupted. 'There's no phone signal, no landline while the generator is down. I need to go and get help for her. You said there's a village at the base of the mountain. I can call for the air ambulance from there.'

'No. It's too risky.'

'We don't have any choice.'

'I need to go and fix the generator. I can do it, I know I can.'

'And if you can't?' Allie countered. 'You wouldn't have followed me back inside if you were certain about the generator.'

A flicker of sadness danced across Gail's face. Then with one hand, she swept the expression away and her eyes resumed their steely focus.

'Fine, you're right. But you'll need to hurry.' Gail's gaze flicked from Allie to Emily and the line of her mouth set more firmly. 'We don't have much time.'

'Are you seriously considering going out in this?' Stacie stormed towards the nearest window and dragged the curtains back, causing them to rattle loudly against the rail.

Even though dawn was still a few hours away, blinding brightness burned against her, causing her to stagger back and shield her eyes. The snow pattered against the glass like tiny fingertips knocking, begging to be let in.

'This storm is crazy,' Stacie continued, throwing her hands up in despair. 'Going out in it would be suicide! There has to be another way!'

'There isn't,' Allie stated stoically as she pulled on her woollen hat. 'I'm going, it's not up for discussion.'

Emily was twelve when she first passed out at school. Getting her first period had thrown her blood sugar into disarray and even her daily injections weren't enough to keep everything in balance. It was during double maths. She'd just asked Allie if she could borrow her protractor and as Allie reached for her pencil case, she heard something slam hard against the tiled floor. Suddenly everyone was screaming as though a grenade had just been flung into the classroom.

That was the first time Allie truly knew fear. When she looked down at her friend, eyes closed, lips blue, she felt the ground opening up beneath her. As Allie stared at her through her tears and clasped her cold, clammy hands within her own, she prayed to anyone who was listening to bring her friend back to her. Teachers rushed in and knelt at Emily's side, pushing the students back, but Allie refused to move, no matter how many detentions she was threatened with.

'We've called an ambulance,' Mr Rogers said.

'Everything is going to be all right,' Mrs Albrighton told an unconscious Emily.

Allie held on, squeezing Emily's hand tighter and tighter and only finally letting go when the paramedics arrived.

'What happened?' they demanded, looking at the worried teachers' faces.

'She suddenly passed out and—'

'She's diabetic.' Allie didn't care that she was cutting Mr Rogers off. She knew that she needed to relay the vital information to the paramedics. No one chided her for speaking out of turn. The paramedic nodded briskly at her and then focused on Emily, calling out her name and reassuring her that everything was going to be fine.

Now, the compulsion to react felt so normal, so natural, that she wasn't really considering what she was actually about to walk into.

'We could call for help,' Stacie suggested, face still turned to the blinding fury of the blizzard.

'On what?' Gail kicked a door closed behind her as she emerged from one of the bedrooms carrying a dark green plastic box. 'There's no signal up here. The landline operates on a satellite system because of the remote location. It needs power to work. Power we don't currently have.'

'So what do you do in an emergency?' Stacie demanded, hands falling to her sides as she spun round.

'I need to fix the generator,' Gail said for what felt like the hundredth time, placing the box on the sofa and by the light of the fire popping it open to begin rooting around inside it.

'Well that doesn't look like a tool kit,' Stacie observed as she edged closer. 'Why aren't you already out there fixing the damn generator?'

'It's a first aid kit,' Diana remarked flatly from where she stood beside the fire, staring intently at the flames, her dark hair gathered at the base of her neck in a messy ponytail which she hadn't bothered to tidy since waking up.

Gail's long fingers dug through the rolls of bandages, plasters and surgical tape. She cursed as she straightened and gave a shake of her head. 'Just like I thought – nothing of any use in here.' She looked up and locked eyes with Stacie. 'I'll return to the generator once we've made sure it's not our only resort.'

'You mean once you've sent Allie out to her doom?' Stacie pressed. 'This is all just ridiculous. There has to be a better way to help Emily. Let's check her suitcase again.'

'No, no insulin,' Gail slammed the box closed, ignoring Stacie's suggestion. 'It doesn't exactly come as standard in a first aid kit,' she added with a sigh.

'Well then we wait. Help will come eventually, right?' Stacie looked over her shoulder, at the snow trying to attach itself to the smooth glass of the cabin window.

'We can't wait.' Allie's jaw clenched so tight she could barely prise it open to speak. She zipped up her coat, hoping it would live up to the waterproof promises it had boasted on its label when she had bought it the previous winter. 'Emily needs her insulin. I'll get to the village at the base of the mountain and I'll—'

'It should really be me going . . .' Gail divided her attention between the crackling fire and the front door. 'But if I fix the generator, I can call for help and they'll get here quicker than you'll get down the mountain.' Hands lifted from the first aid box, she continued to glance between the hearth and the threshold to the cabin, caught in a vice of her own indecision. Allie knew what thoughts would be racing through her friend's mind.

Where will I be most useful?

Which option will give Emily the best chance?

Gail would have already clicked into survival mode, weighing up her options with complete pragmatism.

'Can't someone else fix the generator?' Stacie kept glancing at the window. 'I mean, no one knows this mountain as well as you do, Gail. You'd be the fastest getting down it.'

'Yes, but no one else can fix the damn generator, it's temperamental at the best of times.' With a sigh Gail turned to Allie, jaw clenched. 'When you get to the village knock on the green door that's next to the bungalow on the bend in the road. The one marked two.' Gail was massaging her hands together, her brow furrowed in thought. 'Ewan Cole lives there. He's a local police officer and he has a satellite phone and an emergency radio. One of those has to be working. The storm can't be as bad down there as it is up here. Tell him we need either an emergency evacuation, or if that's too risky, to get a supply of insulin up to Emily immediately.' She grabbed at her left hand, began absently rubbing the now vacant spot upon one of her fingers where a diamond had once sparkled. 'Get ready.' Her hands suddenly dropped to her sides as the trance was broken, a fierce gaze latching on to Allie. 'Dress as warmly as you can. I'll be right back.'

It was a routine Emily should have known well. At fourteen, she had, after all, been doing it herself for almost two whole years. Alcohol wipe to clean a patch of skin on her stomach. Get the auto-injector pen. Check the expiration date. Check for surplus bubbles. If all okay, administer.

She was on the toilet in the upstairs bathroom at Allie's house. A room which always smelt of lavender. Everyone else was in the lounge watching a video so Emily knew it would be quiet. And she needed quiet. Liked quiet. Still . . . she thought about them having paused the film. Waiting. If she was too long, would they be mad at her? When she went downstairs would they pretend they were okay with her, even if they weren't?

'Same time,' Emily whispered to the injector pen she was holding above her exposed stomach, her pyjama top bunched up just beneath her breasts. 'Every day, same dose, same time.' She was repeating what she already knew. The routine which had been drilled into her by her consultant and numerous doctors. It was all about routine. And diet. That, they promised her, was the key to maintaining a healthy, normal life.

'And you're basically fine,' her parents would continually say her, 'absolutely fine.' At every hospital appointment, they only ever smiled as though they were at Disneyland instead of paediatric outpatients. 'Appearances,' her dad was keen to remind her, 'are everything. God gave you this, so handle it with grace and gratitude, you understand?'

A golden cross hung around her neck. Emily sighed and reassessed the injector pen in her hand, palm growing sweaty. She wanted to ask her dad why if God had given her this, he couldn't come and help with the needles? Why leave her alone?

She knew her friends were waiting.

'Do it quick so it won't stick,' she quietly sang to herself the mantra her mother had given her after her initial diagnosis.

Footsteps. Beyond the door. Out on the landing.

Shit. She'd taken too long. They were mad at her. Everyone else wanted to carry on watching the film and she was up here, dawdling over her injection and holding them up.

'Urgh.' She pushed the tip of the pen into her stomach, misjudging the angle. Her muscles clenched in pain. Emily bit down on her lip and scrunched up her eyes. With a gasp, the auto-injector clicked and she withdrew it and then threw it at the door, hunching forward, panting.

'Em, you okay?' A swift knock at the door, Allie's concerned voice threading through the wood.

Tears on her cheeks, moving towards her chin. Emily sucked the last of them back in and scraped the back of her hands over her eyes. Her stomach smarted like she'd been stung by a very large, very angry bee. Softly she padded over to the door, grabbed the pen she had thrown and returned it to her medicine bag resting beside the toilet on the pink, carpeted floor.

'Em, you feeling all right?' Allie persisted in her enquiry. Emily felt her face dampen with fresh tears.

Now it was even worse than angering her friends, she was worrying them, making herself too much of a burden. Quickly she flushed the toilet and hurried to the sink, running the cold tap and flicking cool water against her cheeks.

'Emily?'

She took one final second to look in the mirror above the sink, checking that her reflection held enough credibility. It did. Smiling, Emily approached the door and opened it, her medicine bag held neatly at her side.

'Hey, Em, you were taking a while, wanted to make sure you were okay.' Allie was in soft plaid pyjamas, long hair hanging over her shoulder in a plait.

'Yes, Allie Bear, I'm absolutely fine.' Emily grinned widely at her. 'Now let's go and watch the end of the film, I'm starving for some popcorn.'

'I got some salted in just for you,' Allie told her brightly as they walked down the stairs together. Emily hung back, just a fraction, so that she could discreetly press a hand against the point of her stomach still throbbing uncomfortably.

Twenty-Three

Allie was starting to feel hot within her numerous layers and coat. She needed to leave. She needed to start picking her way down the mountain and head for Ewan Cole's green door as soon as possible. She tried to remember the route the taxi had taken. It had bounced down several back roads before taking a sharp left and crawling up an extremely steep incline. That part of the journey had lasted almost fifteen minutes. Then he'd stopped and said he could go no further. If Allie could just find that road and follow it then—

'The roads will be gone.' Diana didn't turn away from the fire when she spoke. 'They'll be hidden under a few feet of snow by now. Besides' – she lifted a hand to massage her neck – 'the road won't be the quickest way down to the bottom.' In the firelight, Diana's pink streaks looked like copper, rustic and burned against her dark hair. She kept her head bowed towards the flames. On the sofa beside her were stacked some of her own clothes; a coat, hat, gloves. Allie assumed they were there for when the heat began to leave the cabin, a necessary precaution.

'Just keep heading down,' Stacie suggested. 'It's a mountain after all. You can either go up or go down.'

'I guess.' Allie scratched at her arms. Her abundance of clothes was making her feel claustrophobic. She was ready to go but felt that she needed to wait for Gail's return.

'Do you remember when Emily passed out in maths class?' Diana was still turned away from them. Allie stiffened, growing suddenly cold at the recollection. None of the other girls had been there when it happened. It had just been Emily and Allie. The rest of them heard about it second hand from eyewitnesses.

'Didn't they mention something about the risk of a diabetic coma?'

'That's . . .' Allie's tongue felt too big for her mouth. 'I think it happens if someone goes hypoglycaemic and doesn't get help.'

'A coma?' Stacie peered over at Diana, her head cocked with frightened interest.

'Her body will start to shut down,' Allie quickly explained. 'She'll go into a coma and without medical intervention . . .' her voice trailed off. She was unable to finish her own sentence.

'She won't wake up.' Diana spun round and stared down her friends. 'Hence why it's called a coma.'

Bluntness. It was always Diana's favoured approach to any discussion. There had been a time when Allie loved that about her. She could ask her anything . . .

'How's my outfit?'

'Awful. Change it.'

'Should we watch this film?'

'No. It's shit. Pick something else.'

The honesty was always helpful, never offered out of spite but, with Diana, out of utter boldness. Diana would tell her friends that every time she found her mother bloodied and beaten at the kitchen table, her bruises bright in the morning sunlight, she'd tell her that she needed to leave her father, ignoring any platitudes to the contrary. Allie longed for Diana's strength and stoicism, especially in the face of such grave circumstances. Yet where had that determination been when Allie had needed it the most?

'Shit, you mean . . .' The colour drained from Stacie's face even though she was within the warm embrace of the fire.

'Hence the need to get down this mountain as fast as possible.' Diana grabbed her clothes, left the fire, left the circle of sofas and headed for the stack of suitcases and holdalls.

'Diana, are you okay?' Allie nervously called after her. Over the years, bluntness had turned to unpredictability.

'I'm going with you.' Diana knelt beside her silver suitcase and began pulling on her trapper hat, coat and gloves. Finally, she tugged on a heavy pair of boots.

Allie swallowed, feeling a roughness gathering at the back of her throat. She must have misheard. There was just no way that Diana would help her. Perhaps if it was any of the others going. But for it to be Allie . . . no, it just wasn't plausible.

'You are?' The question came out pleading and confused. Allie gnawed on the side of her cheek, wishing she could be as blunt as her friend had once been and demand to know exactly why she wanted to go.

'We stand a better chance of reaching that officer's house if there are two of us searching for a way down.' Diana plucked off one of her gloves with her teeth to free her hand so that she could lace up her boots. 'And I'm tired of sitting around here doing fuck all to help.'

'Okay, but . . .' Allie was about to question if there was some more hidden motivation to Diana's offer when she was cut off.

'Right.' Gail burst back into the room holding a large black box against her chest. Her cheeks were wet and snowflakes glistened in her hair. Turning, Allie saw that she was wearing a pair of Hunter wellingtons which looked damp up to the calf, with snow still clinging to parts of the dark green material. 'Allie, come here.' Gail dropped the box onto the pine table and with a single sweep dusted off the snow which was sprinkled atop it.

'Diana is coming too,' Allie explained a little shakily. Would everyone else be as shocked by that revelation as she was?

'She is?' Gail looked over to the far corner of the room, where Diana was stooped over, still fiddling with her boots. A frown briefly crinkled her features. 'Okay then.' She sucked in a breath and squared her shoulders. 'Diana, you need to get over here too.'

Of course, Gail wasn't about to get into a discussion regarding *why* Diana wanted to go down the mountain with Allie. That would be wasting what precious little time they had. But Allie so dearly wished that Gail would push the topic, at least to help silence her own concerns.

'What's in the box?' Allie looked at its glossy black surface and tried to focus on what she was about to do. With Diana. She literally couldn't remember the last time they'd done something just the two of them. Not that this was catching up over coffee or going to the cinema but still . . .

Gail raised a hand and popped the black box open.

'Some more emergency supplies.' She explained, 'Nothing medical, unfortunately. I dashed out to the generator shed where this is stored. It's getting worse out there. I need to get it fixed before the place fills up with too much snow and the generator completely freezes.' Gail let out a strained sigh. 'I don't hold out much hope for getting it fixed. Dammit.' She gritted her teeth and bowed her head.

'You weren't to know how bad the storm would get,' Allie offered kindly as Diana joined them at the table, bristling at her friend's sudden proximity. It was both welcoming and alarming in equal measure. Allie knew that this was certainly not the time for people to begin acting out of character.

'I didn't *want* to know how bad the storm was getting,' Gail muttered stiffly as she opened the ebony box, its hinges wheezing. 'I was just so desperate to have all you guys up here on my birthday. It had been so long since we were all together. Too long.'

'What is all this stuff?' Diana reached into the box and pulled out a red flare.

'Emergency supplies. Torches, flares, matches, maps.' Gail tapped each of the items as she spoke. She pulled the map out and unfolded it across the table, resting her finger against a point which was marked with an X. 'This is us.' Keeping her finger pressed to the thick paper of the map she traced a route down to the base of the mountain which seemed simple enough in theory. 'And this is where you need to get to. Shit.' Retracting her hand from the map Gail pushed her teeth into her lower lip and turned away from the table and its contents. 'It should really be me going down there. I know this mountain better than any of you do.'

'Then go,' Diana urged flatly.

'I . . .' Gail looked up at the ceiling, flailing as she stood trapped between two conflicted feelings. 'Really, I need to repair the generator. If I can do that quickly enough, we can call for help before you two are even halfway down the mountain. If I can cut the tree up, move some of it out of the way, get eyes on the generator – it might be in better shape than I think. The more chances we give Emily of getting help the better.'

'And how long will that take?'

Gail shrugged helplessly. 'I'll go as fast as I can.'

'So, you stay here, got it.' Allie nodded.

'What exactly is wrong with the generator?' Diana pressed.

'From what I can see a tree got too loaded down with snow and crashed through the roof of the shed, knocking out the generator's main control panel. It'll be tricky but as long as no more of the shed gets torn down, I should be able to fix it.'

'And if you can't fix it?'

'That's why you two are heading down the mountain.' Gail returned to the map and the black box and pulled out five flares. She rolled three across the table to Allie and Diana. 'Take these. I'll set two off up here. Light up the rest of them at intervals as you go down the mountain. Hopefully, someone will see at least one of them and send help.'

Gail divided the matches, flares and torches into piles. Then she carefully folded up the map and passed it to Allie. 'Follow it as best you can,' she advised, 'but if all else fails, keep heading down. If you reach a river, you're going the right way. Track its banks south and you'll reach Ewan's house. If you leave now you should get there by dawn.'

Dawn. A new day. To Allie, it seemed impossible that this endless night would ever relinquish its grip over the world. The wind howled like a banshee, pressing against the walls of the cabin.

'We'd better get going.' Diana plucked the map from Allie's grip and tucked it into her own coat pocket.

'Not in those you don't.' Gail was staring at Allie's feet, at her Timberland boots which she'd pulled on earlier.

'I didn't bring any other shoes.' Allie looked down, wondering what was wrong with her footwear.

'You won't get far in those.' Gail was pacing across the living space. She disappeared up the stairs, her footsteps ringing out through the cabin.

'I don't have any other shoes,' Allie explained again, looking to Diana for support. But Diana was already stalking over to the front door, flashlight in hand.

'What am I supposed to do while you're off taming the mountain and Gail is bashing away at the generator?' Stacie jumped to her feet and tossed her long plait over her shoulder, pouting. 'You can't just leave me here alone.'

'You're not alone,' Diana declared in a scolding tone. She turned and pointed her flashlight at her friend. 'Think about someone other than your precious self for one minute. Emily is upstairs, very unwell and very scared. While we are off *taming* the mountain, you should be by her side comforting her. Be useful for a change.'

'Wha—' Stacie's mouth dropped open as a stunned sound drifted up to her throat.

'She means that comforting Emily is a really important job.' Allie tried to smooth things over, making her voice as silky and free from conflict as possible. She went over to Stacie and gave her a quick, reassuring hug. 'I know that you'll take good care of her. Tell her we'll be back soon. With her medicine.'

'I will.'

'You can wear these.' Gail was hurrying down the stairs, a pair of hiking boots in each hand.

'Oh, um.' Allie looked at her feet and chewed her lip. 'I'm not sure we're the same size, Gail.'

'Doesn't matter,' Gail declared briskly. 'Pull on a couple of extra pairs of socks and they'll fit fine. You need these.' Gail turned over one of the boots to prove her point, 'You see these here?' Sharp spikes were poking out from the sole of the shoe. Like a sinister version of a football boot. 'These spikes will save your life out there, trust me. There's ice about. And ice can be deadly.'

Allie took the boots and then crouched down to untie her Timberlands.

'You got a pair for me?' Diana held out a hand expectantly.

'Of course.' Gail handed her the other pair of boots. 'Make sure you do them up good and tight. And seriously, you two, be careful out there. The mountain can be treacherous even when it's not covered in snow. If things get dicey, if you get injured, just light the flares and double back if you can. We need to keep ourselves safe and in one piece.'

'Emily needs us to reach Ewan Cole.' The hiking boots felt loose, but at least Allie's feet were warm within several layers of thick socks. She joined Diana by the front door, the flares stowed in her pocket.

'Just be safe out there,' Gail pleaded.

'We will.' Allie nodded. 'We'll be back before you know it.'

Twenty-Four

Leaving the cabin was like jumping off a cliff – Allie's breath was crudely pummelled out of her lungs by a powerful wind, which struck her head-on the moment that she stepped outside. As the door shut behind them the air instantly felt as thin and sharp as the ice it carried, mirroring the cold which had already crept into Allie's bones. Her body hummed with the wrongness of it all – of going outside in those conditions, of leaving Emily in such a fragile state. She ground her teeth together in frustration and against the snowy assault that was harassing her from all angles. As enamel crunched against enamel, she tried to settle her nerves by focusing only on the task ahead.

Trudging forward Allie raised her arm to shield herself against the stinging of the snow which barraged her with frightening fury. She'd barely walked three paces and already the blizzard was upon her, snapping and snarling. Her hair, which stuck out beneath her woollen cap, was already sodden, even the hat itself saturated, no longer providing any warmth. The cold from the wind burrowed down through her clothes and settled in her muscles, against her skeleton. Gritting her teeth together even harder she tried to think of something warm; a roaring fire, a white sand beach bordered by a turquoise ocean. But these thoughts didn't help. The blizzard had her in its grip and she struggled to even recall what being warm felt like.

After a few minutes, she could no longer feel her hands. After another ten her feet also became numb. With each step forward she felt herself become more claimed by the storm, more lost to its frozen power.

'We just have to keep going down,' Diana shouted from behind, her words carried on the bitter wind.

Why had Diana offered to come along?

There was still no answer and the wind was a third person on their journey, howling over any words they tried to utter to one another. Allie fought her way along what she assumed was the path she'd previously ascended after the taxi ride up. But beneath the icy blanket of the storm everything on the mountain had lost its individuality. It was all one endless slope of snow, each inch that was exposed to her as she pressed on indiscernible from the last.

There was just so much of it. So much snow. Allie felt it settle in her lungs each time she breathed in. The visibility was terrible. If she held her hand at arm's length it disappeared into the whiteout. Tugging up the hood of her coat, she tried to keep out some of the cold, but it was futile.

Where was the dawn? It was just past four when they left the cabin, which meant it was still hours away. But the snow, glistening all around them, held the lustre of midday, transformed a black night into a strange, sparkling twilight.

'Should we set off a flare yet?' Diana's hands were suddenly on her shoulders, her voice a roar against the wind even though she was close to her ear. The shock of her touch, her proximity, was like receiving several unwanted jolts of electricity.

'No.' Allie had to lean back to shout her response else Diana would never hear it. 'We're too close to the cabin. We need to go further down.'

She was guessing. What did she know about flares and their radius of visibility? But where they were, the air was chaotic and clustered with snow. Surely nothing they set off there would be seen? Lower down the snow had to be less dense, only then would the flares stand a chance of catching someone's eye.

Each step forward, they dropped into fresh powered snow. Allie grunted as she hauled her boots up and pressed on, deeper into the storm. Now the snow was over her boots, darkening the base of her jeans. She could feel a damp chill creeping up the fabric, pressing against her skin. Her cheeks had gone numb. So had her hands, despite her gloves. She could still just about feel her toes and was thankful for the extra socks she'd put on.

'We should check the map,' Diana yelled, her words struggling to reach Allie over the growl of the wind. Allie shook her head, then realised Diana wouldn't see it.

'No. Not yet,' she cried back. 'We need to get out of the worst of it.'

Allie hoped there was a way to get out of the worsening storm. The cabin was at the peak of the mountain, exposed to the full might of the wind. She figured that if they got lower down the blizzard might lose some of its strength.

Time passed in a burning white haze. How many minutes had slid by while they descended the mountain? Ten? Twenty? Allie tried to think, tried to anchor her mind to something rigid and reliable, like time. She wasn't completely numb, not yet, so she hazarded that they'd probably only been walking for half an hour at most. They still had a long way to go.

Allie's legs rigidly kept pressing forwards, kept finding safe footing in the snow. The marrow in her bones seemed to have iced up and Allie feared that she had become woefully brittle – that she could snap under the slightest pressure.

At first, she didn't notice that the wind had weakened. She was so focused on placing one foot in front of the other, head bent towards the snow.

'Should we check the map?'

Allie straightened and turned to look at Diana, who no longer needed to shout. Snow fell densely around them, but it wasn't being swept into their eyes with painful force. The whole world was calmer, quieter, as the storm had lost some of its sting.

'The map?' Allie felt like she was waking from a dream. She became aware of the way the snow muffled all sound. Of how chapped her lips were. She licked them and shook out the icy ache from her arms.

'Yeah.' Diana stepped closer to Allie, producing the map from her pocket and carefully unfolding it, her soft cheeks rosy on the cusp of raw. 'I figured that we've been walking for almost half an hour so we should be getting close to the river by now.'

The snow created an eerie glow. It made everywhere feel bright even though the sun had yet to rise.

'Okay.' Allie pulled her hat lower against her ears and peered at the map as Diana approached, raising the torch which had been in her pocket, casting its beam against the paper. She was being so calm, so cool. Not her usual hostile self. This was the most direct interaction they'd had in a long time and Allie knew to treat it carefully, like a fragile china cup that had only recently been glued back together and could easily shatter anew from even the slightest jolt. Clearing her throat, she stared at the map which fluttered against the weakening wind. Rugged lines cut across the folded page. Some were dotted, some thick and black. Hiking trails. Halfway down the map, a thick line of blue cut across the mountain. The river. 'So where do you think we are?'

'Well . . .' Diana shivered and stamped her feet in the snow, her lips now more purple than red. 'This is the cabin . . .' She angled the beam from the torch on the black X on the map. 'And if we've tracked a route south from there' – she dragged the halo of light down the page, towards the blue line – 'we should be pretty close to the river. Gail said we can just follow that down to the base of the mountain, right?'

'Right.'

It seemed like a reasonable plan. Diana folded the map and shoved it in her pocket along with the torch. Allie dared to peer directly at her from beneath the wet rim of her hat and fringe. 'Maybe we should light our first flare?' she suggested as she occupied her hand by delving into her pockets and pulling out one of the red sticks and some matches.

'Good idea.'

Allie had never lit a flare before. She wasn't sure what to expect when she struck a match and held the little flame towards the tip of the ruby stick. As the flare hissed and crackled to life, burning crimson and releasing masses of smoke Allie thought of the sparklers she used to dance around her garden with on bonfire night. Standing outside with her friends, clutching a sparkler each in their mitten-clad hands as they braved the chill of an autumnal evening. They'd write out their names with their little wands of crackling firelight. It was magical.

'Like a sparkler,' Diana said with a dry laugh as Allie let the flare fall to the ground as it continued to burn away.

'Yeah, it is.' Allie smiled, wondering if they were now basking in the same shared memory.

The red glow from the flare revealed just how much snow was still falling. Tinged blood-red the flakes seemed more sinister than they had before. Smoke billowed away from the flare, swirling with the snow.

'I really hope someone sees it.' Diana banged her hands together and hopped from foot to foot.

'We always used to have sparklers in my garden on bonfire night, do you remember?' Allie dared to push the connection she was sure she'd just felt.

Diana shoved her hands into her pockets.

'We'd stand outside and write out our names with them. And then we'd go inside for hot chocolate. That was our tradition. Every year.'

'Yeah, Allie, I remember.' Diana sounded annoyed, not nostalgic.

With a sigh of resignation, Allie turned and began to walk away from the burning glow of the flare.

Allie's hand reached around to her back, to the base of her spine. She didn't stop it, letting it push against her old wound, hoping to feel something. An ache, a sting. Something. They'd been walking in deep snow for over half an hour. Her back should be responding. But just like her cheeks and hands, her back felt numb.

'You all right?' Diana noticed the action and quickened her steps to reach Allie's side.

'I'm fine.'

'Is your . . . back okay?' Diana cleared her throat in the silence that ensued.

The lie was instantly on Allie's lips. 'I'm fine. Really.'

'Because it's a long walk down and if you're not up to it then just say so.' Diana was staring ahead as she spoke. The tree line was getting denser and they began to have to navigate their way between snowy branches.

'Is that why you're here? Why you came along? Because you thought I couldn't make it?' Allie tried to sound indifferent as she pushed her way through the snow which was now completely over the top of her boots, but she could taste the bitterness of her words on her tongue along with the biting sharpness of the cold.

'Like I said, it's a long walk down and—'

'I said I'm fine.' The words snapped out of Allie as a branch split underfoot, buried deep beneath the snow but still vulnerable to the pressure of her presence.

'Okay, well, great. Whatever.'

The heat of indignation began to burn beneath Allie's cheeks. Knocking her hands together, almost applauding herself, she turned to stare back at her friend.

'Do you even care?'

Allie felt emboldened by her own directness. Finally, she was saying something. Granted, this was most definitely neither the time nor the place, but her words had taken on a life of their own, flying freely from her mouth as she stood rooted in the snow.

'About my back? Do you actually care if I make it or are you hoping I'll fail?' Allie continued, mist unfurling from her lips as she delivered her heated torrent of thoughts. 'If you were that concerned, don't you think you should have mentioned it back at the cabin? But how could you when you pretend I don't exist. The last time we even bloody spoke was at my *wedding*. And even then you were . . . were . . .'

'Honest?' Diana's expression was as smooth as the unblemished snow that surrounded them. Her eyebrows remained locked in a steely line and there was an enviable calmness behind her eyes.

'Seriously, I—'

'You confuse being honest with not caring.'

'There isn't time for this,' Allie scoffed, regretting opening this can of worms now. 'We need to keep going.'

'Is it true Lucas left you because you can't have kids?' Diana didn't even blink as she spoke. 'The others aren't here now, so I don't need to tiptoe around you.'

The question was so blunt, so unexpected. Allie sunk deeper into the snow. The fire in Diana's retaliation had rendered her mute.

'It's what we all think,' Diana said, tilting her head to take in Allie's stunned expression. Is that why she'd volunteered to come down the mountain, so that she could bully and interrogate Allie in private, without Gail to intervene? 'You just said that he left, but you didn't say why. I thought . . . maybe . . . maybe you'd finally, you know. And honestly, Allie, I refuse to be part of the blame game when it comes to your marriage.'

'I . . .' Allie staggered forward and reached for a nearby tree, leaning her hand against it for support. 'This . . .' She shook her head, shaking away memories of him and noticing as she did that the tips of her hair had turned to ice. 'This isn't the time to talk about it.' She calmly straightened up, wishing she shared her friend's sleek, commanding posture. Instead, she looked like she felt; small and afraid. 'And neither was my wedding day,' she added, feeling her own vitriol burn against her tongue. 'We need to get down this mountain and get help for Emily. That's all that matters right now.' Allie drew strength from her task. She continued pushing her way through the snow.

'Don't blame me for all the things you didn't say. I was just trying to help you, Allie. But like always you wouldn't listen.'

'I listen!'

'You don't listen and you don't move on,' Diana scolded. 'Accidents happen, it's time to let go.'

The accident. Just the mere mention of it had the power to liquefy Allie's resolve. She swept a hand across her icy cheek and pressed on, being doubly careful of her footing for fear of falling into past memories.

Allie bowed her head and forced herself to speak though her mouth tasted like copper as she remembered what it was like to almost choke on her own blood. 'We have to get to the base of this mountain. We have to get help for Emily.'

Twenty-Five

The sun was shining on the day it happened. The day of the accident. It had been burning down, warping the air above the tarmac on the road. Allie's skin smelt of the suntan lotion her mother had insisted Allie slather herself in that morning. 'You need to keep safe,' she'd stated as she handed her teenage daughter the plastic bottle. Cocoa butter. Allie smelt good enough to eat. In her favourite denim shorts and yellow T-shirt, she had gone with Diana into town. They'd bought a 99 cone each, laughing as they dipped the tips of their noses into the soft-serve ice cream. It was one of those days which felt like it would be never-ending. But there were shadows on the horizon.

They hadn't seen Emily in weeks. Her parents had suddenly announced that she was going away for the rest of the school year, stating something about stress. Emily didn't return their calls, didn't turn up for sleepovers. It was like she'd vanished. Stacie was completely absorbed with her boyfriend, Oliver, and Gail was in the South of France with her family, so it was just Allie and Diana heading into town. And Diana had been acting strangely, more unruly than usual. First, it had been little things like smoking a cigarette behind the bike sheds after double maths, but by the start of the summer holidays, she was bringing big plastic bottles of cider to the park and drinking most of them herself.

Allie wondered if somehow Diana's dad was back on the scene. But she banished such thoughts almost immediately as he was locked up behind bars and would remain that way for many years to come. Something else had to be bothering her.

There was a motorway that ran along the outskirts of town. It was a favoured route with lorry drivers. Like a crucial vein to a heart, it carried commerce, vitality, commuters. It put their little town on the map.

'I'm bored.' Diana strode along a bridge that crossed the motorway, mainly used as a cycle path. The sun was on her back as she looked at her feet, at the battered pair of Converse she was wearing with a blue dress.

Diana had been getting bored with more frequency like she couldn't bear even a second of unfilled time with her thoughts. She was always suggesting they did something. Cinema, bike rides, drunken afternoons in the park. Allie was getting exhausted keeping up with her demands, but since no one else was around, she felt compelled to agree in the interest of being a good friend.

The rush of traffic blew up warm, disorientating gusts of air and it was loud, like standing on the shore beside roaring waves that battered the rocks.

'Hey, let's hang off the bars.' Diana suddenly had a spring in her step as she approached the railing that bordered both sides of the bridge, bellowing her words to overcome the thrum of the cars. 'We can pretend we're in Titanic and lean out over the traffic.' She was already dreamily humming the theme tune from the film.

'I don't think so,' Allie objected loudly. The lingering taste of the ice cream in her mouth suddenly soured. 'Let's go back to mine and get the paddling pool out.'

'We're not five, Allie Bear. We're fifteen.' Diana had looked down at her long body with contempt, as though she hated the curves which were blossoming beneath her navy tennis dress. 'Fifteen-year-olds do fun, exciting things. Fifteen-year-olds take chances, embrace adventure.'

'Look, Dee, I—'

166

A huge lorry came barrelling down the road. Its engine grunted like a bull at a red flag.

'I'm going.' Diana lifted one leg over the railing and then the other, hooking her arms behind her back to hold her in place.

The lorry blared its horn as it rumbled along beneath them, an ugly sound that shook Allie's bones.

'This is dangerous,' Allie protested. 'What if you fall?' Her heart was in her mouth as she watched her friend hanging above the fast-moving lanes. Car horns punctured the balmy afternoon air as drivers looked up at Diana with disdain or concern for her recklessness.

'Come on,' Diana demanded. 'Stop being a baby and live a little.'

'Dee, I—'

'This summer has been completely shit. First Emily disappears and now Stacie is so into that creep Oliver that we don't even exist to her anymore. Don't let me down, Allie Bear. Climb over, hold on, it feels like flying.' Diana was having to shout over the noise.

Allie missed Emily terribly. Each time she called her home the clipped voice of either her father or mother would inform her that Emily wasn't in and that she was to stop calling.

But why? Allie wanted to demand, but they always disconnected before she could get the words out. Emily had been fine, hadn't she?

'Fine.' With a shaky breath, Allie looped her leg over the railing, holding on as tight as she could with her hands. She pulled her other leg over and then she was beside Diana, feeling the rising heat from the stream of traffic against her cheeks. Her stomach dropped into her feet as her palms became slick, their grip unsteady.

Another lorry was thundering towards them. Diana playfully released one of her arms from behind her.

'Ooh, look at me, one-handed!'

'Dee, stop.' Allie was holding on to the railing so tight, her fingers were already starting to go numb.

'This . . .' Diana grandly stretched out her free hand as car horns shrieked at her in judgement. 'This is the closest we'll ever get to flying, to being free.'

Then she slipped.

Allie felt like she was watching it happen in slow motion. Diana's feet billowed away from the rail and she was holding on with just one hand. Allie instantly reacted. Unhooking her right arm from the rail she reached across and grabbed Diana, pressed her back against the bars. With only her left hand remaining connected to the bridge Allie felt her shoulder shake, the tremor of her precarious position passing through her. Her back was to the road, her right hand pressed to Diana's chest, her left clutching the sun-warmed metal. A lorry powered beneath them, causing an updraught. The wind knocked Allie off-balance, loosened her already weak grip. Her sweat-clad hand slid away from the railing, her right reaching out, but finding only empty air to cling to. She was already falling.

Allie's hand found the base of her spine once again and desperately prodded against it. She'd broken her back that day out on the road. It was ten months until she'd been able to walk again. And that wasn't the only part of her that had been broken. Her abdomen had endured extensive damage during the impact. Irreparable damage. 'It has to come out,' she'd heard the surgeon say as he stood at the foot of her bed in the HDU while her parents wilted against one another as though they'd both forgotten how to stand on their own two feet. 'All of it,' the surgeon repeated, a hint of regret in his voice. 'The extent of the damage goes too far to salvage anything. I know she's only fifteen, but this really is the only way. Your daughter needs a hysterectomy to stem the risk of further internal bleeding.'

'Allie?' Diana stood in the falling snow, looking back at her. With a start, Allie realised that she'd stopped walking, had let her thoughts freeze her to a standstill. 'You okay to keep going?'

'I'm fine,' Allie snapped. She was getting really good at telling the lie. If only she could start believing it.

As she walked, her thoughts drifted back to the cabin, her heart aching with the fragile hope that her friends were okay, that Gail had somehow managed to salvage the generator and that Emily was holding on. She'd seemed so pale and withdrawn when Allie had left, so weak. And so afraid.

Allie's movements were robotic. Her feet kept awkwardly landing in the snow, kept dragging her forward with each step. Everything beneath her was banked at a steep incline. Twice in the last ten minutes, she'd lost her footing and fallen back into the snow. It hadn't cushioned her collapse. Landing on the tightly packed flakes wasn't like landing in a soft, fluffy cloud of white. The snow was hard, like ice. And it met Allie with rough, unfeeling hands. Staggering to her feet, she dusted off what she could of the snow. The cold had become like a rot in her bones, deep-set and unmoving.

'Doesn't this seem pretty steep to you?' Allie called out after she'd almost tumbled down the third time. She planted her feet firmly in the snow, found her core and straightened. It was still dark, but the whiteout coating the mountain made it feel more like twilight than near dawn. The luminosity of the ground made it difficult to anchor the darkness to a specific time.

'Allie . . .' Diana scrambled through the snow towards her, keeping her body low. 'I've been asking you if you're okay for like ten minutes straight and all you can say is how *steep* it is?'

'Sorry, I . . .' Looking down Allie saw just how steep their current path was. She hadn't been exaggerating. They'd been painstakingly picking their way down an almost sheer face of the mountain. Gail hadn't mentioned terrain like this. Had they strayed from their route? How far was the river from here?

'Allie!'

'I got distracted.' She wiped a gloved hand against her nose but couldn't feel the fabric connecting with the tip. So much of her was now numb.

'That makes two of us.' Diana dropped down onto a nearby rock, pausing to swiftly dust it down, and dipped her chin against her chest.

'Are we still going the right way?'

Diana drew in a ragged breath.

'This just seems so steep, but maybe it levels out not far from here and we'll reach the river.' Allie surveyed the landscape around them. She felt like she was standing on a ski slope. Any second she expected neon-clad holiday-makers to zoom past her like racing cars.

'But he knew, right? Before you married him?' Diana remained on the rock, head bowed, hands clasped together. 'Tell me he knew. Tell me I was wrong about what I saw at your wedding.'

'Why? To save your fucking conscience? Diana, come on, we need to keep going. I'm not talking about this.'

'Lucas. He must have known that you can't have children.'

Allie felt sick. There was a buzzing in her head as though Diana's words had disturbed a hornet's nest.

'Diana, enough!'

'No, Allie, not enough. Last time we spoke alone, just you and me, was at your wedding.'

'And whose fault is that?'

'I'm not doling out blame. I'm just saying that I overheard something troubling and fast-forward a few months and Lucas is out of your life. Doesn't take a genius to put two and two together.'

'Doesn't take a genius to misread things, either!'

'So I'm wrong then, he left for some other reason?'

'Jesus, *why*?' Coughing, Allie strained to find her voice. 'Why do you keep asking about him? He's gone, can't you just leave it at that?'

'No, I can't. Because I'm worried,' Diana stated but refused to meet Allie's bewildered gaze. 'I'm worried that you blame me for your husband leaving. And I'm done, Allie. I'm done being the reason your life is a mess.'

Twenty-Six

Rustic and rural. That had been what Allie was going for with her wedding, and as she breathed in the scent of sun-warmed hay and heard a breeze rustle through the long grass in a nearby field, she knew she'd achieved her theme. Lucas had wanted something glitzier, something held in the heart of London which all their friends in publishing could attend. But ultimately, he'd bent to Allie's more humble wishes, as he always did.

The renovated barn made for a perfect venue. Its aged beams were adorned with fairy lights that sparkled in the dwindling light. Soon the sky would be thick with stars and the four-piece jazz band they'd hired for the evening would commence playing.

With a champagne glass in hand, Allie lingered at the edge of the party, her long lace dress drifting away from her as it was playfully tugged by the heady summer evening air. She was now a married woman. Her mother had wept during the subdued ceremony and it had pleased Allie when she noticed her father offer her his handkerchief. The child within her fluttered in excitement at the thought of her parents possibly reuniting over their shared love for their sole daughter, but the adult Allie knew better. But for a day she could revel in the fairy tale that things were as they once had been.

'Allie . . .' Lucas's hands found the small of her back as he nuzzled into her long hair, as golden as the hay bales stacked up in the surrounding fields. 'Come back and join the party, it's almost time for our first dance.'

He was handsome in his grey suit, his blue eyes bright. Freshly shaven he looked younger than his thirty-six years. Allie felt that if she stared at him hard enough, she'd find the boy lurking within the man. Drawing close to his side Allie leaned into him, liking how her head fit almost perfectly against his shoulder. Lucas was built like the barley she could smell — tall and lean. The air had a lazy sweetness to it which reminded Allie of home. It wasn't like London, where a million different scents fought for dominance. Here, there was a crispness, a cleanness. It felt pure. And Allie wanted that purity for her marriage. For everything to remain as perfect as it currently was. Because this could be perfect. Couldn't it? Lucas loved her, she saw that in the smile he reserved solely for her, the one which made his eyes crinkle with mirth as though he was permanently engaged in some private joke.

'You're my wife . . .' He leaned in close enough for her to smell the beer on his breath. His kiss upon her cheek was soft, yet the sensation lingered, as though he'd branded her. Allie smiled. This was what she'd wanted for so long — normality.

'Hey, Allie.' Diana joined them in the shadows, glancing over her shoulder at the illuminated barn. In her full-length beige bridesmaid dress, Diana was demurely beautiful. As were all of the girls in their gowns. Emily, Gail and Stacie too, had followed Allie up the aisle smiling dutifully.

On Diana, the silk of the dress gathered against every curve and her silhouette made Allie think of mermaids out of the sea, with their long dark hair and dangerous nature. 'They are about to do the first dance.'

'Right, okay.'

'You know.' Lucas's smile was so wide as he addressed both bride and bridesmaid that it was in danger of engulfing his entire face. 'I hope our kids get Allie's eyes.' He was drunk. Allie chewed her lip and tried not to overtly notice the way he swayed as he pointed at her. 'Her eyes make me think of caramel. Like

173

the delicious, really rich kind. She has caramel eyes. Caramelise.' Lucas laughed richly at his own joke.

'Uh huh . . .' Allie rolled the objects of interest and heard the band start to play, the music swelling across the night air to greet them. 'That's our cue.' She stepped forward and reached for her husband's arm, but Diana stopped her with cold fingers that wrapped around Allie's wrist and held her in place.

'She'll be right there,' Diana told Lucas without looking at him. He shrugged and then began to amble over to the barn, his humming graduating to a full-on singing session.

'They're playing the song for the first dance,' Allie tried to pull away from her friend. 'I need to go.'

'He wants your kids to have your eyes . . .' Diana's grip tightened. Allie could feel the tips of her nails almost piercing her skin. 'How is that going to happen? Allie, you said you were going to adopt.'

'We are, he's drunk.' Again, Allie tried to break free, again Diana refused to let go.

'You told us he was okay with adopting.'

'He is.'

'Doesn't sound that way.'

'Seriously, Diana, I need to go.'

'You haven't told him, have you?'

Allie put her back to the barn and stared at her friend. 'I—'

'Jesus Christ, Allie!' Diana took a step back from her and finally released her wrist, letting her now freehand clasp at first her throat and then her mouth. 'You've really not told him?'

'Diana stop, I—'

'How can you not tell him something like that? Allie, what the hell are you thinking?'

'If I tell him, he leaves!' Allie dragged a hand across her eyes, not caring about the damage the gesture might do to her make-up. She looked up, expecting to see stars but they were blotted out by thick, velvety clouds which had slid unnoticed as dusk turned to night.

'So, so what? You're just going to lie?'

The song, their song, had begun. Allie was supposed to be beneath the fairy lights in the barn, wrapped in her new husband's embrace as they swayed drunkenly together.

'Diana, just drop it!'

'You can't keep playing the victim, Allie, making yourself a martyr. Lucas loves you, just tell him the bloody truth!'

'Stay out of it. It's my life and you've already done enough to ruin it.'

'Okay.' Diana threw up her hands and raised her voice as though addressing some invisible audience. 'It all comes out now, doesn't it, Allie? You hate me, you blame me, blah blah blah. And you wonder why I avoid hanging out with all you guys anymore. But think what you will of me, you still owe Lucas the truth.'

'He'll leave!' Allie cried, gripped by her own mortification that this argument was even happening. Secrets, her secrets, weren't supposed to be spoken about on summer nights with the sound of crickets chirping and a distant jazz band in the background.

'He won't!'

'You did!' Allie could almost choke on her fury, her disdain. 'You left me,' she whispered through gritted teeth. 'You . . . you . . .'

'Write a book about it,' Diana advised breezily as she began to saunter back to the party, one hand wafting through the air in a dismissive gesture. 'You're good at that.'

'Diana, I—'

'You're drunk, we both are,' Diana called back to her. She was now close enough to the barn for its lights to glow through the edges of her dress, turning the satin to golden honey. 'Let's just go inside and pretend that everything is fine. You like pretending, don't you, Allie?'

Twenty-Seven

Officer: The absence of medication was a concern for you all.

POI: Yes! A huge one. Hence everyone's frantic attempts to contact the emergency services.

Officer: The weather prevented any immediate access to the cabin.

POI: Yes, the snow had successfully sealed us off.

Officer: Successfully?

POI: Just my phrasing, don't read anything into it.

Officer: This is a murder investigation; it's my job to read into everything you say.

POI: We knew that the medication wasn't coming, either someone went to get it or it simply wouldn't arrive.

Officer: And the consequences of that would be . . .

POI: Dire. We all understood that. Time wasn't on our side.

Officer: The weather certainly left you girls in an unlucky situation.

POI: On that we can agree.

Officer: But perhaps not that unlucky.

POI: I'm not sure I follow.

Officer: The storm offered cover. Solitude. No one could get to you.

POI: Right. What is your point?

Officer: It was just the five of you up there, all alone.

POI: Exactly. We were all alone. And vulnerable. We were at the mercy of the storm.

Officer: Anything else?

POI: Excuse me?

Officer: Were you at the mercy of anything other than the storm?

POI: I don't like this line of questioning.

Officer: So you won't answer?

POI: Shall I just continue?

Officer: Fine. Yes. Continue.

Twenty-Eight

'Just us for breakfast this morning?' Diana asked as she entered the kitchen, the air already thick and claustrophobic with cigarette smoke.

'Uh huh.' Her mum nodded and then slid her cigarette from between her lips and tapped it against the mustard-yellow ashtray perched in the centre of the small kitchen table, which struggled to accommodate the two chairs wedged beside it. 'Why, you trying to be smart?'

'Wouldn't dream of it.' Diana squeezed behind her mum's chair and reached up into a cupboard for a box of cereal.

'You got much planned for today?' her mum asked as she took a long drag, the smoke rising up and curling above their heads. She was dressed in her smock for work which meant her day would consist of helping the elderly at the care home in the centre of town. 'Wiping arses and cleaning up piss and getting paid a fucking pittance,' she loved to moan.

Still clutching the cereal box, Diana bristled, wishing she'd trusted her instincts and stayed upstairs, forced herself to remain in bed for at least another hour, until the house was empty. But sleep was evading her. It had been since that day on the bridge. Her mum was treading old, worn ground and Diana was too exhausted to resist, but also too exhausted to dance through the steps to the argument.

'I'm not going,' she declared sharply, throwing open another cupboard and reaching for a bowl with her spare hand.

'Diana.' Her mum said her name slowly, despairingly.

'I'm. Not. Going.' Diana's voice was a razor, she hoped it was sharp enough to cause her mum to flinch, to stray off track. 'I've told you, so stop asking.'

'I will not stop asking.' Her mum began waving her cigarette around as she gestured wildly, the white, smoking stick making her appear like some macabre conductor. 'That poor girl is up there in the hospital, spending her summer locked away, can't even walk and—'

'I've heard it all before.' Diana quickly tipped flakes of corn into her bowl, eager to leave the cloying air of the kitchen and her mother's tirade.

'You put her there!' Her mum's cheeks flushed, tired eyes almost bulging out of her head. 'Diana you need to show some . . . some fucking decency and go and see her!'

'No!'

'She's your friend!'

'What do you know about friendship?' Diana slammed her bowl down, causing some of her breakfast to slop over the edge and splat against the grimy kitchen countertop.

'Clearly a damn sight more than you,' her mum countered coolly, drawing on her cigarette. 'If you gave a shit about her, you'd go and visit.'

'I'm not going, stop asking.' Diana grabbed the bowl, clutched it to her chest and stormed towards the door.

'You'll regret this,' her mum was shouting as she slammed the door shut, managing to muffle her voice but not drown it out entirely. 'Mark my words, Diana, you'll regret this!'

Diana stomped up the stairs, exerting too much pressure on already well-worn floorboards. She went into her bedroom and added the bowl full of cereal to her pile of meals she'd yet to eat. Old microwave pizza, cold toast, they made an inedible Tower of Pisa in the far corner. Dropping back onto her bed, Diana felt *down the side for the familiar shape of her Walkman, grabbed it and put the headphones on, keen to lose herself to this part of her daily ritual. While The Cure played she let hot, sticky tears fall down her cheeks. She just wanted the summer to be over.*

Twenty-Nine

'*What?*'

Allie demanded as she hugged her arms against herself. They'd stopped walking, which had allowed the cold to penetrate her bones even further. The air was so frigid it was choking. Each breath burned her lungs with icy fire.

'You're bringing this up now?' Allie knew that they needed to press on, that they didn't have time to stand and deliberate things that had happened in the past. But her feet remained rigidly in place and her heart couldn't ignore the shadow of guilt that hung across Diana's face. Did she truly blame herself for Lucas leaving? Old feelings stirred within her like poisonous eels, feelings she was constantly striving to ignore.

'You've never got mad at me.' Diana sighed and shook her head, raising her gloved hands towards her forehead as though it was suddenly too heavy for her neck alone to support. 'Not once. I guess everything you needed to say, you said in your book. But' – she inhaled sharply – 'if he left because of the whole kid thing then it's my fault, isn't it? And I'd rather you hurled your blame directly at me than write another bloody book about it.'

'So you're worried about how my husband leaving me affects *you*? Is that it? You're trying to manage your own guilt?'

'I don't want to be the one to blame for his leaving.'

'Do you even care, really?'

'I care about always being bloody blamed. About being made to feel like a pariah. Again. Tell me the truth, Allie, stop locking us all out. Why did he leave?' Diana said each part of her question with slow deliberation.

Allie stared down the slope of snow, unsure if the dampness on her cheeks was melting flakes or tears. She'd never locked any of her friends out. Had she?

'He left because of me, not you.' Allie owed the truth to herself even more than to her friend.

'So it wasn't about the whole not having children issue?' Diana was still pushing, the disbelief thick in her voice. 'You think I'm being difficult but . . .' Diana crossed her arms against her chest. 'I can't deal with any more guilt over the accident. I'm carrying enough as it is. If only you'd open up more, I wouldn't have to pry like this. You're such an enigma, Allie. It's so hard to know anything about you. You keep us all at such a distance.'

'*You* put the distance between us,' Allie seethed. 'You're the one who pushed *me* away.' Allie was continuing with her descent, ploughing through the crystallised snowflakes. She couldn't afford to lose another friend. Emily was back up in the cabin depending on her.

'So Lucas did know?' Diana stood up and towered over Allie. 'Is that why he left? You have to tell me. The others have been talking and I'm not going to be demonised again over—'

'Does it even matter?' Allie wanted the wind to grow in power, for it to sweep her off the mountain and carry her away from the ice and the snow on a stiff breeze. She wanted to feel weightless. Free.

'It matters because I told you, back at your wedding, I told you this would end in tears.' Diana caught Allie's arm and pulled her close. 'You keep hurting yourself, Allie. And you don't need to. But it's like you can't escape that day on the bridge. And I so badly want to forget it, don't you?'

'Yes.' Allie shook off her friend's grip. 'But I can't forget it. I'm covered in reminders of it.'

Diana took a step back. 'You've been touching your back a lot since we left the cabin. Does it still hurt or something?'

Fire lashed over Allie's tongue, singeing her next words. 'Are you going to interrogate me about that too?'

'Allie—'

'Lucas leaving isn't any of your business. Maybe if you hadn't ghosted me the entire time I was in hospital you wouldn't feel so shitty now. Stop pretending to care, it doesn't suit you.'

Diana flinched. 'I'm trying to help you like I was at your wedding.'

'You weren't trying to help.' Allie stalked away from Diana. 'You were trying to appease your own guilt, that's all.'

'I was trying to make you be reasonable. You're the one giving power to the accident, to what happened to you, no one else.'

Allie was silent, watching the snow fall down between them.

'Let's just get to the base of the mountain.' Diana kicked her way through the snow, her movements filled with frustration. 'I'm done trying to talk sense into you.' As she moved away she scanned the mountainside, the new-fallen snow. 'We should light another flare.' She tossed the command over her shoulder. Then, her words almost getting lost as she turned away, 'We've been walking for a while now.'

Looking up, Allie saw that the sky was no longer infused with the pinkish-red hue which had accompanied the lighting of the first flare. She reached into her pocket and closed her fingers around the second flare. Retrieving it she struck a match. The wind whispered past her ears and blew it out. 'Dammit.' She dropped the match and lit another. A weak flame bloomed at the end but it too was swiftly snuffed out.

'Here . . .' Diana dramatically stomped back over and cupped her hands close to the third match Allie had plucked from the box. In her gloves, everything was taking twice as long as usual as she'd lost so much of her dexterity. It took five swipes for the match to properly catch against the box and light. She held it towards Diana's hands and the flame flickered reluctantly and then came to life. Allie carefully raised the flare to the flame and then extended her arm full length. The red stick sputtered and sizzled. Its scarlet light burned hotly against the snow. 'Leave it where it will be most visible,' Diana instructed.

Did such a place even exist? They were on a snowy mountain, held in the clutch of a powerful blizzard. Would the people at the base even be looking out their windows at such a time or would they be curled up warm and safe in bed, blissfully oblivious to what was happening up at the cabin? What would they even see? Allie lowered the flare towards a rock and left it to rest there, like a burning rose upon a gravestone, hoping it would turn the sky red, or at least pink.

Red sky in the morning, shepherd's warning.

It was the old saying her dad would repeat whenever dawn turned the horizon to blood. Allie figured it was weather-related, that the colour of sunset or dawn somehow determined the forecast for the following day. But when

Ewan Cole and his neighbours looked up towards the mountain and saw a faintly crimson sky it would truly be an ominous sign; a desperate cry for help.

'We should get off this steep bit before we light the final flare.' Diana tightened the hood of her coat around her chin and began picking her way forward, away from the ruby glow of their SOS signal. Allie reached around for her hood which kept getting blown back by the wind. She secured it beneath her chin, grimacing as it pressed down on the dampness of her hat. She wished she'd had the foresight to put her hood up as soon as she left the cabin, to take the time to properly tie it in place. But then she wasn't prepared for this. Each step down the mountain was a step into the unknown.

'Tell me why . . .' Allie wanted to walk in stony silence but her desire for the truth took control of her tongue. 'Why keep bringing up the past, my infertility? Tell me why you so readily hurt me, because it makes no sense to me.'

'Of course, it doesn't.' Diana's words were as sharp as flint. 'All you see is what goes on in your little bubble of a world.'

'That's not fair.'

'You think you saved me, don't you?' Diana spun round, her pretty features hardened with rage, her tone suddenly confrontational. 'That day on the road, with the lorry, you think that you pushed me out of the way – that you saved me. That all your ongoing health problems are because of me, that I'm solely to blame.'

'But that's what happened! I fell as I was trying to save you!'

'You pulled me back, you got to be the hero and then you wrote a fucking book about it all. About your ordeal. What was it the *Guardian* said about it? Oh yeah, "harrowing and raw, a truly poignant account of a teenage tragedy". Only it was never that, Allie. You never saved me. And you took all your lies and bundled them together in that bloody book and made money off us all. You demonised me to glorify yourself.'

'I saved you!' Allie could feel all her muscles tightening as fresh hurt coursed through her veins like poison. She had flung herself forward off the bridge to grab her friend before she could fall in harm's way; she still had the scars to prove it.

'No, you didn't!' Diana was shouting. Her voice a match for the wailing of the wind that swooped down the mountainside and tried to knock them both off their feet. 'You never saved me, Allie.' Something in Diana broke then like her batteries had suddenly fallen out and she was now just a shell. Her whole body sagged; tears shone in her eyes. 'You didn't save me, because I wasn't falling, I still had a grip. One hand was still on the rail. But, Allie . . . you saw what you wanted to see.'

'From where I was it looked like you were falling! I was trying to help! What did you expect me to do? Nothing? You expected me to just keep hanging on while you dangled yourself over a fucking motorway?'

Diana shook her head and ignored Allie's words. 'You barrelled forwards and in doing so you condemned me. I got to fail not only Emily that summer but you, too.'

'Emily?'

'You made me let you down, you made me a monster. Don't you see that?'

Thirty

The air was cool in the London meeting room that belonged to Allie's publishers. Rain splashed random rivers against the large windows which peered out onto a steel-grey morning.

'It's brilliant.'

Allie sat with her hands clasped on the table as the bespectacled woman across from her showered her with praise.

'I mean, truly. It comes from such a place of pain and is so beautifully written. You did an amazing job on your edits and we can't wait to release it.'

'Thank you.' Allie smiled politely at her editor. There were a pile of books on the table. Her books. Proof copies, ready to be sent out to reviewers.

Wilted Rose. That was the title. Beneath it, a blood-red flower hung limply in the centre of the cover and then Allie's name was in embossed lettering along the base. 'A haunting account of a teenage tragedy', the tag line read.

'We've had interest from The Times *and the* The Guardian *already. They want to interview you before the release. We anticipate that this book will be huge, Allie, and we're thrilled.'*

Keeping her hands clasped, Allie nodded courteously. It felt strange to be complimented about her book. About her pain. She had written it two years ago, when she turned twenty-three, when all the emotions from her teenage trauma came tumbling out. All the things she'd never said, all the times when she'd buried her anguish rather than dealing with it. Now it was splashed across three hundred and twenty pages and soon people would be reading it. Her family would read it. Her friends would read it.

'I mean, you've been through so much.' Her editor adjusted her glasses as she smiled at Allie.

But it wasn't all within the book. Allie told herself it was poetic licence when she didn't discuss her hysterectomy when she just focused on what happened to her spine.

People didn't need to know all the gory details, she'd decided. The truth was that she didn't want to add any more depth to the pitying glances she already received because of the accident. Whenever she stumbled a step or winced as she rubbed at her back people tilted their head and gave a sad smile. A look she'd grown to resent.

'I think we should also be able to secure an interview with Radio 4. People are really keen to hear from you since this is your personal story.'

Allie looked at the books. At their black-and-red spines. It was exactly the sort of story she'd have wanted to lose herself in as a teenager. A story about friendship. About bravery.

'Your friends, Deena especially, she has a pivotal role in the book, and soon she'll get to read it.'

Deena. Allie suppressed a snort of laughter. Deena was Diana. Everyone's names had been changed in the book, even her own.

'To protect the innocent,' her editor had said with a wink and a smile.

The innocent.

Allie looked at the books. The girl at the centre of the story, Angelina, she was innocent. She was pure and noble and just looking out for Deena, just trying to save her.

Diana hadn't called in over a year. She barely even bothered to text. The only time Allie even saw her was when everyone met up, despite she and Diana living in the same city. Allie knew that Diana wouldn't care about the book. If she was given a copy *she wouldn't read it, just shove it up on some shelf somewhere to gather dust.*

'This is your story, Allie. You must be so proud to get it out into the world.'

Allie smiled through clenched teeth. This was her story but now that she saw the copies on the table, knew that they'd soon be flying from the meeting room out into the world, she questioned her decision to share this part of herself with everyone. This had been her intimate tragedy. One she'd lived through agonising day after agonising day. Writing the book had been cathartic, a way to exorcise the demons that still came for her every night when she closed her eyes.

'And your dedication is so beautiful.' Allie's editor reached for a copy of the book which smelt so fresh, so new, and reverently opened the cover. 'For all the fallen.'

'Yes . . .' Allie's smile still felt forced. 'May they forever have the strength to get back up.'

'What the hell are you saying?' Allie feared that the anger welling up within her might suddenly tear her in two.

Cold. It was still so dreadfully cold, the air brittle with it. But her indignation, her rage, burned beneath her skin, briefly flushing her cheeks red.

'It started as a game, we were just messing about and then we were *hanging off the bridge*, Diana. It had been *your* idea. You kept doing it, kept taking things to weird places. You were the one who was bored. You were the one who wanted to pretend to fly to show how brave you were. You'd spent that whole summer doing strange shit like that.'

'No!'

'Then what? I wonder what book I'd have ended up writing if I'd had to witness you getting splattered across the front of that lorry. I'd have ended up soaked in your blood and broken. You're being fucking ridiculous. You were deliberately being reckless that day. Stop trying to turn it into something it wasn't.'

The wind howled between them. Diana's hair swept across her face, she fought to push it back, to keep her gaze on Allie.

'I just wanted to feel . . . something. Something other than . . . it doesn't even matter. You wrote that book and you rewrote history.' Diana jabbed a finger in the air, pointing at Allie. 'Yes, I said let's play on the bridge. Yes, I was being reckless and stupid. Emily was gone and it kept eating at me. I couldn't talk to Stacie, Gail was in France and all I had was you. And then you fell and I became the girl who hurt you, the girl who made you lose your grip and suddenly I was a villain in my own house. My own mother *detested* me, accused me of being just as evil as *him*.'

The ground was steep, a slope of fresh white tumbling away into the deep shadows which gathered around them. Diana was shaking, hands hanging impotently at her sides as she stared at her friend, teeth chattering loudly together, the tip of her nose shining like a ruby. Allie dared to glance behind, noticing how their footsteps were already stolen by shadows and yet more snow. It felt as though they weren't even really there, as though their moment on the mountain, within the storm, was strangely temporary.

'Years . . .' The word rattled out of her, carried on trembling, sore lips. 'You've had years.' She drew in an icy breath to inject more power into her voice. 'You've never spoken to me about what happened that day. Never—'

'Never what?' The mountain delivered Diana's rebuttal with brutal swiftness, letting it brush against Allie's bare cheeks with an icy blast. 'Never *apologised*?'

'Anything, you never said *anything*!' Allie was almost screaming, tasting the salt of her tears each time she spoke.

'How could I?' Diana demanded, stepping forward, attempting to destroy the space between them. 'Gail would have crucified me. "Poor little Allie." "Weak, broken, Allie." Everyone . . . they told me not to hurt you even further.' Diana's face was concealed in shadows and Allie couldn't tell if she wore a scowl to accompany her scornful tone. She stepped closer still. 'So I kept quiet. Kept my distance. Said nothing.'

'You should have spoken to me.' Allie dragged the back of her gloved hand across her eyes, trembled against the wind.

'I watched you fall.' Diana stumbled as she moved, staggered to her knees, the air knocking from her chest as she connected with the snow.

'Hey . . .' Allie hurried to her, snow crunching, crouched low and helped to haul her back onto her feet. Around them, the barren trees rattled as though in cheerless laughter.

'Do you know what that does to someone?' Diana asked as she dusted herself off. 'Almost seeing one of your best friends die?'

Allie swallowed.

'It fucks them up,' Diana continued. 'Really fucks them up. Emily . . .' She released a shaky breath as she glanced beyond Allie, back up the mountain. 'I want her to be okay. Thinking about her, about what might happen, as we walk through all this' – she kicked at the debris around her – 'all this bloody snow, it made me realise I should have spoken up long ago. Life is too short to keep secrets, to keep things in.'

'I thought you were going to fall, I thought I was saving you. And you blame me for that?' Allie's voice had shrunk in size. Now she felt numb all over and it was from more than just the cold. Her anger was being swept away with the bitter wind. The darts Diana had fired with her words had hit their targets and their poison was slowly sinking in.

'Yes.' Diana raised her chin and Allie noticed that it was trembling. 'I blame you for that. I was never going to fall, my grip was a lot stronger than yours.'

'Not many fifteen-year-old girls would risk their own lives to save a friend like that.' The reporter stared at Allie over his cappuccino, his pen poised atop his slim notebook. 'They'd just let them fall.'

'It's hard to say what someone would do until they're put in that position.' Allie shyly tucked a long strand of golden hair behind her ear. The reporter smiled at her, his stubble-laced cheeks lifting.

'I think you did something remarkably brave for a girl of fifteen. Because this story is about you, isn't it?'

'Yes, it is.'

'And all the other characters; Deena, Gigi, Sarah and Emma are they based on real people too?'

'Pretty much.'

'Your friends must be excited for you, for this book.' The reporter scribbled in his pad. 'You've been on quite the journey. Are you fully recovered from all your injuries now?'

'Yes.' Pain stabbed at the base of her spine, which Allie ignored. Pain was good. The doctors had told her that. Pain meant that things were still working. Still connecting. 'It took a long time, but I'm fully recovered now.'

Jasper had left when she told him the part that was missing from the book, the part about her infertility.

'It's just better I leave now,' he'd said as he packed up his things. 'Because I want kids, Allie. Someday. I at least want to know it's possible.'

Allie didn't chase after him. Didn't beg him to stay. She just stood at the window and watched him leave. She was used to managing her pain alone. She'd got incredibly good at it over the years.

'Any regrets?' The reporter's pen had briefly grown still.

'Sorry?' Allie blinked at him, wondering if she'd misheard the question.

'Any regrets?' he repeated, tapping the pen against the edge of the notepad. 'I mean you saved your friend but at an excessive cost to yourself.' He paused to check his notes. 'You spent over a year in hospital and for a time there was a good possibility that you wouldn't walk again. You sacrificed being a normal teenager.'

Allie wanted to point out that she hadn't been all that 'normal' to begin with. What did normal even mean?

'No.' She reached for her coffee and cradled it between her hands. 'No regrets.'

'Well, I look forward to the next book.' The reporter stood up and offered his hand which Allie duly shook. 'I wonder which one of your friends you'll have to save for the next one.' He winked and then walked away.

Thirty-One

The icy wind scratched against Allie's cheeks. She embraced the pain. It distracted her from the ache in her heart. Diana was a few feet ahead, almost absorbed from view by the falling snow. She was walking fast, head tucked against her chest, fists clenched at her sides.

'Okay, maybe I don't completely blame you.' They had been walking in silence for ten minutes, only the wail of the wind stretching between them when Diana abruptly stopped and turned round. She peered up at Allie from her lower position on the mountain, shielding her eyes to stop snow clumping in her lashes.

'What?' Allie had been so busy internalising what had been said that she almost tumbled straight into her friend.

'I said I don't blame you.' Diana grabbed her shoulders just before they collided. Allie blinked, feeling dazed by the sudden intervention.

'You don't?'

'No, I . . .' The cold had done little to weaken Diana's strength. Her grip was tight against Allie's shoulders, anchoring her in place. 'That day when you fell, you were right, I'd spent a whole summer being a bitch.' She released Allie and let her hands drop to her sides where they began to twitch with unease. Diana's entire body seemed to be prickling with discomfort as she looked towards her friend with a troubled stare. 'Remember that party at Ashley Smith's house over the Easter holidays?'

Allie remembered. Vaguely. That night now existed in a drunken haze as so many of her teenage exploits did. She'd enjoyed drinking, downing shots eagerly with Stacie, keen to feel the intoxicating numbness after the alcohol entered her system.

'The one where we all tried tequila for the first time?'

'Uh huh.' Diana's expression darkened and her hands became still. 'I saw something that night.'

There was an edge to her voice, a wariness.

'What?' Intrigue prickled at the base of Allie's neck. Along with fear. She shivered as though the temperature had dropped several more degrees in the space of a second.

'Something I . . .'

A snap. Loud and sudden, almost a gunshot. Allie leapt back from Diana's grip as a branch was released from a nearby tree, overcome by the weight of the snow upon it. In a cloud of icy dust, it landed on the ground beside them and Allie raised a trembling hand to her chest. Her heart was beating a frantic rhythm.

'Shit.' The word fogged before her as she glanced between the tree and Diana, wide-eyed.

'It's getting dangerous out here.' There was fear in Diana's voice but also a steely stoicism that shone in her eyes. She nodded beyond Allie, to the descending mountainside. 'We really need to keep moving.'

'Sure.' Allie nodded and took a single step before turning herself back round, cocking her head to the left, eyes narrowing. 'But what did you see, at the party?'

Diana had paled, becoming a ghost even amongst the whiteout of the snow. 'Nothing. Forget it.'

'Just tell me. What was it you saw?'

'Now isn't the time.' Ice crunched beneath her boots as Diana pushed her way past Allie and kept moving downwards.

'Diana?'

'Let's keep going, okay?' Although she presented it as a question Allie knew that it wasn't, that it was a directive.

As they walked on Allie did her best to recall the party Diana had mentioned. But between the tequila she'd so easily downed that night and the passing of so much time, her memory was far from reliable. Emily had been the worst of them, that much had stuck in her mind. Back when Emily didn't, or wouldn't, understand the limits of her diabetes. It was unlike her to drink, to let loose, but when she did she went all out, Allie remembered that much. It was a rare spectacle to behold, a shooting star of social events, like when they went on their girls' holiday and Gail was left holding the injector pen. It was as though Emily figured that if she was going to dance with the devil it might as well be a rave, not a waltz. Allie forced herself to polish off the remnants of the memory, to make what remained shine.

Emily had danced to The Fugees, arms wide and free above her head as she spun around the room, blonde hair fanning out around her. But as the drinks became multiple Emily had disappeared. Had she gone upstairs to lie down? Allie couldn't be sure. Other once familiar faces, all forever fifteen, came back to Allie. They had all been there as a group, the once regular ensemble of the Fierce Five. And Oliver, he had been there. Back then he was Stacie's boyfriend and she'd adored him with the kind of intensity reserved only for the young and unjaded.

Oliver Henderson with his boy-band good looks and penchant for polo shirts. He had a square jaw speckled with fine blond hairs and drove around in a white Ford Fiesta even though he was too young to legally drive. It was like the rules just didn't apply to him. Many girls became moths to the flame around him but Allie had never seen the appeal – he always seemed too clean-cut, too perfect. Too dull.

And Ollie's friend Steve, he'd been there too. The snow stung at Allie's eyes, at her tongue, as she sucked in vital breaths and let her mind wander back in time. It was nice to be distracted from the cold and the ice.

Steve Michaels had been built thick and strong like a tree trunk. Allie remembered his guffawing laugh which grated on her during her English Lit classes. He'd throw back his head, mouth hanging open wide enough to show the glint of silver fillings and then he'd bellow his laughter across the classroom until his cheeks were rosy. Steve used to flirt with Diana, used to wait for her in the corridor and sheepishly follow her. He was the one guy at school Diana seemed willing to tolerate and Steve was wise enough to notice this and be grateful for her attention.

But he changed after Oliver died. His laugh flattened and he seemed to slip from Diana's sphere of awareness, forgotten like an old toy that had dropped down the side of the bed, gathering dust.

Diana swiped a gloved hand across her mouth and cleared her throat noisily before glancing back up towards Allie. 'You're dawdling, you need to hurry the hell up.'

'I'm going as fast as I can.' Allie sped up marginally, hurriedly dragging her feet through the snow.

'I just want to get down this bit as quick as we can, okay?'

'Look, don't rush. We need to be careful.'

'We need to go faster.'

'Tell me. Tell me what happened at the party.' Allie couldn't disconnect from her curiosity. There had been a time when she'd known everything about her friends, nothing occurred between them without the others knowing. And the party had fallen into this time bracket so what was Diana even referring to?

'Later, Allie.' There was gravel in Diana's voice.

'I know we were all pretty drunk, Emily especially . . .' Allie kept pressing, compelled to pick at the scab of the memory. It had been strange to see her blonde friend so intoxicated but when they were fifteen three shots of tequila could be extremely potent and they were all such novices when it came to drinking – believing shots were weak because they were so small.

'Fuck, just forget I said anything,' Diana ordered with an exasperated sigh. 'I shouldn't have brought it up, I just . . .' Her shoulders sagged and she craned her neck to peer up at the sky, at the snow which fell against her. 'The prick died anyway, that's the main thing.'

'Wait, what?' Allie's brow became knitted, with the now numb tips of her fingers she needled the bridge of her nose. Was Diana talking about Oliver Henderson? But why? And why in such a callous way? It was common knowledge that she'd never been fond of him but that was then and this was years later. Allie knew all too well that time rarely operated as it was supposed to in theory. Pain that should be fleeting could last a lifetime, friendships that were supposed to endure could all too quickly decay.

'Maybe he rammed himself into that wall on purpose, finally let his guilt get the better of him. Or maybe it was all some awful accident, who the hell knows?' Diana was ranting, kicking up clouds of snow as she walked. 'And by then my mum was so busy blaming me for your hospitalisation that she probably blamed me for any rumours surrounding Ollie too. Over and over again she told me that I was no good, that I was evil, just like my dad.'

Allie's gut wrenched with guilt. 'Are you talking about Oliver Henderson's car accident? Diana, what aren't you telling me?'

Ignoring the questions, Diana continued her lament. 'Every night at dinner she'd pull this face. She'd sigh, tut and purse her lips and then remark on your situation. "Poor little Allie up there in that hospital, it's so awful," she'd say. And she'd stare at me like she wished I was the one up there wrapped in casts. She was right, it should have been me. But you were the martyr. I was the wicked witch who had led you to your demise and my mum never let me forget that, not for one second.'

'Diana, I—'

'Remember what our English teacher Mrs Hibbert would say? About how we should all be the heroine in our own stories? Well, I learned that I was the villain. Mum made me see that. I sent Emily away. I put you in the hospital.'

'What do you mean you sent Emily away? She just disappeared, no one ever knew why. She just spent a few terms at one of those strict Catholic schools, right?' Allie could feel the doubt growing within, new and unsettling.

'I owe it to Emily to save her. To do something.' Diana sounded more than just determined, she sounded like someone on the verge of being possessed. With a grunt she sped up, kicking her way through the snow.

'Diana!' With a surge Allie dashed forward, forcing the space between them to fold into nothing. Hand outstretched, she grabbed her friend's shoulder and dragged her back, disabling her from stomping onwards. 'You're not making any sense. Either stop speaking in bloody riddles or tell me what's bothering you.'

'Nothing I say can change what happened.'

'Jesus.' The word was pushed through Allie's lips in a terse breath. 'Do you know what happened to Emily? Where she went that summer? Why she didn't come back to school?'

Diana withdrew from the question, eyes becoming wide and wild. 'Forget it.'

'Does her going away have something to do with what happened that summer? Why you were behaving like you were?'

The wind tried to prise them apart but Allie remained rooted to the spot, a single hand on Diana's shoulder.

'Please,' Allie pleaded, 'you're not making any sense.'

'I accept that I shouldn't have been hanging off the bridge like that.' Diana pursed her lips and squared her shoulders beneath Allie's grip. 'I wish I could go back, do it all again differently. And I wish you could let go, move on from it all.'

'Diana, what happened at the party?' Allie deflected.

'There's so much I should have done. I should have stopped Emily drinking for a start – how could we have been so dumb, so reckless, to let her do fucking shots with us?'

'We were all young, Diana. So very young. We didn't understand how dangerous it could be for her.'

'We put her in danger, we—'

'What happened? What did you see?' Allie applied pressure to her touch, clenching her fingers against her friend's shoulder. But Diana staggered back, physically detaching from the conversation. Allie let her hand fall to her side, admitting defeat.

'We can't change the past,' Allie noted sagely as the cold began to seep into her bones anew, hoping her words might bring both her and Diana some semblance of comfort no matter how fleeting. How long had they been out on the mountainside? How long until Emily slipped too far out of reach?

'It seems we can't move on from it either,' Diana stated sadly.

'It could be residual nerve damage.' Dr Otterman stroked his ginger moustache as he eyed Allie from behind his grand dark oak desk. She shifted nervously in her plush armchair, the cup and saucer of tea she'd been given on arrival left untouched nearby. Freshly thirty-four, this wasn't how she'd been intending to spend the day after her birthday, revisiting old ghosts, assessing old wounds. But the numbness was spreading, each time Allie pressed her fingers against her spine and felt nothing she knew she was edging closer to something she refused to even consider.

'Could be?'

'Or it's more likely to be new damage, from scar tissue. This can be quite common as it's had time to accumulate.'

'I see.' Allie slumped back in the chair. The room smelt of lavender and old books. The golden glow of an autumnal afternoon filtered in through the single window behind her, painting a pattern upon the ornate rug beneath her feet.

'The problem we have is that your initial surgery was messy, as all emergency surgeries tend to be. And then all the subsequent surgeries increased your risk of the build-up of scar tissue. The numbness you are experiencing is, like I said, unfortunately very common.' Dr Otterman's voice remained calm and level, as though he were merely remarking about the state of the weather with a stranger.

'Will it go away?' Allie wanted to reach round and press at the base of her spine, to use her fingers to needle through the scar tissue which was causing her so much concern.

Dr Otterman cleared his throat and shifted in his leather chair, causing the waxy material to squeak softly. His fingers found his moustache and ruffled the coarse hair. Allie had learned over the past seven months that it was a habit he adopted whenever he was nervous. 'Possibly,' he replied vaguely.

'Possibly?'

'The results of the MRI were inconclusive. There is too much damage and scar tissue to get a clear view of the nerves. The numbness may well remain as it is: a mild discomfort. However . . .'

Allie knew this tilt of the head. The setting of the mouth in a firm line. Bad news was coming. She gripped the arms of her chair in preparation. Lucas should have been there. He should have been at her side, holding her hand and saying all the right things. But somehow he'd slipped through her fingers, like so many good things seemed to. While she was sitting in Dr Otterman's office, he was back at their flat packing up his things. He'd most likely wait for her to come back, to have one last-ditch attempt at saving their marriage which was still in its infancy. But all his words would be in vain.

'The numbness may spread.' Dr Otterman looked remorseful behind his glasses even though he didn't sound it. 'We will closely monitor it and—'

'Real talk,' Allie blurted. She didn't have time for this. There were currently too many fires in her life that were demanding her attention, needing to be snuffed out. 'Worst-case scenario, will I end up in a chair again?'

'Worst case?' The doctor raised his pale ginger eyebrows at her. Allie nodded. 'Then yes, you may. It's certainly an outcome we should be prepared for.'

'Prepare for the worst and hope for the best, right?'

'Right.'

Allie sounded like she was getting ready to go to war. Which she figured she was, in a way. Ever since the accident she'd been in a constant battle with her body. Every time one thing mended, something else broke. She was like a china doll that had been smashed and then painstakingly glued back together. But you could always see the cracks. And it would only take the slightest knock for all the pieces to fall apart again.

'We'll see you again in a month and assess things then.' Dr Otterman was rising up out of his chair and extending a hand to her. The appointment was over.

'Yes, thank you.' Allie genially shook it as though she were agreeing on a business deal. It was all very amicable. Very formal.

'Perhaps next time, if we need to discuss possible future measures, your husband might like to be present?' Dr Otterman walked her to the door.

'I doubt it.' Allie didn't turn back to see if a look of surprise had spread across the doctor's face.

Thirty-Two

'Allie, are you all right?' Diana was standing so close that Allie could feel the warmth of her breath blowing against her face.

'W-what?' Allie snapped back into the moment, snatched her hands away from the base of her spine. She felt nothing back there and she feared that the nothingness was spreading. The fear gnawed at her, hollowed her out until it had won until there truly was just nothing left. No sorrow. No joy. Just . . . emptiness.

'I said are you all right . . . your back?' Diana nodded at Allie's hands with a grim look on her face. 'You were standing there, zoning out and you keep touching it, do you need to stop and rest?'

'It's fine.'

'Allie—'

'Really, I'm good. Let's keep going. There isn't time to be talking, right?'

'Allie, I'm sorry.' Diana remained rooted to the spot.

'Look, let's just—'

'I shouldn't have pushed you. Lucas left and it's up to you if you share the reason for that, you don't have to. I should never have let my anger over what happened that day on the bridge colour my view of you the way it has.' Her brow furrowed into a hard, thick line. 'I know you were just trying to help me. I get that. But I spent *years* being berated for your actions, being made to feel guilty all the time, having to live with failing both you and . . .' She let the wind carry away the words she refused to say, the truth she couldn't yet impart.

'It's fine,' Allie sighed, keen to press on. Each second spent idling was prolonging the moment when Emily could be reunited with her vital medication. 'Really. It's fine. Lucas is gone. It doesn't matter anyway.'

'But is that why he left?' Diana reached for Allie's shoulder to draw her back, her eyes wide and desperate. 'Because you can't keep living like this, Allie, forever being a victim. That's what I was trying to tell you on your wedding day, that you need to let go. If you told him the truth and he left that's on him, not you. Don't make it about you.'

'No.' Allie shrugged her off. 'I mean . . .' She flexed her hands within her gloves, trying to restore some feeling to the tips of her fingers. 'That's not why he left. It wasn't about me not being able to have children.'

'Oh.' Diana sounded relieved and confused. 'Then . . .'

Allie filled her lungs with bitterly cold air as she braced herself for the inevitable question.

'Then why did he leave?'

It was the question Allie had been avoiding ever since her husband of just a few months had packed up his designer clothes and MacBook and left her flat that summer. His scent still lingered in the bathroom; cedar-wood and lime, she still couldn't sleep on his side of the bed. Her parents demanded answers, but it was easy to avoid their calls. With them, she could always keep insisting she was busy, that everything was just fine. Living in her little writing bubble Allie could conceal the truth from almost everyone.

She knew that it would be different with her friends, with the girls who knew her better than she knew herself. She was certain they'd see the truth written all over her face so she worked hard to hide it, to always look and sound *fine*.

'I lied to him.' Allie felt the weight of her words on her tongue, causing her head to droop.

'You lied to him?' Diana wondered. 'About what? About—'

'So I'm the reason,' Allie blurted. 'I'm the reason he left. Satisfied?'

The wind tugged at Allie, urging her forwards. She responded, letting her boots sink deep into the snow. Her mind drifted back up to the cabin, thinking of Emily, hoping she was okay, that she was still holding on.

'Allie, I . . . I'm sorry.'

Snow crunched underfoot and Allie kept walking, moving with forceful determination. 'Don't pity me,' she seethed, throwing the comment over her shoulder like a grenade. 'Don't ever pity me.'

They continued walking down the steep mountainside.

'Allie, I can't help but pity you.' Diana's voice ripped through the growl of the storm after several minutes had passed. 'I pity you because you can't seem to stop making choices which make you the victim. If you'd just told him the truth from the beginning then maybe—'

'Stop! Okay? Can we just . . .' Allie sighed and felt the cold reaching down to the base of her lungs. 'Can we talk about something else? Anything.'

'Like the party?'

'I thought we weren't discussing that?'

'We're . . . we're not.' Chewing on her lip, Diana paused to stare at her friend, expression pinched and serious. 'But

I do owe you the truth. What happened at your wedding between us, Lucas leaving, being out here with Emily depending on us, waiting on us, it's all got me thinking. I'm done hiding things, aren't you?'

Allie bristled but said nothing.

'Keeping things in only causes pain.'

'So what have you been keeping in?'

Secrets.

'Too much.' Dropping her gaze, Diana kicked around the snow gathered at her feet, seemingly needing the distraction. 'At the cabin . . .' Inhaling deeply she straightened anew. 'When we're back when Emily is safe and has her insulin, I'll tell you what happened at the party. Both of you.'

'So it involves us both?'

'It involves all of us.' Diana shook her head wearily. 'Isn't that always the way with us?'

Thirty-Three

Officer: What broke the windows in the cabin?

POI: I believe it was the force of the storm.

Officer: So things started to get dangerously cold in there?

POI: Seems to be the natural order – the window breaks, the cold comes in.

Officer: I'm just trying to ascertain what happened.

POI: I've explained what happened.

Officer: At the cabin the windows were all broken, most of the building already succumbing to the storm.

POI: That sounds about right.

Officer: Were you worried you might freeze to death?

POI: We all were worried about that.

Officer: Did you think help was coming?

POI: Honestly?

Officer: Of course honestly. Need I remind you that you're being interviewed as part of a police investigation?

POI: No reminder needed. And with help coming, I wasn't sure at that point. Things seemed to just be going from bad to worse.

Thirty-Four

It was getting colder. Though the sky grew marginally lighter, the wind became sharper. It buffeted Allie as she picked her way through the snow, trying to knock her off her feet. Diana was a few paces ahead taking long, confident strides. The ground was still steep beneath them, an endless glistening slope that was supposed to level out into a river at some point.

Gritting her teeth, Allie kept going. She had no idea how much time had passed since they'd left the cabin. One hour? Two? The snow seemed to absorb everything; sound, time. It blanketed the world and transformed the mountain into an icy prison.

'We have to be close to the river.' Diana paused to throw her comment over her shoulder, back towards Allie.

'Yes, hopefully!'

Diana withdrew the map from her pocket as Allie caught up to her. Even held securely it flapped madly in the wind like an unfurled flag, making it difficult to trace the web of markings across it.

'Where do you think we are?' The friends bowed their heads towards one another as Allie held the torch over the map. The beam of light revealed all the hiking trails, the blue line of the river. But there was no key for deciphering landmarks when everything was covered in several inches of snow.

'Um . . .' Diana dragged her gloved fingers over the map. The black X was in the top corner. Allie peered back up the slope, hoping to see the crimson glow of a distant flare burning. But, to her disappointment, all she could see was snow falling upon more snow. Trees bowing beneath the weight of loaded branches. The slope lifted up out of her vision, meeting the leaden sky. 'Crap.' Diana closed her fingers against her palm, making a fist. 'I really don't know where the hell we are. We kept going down.' She jabbed a single finger at a line that was marked in red. According to the key in the left-hand corner, it was a 'hazardous hiking trail, only to be ventured by the most seasoned explorers'. 'I'm worried we've somehow ended up here.'

Allie focused the beam from the torch on the red route. It peeled away from a yellow line up near the cabin, traversing a sharp incline of a forested area before dropping to a point marked as treacherous in bold letters. They were surrounded by trees. Allie withdrew her torch from the map and let it shine upon the nearby pines. They stood all around them, their presence feeling oppressive.

'I think we came down the red route.' A tense breath slid through Diana's clenched teeth. 'Dammit.'

'It's easily done.' Allie studied the map, trying to find a safe route back to the yellow or blue lines that snaked across it. The cold worked in tandem with her nerves to cause her hand to shake as she held the torch, casting an erratic beam of light over the flapping piece of paper. 'We can't see anything out here in all this snow. Besides, taking the more dangerous route probably got us down quicker.'

'Yeah, that's true.'

'If we head left instead of down, we should connect with the yellow trail.' But Allie wasn't Gail, she couldn't be certain of where a different route would take them.

At that moment she envied her friend's affinity with the wild, the way Gail could read the stars like a map, meaning that wherever she was in the world, she was never truly lost.

'No.' Diana started to fold up the map with her gloved hands. 'We keep heading down.'

'But the map says that way is—'

'We've wasted enough time as it is. We need to get to the base of this bloody mountain and fast. We keep going down.'

'Diana, I—'

'Do you trust me?'

'Should I?' Allie asked, openly sceptical.

'Fine. Whatever. It doesn't matter. Emily needs us. We can't waste any more time.' Diana shoved the map back into her pocket and boldly stepped forward.

'We thought you were going to die.' Stacie sat in a chair by the window looking out at the setting sun. She was still in her school uniform, red hair pulled back in a tight ponytail. In her hospital bed Allie reached for the controls and slowly altered the incline of the mattress so that she was completely sitting up. Changing position made the stitches in her stomach ache and strain. She was thankful when the green light on her morphine drip shone bright, eagerly pressing it down and drinking in the rapture of release the pain medication brought her.

'I'm not dead,' Allie assured her friend, her body relaxing against the inflated mattress which continually wheezed like an eighty-year-old smoker.

'You nearly were.' Stacie looked away from the sunset. She uncrossed her legs and leaned forward in her plastic seat. 'When they found you, they said you were CTD.'

'I'm pretty sure that's just from TV.'

'No, circling the drain. It's a thing. Like the golden hour.'

'Uh huh. Been watching a lot of ER lately?'

'I raided the mothership's box sets so that I could bone up on the lingo especially for you.' Stacie smiled proudly.

'Thanks.' Allie was tired. It was a fight just to keep her eyes open. She felt like she'd been tired forever like she could no longer remember a time when her body was full of youthful energy.

'You really scared us.' Stacie dragged her chair closer to the bed. 'Like, seriously scared us. We're a five, Allie. We're like the Spice Girls; we don't work as a four.'

'I'm sure you'd have figured something out.' Allie allowed her eyes to seal shut, just for a moment. Then she blearily blinked them back open. Stacie was leaning her elbows against the bed, staring up at her.

'You're not allowed to die before the rest of us.'

'What?'

'I was thinking about it . . .' Tilting her head Stacie narrowed her blue eyes. 'I've not told the others about it yet, but I figured I'd speak to you first since it involves you at some point.'

'Right?' Following the conversation was draining Allie. It wasn't just her body that was currently sluggish. Even the simplest acts, like eating dinner or being hoisted into a wheelchair and exploring the ward could prove exhausting. Sleep. Her body craved it like an addict.

'I think we should all vow to go together.'

'Go where?'

'When we die. We all die at once, that way no one is left to miss anyone else.'

'Huh.' Allie closed her eyes again, her breathing deepening.

'I mean, when I thought you were dead I just – I lost it. I don't want . . . I can't lose anyone else, Allie Bear. I need you all to promise that you won't leave me. You especially, since you were CTD and all.'

With effort Allie's eyes flickered open and she saw that Stacie had returned to the window, legs held against her chest as she balanced her chin on her knees and peered tearfully at the sky which looked like it was burning.

'Ollie is dead,' Stacie stated stiffly. 'I'm not sure if you heard.'

'No.' The drugs in Allie's system were distorting everything. Oliver. Ollie. Stacie's Ollie. The news of his death tangled itself around her like a net, trapping her against the bed. He was dead. How? When? Why? She incoherently babbled her questions at her friend.

'No one really knows.' Stacie wiped away her tears and focused on the sunset. 'That's the point of the pact. I can't lose anyone else, Allie.'

'So . . .' Allie was fighting her fatigue, trying to get her weary mind to process the news about Ollie's death. Had he been in a car accident? Been sick? 'He's dead . . . how? I'm . . . I'm so sorry.' Being in the hospital was like being in another dimension. News didn't find her the way it did at school, didn't travel along corridors like nits eagerly darting from scalp to scalp.

'He ran his car into a wall.' Stacie tightened her grip on her legs and pressed her chin more firmly against her knees.

'He . . . what?'

'He was drunk. High. Out of his fucking mind. Maybe it was an accident. Maybe it was . . .' Stacie's voice trailed off as she stared absently at the sunset. Allie coughed against the taste of plastic that seemed to constantly coat her throat. She needed to lift Stacie's spirits somehow.

'So . . . the pact is . . . we all go . . . together?'

'Exactly.' Stacie brightened but she sounded manic. Unclasping her legs, she hopped back over to the bed. Or perhaps she didn't hop. Reality was starting to merge with Allie's dreams, the way it always did when there was fresh morphine in her system. 'All for one and one for all and all that crap.'

'O-Okay.' Allie wasn't even sure what she was agreeing to.

'Great, I'll fill the others in. We're taking it in turns to come and sit with you every day. Although Emily and Diana have been a bit MIA lately. But don't worry, Allie, we won't leave you alone in here. Not ever. We're best friends. Forever.'

'Forever,' Allie muttered, eyes firmly closed now.

Thirty-Five

Allie's attention was focused on her feet. She was carefully shadowing Diana's foot holes in the deepening snow. 'Don't rush,' she ordered loudly. 'It's really steep here, be careful.'

The wind had finally receded, preferring to batter the upper regions of the mountain, the flanks of trees offering protection from its coarseness in these lower regions. Which meant that they had to be winning – that they had to be drawing ever closer to the base. The snow was still softly falling and Allie had become numb to the cold. But each time she spoke, she felt its icy presence anew against her teeth, making the strong enamel suddenly feel like delicate china.

There was no crunch in the snow up ahead, Diana was moving too fast. With a quick glance, Allie saw the way ahead of her was clear, her companion having moved out of her eye line. With a grunt Allie tried to quicken her pace, internally bemoaning her old scars, her limitations.

'Diana, slow down, just—'

A scream. Disturbing the snowy silence with jarring force, like the striking of an incorrect chord during a peaceful harmony. The sound struck Allie in the chest, curdling her blood and knocking the air from her lungs. She took a second to recover and then she surged forwards.

'Diana?'

It had to have been Diana who'd screamed. They were all alone out on the mountainside. There was no one else around for miles.

'Diana!' Allie was frantically forcing her way through the snow, no longer attempting to trace her friend's steps. 'Diana!' She managed to stop short as the ground gave way beneath her, squealing with surprise at her near fall. Dropping to her knees, Allie peered over the edge of the slope. Now the only screaming she could hear was her own.

There was a steep drop at the edge of the slope, a precarious stretch of a rocky mountain that fell at least ten feet. At the bottom sat an icy ledge surrounded by steep rocks, which gleamed from the touch of the cold. Tree-tops poked up around the ledge, dusted with snow.

'Diana!'

Her friend was sprawled upon the ledge. Face down, arms splayed at her sides. She wasn't moving.

'Diana! Diana are you all right? Get up!' Gripping the edge of the slope Allie leaned forward and scoured the steep rocks for safe passage down to the ledge. 'Diana, I'm coming, okay? I'm just . . .' She swung a leg over the side of the slope and froze. A dark stain was spreading out from beneath Diana's head. She was lying on a pillow of her own blood. As Allie stared, heart thudding and bile rising in her throat, she noticed the awkward angle of her friend's neck, that her face was twisted to the side, facing the mountain, instead of pressed against the ground. 'Diana?' Retracting her leg Allie scrambled back onto the safety of the slope. Tears distorted her vision. 'Can you . . . can you hear me? I'm trying to get down, all right? I'm . . .' Allie grabbed fistfuls of snow in her gloved hands and nearly choked on the sobs that were getting stuck in her throat.

There was no way of safely reaching Diana. The ledge was too far down the mountainside, the rocks too slick and precarious to traverse without climbing equipment. Allie had no ropes on her, no pickaxe. She just had the boots which were meant to keep her safe with their spiked soles. 'Diana, get up, please!' Allie was shaking, her voice growing hoarse, as she sat in a ball looking down at her fallen friend. 'I need you to get up, Diana!'

Her heart turned to ice. The cold had finally broken her, claiming every last part of her body. Diana couldn't get up. Couldn't even respond to her friend's cries. Her neck was broken. Allie could see that clearly from her vantage point, but her brain didn't want to accept what her eyes knew.

'I'll get down and everything will be okay, you'll see.' She again lowered a leg over the side of the slope and a cascade of snow tumbled down. Some of it landed around Diana, the rest kept falling until it met with the treetops below. 'Shit.' Allie scrambled to safety, her cheeks burning as her tears froze upon them. 'Shit!' She looked down at Diana who remained lifeless and still. And the blood. There was so much blood. It created a dark halo around her as it seeped into the snow and ice. 'No!' Allie was screaming. She rocked back and forth and wailed against the wind.

After several long, barren minutes Allie looked over the edge of the mountain and teetered against her own drowning despair, chest painfully constricting with the sobs she wasn't bothering to hold in. Diana had broken against rocks, her secrets forever silenced with her fall.

'No!' Allie staggered to her feet and roared at the mountain. At the snow. She screamed until her vocal cords burned, the sound feral and desperate. Once spent, she dropped against the ground, panting. Lost. Alone. What was she supposed to do now?

A brisk wind swept up some snow, letting it swirl around her in a frantic dance. This was the mountain's response to her question. If she lingered where she was then the storm would claim her. And she could still save Emily.

Awkwardly clambering to her feet, Allie dusted herself down and summoned all the strength she had left.

'I'm going to get to the bottom,' Allie shakily called down to her friend, her voice broken and ragged. 'I'm going to send help back up. You'll be okay, Diana.' Drawing in a pained breath Allie stepped away from the edge of the slope. She could barely breathe. Could barely think. Her mind was screaming the truth at her—

Diana is dead.

But she couldn't let the truth in, not fully, not yet. Not until she'd completed her task, not until she'd helped Emily.

Allie needed to get down the mountain, needed to connect with the yellow route. If she could just . . .

The map. It was in Diana's pockets and had fallen down with her. 'Argh.' Allie dragged her hands across her head and paced back and forth. She had no idea where she was going. No map to guide her.

A powerful surge of wind knocked her clean off her feet. It dropped her against the snow, scratching at her cheeks. The storm had picked up again. Allie managed to get up as the falling snow became thicker, icier. She wondered if there was time to light the final flare, but the wind was too strong, dragging the snow like a current across the mountain. To stay where she was would mean certain death. She had to move.

Thirty-Six

Officer: Did you see Diana fall?

POI: No, I didn't.

Officer: She was found on a ledge, her neck snapped.

POI: Look, I just . . .

Officer: Do you need a minute? A tissue? Some water?

POI: One of my best friends is dead. Gone. Don't you get that? And instead of asking how I am, if I'm all right, how I'm doing, you just keep asking me if I saw her fall.

Officer: In my line of work I have to question everything. People so often have a tendency to lie.

POI: Do you think I'm lying?

Officer: Maybe.

POI: But you found her, out on the mountain. Won't forensics prove that she fell?

Officer: Leave the questions to me. So you didn't see Diana fall?

POI: No. I didn't see her fall. I mean . . .

Officer: As a response the no is sufficient.

POI: What are you actually trying to deduce here?

Officer: Whether or not you saw Diana fall from the mountain face.

POI: Don't dance around it, Officer Fields. If you think we're monsters, just come right out and say it. We are flawed, yes. We aren't the paragons of perfection people liked to think we were. But we are not murderers.

Officer: But you didn't see Diana fall?

POI: For the last time, I didn't see her fall. Nor did I see the storm come in, but it came. It happened. Life is like that – you don't need to be a constant spectator to let the tide take you.

Thirty-Seven

Allie planted her feet deep in the snow and braced herself against the storm. She felt hopelessly untethered as she fought to withstand its might, a kite cut from its string. Inside she was twisting and spinning as wildly as the falling snowflakes around her.

Diana was dead. Had to be.

The reality of the loss turned Allie's blood to ash. Shock was strangling her veins, numbing even the most concealed parts of her body. Allie hiccuped against developing sobs as her hands began to shake.

The truth of the situation was boring into her, trying to weaken her, break her. Allie blinked against the snow, coughed against the ice in her lungs. Her tears brought a brief feeling of warmth to her cheeks as she forced herself to stagger on.

Allie was on all fours crawling through the snow. It was too steep to be on just her feet, her legs too leaden to withstand the demands of trekking back up the mountain. And she was going back up. With each desperate surge forward, Allie knew she was taking herself further away from Diana, further away from the base of the mountain, from help. But what choice did she have? Without the map, she was lost. The storm was worsening. Her own footprints were quickly disappearing as she dragged herself back up amongst the trees. She needed to return to the cabin, to the others. She'd tell them what had happened and they'd know what to do. Gail must have ropes, climbing equipment. Together they could return and safely hoist themselves down to Diana.

'Come . . . on.' Allie gritted her teeth. Her mouth was dry, but she tasted the ice in the air. Muscles trembled as she forced them to keep going, to build momentum as she scrambled through the snow like a wounded animal. There was no way she could stop. If she stopped, she would freeze to death.

But stopping would be so blissful. Her body ached with longing when she considered leaning up against the base of a nearby tree, just for a moment. She'd close her eyes, let herself fall into darkness for a few minutes, nothing more. She needed to rest, to recharge.

'Diana needs me,' Allie whispered to herself through chattering teeth. Help. She was going to get help. And maybe, if they could get to Diana then everything else would work out. The insulin, they'd find some somehow. They had to. 'Emily. Needs. Me.' She powered through the snow, her gloves soaked through and her hands raw. None of her pain mattered. All that mattered was getting back up the mountain and saving at least one of her friends.

Diana might be okay.

The last hopeful part of herself clung to the possibility. It was the same part that liked to believe that her parents would one day reconcile, that her father would discard his new wife and remember that it was Allie's mother that he truly loved, who he truly belonged with.

And perhaps Lucas too would return.

That was a thought too far. Allie angrily shook her head, letting it get flung from her mind and carried away by the wind. Lucas wasn't coming back. He was gone.

His drawers in the dresser were empty, his side of the bed hadn't been slept in for months. He was gone and Allie needed to move on.

'You did this.' Those had been his parting words to her. 'You did this, Allie.'

She kept crawling, unaware that she was sobbing, that her whole body was heaving and trembling as she inched forwards. She was supposed to save Diana. That day in the sunshine she'd pulled her out of harm's way. She was supposed to keep Diana safe, not watch her fall.

'I'm sorry.' The words kept falling from her chapped lips. 'I'm sorry, Diana. I'm so sorry.' Allie wore her failure like a cape, letting it shield her from the worst of the storm. She tried to focus on the rhythm of her movements, on taking the crucial next step and then the next. But her mind kept drifting away from the mountain, to moments past. And her memories were like quicksand, eager to drag her down. Too easily she was drawn back to that fateful summer when she was sixteen . . .

Emily had just gone, disappeared, pulled out of school with barely a whisper of an explanation.

Meanwhile, Stacie became increasingly distracted by Oliver, following him around the school like a little lost lamb.

'She's a fool,' Diana would openly seethe. 'She needs to see him for what he really is.'

But what was he? To Allie's eyes he was cocky and arrogant but nothing more. Yet Diana seemed to loathe him with a frightening intensity. There had been a party at Ashley Smith's house. She remembered that much.

Thinking back, Allie could vaguely recall the drunken revelry, the couples who stood in corners with their mouths glued together. Stacie had all but kept pouring tequila and beer down her throat until Allie felt like she was floating. And Emily. She was the worst of them, barely able to remain on her feet.

'Upstairs,' she'd declared at one point, hanging off the back of the sofa. 'I need to lie down.'

'I'll take you,' Stacie had swiftly offered and Allie had watched them leave. Had noticed Gail's scowl as she stood in the doorway, disapproving of Emily's behaviour. The music kept playing, people kept dancing, joking, drinking. Stacie returned, sans Emily, and continued to knock back shots. At some point had Diana left the living room? Oliver too? Allie wished her fragmented memories were sharper, clearer. She could just about recall Oliver slinking out of the room, Stacie staring after him in a puppy-like trance but not following. She'd followed him out of rooms before at parties and been berated for not giving him his space. So she stayed at Allie's side, but her eyes all but burned a hole through the living-room door as she desperately waited on his return.

'He's gone to the loo,' Allie slurred, wishing the fun, carefree Stacie would return, the one who liked to show off for the audience of her older boyfriend.

'He's been gone ages.'

'Has he?' Allie couldn't tell. Tequila made time flow by in a deluge rather than a trickle. The last hour felt more like a second.

'Yeah, he has.' Stacie lashed the words from an impatient tongue and kept frowning at the door. 'And where the hell is Diana?'

'She's upstairs, passed out.'

'No. That's Emily.'

'Right.' Allie was giggling. For some reason when drunk everything became hilarious. She felt Gail's presence at her side. When had she appeared?

'I think we've all had too much,' the Girl Guide of the group was stating with open contempt.

'What's with your face?' Stacie snapped at Gail.

224

No, Allie blinked through the fog of liquor that was slowing all her senses. Stacie was addressing Diana who was back in the living room, skin ashen.

'Nothing,' Diana insisted as she hoisted Allie up by the armpit, Gail grabbing her other arm. 'Let's just get the hell out of here.'

'Did you see Ollie? Where is he?' Stacie delivered her questions with quick intensity, a machine gun firing.

'Fuck Ollie,' Diana seethed. 'He's a prick. You can do better.'

'Hey, how dare—'

Gail became a physical barrier between the warring friends. 'Now is not the time for a domestic,' she told them both sternly. 'We need to get Allie home. Emily, too. Someone go and get her.'

'Not me,' Diana barked her refusal directly into Allie's ear as they all headed towards the front door.

'Fine, me then,' Stacie exclaimed with a haughty sigh. 'Be right back.'

The front door opened and the velvety cloak of the night wrapped around them. Allie all but blacked out. Next thing she knew, she was huddled over the toilet at home watching as she threw up green liquid against the inside of the bowl. She never cared for tequila after that.

Thirty-Eight

Allie crouched against the snow, burying her teeth into the painful cold. There was an emptiness in the air. Allie had seen three people die before, all while she had been in hospital. Two of them had been elderly. Late in the night, their thin voices had screamed out in protest, not yet ready to meet their maker. Come the dawn they were silent, their eyes wide and vacant as the life had steadily seeped out of them. The third person had been accident victim, like Allie. He'd been stowed in the room opposite and he didn't scream or berate whoever he chose to worship for his predicament. He just lay upon his bed and silently waged a war against his broken body. A war he ultimately lost. The sound of his mother weeping when she heard that he was gone still haunted Allie.

Her hand slipped round to her back and she let it hang there, refusing to allow her fingers to push down against her spine. She needed to be strong. She could return to the war against her own body later when . . .

Allie fought against the weakness in her limbs and crawled up through the snow, using what energy remained to make haste for she knew that death was still stalking the mountainside. She was about to return to the cabin empty-handed; no insulin, no completed delivery of an urgent SOS message. She was going back with nothing, which meant that Emily would be teetering ever closer to her own end.

'No!' Allie spat the word through sore lips and focused on increasing her speed. 'Not here, not like this.' Her muscles had turned to ribbons of fire which burned with every surge forward. Her toes, fingers and nose were so numb that Allie began to doubt if they were even attached to her anymore. She kept looking down at her gloves, checking. She knew that numbness was bad. For her spine and everything else. What if her skin was starting to blacken like she'd seen happen in a documentary about explorers who got trapped while climbing Everest? How long did she have once frostbite set in? And if she never made it back to the cabin, how long until she shared Diana's fate?

Snow tumbled down the mountain in a drift, a vast cloud that swept around Allie. Squeezing her eyes shut, she sunk low to the ground and braced herself against it. Dawn had arrived. She saw its presence in the receding shadows, in the pale light which now hung overhead. But there was no sunshine. No reprise from the battering of the storm.

Creeping ever forward Allie dug through the snow. It was up to her elbows and still she had to keep digging.

Her world became a tunnel. A steep, snow-filled tunnel through which she had to burrow her way to the surface. Allie kept burrowing, kept moving. Her arms and legs stiffened into the rhythm of it. Choking on the frozen air, Allie pushed on, kept dragging her exhausted body upwards. Up towards the summit. Up towards the cabin.

She had to banish all thoughts of Diana to the back of her mind. Because when she thought about her the tunnel quaked, at risk of collapsing. Allie endured the lashing of the wind, ignored its cackle as it blew past her. The storm doubted her commitment. It continually tried to drive her back, tried to take her towards Diana, but Allie's resolve was strong. Allie was a warrior. She wore her war wounds on her body, across her heart. Releasing a scream, she dared the storm to stop her, dared it to try to keep her cowering in the snow. Because she was going to get back. She was going to reach the cabin and then, with Gail, she would journey down to where Diana had fallen and they'd hoist her back up.

'You can't stop me,' Allie told the wind. 'I won't let you.'

'How did you do it?' Emily's hands rested atop the swollen mound of her pregnant stomach. From the neck down she was perfectly serene and maternal. But in her eyes there was too much movement, the way her gaze flitted between Allie and the surrounding living room.

'Do what?' Allie placed her mug of tea back down upon its coaster and fought to hold in a yawn. It had been a long day. Just four hours ago she had been in London amid the throb of activity in Euston Station with Lucas at her side.

'Are you sure you're okay to go on your own?' It was the third time he'd asked the question since they'd left the flat.

'Yeah, I'm fine, it's just a train journey.'

'Because I could go with you if you want.'

'I thought you had a deadline on your script.'

'I do.' His hands were on her shoulders as he looked down at her. Allie noticed the way passing heads turned in her husband's direction, almost involuntarily. He surpassed six feet in height and had thick, chestnut-brown hair which had been curly in his youth but was now straight and forced into a stylish forward flick. She knew too well how easily he cast a spell on all who he met. 'But I could work on the train. I could—'

'It's a girly catch-up, just me and Em. You'd be a third wheel.'

This made his mouth lift into a half-smile, the slightest impression of a dimple appearing in his cheek. 'True.'

'Honestly, I'm fine.' She stretched up to kiss his cheek. His smile widened.

'Okay then, but say hi to her for me, and text me when you get there.'

'I will.'

'And just think, next time it could be you.'

'Huh?' Allie had been looking up at the departure board. She turned back to him, puzzled. 'What could be me?'

'Pregnant.' He swept forward and kissed her hard on the lips. 'I mean, we've been trying. It could happen anytime for us.'

Allie stepped back from him, pressing a hand to his chest and straightening out her arm. 'Yeah, totally. Anytime.'

'Allie?' Emily was waiting patiently on her response but now the agitation from her face had crept into her voice.

'Sorry.' She shook her head and this time allowed her mouth to widen with a yawn. 'Travelling kind of wiped me out. What were you asking?'

'How you did it,' Emily repeated. 'How you kept going when things were . . . were hard. When you were scared.'

'Oh.' Allie quickly reached again for her mug, needing something to hold on to. 'I mean . . .'

'I know I've no right to ask.' Emily smoothed her hands across her stomach, but there wasn't anything tender about her movements. As she caressed her large bump, she grew tense, protective. 'And if you'd rather not answer that's fine but . . . I suppose I'm just wondering.'

'Are you scared about having the twins?'

'Yes.' Emily permitted herself to laugh nervously, a delicate, soft sound which so suited the home she'd made for herself which was all plush, expensive fabrics and scented candles. 'I'm bloody terrified. I'm scared of having them, I'm scared of . . .' Finally she lifted a hand from her belly to twirl the diamond-encrusted wedding band upon her ring finger. It caught the late afternoon sunlight, winking seductively like a star. 'I'm scared of all of it,' she admitted with the release of a long breath.

'Well . . .' Allie tightened her grip against her mug, felt the warmth from the contents within pass into her fingertips. When she returned to London, Lucas would be waiting for her, grinning excitedly and talking through their plans for the impending weekend. He always liked to have plans, to be looking ahead. 'I guess I did it because I had no choice, I just had to keep going, even though it was hard.'

'No choice,' Emily repeated, nodding her head and twirling her glittering band faster and faster so that the sparkle became a blur of light. 'Yes, yes I get that.'

'Sometimes you just have to keep going. It's keep going or just stop altogether. And no one wants to stop, everyone wants to keep moving one way or another.'

Thirty-Nine

Stumbling forward, Allie noticed that the ground beneath her feet was no longer quite so steep. Head bowed she moved on, boots sinking into snow. Glancing up, she thought for a second that she was hallucinating. Was she actually currently slumped beneath a tree further down the mountain, slowly freezing to death, her mind trying to take her somewhere familiar for her final moments? Allie blinked, but the scene before her remained. It was no mirage.

Ahead of her, at the top of a short hill, stood the cabin. No light radiated out from it, but it looked tall and proud with its wooden walls and snow-capped roof. She doubted if she'd ever seen a more welcome sight.

The wind sang off-key. It whistled through the trees, picking up some of the snow from their overloaded branches and scattered it across the mountainside. Allie was on her knees. She knew that this was the last push, but her body was refusing to cooperate. Everything felt numb, had been claimed by the cold.

'Come . . . on,' she urged herself onwards with what little breath remained in her burning lungs and clambered to her feet. She awkwardly cut a path through the snow, making for the front door of the cabin.

There were no lights. The absence of light needled at her, but not enough to slow her progress. No welcoming glow bled out from the windows or from beneath the door. The cabin was a slave to shadows, just like the rest of the mountain. Pushing open the door, Allie stepped inside. No warmth greeted her. No flickering candlelight lingered to guide her through the darkness. Glass crunched underfoot and Allie tensed, twisting her neck to look at the nearest window. A tree branch sagged through a fresh hole in the glass. Two flimsy pieces of wood bordered it, clearly having failed at keeping the elements out.

'Shit.' Allie surveyed the damage. The storm had broken into the cabin. There was no light. No fire. Where were the others? Opening her mouth, Allie was about to call out for them when something silenced her.

It echoed through the cabin with brutal clarity. The sound turned Allie's heart to glass. It sounded like a car backfiring. Only it couldn't be.

Which meant that it was a gunshot.

Standing near the doorway, Allie's body tried to break itself in two. A part of her instinctively wanted to run, wanted to sprint back out into the cold and take her chances out there. But another, stronger, part of her knew she owed it to her friends to investigate. They might still be in the cabin, though it was looking less and less likely. The building was just an icy shell of what it had been.

There were no further gunshots, but the sound had sunk deep into Allie and reverberated through her bones. Summoning up what was left of her dwindling store of courage, Allie clenched her hands into fists and crept deeper into the cabin.

Forty

Officer: So you heard a gunshot?

POI: Yes.

Officer: Can you be certain?

POI: I mean I was there, in the cabin. I'm pretty certain I heard it.

Officer: Only pretty certain? Not completely certain?

POI: I was . . . things were . . . loose. I don't know. I was exhausted. I remember hearing it. But . . .

Officer: But?

POI: I don't know. I'm struggling to trust my memory. It was like being in a dream.

Officer: Did you see who fired the shot?

POI: No, I only heard the first shot.

Officer: So you can't say who fired the gun?

POI: No, I can't.

Officer: And the second shot?

POI: Everything was happening so quickly . . .

Officer: Were there multiple shots?

POI: You already know the answer to that.

Forty-One

Allie froze in the darkness, every nerve electrified as she waited for whoever had fired the gun to hear her, to burst through the shadows and shoot again. The wind whined through the broken windows and the walls creaked.

Allie waited.

One breath. Then another. Her blood was roaring so loud in her ears it was almost blocking out the storm.

Everything was tight. Her hands were fists. Her shoulders raised. Her body coiled like a spring about to be released.

She strained to hear over her own anxious heartbeat, over the soundtrack of the storm, but no additional gunshot came, no footsteps thundered towards her. Exhaling nervously, she forced herself to hurry on.

Allie was on the staircase, taking the steps two at a time. All her exhaustion had burned off and now she was just exhilarated, fuelled by the adrenaline being pumped into her system. It made her feel wild. And nervous. Like stage fright laced with a terrifying sickness. Allie wanted to just explode, to spread herself across the cabin as much as she could because her body suddenly felt too small. There was too much energy, too much fear for one skeleton to carry.

The cold followed Allie up the stairs. From the small landing, she saw that the bedroom door was open. Without thinking, she hurried through it and then stopped. There was a sudden ringing in her ears as her body turned to stone.

Gail stood with her back to Allie and Stacie was beside the bed, arms raised, palms exposed. 'Jesus Christ,' she rasped, seemingly unaware of Allie's arrival. 'What the fuck, Gail, like seriously, what the fuck?'

'I said step away from her.' Gail growled the order with such venom that Allie felt the hairs on her arms prickle.

'Look I—'

'Away from the bed, *now*!'

'What's going on?' Allie stepped over the threshold into the room. Stacie shot her a panicked look, but Gail remained rigidly in place.

'Ask her.' Not moving her arms, Stacie nodded manically at Gail. 'She's the one who brought a fucking gun in here.'

Allie stepped deeper into the room and cautiously moved around Gail. Sure enough her friend was holding a shotgun, its barrel aimed at Stacie's chest. The sight of it caused Allie to whimper. 'Gail?' She had to strain to whisper her friend's name. 'Gail, what is going on? W-why do you have a gun?'

Still Gail remained perfectly erect, as though her spine had been fused with cement. Her eyes never left Stacie, a hunter stalking her prey. Allie could almost taste the fear in the air, it was clotting and thick. Gail's finger grazed the trigger of the gun. Her expertise was visible in her stance – the way she could hold the weapon without wavering even slightly.

'Gail!' Allie had to shout to be heard over the fury of the wind which rattled at the walls of the cabin. 'Gail, what the hell?'

Her friend blinked once. Twice. But still, the gun did not move. 'I heard her,' Gail spoke slowly, her voice was level as the barrel was directed towards Stacie's chest. 'I heard everything she said. And like I told Stacie – I'm going to turn her in. She won't get away with this.'

'Get away with what?' Allie's fingertips tingled as sensation slowly began to return to them.

'I heard her! Heard her talking to Emily. Asking her about . . . about that *prick*. Heard her admitting that she'd taken her medicine, had binned her insulin back at the airport.'

Allie baulked. 'Wh-what?' Beside the bed, Stacie's head was thrashing back and forth, arms still raised.

'She's . . . she's lying. I didn't—'

'*I heard you!*' Gail's usually calm exterior had been shattered. 'You were taunting Emily, asking her about that damn summer and that awful party. Don't pretend you didn't know, Stacie. That's why you did this, that's why you took her meds!'

Party.

Diana had spoken of that party. Allie could feel pieces of some sick puzzle slowly slotting into place. Flexing her fingers, she reached out a hand to Gail, to the gun. 'Whatever Stacie did, this isn't the way to solve it.'

'She tried to kill Emily.' The barrel of the gun lowered, just a fraction, as Gail spoke against a sob. 'She did this on purpose, binning her insulin. She's finally snapped, finally gone too far.'

'It . . . it was an accident, like I said,' Stacie whispered pleadingly, edging herself closer to Allie with tiny, shuffling steps. 'I just wanted to scare her, that's all. I figured she'd have some spare in her suitcase and—'

'Why can't you let it go?' Gail demanded, gripping the gun with a renewed force so that Stacie resumed being frozen in place. 'All these years, Stacie. Why hold on to it? Why hold on to *him*?'

'Why lie?!' Stacie raged, nostrils flaring as she stared down both the gun and Gail. 'You're right, it's been years. So why keep lying to me?'

'No one lied to you!'

'No one told me the truth, either, isn't that as bad?'

Stacie edged back and a small handheld mirror crunched underfoot, debris from when Emily's handbag had earlier been emptied. The mirror cracked into three shards and Stacie glanced down at her fractured reflection and then kicked it away, banishing it to beneath the bed.

'Stacie, don't test me,' Gail hissed through clenched teeth.

Allie was between her friends, a flimsy barrier in their battle. She reached out a hand to each of them, trying to create some sort of bridge. 'Look, let's all just calm down. Is Emily okay? Let's just take a second, take a breath and—'

'I'm turning you in,' Gail seethed, looking over Allie at Stacie. 'This time you've gone too far. You won't get away with this.'

'Look, let's see what Allie thinks. You don't get to be judge, jury and executioner here, Gail. Wait.' Stacie began lowering her hands, cocking her head at Allie with bird-like interest. 'You're alone?'

The question hung in the air for several seconds. Allie looked between her friends, at the darkened barrel of the gun.

'Where's Diana?' Gail latched on to the enquiry, her gaze flicking over to Allie for barely a second.

'She . . .'

'Yes, Allie, where is Diana?' Stacie seconded. Allie swallowed against the bile which now lined her throat. The truth was so terrible, so awful. She'd left the cabin as a duo and returned alone. And without help. She'd failed.

'Diana . . . she . . .' Allie wasn't sure she could find the words.

'Is she downstairs?' Gail was speaking quickly, shoulders still square as the gun remained trained on Stacie. 'Because the wind blew all the windows in, she'll freeze down there. Bring her up here.'

'I can't.'

'Why the hell not?' Gail was several shades past annoyed. Clenching her jaw she permitted herself a longer glance over at Allie. Her eyebrows lifted fractionally as she took in her friend's ghostly appearance. 'This isn't the time for games, Allie. Where is Diana?' she asked the question slowly, carefully.

'She fell.' Allie hated the truth which dripped from her lips, hated the way it twisted the expression on Gail's face to something between despair and disbelief.

'She *fell*?'

'Out on the mountainside. We took the wrong route down, the more dangerous one and there was a ledge and she was ahead of me and she just . . .' Allie had been speaking quickly, running her words together, but she suddenly stopped as though crashing against a verbal brick wall. 'She fell.' Her conclusion was breathy, panicked.

'Is she okay?' Gail frowned and cleared her throat before proceeding. 'Where is she? We need to go and help her. Tell us where she is.'

Allie could feel the heat of her tears upon her chapped cheeks. They burned against her raw skin. 'No.'

'Why not? Allie, if she fell, she needs our help.'

'We can't help her. She's . . .' Allie squeezed her eyes shut and breathed in deeply, but her lungs still felt empty and dry. 'She's past saving.'

'And you dare point the gun at me!' Stacie darted an extra foot away from the bed. Now she was shoulder to shoulder with Allie, staring at Gail. 'I never meant to hurt anyone. Here is your real criminal, Gail, here is the one you should be threatening.'

'What?' Allie yelped, flinching at the vitriol in Stacie's statement. 'No, she fell. It was an accident. I didn't—'

'You read the book.' Stacie was talking directly to Gail. 'You know how Allie feels about Diana. And we all know why Lucas must have left, and how Allie would blame Diana for that too.'

'I—'

'Is that true?' Eagle sharp, Gail's gaze was back on Allie.

There was a pause of a second, a moment, and Stacie seized it. She sprung forward, hands extended and reached for the gun. Gail reacted, turning both herself and the gun out of Stacie's reach but she wasn't fast enough. Soon four hands were on its hilt, battling for possession. Allie screamed for her friends to stop. The echo of the initial shot was still in her ears. The gun was loaded, dangerous.

Stacie's cheeks grew pink as she tightened her grip, refusing to submit. 'I did . . . nothing . . . wrong,' she panted as the shotgun slid perilously close to being in her possession. 'It was an accident.'

'Just put the gun down!' Allie shouted.

A shot boomed in response to her demand. The sound was so sudden, so shocking, that it knocked the air from her lungs. Gasping, she struggled to recover. Her ears hummed to a pitched frequency as her heart beat an erratic rhythm.

'Just . . .' She had to remind herself to breathe, to focus. And then she saw Gail. 'No.' The word left her as she dropped to her knees. 'No, no, no.'

Gail crumpled to the floor as though she were made of paper, hands desperately pawing at her chest out of which a river of blood ran out. With wide, pleading eyes she glanced up at Allie as she spat out a mouthful of crimson.

'No!' Allie reached out and grabbed her, thrust her hands against her friend's chest, felt the warm pulse of her even through her gloves. 'Gail, it's okay, you're all right.'

'She should have just given me the gun.' Stacie was speaking from somewhere behind her but Allie didn't look up. 'If only she'd . . . she'd listened to me. I didn't mean to hurt Emily I only—'

'Go and get some towels! Bandages! Something!' Allie cried. There was blood everywhere. It had soaked through her gloves and was pooling beneath Gail on the floor, darkening the exposed wooden boards.

'A-Allie.' Gail's entire body twitched and her hands kept grasping for her chest, fingers shaking as they became drenched in her own glossy blood.

'I'm here.' Allie was pressing against the hole in her friend's chest with all the force left within her. 'Gail, I'm here, it's going to be all right. Just stay with me, okay? Stacie!' she screamed at her other friend. 'Fucking help me! Help me!'

Stacie didn't move. She remained on her feet, staring down at the grim scene as all colour drained from her face, lips limply twitching but forming no words.

'Stacie! Fuck!'

'It's such a fucking mess,' Stacie eventually panted, eyes wide and bloodshot. 'I didn't mean to shoot her. The gun it . . . it just went off.'

'I . . . I know.' Allie didn't want to comprehend what was happening. She kept hoping she'd find herself back on the mountainside resting against a tree and delirious from the cold. Where was the cabin she'd left, the one filled with candlelight and the glow of a warming fire? Gail was coughing, blood spluttering upon her lips, shining in the dim light like precious rubies.

'Just . . . just hang in there,' Allie begged. She could already feel her friend's pulse slowing beneath her hands, yet Gail kept gasping like a fish pulled out from a river, desperately trying to endure its final moments. 'It's going to be fine, just fine, just hang on, okay? Stacie, we need to stay calm, I need you to help me, okay?'

Blood. There was too much of it. Allie could see that. She looked into Gail's eyes, but her gaze was flat and growingly increasingly vacant.

'Stacie, don't just stand there! Help me!'

'I . . . I didn't mean . . .' There was a tremor within Stacie's words which extended to the hands holding the gun, causing the weapon to rattle. 'I was just trying to get the gun and . . .'

'I *know*, okay? Reasons don't matter anymore. What matters is helping Gail.'

If it were Allie on the floor, Gail would be springing into action, barking orders and taking charge.

'Stacie! For God's sake, move, help me!'

'She's dead.'

'What, Stacie, no, there's still time. Help me!'

'Emily. Gail. They're both gone.'

'Jesus, Stacie, just help me just—' Allie looked down again at Gail as the blood pouring from her chest began to pump more slowly, a river becoming a stream. Gail's cheeks had paled and grown glossy as though made of porcelain. And in her eyes – in her wide, knowledgeable eyes – there was only emptiness.

'No!' Allie barely registered the sting of her tears as she flung off her gloves and grabbed Gail's wrist, manically searching for a pulse. Her friend was cold. And still. 'No! This can't be happening.' She began pressing the heels of her hands against Gail's brutalised chest. As the blood settled beneath her, the extent of her wound was beginning to become more apparent. But Allie wouldn't look at it, wouldn't acknowledge what had happened. 'Gail, come on, it's going to be okay.'

Pressure. She kept applying pressure to Gail's chest. Isn't that what you're supposed to do? When that failed to bring her friend back, she turned towards to Stacie with fire on her tongue. 'Towels!' she ordered. 'Go and get some, now! We need to stop the bleeding.'

'Get up.' Stacie's words were ghostly, detached.

'Towels,' Allie repeated, resuming the task of pumping Gail's chest. 'Get some towels or at least pass me the duvet.' Her clothes were soaked with blood, its warmth a woeful caress against her frozen body. When she didn't hear footsteps behind her she shouted again – 'Towels!'

'I said get up.'

This time when Allie turned, she noticed that Stacie had raised the gun, her stance stoic. And the barrels were pointing down at Allie who was crouched on the floor and elbow-deep in Gail's rusting blood.

Death was so impossibly final. Allie could feel the weight of it creeping into the room, applying pressure as though they were now standing at the bottom of the sea. Still, her lungs ached as her anxiety squeezed against them, turning each breath into a gasp.

'Just, just help me,' she placated slowly, lifting her hands and willing them to cease quaking as she struggled to her feet. 'We can still save Gail. Everything is going to be okay, I swear. Is Emily all right, can we just—'

'You're too late.' Stacie was frantically shaking her head. 'You've not brought help. You're too late.'

'You don't know that.' Allie was glancing back at Gail and thinking of Diana. She willed her freshly fallen friend to move, repeating the same plea internally as she had done out on the mountainside, but Gail was just as frozen as Diana had been.

'Diana was supposed to come back.' Stacie's words were gaining strength. 'She was supposed to come back. With you. But she hasn't.'

'Stacie, I can explain, let's just—'

'You made your own mess, out there on the mountain.'

'Stacie, let's just take a minute to—'

'It wasn't supposed to be like this. I just wanted to scare her.'

'What? Why?'

'You know why.'

'Stacie, you're not making sense.' Allie felt her muscles tightening with fear.

'Everyone knew but me.'

'*Knew* what?'

'But this summer I found out about it all. And I knew I'd make her pay.'

'Emily? Pay for what?' Allie sensed the loaded presence of the shotgun without looking directly at it. The weapon had the potential to do so much more than just scare someone, Gail was already a tragic testament to that.

'Her lies, her whole life was built on them.'

'Did you want to . . . hurt Emily?' Allie heard the tremor in her voice.

Stacie threw her head back and forth in agitation. 'No! Not like this. It was a prank. A way to make her realise she couldn't . . . shouldn't keep lying. A fucking prank.' A shudder rippled through her body. Her head was still bowed, but her shoulders were squaring as she regained her composure. 'I was just . . .' She inhaled deeply and briefly regained her composure. 'He died because of her. You know that, don't you?'

'Ollie?' Allie felt herself frown.

'The rumours. They were too much. And he . . .' Stacie blinked rapidly, chest rising and falling against her internal sorrow. 'You get it . . .' Black streaks of mascara swept down her pale cheeks as her body shook. 'You know what it is to hate someone for what they took away from you. That's why you did it. You killed her. You killed Diana.'

'No.' Now it was Allie's turn to shake. 'No, no, Stace I didn't. She fell.'

'She *fell*?' Iron coated Stacie's words. Allie sensed the situation moving in a dangerous direction, her senses hummed with the threat of it all. Taking a tentative step back from Gail's body she spun round and eyed the door. 'Do you know how fucking pathetic that sounds as an excuse?'

'Emily . . .' Allie was nodding at the bed. 'Is she all right? Have you checked her have you—'

'Of course, she's not fucking all right!' As Stacie's tears flowed freely, she wilted like a neglected flower, the gun lowering in her grip. 'Why do you think Gail came in here like she did? Emily . . . she . . . she lost consciousness. I wanted to scare her, that's all! Make her pay for what she did. Now she's going to die up here and no one will believe I didn't mean to kill her!'

'I believe you.' But Allie could hear the doubt in her own voice. Stacie had shot Gail, was now aiming a gun at her, it was hardly a stretch to believe that she'd also intentionally tried to kill Emily.

But there was still time. There had to be. Allie could run back down the mountain, try to find the way down to the river, to the little village at the base. All could surely not be lost already. Gail's pulse might just be so weak she'd been unable to find it and all Emily needed was her insulin.

'Stace, we can still save them.'

'And Diana, can she be saved?'

'I . . . I don't think so. We accidently took the . . . the most dangerous route down the mountain.' Allie's explanation became a waterfall; gushing and fast as she kept advancing towards the door, having every intention of leaving. 'I didn't see it happen, but she fell . . . she fell down the cliff and landed on a . . . a ledge.'

Stacie's words came like a whip, 'And you just *left* her there?'

'No.' Allie fiercely shook her head. 'I mean, yes.' Her words were failing her. She mentally envisioned her sprint through the cabin, towards the front door and out into the icy embrace of the storm. Help. She needed to get help.

She could stay. But something feral was guiding her limbs, urging her to make haste and leave. Gail had been shot and her killer was now aiming that same gun at her. It was no longer safe in the cabin. Help was at the bottom of the mountain. If she could just get there . . . but if she failed again, they'd all be doomed. She'd freeze out in the snow, Emily would never awaken and Gail . . . she was gone. Allie needed to save who she could. Who was left. And Stacie . . . would she freeze to death too?

She needed a clear head. Her feet were guiding her out of the room. She needed to do what Gail would – needed to take command of the situation while she still could. Taking an uneven breath, Allie paused in the doorway and turned back towards the bedroom and stared down at her friend. 'Diana fell and I think she . . . it was instant. There was a lot of blood and her neck was twisted at a terrible angle.'

Stacie was now standing over Gail, the shotgun in her hands, aiming it squarely at Allie's chest.

Allie had to keep reminding herself how to breathe, that everything was fine; the situation was still under control.

She was just carefully and calmly explaining what had happened to Diana. But the words became barbs in her mouth and they pricked her tongue and throat, piercing her so sharply that she began to wonder if the blood she could taste in the air was Gail's or her own.

'Stacie, I really think she died.' She breathily gave her conclusion. 'I came back up here to get . . .' She blinked rapidly, her gaze barely daring to leave the tip of the shotgun's single dark cylinder.

'To get some ropes and climbing equipment and—'

'So that's your story, you're saying Diana *fell*?' Stacie peered at Allie down the barrel of her gun. Her stance wavered, like a weak sapling in a rugged wind.

'Yes, yes she fell,' Allie gushed. 'I didn't see it happen but' – her hands reached for the base of her spine – 'I heard it.' She pushed hard against her back and felt nothing.

The scream. It was a blade that would only grow sharper with time. It continued to slice through Allie, to tear her in two.

'So you're telling me that Diana fell? That the mountain was treacherous enough for her fall to be fatal and yet you've made it back up here without a scratch on you?'

'She fell. Yes. That's right. And I . . . I came back here to get help.'

'You see, the thing is, Allie Bear,' Stacie's eyes narrowed as they darkened. 'I don't believe you.'

Forty-Two

'How can you not believe me?' Allie was somehow managing to hold in her tears. She couldn't look down at Gail again because if she did, she knew she would fall apart, shatter like a vase that had been knocked to the ground. 'Diana *fell*. There was nothing I could do. We need to stop arguing and help Gail.' She hiccuped against the painful realisation that Gail was already beyond saving. 'Help Emily,' she sputtered, as hot tears warmed her icy cheeks.

'So you came back here rather than continuing to find your way down the mountain?' Stacie didn't seem to care about her friends in the room, only the ones beyond it.

'The storm it . . . it got worse.' The wind rattled against the walls as though corroborating Allie's story. 'Diana had the map and I knew if I came here I could get rope and climbing boots and . . .' She looked at the bed. A pit opened up beneath her as she realised that Emily hadn't moved the entire time she had been in the room. Not even the flutter of a ragged breath had escaped from her lips. 'Emily? Is she okay? When was she last awake?'

'Did you find help?'

'What? Um . . .' Allie wanted to go to the bed, to pull back the sheets and check on Emily but the gun was still on her, holding her in place. 'No. I came back up after Diana fell, but we set off the flares.'

'Oh, the flares,' Stacie repeated in a mocking voice. 'Good job you set them off. Someone is *bound* to see them through all this snow.'

'You don't know that they won't.'

'And you don't know that they will.'

'I need to check on Emily.' Allie boldly approached the bed. 'When was she last awake? Stacie, answer me, please.'

'Don't do that.' The tip of the gun followed her movements, shadowing her. There was something desperate in Stacie's voice, something raw. Allie paused, the duvet within her bare hands, poised to draw it back.

'We need to check on her.' She could do this. She'd managed to be strong even when her body was weak and she needed her strength now more than ever.

'No one's coming, we're all alone up here.'

Allie steeled herself, hating the sensation of guilt that was now grating against her, trying to tear the flesh from her bones.

'Someone might have seen the flares.'

'You're too late, we've failed.' Stacie's voice was a dejected wail through the room. 'Emily is gone and now so is Gail. And Diana too. What have we done?'

Bowing towards the bed, Allie clenched the duvet within her hands. This couldn't be happening. There was no way that three of her friends were dead. It was just impossible. She needed her friends to exist. They were all points on the same star. Without them she was just drifting. Alone.

'Step away from the bed and tell me what really happened to Diana.'

'I've told you.' Allie ground her teeth together.

'I want the truth.'

'She fell.' Her tears burst their banks and powered down her cheeks. 'She fucking fell, Stacie, and it was awful.

249

She's down there on some ledge and . . .' Staggering back from the bed Allie pressed her hand to her temple. She was breathing too hard. Too fast. The walls felt like they were closing in on her.

'It's just you and me now.' Stacie's eyes were wide and fearful as she navigated the knife-edge of terror that she was standing on. 'So stop with the games and tell me the truth.'

'I *am*. Stacie, you've got to believe me. She *fell*.'

'You see.' Strengthening her grip on the gun Stacie regarded her with cold intensity. 'The issue I have with your version of events is that they don't add up. And they don't add up because I know.'

'Know what?'

'Everything.' The word entered the room like a grenade. 'Allie, I know everything.'

The ice in the air was now flowing through Allie's veins, cutting her. Her heart pulsated painfully in her chest as she stared at Stacie, seeing grief swirled with madness in her friend's eyes.

'What? What are you talking about?'

'Like I said, I know everything.' The gun remained angled at Allie's chest. All it would take was one shot, one squeeze of the trigger and she'd join Gail on the floor, eyes frozen open.

'What does that even *mean*?'

'You kept looking at that door. Kept waiting for her to show.'

'Stacie, what are—'

'Not once did she visit you in hospital. How can you *not* hate her for that?'

The question was an axe. Allie gasped as it plunged into her chest, causing her to stagger backwards. Frigid air was trapped in her lungs. She couldn't breathe. Couldn't move.

'You fell for *her*. You lost your choice to be a mother, for *her*. And she abandoned you.'

Clenching her hands at her sides Allie managed to find her voice. 'Look . . .' She squeezed her eyes shut, savouring the moment of seclusion the darkness afforded her.

'You had every right to be mad at her,' Stacie continued, relaxing her hold on the gun. 'Every damn right.'

'Wh-what?' The ice was invading every part of Allie. It was trying to bring her to her knees. Her teeth gnashed together as a tremor rippled through her bones.

'God knows that I'd have been furious. Beyond furious.'

'Stacie—'

'I *saw* it in your eyes, Allie. Every damn day. She betrayed you, should have come to visit, been at your side.' Stacie shook her head in woeful dismay. 'And then Lucas leaves, because you can't have children, right? We all know about what happened in the hospital after your fall, about the emergency hysterectomy. I mean, it's why Jasper left. You told us that. And history likes to repeat itself, doesn't it? Which leads your trail of pain and misery right back to Diana. Of course you hate her. I'd hate her for denying me that choice. The choice to be a mother. It's okay, Allie, you don't need to say it, you never did, but I've always understood how you must hate her.'

'N-no.'

'So when you two were out on the mountainside, finally alone together, you had all these thoughts pounding in your head, making it a struggle to even hear yourself think. You saw a chance to settle an old score and you took it. This time when she fell you didn't reach out to save her; instead, you gave her the nudge she needed.'

'What, no, I didn't. I'd never—'

'I'd have pushed her heartless arse off a ledge too. She should have been there for you, been by your side.' Stacie's gaze slid towards the bed. 'Seems we all felt like we had old scores to settle.'

Allie surged towards the door.

Fight or flight.

She chose flight.

Her limbs exploded into a sprint as she powered towards the open door, determined to flee. She was almost out, one foot on the small landing when the barrel of the gun pressed sharply into her back. Just up from the base of her spine, where she still retained enough feeling to recognise the sensation and freeze.

'I didn't say you could leave.' Stacie's voice was colder than the ice which gathered around them. Panting, Allie watched her breath fog before her. A hand clasped her shoulder and she allowed herself to be guided back into the bedroom. What else could she do? If she ran, the storm would claim her. That or a bullet to the back. She swayed uneasily when she knocked against Gail's feet.

'Did you mean to kill her?' Allie turned, her question barely a gasp upon her lips. Stacie blinked back tears and then looked away from her.

'Are you asking about Emily?'

It was snowing in London. Delicate flakes pirouetted outside the window of Allie's flat, twirling their way towards the street below. The flames of the little electric fire across from the sofa danced as Allie sat curled against a plump silver cushion, a heavy book open in her lap.

'You staying in tonight?' Lucas's keys jangled as he slid them into his trouser pocket. He wore a navy suit, hair slicked back and jawline freshly shaven. Allie sunk back against the pillow, feeling woefully underdressed in her joggers and fleece hoody.

'I figured I'd catch up on some reading.' She casually turned the page in her book, keen to have her husband leave so that she could get well and truly lost in the story.

'It's Saturday night.'

Allie rolled her eyes as he stated the obvious.

'Why don't you ever make plans with your friends?' Lucas was doubling back towards the sofa, bringing with him a thick cloud of cologne. With a resigned sigh, Allie marked her page and closed her book, letting her palms gently rest atop its embossed cover. 'Stacie lives in London, right? Why don't you give her a call?' Lucas sat down on the far end of the sofa and scanned her face. Allie blushed at the scrutiny, knowing that he was searching for something she wouldn't let him find. 'I don't like how you sit home alone every night. It's not healthy. Where are your friends, Allie?'

He might as well have grabbed a steak knife from the kitchen drawer and come and wedged it between Allie's ribs. Somehow she managed to smile sweetly at him. 'You know how it is, life gets in the way. Husbands' – she paused and pulled her smile even tighter – 'kids.'

'But you guys were thick as thieves back when we met,' Lucas insisted, a crease forming between his eyebrows as his face became marked with concern. 'What was it you called yourselves? The Fierce Five?'

'I still see them.' Allie began to tightly grip the edge of her book. 'Barely.'

'I see them plenty.' Why was she lying? Was she trying to convince Lucas or herself that everything was fine in her friendship?

'Allie.' He placed his hand on her leg, his voice tender. 'I'm just worried about you, sweetheart. You spend all week holed up here alone and then at the weekends you just sit and read and—'

'I like my own company.' There was too much snap in her response, but Lucas didn't seem deterred.

'I know that, Allie, but still. You hardly ever see your best friends anymore and it worries me. That's all.'

Allie ground her teeth, internally ordering the tears which were gathering behind her eyes to go back where they'd come from. What did Lucas want her to say?

I've drifted away from my friends.

They've all but forgotten about me.

It used to be that an hour wouldn't go by without her hearing from one of them. Now it could be days, even weeks before someone would respond to a text or email. She had become an afterthought, an echo from their childhood they seemed to prefer not to listen to.

'Isn't Diana still in the city? Why don't you give her a call?'

Because she won't pick up.

Nothing casual happened between them anymore. Every reunion had to be a pre-ordained appointment arranged via invitations with gilded lettering.

'I mean, it's snowing.' Lucas gestured towards the window. 'Allie, you love the snow. Why don't I hold off meeting Mike and the guys for a while and we'll walk around in it together for a bit? What do you say?'

Hold off for a while.

Allie almost snorted. Of course Lucas wouldn't cancel his plans entirely. He was concerned about her, but not that much. He had his own life to live. His own friendships to maintain. 'Go.' She flicked her hand towards the ruby-red door to their flat. 'Really, I'm fine.'

'Call Diana then,' Lucas urged as he stood up. 'Or Stacie. I just don't want you to always be so alone.'

He left a few minutes later. Allie reopened her book and stared down at the words on the page which no longer made sense to her. She could barely make out any of the letters through her tears. They splashed against the page, wet and angry.

Forty-Three

'Yes, I'm asking about Emily! Stacie, what the hell is going on here?' Crouching down, Allie carefully cradled Gail's head and shoulders in her arms, willing her friend to open her eyes, to come back to them.

'We don't have time for this.' Stacie was still holding the gun. 'If help doesn't come soon then we need to figure out what to do.'

Gail's blood still held a fragile hint of warmth. Allie shuddered as it coated her hands, sank into her clothes. A river of tears ran down her cheeks.

'Why? Christ, Stacie, why? Why did you shoot her?' Allie demanded between sobs.

'I didn't!' Stacie countered emphatically. She stood just inches from Gail's body, between her fallen friend and the bed, the gun clutched in both hands and angled at Allie. 'I mean, it just fucking happened when I reached for the gun. You saw! I didn't do it on purpose! She should never have threatened me like she did, maybe then I wouldn't have felt like I had to defend myself!' Stacie was panting heavily, her chest swelling and then falling at a frantic pace. 'Why did you push Diana?' she gasped.

'I've told you I didn't push her! What did Gail ever do to you? She's your *friend*, Stacie, how could you do this? She was just trying to protect Emily.' Allie wished Gail didn't feel so cold and limp in her arms. Wished she had never returned to the cabin. If she'd kept descending the mountain, she might have happened upon the little houses at its base. She should have kept going, should have hammered upon the green door until her hands bled. If she'd reached the satellite phone, help would definitely be coming. Instead . . .

'I didn't mean to shoot her.' Yet Stacie stood clutching the shotgun, the guilty article still in her possession.

'When I left, everything was okay here and I come back and . . .' Allie couldn't even find the words to describe what she had returned to. It was like leaving a chick flick and stumbling onto the set of a horror movie. Only this was her life. This was *real*. Her stomach reeled with the horrendous enormity of it all. 'Why did you do it, Stacie?'

'See, you think I'm to blame, that this is all my fault. Fuck.' Stacie's lips curled with internalised contempt. 'Maybe it *is* all my fault.'

Allie traced a finger along Gail's cheek as her entire body shook with grief. But this wasn't the time to mourn. Nor the place. She needed to stay in control. Several of her tears dropped onto Gail's pale skin. Allie bundled up her pain, pushed it down deep into her gut and breathed deeply to control the freight-train tempo of her heart.

'And what about Emily?' After bending down to kiss the tip of her nose and carefully lowering Gail against the ground, Allie scrambled to her feet, almost slipping in all the spilled blood. 'Emily is the best of us all.' She approached the bed, aware that the gun was tracing her every step.

'I know I shouldn't have taken her insulin.'

Allie was handling the duvet, preparing to draw it back. Her gaze snapped towards Stacie as her voice dropped, 'But you did.'

'At the airport . . .' Stacie squared her shoulders and made herself as tall as possible as though preparing for a fight. 'I did it in haste, it was a mistake, a huge fucking mistake. I just wanted to teach her a lesson, scare her a bit. She'd been so smug about Adam and the twins and I . . . I snapped.'

'You snapped?'

'That life . . . her life . . . it should have been me and Ollie. We were supposed to be forever, we were supposed to have the big house, kids.'

'Look, Stacie, being jealous isn't—'

'I'm not *jealous*, Allie. I'm furious. Don't you get that? Ollie died *because of her*. I lost my chance of happiness *because of her*. And she struts around like she's in a fucking fairy tale not giving a shit about the damage she caused!'

'So you took her *insulin*?' Allie whispered in angry disbelief.

'She took my dreams,' Stacie replied through gritted teeth.

'You didn't just snap,' Allie challenged. 'You planned to take her meds. You planned all this shit. The airport just offered you the opportunity you needed.'

Stacie was silent.

'She . . . she trusted you.' Allie's legs became jelly but her anger kept her rigid, kept her on her feet. 'She's your *best friend*, Stacie. How could you do that to her? You know that without her medication she risked slipping into a diabetic coma and—' Allie pulled back the duvet and sucked in a panicked breath.

Emily was in the bed, but she was so still, like a waxwork of herself. Her lips were blue and parted but no rattle of breath escaped through them.

'No, no!' Allie jumped onto the bed and huddled over Emily, leaning her ear against her friend's chest, reaching for her wrists to check for the faint throb of a pulse. But there was nothing. 'How could you do this?' Allie's tears were flowing freely as she turned on her remaining friend. 'You fucking monster. You—'

'I thought she'd have some spare insulin in her suitcase! How was I to know that all she had was in her flight bag? I never meant to hurt her, just scare her a little. That's why Gail came in with the gun because she heard me confessing to Emily and . . . and read it the wrong way.'

'Do you really hate her *that* much?' Allie demanded. 'That you'd *steal* her medication? I mean, Christ, Stacie, what the hell? I know that there's a lot of resentment between us but *this* . . .' Swiping the back of her hand across her eyes Allie staggered back from the bed.

'I blamed her.'

'Blamed her for *what*? For being happy? Ollie killed himself, remember? His death isn't on Emily.'

'Yes . . . it is.' Stacie tipped her head to the ceiling and tears pooled at the base of her eyes. 'Remember the rumours when Ollie died?'

'I . . . I guess, yeah. But that was years ago, Stacie.'

'People were talking about him, saying he'd done something awful. But no one seemed to know what. They were just speculating like bored people in small towns like to do. Emily was gone and there were whispers about something happening at the party. And I . . .' With a sob, Stacie shook her head and let some of her tears fall. 'I didn't want to hear it. Refused to hear it. And Emily wasn't talking, she was keeping all her truth to herself which meant it was easy to believe his version of events. Because if it was true, she'd have told me, right? After all, I was meant to be her best friend. So I accepted Ollie's truth over her non-existent one.'

'Which was?'

'That he'd done nothing, that what everyone was saying was lies, that Emily was just at some convent like her parents said.'

'Emily never talked about why she went away,' Allie recalled quietly. She had always accepted that Emily's absence was a deeply buried secret which they all knew better than to try and excavate. 'She never told us what happened and we never asked.'

'I *know*,' Stacie agreed with emphasis. 'But here, in the cabin, she finally told me the truth.'

'I . . .' Allie held up a hand, unsure if she was ready to hear the revelation Stacie held on her tongue.

'He was falling apart that summer, Ollie, but I refused to see it. Then you had your accident and—' She freed a hand to grasp at her throat. 'Lies. So many lies. If only we'd told each other the truth.'

'No one lied to you, Stace.'

'You all knew about Ollie. I know you did. What you said at the christening, about it being hard for Emily, that was when I knew. Really knew, that you'd all betrayed me.'

'You're being paranoid. You're fucking crazy!'

'Am I?'

Stacie snapped her gaze towards her friend, looking like a viper about to pounce.

'I didn't know about Ollie. About the party. I guess I speculated about it but then we all did. But the truth . . . shit, Stacie, it is ancient history. You hate Emily for lying? People lie all the time. Are you going to kill me too?' Allie demanded heatedly. 'Is that what this is all about? How long have you been wanting to end us all?'

'I didn't want to *end* anybody.' Stacie's anger fell away and she was sobbing. 'I'm not like you, these were accidents.

I merely wanted to scare Emily, to punish her and if . . . if she'd just been open with me in the first place, we wouldn't even be here. And Gail, she wouldn't listen when I told her it was a mistake, that I never meant to hurt anyone. You saw that.'

'I saw Gail trying to control you, trying to keep you away from Emily before you could hurt her even more.'

'*You* killed Diana in cold blood. You're the monster here. Not me!'

'No!' With one swift movement Allie leaned back and swept the duvet up over Emily's face. 'I'm not a killer, Stacie. I didn't come up here to murder anyone.'

'Yet you did.'

'No.' Allie was shaking her head, the word getting old on her lips and starting to lose its impact. 'I . . .' Her head was spinning, making her feel like she needed to throw up. Shaking, she got up off the bed, constantly aware of the gun in Stacie's grasp. 'You lashed out at Emily through jealousy, nothing else.' Allie was levelling her voice, trying to restore some calm to the situation.

'No, it was because of all the secrets,' Stacie snapped. 'She built her entire fucking life on them.'

'You're wrong.'

'How can you even defend her? When you were stuck in hospital for almost a whole year, where was she? Did she come and sit at your bedside? No! She was too busy looking after herself, protecting her secrets. If only she'd told me the truth about Ollie I'd never—' A gasp left Stacie's throat and she uttered nothing more.

'You're right. There should never have been all these secrets between us.' Allie was crying, her tears cascading down her cheeks. She didn't bother to wipe them away. They were already hardening, turning to ice. It was bitingly cold in the bedroom. The fire had died and every panicked breath she let out misted before her.

'I lashed out at Emily because I resented her like you resented Diana.' The gun rattled in Stacie's hands. She was without the protection of a coat and gloves. Her skin was as flat and white as the fallen snow outside.

'You're wrong.' Allie protectively held her hands up in front of herself. 'Diana fell. I never pushed her, it was an accident.'

'Your . . . y-your husband left because of her.'

The gun shook again and Allie used the moment to sneak in a few more steps, increasing the distance between her and Stacie. 'The only person to blame for him leaving is myself.'

'You blame Di-Diana, you—' Stacie's pale lips were stretched thin over her chattering teeth as she lost control of her speech. Turning on her heel, Allie made for the door. She no longer cared about creaking floorboards. Another chance to get away might not present itself. Stacie was freezing in the cold which meant that her trigger finger would be weak, her aim unreliable. There was only a slim chance that Allie would make it down the stairs, but it was a chance she was willing to take. She reached for the bannister, skidding across the landing, about to take the first step down when something hard connected with the back of her head. With a spluttered gasp, she stopped running and dropped to the ground. She was about to reach round and survey the damage caused by the blow when everything went black.

Forty-Four

'Time.' Gail was standing with her back to the fire, facing her four friends, her Girl Guides cap pulled low on her head. 'So often that is all that separates us from life and death.'

'I'm pretty sure we are all separated from death by time,' Diana noted philosophically, hair still the vibrant shade of pink she'd dyed it the previous week to mark her eighteenth birthday. She yawned and gave a feline stretch in her foldout chair.

'I'm being more specific,' Gail replied haughtily. 'I'm talking about what to do in an emergency. Hence this trial run.' She opened her arms and gestured to the small campsite around them. Two tents had been painstakingly erected that afternoon and a fire crackled a few feet away. Soon the girls would toast marshmallows over the flames and tell ghost stories, but not until Gail was done with her training.

'Trial run?' Stacie pulled up the hood of her bright pink bomber jacket and sank deeper into her chair. 'We're going to V Festival, Gail, not climbing Everest.'

'With some of you guys, it's one and the same.' Gail's gaze pointedly lingered on Emily who fidgeted with a loose thread on her jeans. 'We've not all camped together before. It will be a first and I think we need to be prepared.'

'No prizes for guessing who was the Girl Guide amongst us,' Diana muttered with a roll of her eyes.

'I'm trying to do you guys a favour.' Gail's hands dropped to her hips.

'What exactly do you think will happen at the festival?' Leaning forwards Diana rested her elbows on her knees, eyes narrowing with interest. 'Will we risk starvation? Exposure to the elements? No. The main thing we'll be battling is a hangover. Your Girl Guides teach you any quick fixes for that?'

'Diabetic. Back problems.' Gail listed the ailments of the group with rapid-fire militancy, pointing at the afflicted members in turn. 'If Emily or Allie encounter a problem we need to know how to act. We need to know how to buy them time.'

'They have paramedics there you know,' Stacie stated as she glanced longingly at the fire, wanting to settle around it and commence the toasting of sweet snacks.

'And I don't want to go if I'm being a burden,' Emily quickly offered.

'Me neither.' Allie hugged her arms against herself. Her parka coat wasn't quite thick enough to shield her from the lingering chill in the air. Even though it was late June a mild day had turned into a brisk evening.

'Neither of you are burdens.' Gail looked between them, eyes shining. 'Like we agreed, either we all go to the festival or no one does. All I'm doing is ensuring that once we're there we are prepared. There's nothing wrong with that.'

'We'll be prepared,' Diana noted grumpily. 'Please don't give us checklists again. My mum freaked when she saw the last one since we didn't have half the stuff on it.'

'No checklists.' Gail held her hands up in submission. 'Promise.'

'Then what's this training session for?' Stacie asked as she burrowed deeper into the fabric of her padded coat. 'My back will not forgive you for an unnecessary additional night sleeping on the ground.'

'Tonight isn't unnecessary. It's about preparation. It's about knowing what to do if Emily or Allie get hurt or sick.'

'They have paramedics there.' Stacie gritted her teeth as she repeated her objection.

'And you can't always rely on them,' Gail snapped. 'In a sea of tents, how will they find ours in time? Sometimes minutes can be the difference between life and death.'

'Emily . . .' Diana got up and went to stand beside Gail. 'You on top of your meds at the minute?'

'Uh huh.'

'You'll bring extra with you to the festival?'

'Yes.'

'And, Allie?' Diana turned to the furthest chair. 'How's the back these days?'

'Still there.'

'Great.' Diana clapped her hands together. 'So now can we finish this little training session and actually start to have some fun on our first night together beneath the stars.'

'But we're not done.' Gail was facing her friends in turn, but they were already picking up their chairs and taking their places closer to the fire. Stacie gleefully opened a huge bag of marshmallows as Emily handed out skewers. 'Fine.' Throwing up her hands in defeat Gail dropped down into her own chair in a cloud of dismay. 'I'm just trying to save you, so that you know what to do in case you run out of time.'

'You're always trying to save us.' Stacie's voice was gentle as she offered the bag of marshmallows to Gail. 'Why not give yourself a night off for a change?'

'I just . . . I want us to be prepared.' Gail grabbed her sweet treat and stared sadly into the flames of the campfire.

'We are prepared.'

'And if something goes wrong?'

The fire began to blacken a thick piece of wood. The flames spat and hissed as they tore through it.

'Paramedics,' Stacie sounded around the marshmallow which she'd just shoved into her mouth.

'What if they don't come in time?'

'They will.'

'How can you be so certain?'

'It's V Festival.' Diana threw her marshmallow over the fire so that it landed squarely against Gail's chest. 'We'll be fine. Quit preparing us for Armageddon. It's not coming, you know? We're all going to grow old and wrinkly together.'

'I hope you're right.'

'I am,' Diana declared with a grand smile. 'Just wait and see.'

Allie woke up. She felt like she was coming round after a particularly messy drunken night out. Her head throbbed and her mouth was too dry.

'Urgh.' She twisted to look around. The cold rushed against her. A frozen wind blew and scratched her cheeks, burned her eyes, banishing the lingering fog of fatigue. Blinking furiously, Allie managed to open her eyes fully even though her eyelids felt brittle. 'What . . .?'

There was a pain in the back of her head that was drilling through to her brain and banging against the space between her eyes. She went to lift a hand, needing to apply pressure to the bridge of her nose, only no hand came. 'What the hell?' Allie squirmed and felt the tightness in her arms, the rope against her wrists. 'Argh!' She tensed and realised she was seated in a chair, her legs spread, ankles tied, her hands gathered together behind her back. 'Argh!'

The cabin came slowly into focus as she frantically looked around. The trio of sofas had been pushed back from the fire so that Allie could sit beside the dying embers. There was the faint smell of smoke in the air. And blood.

'Fuck.' Allie tried to free her hands and felt the bristled caress of the rope. The rough fibres of her ties grazed against her exposed skin. 'Fuck!' She cried louder, turning her head as much as she could, trying to find something to get her out of her predicament.

'Squirm all you want but I made those knots good and tight.' Stacie stepped out of the shadows, the heavy echo of her footfall bouncing off the wooden floorboards.

The cabin seemed too hollow, too cavernous. What had once felt warm and welcoming was now as desolate and forbidding as the bottom of an abandoned well. And for Allie, it was going to be almost impossible to get out. She twisted her wrists against the rope; it was so tight she could feel it squeezing the sensation out of her fingers. Soon they'd go numb from either the restriction or the cold and be useless to her.

'Gail would be proud.' The gun wasn't in Stacie's hands. Allie's head throbbed painfully as she tried to figure out where it was. 'She taught me how to tie knots, you know. The only Girl Guide lesson of hers I ever paid attention to.'

'What?' Allie fought against her restraints, tears of frustration glistening in her eyes. 'What is this?'

'You were going to leave,' Stacie replied darkly. 'I know what you'd do to me. You'd ruin me like you did Diana. You'd tell everyone that it was all my fault, that I killed Emily, shot Gail, and once again you'd come out of it all like some little hero. And I can't have you going anywhere. Not yet.'

'Stacie, please—'

'I mean where would you even go?' Stacie demanded shrilly. 'We're pretty trapped up here in case you hadn't noticed. I figured that's why you turned yourself round after you saw Diana off. The mountainside must be pretty impassable. So stop fighting this. Maybe *you're* the one who came back here to finish *me* off. Were we all a last loose end? Get rid of us and you can tell any story you want to. First, you pushed Diana . . .'

'I didn't . . .' Allie sighed and let her chin drop to her chest. She hadn't killed Diana, but there seemed to be no convincing Stacie of that.

'I need you to sit tight while I get everything we need.'

'We need?'

'I won't be long.' Stacie was zipping up her jacket. She now wore hiking boots, a hat and gloves. The faintest trace of colour had returned to her cheeks. 'You just sit there, no running off.' Her footsteps rang out behind Allie, growing weaker. A door slammed and Allie began to writhe in her chair, twisting her wrists every possible way to try and squeeze out of Stacie's knots. When that failed, she forced her limp fingers to pick at the fibres. Something warm was trickling down them. With a strained groan, Allie realised it was her own blood. The rope was cutting her wrists to ribbons. But the pain in her hands wasn't as demanding as the pain at the back of her head. It throbbed continually, causing spots to dance before her eyes.

'I have to get out of here.' Allie leaned back, blinked until the spots dispersed and then started to bounce. She raised herself up as much as she could and then came crashing down, turning all the while. Reluctantly the chair inched round. Panting, Allie looked around the cabin. She knew what she was searching for. She saw the shadow of the open luggage still near the door. For a moment the pain in her head was overridden by an ache in her heart. Then she was once again bouncing in her chair, trying to figure a way out. She was facing the kitchen area when she saw it.

The gun rested atop the large pine table, flat and innocuous. When Allie looked at it, she tried not to think of Gail, of the gaping wound that had opened her up.

Allie would never fire it. In her hands, it would be a deterrent, not a weapon. But first, she needed to get hold of it. Grinding her teeth through the pain, she frantically twisted her wrists and pulled at the rope with the tips of her fingers. The cold was beginning to make its way up her arms. The blood that trickled from her wrists no longer held any warmth. Still, she twisted and turned, determined to break free.

Behind her a door was thrust open, announcing Stacie's return. It slapped hard against the wall, wood on wood. Heavy footsteps rang out and then Stacie came into view. Her hood was pulled up so her face was partially hidden. Fresh snow covered her coat and she was gripping something in her hands, something heavy that made her waddle slowly. With a pant, she reached the table and put down her burden.

Allie tried to swallow, but her mouth was too dry, her throat too parched. She felt her papery tongue move behind her teeth as she looked over at the table. Knocking her gloved hands together, Stacie was standing back, grinning in admiration at her find. Beside the gun were now two petrol cans, their red surfaces streaked with grease.

Fear sizzled in Allie's veins. It tried to lift her out of her chair. Danger was so close she could smell it. Like a rat, she knew that she needed to run, needed to get out before the ship was completely sunk.

'I figured these would be by the generator.' Stacie smoothed her hands down the front of her coat, her gaze worryingly vacant. 'They should work nicely, don't you think? Gail was out there for ages hammering on the damn thing while you were gone. I think she might have even got it working.' Stacie planted her hands on her hips and thoughtfully tilted her head. A second dragged out between them. Then another. 'But I can't hear help coming, can you? Which means that no one heard any calls she made. We're still well and truly alone up here.'

'Please,' Allie rasped. 'Please don't do this. We can talk about it. Gail . . . it . . . it was an accident. The police will believe us. And like you said, Emily was a prank. A joke gone wrong. We can figure something out. I know we can. We can . . . we can get our stories straight.'

'What is there to figure out? You and I are both fucked. I didn't mean to hurt Emily, but no one will believe that, not given our history. I didn't mean to shoot Gail, but no one will believe that, either. Everyone will just see me as some guilty psycho. Our secrets need to burn up here, it's the only way we can truly be free of them.' Stacie unscrewed the cap of one of the cans.

'Don't you remember, Allie, our pact, our promise? To all go together?'

'We were *kids*, Stacie. Stupid little girls who didn't know what we were saying.'

Stacie, holding the petrol can aloft, held Allie in a hard stare. 'I meant what I said back then, Allie. What I did. At sixteen you mean it all.'

'Look, Stacie—'

'Only I'm breaking the pact' – Stacie's mouth lifted into a cruel smile – 'because we won't all go. Just some of us.'

The viscous scent of petrol began to permeate the room. It was a smell Allie used to enjoy. As a little girl, she always hopped out of the car at petrol stations to stand by her mum or dad while they filled up.

'You're a strange little girl,' her dad would remark with a smile.

'I like the smell,' Allie replied, nostrils widening as she breathed in deeply. 'It's so . . . strong. It smells like an escape.'

Because back then whenever Allie got in the car it was to go somewhere exciting. To visit a distant relative, her grandma or to go swimming. Car journeys were thrilling, a portal to adventure. Exotic. Now as Allie breathed in the petrol fumes, they didn't smell like escape.

They smelt like death.

Forty-Five

Emily stared at the ceiling. She breathed in. And out. She still couldn't feel her legs.

'The sensation will come back in an hour or two,' the midwife had told her cheerily. Emily looked down the bed, at the white sheet covering her lower half. From her waist down it seemed there was nothingness, only they were there, two unmistakable shapes beneath the sheet: her legs still attached.

'Are you all right?' Her mother fluttered at her side like an anxious moth, one which Emily didn't have the energy to bat away.

'Fine,' she croaked, still fixated on her legs. They were there only . . . they weren't. What began as a pleasant numbness had graduated into a total removal of feeling. With each press of the green button, Emily slid further away from pain, closer to a blissful place where she wasn't sixteen and in hospital, about to give birth, to a place where she could just be numb.

'The midwife will come and check you over in a little bit. She said not to worry if your breasts continue to leak, if you wear a tight bra and pack it with pads it'll stop in a day or two.'

Emily couldn't see her swollen breasts, they were hidden beneath the itchy cotton of the hospital gown she was still wearing. Back pains at home turned to waters breaking in the hallway, a mad dash to the private hospital over an hour away, Emily sweating and panting in the back seat. It was a blur. The nurses. The lights. The needles. Emily slipped in and out of the moment, catching pieces of conversation which left her with an incomplete puzzle.

'Breathe, just breathe.'

'She's not dilating enough.'

'We'll have to induce.'

'She needs something for the pain.'

'The baby is in distress. It needs to come out now.'

The room sharpened into focus and Emily blinked at her mother who was anxiously smoothing down the sheet on the bed for the twentieth time.

'My baby,' Emily said, blood pressure rising. 'Where is my baby?'

'Oh . . .' Like a nervous cat her mother withdrew from the bed, eyes wide. 'Sweetheart, try not to—'

The door to her room opened and her father strode in, smart in a navy suit. He fixed his daughter with a tight gaze. 'Feeling all right, Emily?'

'Where is my baby?'

She heard her mother whimper.

'Your baby?' Her father's silver eyebrows lifted high on his forehead. 'Emily, you don't have a baby, remember? You had a baby, but it isn't yours, it's with another family now, another mother.'

Her heart felt like it was trying to tie itself into a knot. Emily fought to find her breath, to speak.

'We're not to talk about it, remember?' her father barrelled on. 'Now that it's all done, we can move on and forget about it. The midwife assures me that while it was a messy birth, you'll be recovered enough in a month to return to school.'

Emily began to cry.

'You should be happy, to go back to your friends' – her father's tone was flint, sharp and unforgiving – 'and remember when you return to speak fondly of your term spent at the convent, at how your time there brought you closer to our Lord and Saviour.'

'But . . .' Emily was shaking, the numbness beginning to leave her legs.

Her father approached the end of the bed and gripped the metal frame between his strong hands. 'You're going to be strong, Emily. Do you hear me? This . . . this incident will not ruin you. I won't let it. You're going to be fine. Tell her' – he snapped his fingers at his wife – 'tell her how she'll be fine.'

'Yes.' Her mother meekly returned to Emily's bedside. 'You'll be fine, sweetheart, absolutely fine.'

Emily sniffed and raised a trembling hand to wipe at her face. 'A boy?' She looked at her tired mother. 'Or a girl?'

Her father cleared his throat. A warning.

'Please.' Emily looked into her mother's eyes, felt fresh tears falling from her own. 'Just tell me, please.'

'Does it even matter?' her father barked. 'Sleep. Rest. Pray. You'll be home soon.'

The door opened and a midwife came in, pulling a blood-pressure monitor along with her. Emily's father beckoned for her mother to leave. Together they edged out of the room, towards the open door.

Emily felt an ache in her legs, dull and constant. It drifted up to the burning fire in her groin and above that . . . empty. She felt so utterly, completely empty.

Forty-Six

Officer: There was clearly an intention to burn down the cabin. Why?

POI: It wasn't my intention so I can't explain that.

Officer: Try.

POI: I really don't know.

Officer: Who are you protecting?

POI: No one.

Officer: Yourself?

POI: What? No – I've been telling you the truth this entire time.

Officer: Well let's hope that you're right because once forensics are done at the cabin, we'll have a much clearer view of what happened up there. Will what we find align with what you've told us?

POI: I think so.

Officer: You sound unsure.

POI: I know as much about it as you do, which clearly isn't all that much. Can we move on?

Officer: Reluctantly, yes.

Forty-Seven

'Stacie . . .' Allie's fingers had stopped working. The slick outer coating of her own blood wasn't enough to keep away the gnawing bite of the cold. Her wrists burned and the rope tied against them held tight. 'What happened to Gail . . .' Grimacing at the taste of copper, Allie sucked in frigid air. The ice in her veins sharpened, sweeping through her with freezing agony. It wouldn't be long until what little warmth she still held in her body escaped in one final foggy breath. 'What happened to Emily. We can figure it out. We can—'

'Lie?' Stacie asked with a growl. 'Isn't lying and keeping secrets what got us here in the first place, Allie? Don't you think it's better to finish things now rather than live beneath the shadow of yet more lies? I told you I didn't mean to hurt Emily and I know you don't believe me. Then the fucking gun went off by accident. But you won't accept that, I can see it in your eyes. So like I said, we need to just finish things.'

'Finish things?' Allie stared at the petrol can Stacie was now holding. Its pungent odour was reaching out like invisible tendrils, curling around Allie, trying to choke her.

'The rest of the world doesn't need to know what happened here.' Turning the can upside down Stacie let its oily contents splash against the floor. Then she approached the fireplace, which was now dark and barren, all the while creating a slug trail of petrol.

'Look, there has to be another way, Stacie, give me a moment to—'

'She claims he raped her. It was why she went away.' Stacie ceased spilling petrol to stare at the canister in her grasp, cradling it close to her chest as though it were an infant.

'W-what?'

'This summer, I found out. I had a one-night stand with this guy who was a private investigator and it got me thinking about the past. About Ollie. About what everyone said about him. I wondered if it could be true, if there would be a police report or something. If Emily had told someone, *anyone* about it. Or if it really was just lies.'

'I don't . . .' Allie felt groggy. 'Stacie, what is all this about?'

'Gail knew, I'm damn sure of that. Because Gail knows everything. Gail who was godmother to those little chubby twins. Gail who Emily trusted above us all. Gail who kept her secrets.'

'Stacie, can we just—'

'There was a baby.' The revelation was released like a long-held breath. 'Upstairs, earlier, Emily told me the truth. All of it. There was never a convent, just a swollen belly and a secret to hide.'

'A baby?' Allie thought she was going to choke on the revelation. No wonder Emily adored the twins like she did, having previously been made to give up her firstborn. And it explained why she was unable to visit Allie in hospital because she had been busy dealing with her own trauma. 'Jesus.'

Puzzle pieces slotted into place and Allie didn't like the bigger picture. That summer, when Diana had been so reckless, so restless, as though something was eating away at her, as though she knew about something awful and was trying to forget it when—

'Don't act surprised,' Stacie scoffed. 'You knew, you all fucking knew. And you kept lying to me, kept letting me ruin one marriage after another because I was obsessed with something that never even existed. You all let me go on believing he was perfect, that my one shot at happiness had slammed into that wall with him! You should have told me. *She* should have told me.' Stacie blinked furiously against tears that gathered in her lashes like tiny jewels, one hand beating a nervous rhythm against the canister still nestled at her chest. 'Maybe then I'd have understood. Instead, she let me spend a lifetime believing Ollie was someone he wasn't, thinking that every guy I met didn't measure up to him. I bet he ran his car into that fucking wall on purpose because he knew what he'd done, couldn't live with himself.'

'You can't blame Emily for his mistake.'

Stacie's reply shot like a whip from her cracked lips. 'I don't.'

'Then why—'

'I blame her for *lying*. Don't you get that? I spent a lifetime thinking Ollie was unjustly taken from me and I had to hire a fucking investigator to discover the truth. My *best friends* kept it from me. What he'd done. What had happened at that party.'

Allie squirmed against her bindings and the new pain that burned in her chest.

'I mean, you can't even have children and Emily . . . she gave hers away. Like it was nothing. She had a choice. Made a decision. You don't even get to choose!'

A shudder ran through Allie's body, a hand automatically straining within the rope, keen to reach for her stomach. One day, one moment, her entire life changed. 'Emily . . . she isn't cruel, she . . . she understands, she knows what pain is like, she—'

'Maybe she did once,' Stacie interrupted, 'but then she had the twins, her little IVF miracle. Her slate got wiped clean, she got a fresh start. She got a second chance, Allie. And where is yours?'

Allie hated to admit that when Emily had the twins it was like she forgot her other friends even existed, that whatever had previously connected them had been erased. Her world became one of happily-ever-afters while Allie's was still consumed by shadows.

'I didn't want to believe it, even when she told me the truth about that night at that party. Even when I heard it from her own mouth.' Stacie's head dropped abruptly to her chin as though she'd been released from invisible gallows. 'I admitted to Emily that I'd taken her meds. That I knew everything, about that summer. About the baby. I wanted her to tell me I was wrong, that it had never been Ollie's, but of course, it was. I was trying to explain to her how taking her meds . . . it was a reaction. That I was angry . . . that I felt like she'd let me down. Only we weren't alone. Gail was merrily eavesdropping at the door in that way of hers, always circling, always judging. And when she exploded into the room with her gun minutes later it was angled at me, it was me who was at fault in her eyes. She didn't chastise precious Emily for her lies, oh no. Not for a second.'

'She wasn't lying to hurt you.'

'No?' The pitch of Stacie's voice rose an octave. 'In protecting herself she was hurting me, she knew that. Yet still, she did it, went on doing it. And there I was like a damn fool, believing Oliver was some fallen idol. *Why?*' she groaned in frustration. 'Why not tell me? Why not trust me with the truth?'

Allie thought of her final conversation with Diana. They'd been discussing the party at Ashley's house, something she'd seen, something terrible, something which had haunted her for decades. Diana's guilt had followed her down the mountain and to her death. Allie had seen it in her friend's tormented gaze. And now she understood.

Stacie was right – their entire friendship was built on the unstable foundations of secrets. And like a serpent biting its own tail they'd become locked in a terrible, never-ending cycle of concealing the truth from one another. Only now was it all coming out, but so many of the five weren't around to hear it. Allie looked at Stacie, trying to lock eyes with her, but Stacie had resumed tipping petrol about the cabin, scowling angrily as she completed her task.

'He *died*, Allie, because of Emily,' Stacie was lamenting as she walked. 'Whatever truth there was to her claim, whatever he did to her, he didn't deserve to . . .' Her voice trailed away.

'You still love him,' Allie declared accusingly. 'Even after learning the truth this summer, hearing it straight from Emily tonight, you still miss him, still care for him, don't you?'

'Would that make me a monster, too?' Stacie demanded from across the room.

'He's a ghost,' Allie cried, 'he's gone. He's nothing. Let him go.'

'You're one to judge,' Stacie scoffed, carrying on with her task.

'Just . . . just stop! Don't do this!' Allie begged.

Ignoring her, Stacie kept tracing her way around the cabin, leaving in her wake a slick trail of petrol.

'Please, stop.' Allie kept repeating her plea as the pungent odour of the fluid filled her lungs along with the cabin.

Stacie reached Allie and spilled petrol over her feet, then down her back. Allie screamed as some of the cold fluid slipped beneath her coat, journeying down her neck towards her spine. Its unpleasantly cool touch lingered on her skin. 'Stacie, stop! Please!'

'This is how it has to be, Allie. Surely given everything that has happened you understand that?'

Breathing hard, Allie pulled her lips tightly shut and tried not to give way to panic. Behind her back her fingers twitched. The petrol had soaked the ropes, had softened their crude fibres and greased her wrists.

'I'm going to burn this place down along with all our fucking secrets, maybe then we can finally be rid of them. Finally, be free.' Stacie threw the now empty can into a distant corner of the cabin. It rattled away towards the shadows and she returned to the table, eyes narrowed with focus.

'People will say that there was a great accident up here. That something awful happened. Maybe the generator blew up.' She thoughtfully chewed on the inside of her cheek and turned to face Allie. 'Because that's plausible, right? Generators blow up from time to time. A fire was started. A fire that even the storm outside couldn't suppress.'

Allie bowed her head and relaxed her shoulders as she willed herself to focus solely on her hands. She could feel the rope around her wrists releasing some of its tension. She just needed to bide her time. A few more minutes, a few more turns of her hands and she'd be free. What then? She furtively peered up at the table, at the shotgun. She could spring up from the chair, surprise Stacie and knock her over and then reach for the gun. The only issue was the petrol that was soaked into her clothes, her hair. One strike of a match, one spark and she'd go up like a bonfire. She didn't doubt that Stacie had the means to start the fire on her person – some matches stashed away in a coat pocket or a lighter somewhere.

'I'm not going to leave things as they are,' Stacie said stridently. The second petrol can was in her hands and she was marching to the far side of the cabin, tipping more flammable fluid as she went. 'I'm not going to leave this mountain as a monster.'

'Fuck you.' Allie spat out more petrol. Its taste and odour was invading every pore.

'And just imagine . . .' Stacie poured petrol over the luggage stacked up near the door. 'If you were the one to walk out of here this could all be in your next book. And yet again you'd paint such a pretty picture of yourself and fuck the rest of us.'

Allie feverishly slid her sliced wrists against one another, loosening the rope.

'But you're not getting out of here.' The second can was empty. Stacie threw it towards the base of the staircase. 'You're going to burn up in here with everyone else. You're going to burn for killing Diana. Because unlike with Emily and Gail, we both know it was no accident.'

'And you?'

'Me? I'm going to be the sole survivor. They'll find me on the mountain, alone and distraught at how I went out to get firewood and when I came back, boom, the place was a fucking bonfire. I'll cry when interviewed on TV, maybe I'll even take to wearing big black sunglasses for a couple of weeks, to help hide my grief. And hey, who knows' – she dropped a hand to her waist and slowly approached Allie's chair – 'maybe *I'll* write a book about it. I mean, you wrote one. How hard can it be? I'm tired of living in the shadow of past mistakes, Allie, far too tired.'

Forty-Eight

Officer: There is no account of a rape charge being filed against Oliver Henderson.

POI: Well there wouldn't be, would there?

Officer: But there must be proof of the child born during the winter of '95. Our investigators are looking into it.

POI: You should let the past be. Please.

Officer: The alleged rape goes a long way to providing a motive for what happened up at the cabin. Can you talk about that summer?

POI: I won't.

Officer: Why not?

POI: Because I'm here to discuss what happened at the cabin.

Officer: The events with Oliver Henderson seem to have shaped, or at least played a part in what transpired up at the cabin. It would be helpful if—

POI: It was never about Ollie.

Officer: It wasn't?

POI: It was only ever about us, the five of us.

Officer: So you're saying that the alleged rape wasn't a motivating factor?

POI: I'm saying that people were most hurt by the constant lying, that's where their grievances lay.

Officer: So why did you girls keep lying to one another? Why not just be honest?

POI: You've been to the cabin, seen what transpired there. That's why.

Forty-Nine

'It's . . .' Allie's mum sat in the centre of her brown leather sofa, a brand-new hardback copy of Wilted Rose on her lap, her palms neatly resting on top of it. The skin on the backs of her hands looked like it was stretched too thin, giving an almost translucent view of the network of blue veins beneath it. Pursing her thin lips, her mum leaned back, as graceful and as cold as the Persian cats Allie's aunt loved to keep. 'It's very personal.'

Allie could tell that her mum's words had been carefully chosen. She'd probably been rehearsing them ever since her copy of the book had arrived almost a month ago. Now Allie was back home, back in the house where she'd convalesced for what felt like an eternity after the accident. Much had changed. Her dad was no longer there, but his face remained on the walls in framed pictures of happier times. The sofa had been replaced. Gone was the soft mauve velvet that Allie loved to snuggle against. In its place was coffee-coloured leather. Practical. Stiff.

'I mean . . .' Her mum tapped the cover with a long nail which had been painted a deep shade of plum, so rich it was almost black. 'Do you really want people reading about intimate details of your life in this way?'

So much had been spared from the pages: her parents' divorce, her infertility. The book focused on the accident and the aftermath between her and her friends. Only at some point, fiction had overtaken reality. In the book, their friendship grew stronger after the accident, they came together. A fissure didn't open between them, a slender crack that would eventually prove fatal. Allie preferred the version of events in her book to those in real life.

'Well, it's fiction.'

Her mum gave a lacklustre smile. 'Hardly. You can dress it up as that, Allie, but for people who know you, this is auto-biographical. A sixteen-year-old girl breaks her back in a terrible accident and has to learn to walk again with the help of friends such as . . . Deena.'

'Fiction,' Allie repeated, more softly. 'Based on some facts, yeah.'

'What did the girls think?' her mum pressed, tired eyes dancing over her daughter's face.

'They . . .' Allie reached for her cup of tea, needing something to hold to stop her hands from fidgeting. 'They all like it. They've all been really supportive.' Despite the addition of sugar, her tea tasted sour as she swallowed it down with her lies.

'So they were all at the launch in London?'

No.

'Not everyone could make it. What with, you know, work and family stuff.'

'Mmm.'

She and Jasper had broken up a few months prior. He gave her his parting speech on one wet Tuesday evening, leaving only a few unwanted CDs at her flat.

Stacie had showed up for the publication day party and that was it. She'd brought along her boyfriend, parading him around like he was her newest toy. Diana was apparently sick with the flu. Emily couldn't travel down from Manchester at short notice and neither could Gail from Scotland. Emily was a newlywed, besotted with Adam, and Gail had all but disappeared since meeting Melissa. Apologies arrived as tweets, flippant and hastily written on some commute to somewhere more important than Allie's book launch.

'But you liked the book?' Allie's voice lifted hopefully. 'I mean Dad said it was—'

Her mum raised a hand like she was stopping traffic. Allie snapped her teeth together, almost biting down on her tongue. 'It's powerful stuff.' Her mother gave a tight nod of her head — whether or not it was in approval Allie couldn't tell. 'And you write well, Allie. Truly.'

'But?' Allie could feel the counter-compliment hanging between them, tainting the air.

'But . . .' Her mum's shoulders sank low as she released a breathy sigh. 'As your mother, how do you think I felt reading this? All the accounts of the pain you went through, the suffering.'

'You were there, Mum. You already know what I went through.'

'Yes, but . . .' Her mum's hand fluttered between the book and her throat. 'It's just . . .' It finally settled upon her slender throat. 'I know I was there, Allie. I watched you get broken down to nothing and have to rebuild yourself brick by brick. And you did it with a smile on your face. You had this inner strength that shone through, that amazed me and . . .' The hand became a fist and dropped back against the book. 'I'm concerned that you're still holding on to all that pain from back then. You're better now, Allie. Why write a book about it? Why dwell on it? You should just be letting go and moving on with your life.'

'The book is letting go.' Allie lowered her tea and pointed at the hardback. 'I put all my pain between the pages so that I wouldn't have to carry it around with me all the time.' There was some truth to the statement.

'But, Allie—'

'Writing the book allowed me to heal more than just my body. It allowed me to make sense of something really awful that happened to me. Something that no one else should ever have to go through.'

286

'But it reads . . .' Her mum pinched her eyes closed and pulled her lips into a line. 'The pain in it reads so raw. I'm worried about my little Allie Bear.'

'You don't have to worry about me, Mum. Really, I'm fine.'

'I noticed you didn't mention the hysterectomy.'

'I didn't want to put absolutely everything down on the page. Some things I wanted to hold back, to keep private. And I told you, it's fiction.'

'So how are you going to heal regarding that if you don't write a book about it?'

'Mum—'

'It's my job to worry, Allie. The girl in this book.' She lifted the novel up off her lap. 'She is haunted. Tell me that's not my little girl. Tell me that my little girl isn't haunted.'

'Mum.' Allie gave her a level look. 'I'm not your little girl anymore.'

'How long do you think it'll take this place to go up?' Stacie pulled a silver lighter from her pocket and flicked it on and off, transfixed by its yellow flame. Allie imagined that the fire would torch the cabin. It would move along the petrol as fast and as fluid as water. It would gather at her heels and silence the screams that erupted from within her as it powered up her body and reached into her throat. She'd burn along with the walls. The cabin would be turned to ash, carried off by the wind and scattered upon the mountain.

'Is there . . .' The lingering taste of petrol in her mouth made Allie's eyes water. She coughed uneasily and sat up straight, needing to focus. 'Petrol. Is that it?' She nodded towards the base of the stairs at one of the discarded cans.

'I think so. Why?' Stacie pursed her lips with interest.

'Well . . .' More coughing. Allie wondered what the petrol seeping into her system was doing to her. She imagined it didn't need a spark to be dangerous. 'I figure that downstairs will burn up real quick. But upstairs . . .' With some effort she strained to look at the ceiling. 'That will take longer. And people will see the fire. Even through the storm. Help will come. It might arrive before the cabin has completely burned down. What with the snow and everything it might take longer than you think.'

'Huh.' Stacie took a step towards the staircase, studying it. 'So you think one more can upstairs will ensure the place burns up nice and quick?'

'Exactly.'

Stacie stalked back over to the chair and narrowed her eyes. 'Why help me? Why make a suggestion like that?'

'Because you're going to burn me down with this place no matter what I say. I'd rather go quickly.'

Stacie considered that for a moment. 'Makes sense.' Snapping the lighter closed Stacie returned it to her coat pocket. 'And for the record, the only reason you're going to burn in here is because you killed Diana.'

Allie merely grunted, knowing any declarations of her innocence would be in vain.

'I'll go and see if there are any more cans.'

Hearing the door close, Allie set to work. She ground her wrists together, twisted them back and forth as her numb fingers relied on muscle memory to pick at the rope's fibres. Freedom was close. The storm continued to lash at the walls, to blow in through the broken windows with a bitter howl. But Allie would rather take her chances out there. Given the option, she would prefer to freeze to death than be burned alive. It was a grim decision to have to make.

One hand was almost free. She was sliding it up and out of her restraints when the door was thrown open. Stacie hurried inside, dusted with snow and carrying a third and final petrol can. 'What do you know?' She wore a smile as she peered over it at Allie. 'They did have another one stored in the generator shed. I'd best go and give this a shake upstairs.'

Allie watched her leave, not moving an inch for fear of revealing how close she was to breaking free. The staircase groaned as Stacie powered up it. And then Allie was alone. She allowed herself a second to stare at the space where her friend had been. Something had changed in Stacie. Something had allowed the fire within her, the fire which Allie had always envied and admired, to take hold and burn through her until everything was blackened and charred. Where was the sweet girl with the sing-song voice? All Allie saw when she looked at Stacie was a stranger. Is that how Stacie felt? Is that how all her friends had felt? Somewhere along the way had Allie lost herself too?

A fierce wind drove its way into the cabin, knocking over one of the chairs placed around the table. As it clattered to the ground Allie knew she had to act. She slipped her one hand free and then tugged at the remaining rope. If she was going to leave the cabin, she had to do it now.

Allie released a stifled cry as she untangled the last of the rope and let it drop to the ground. She didn't pause to draw breath as she leaned forward, hands reaching for her ankles. The cold had crippled her exposed fingers. They'd become rigidly locked in place, suddenly arthritic.

Biting down on her lip Allie forced out what life remained in her grip, diligently unpicking the knotted ropes still holding her to the chair. The wind concealed Stacie's footsteps upstairs. It creaked along the walls and shuddered through the windows. Allie knew that time was in precious short supply. At any moment Stacie could come back down the stairs and while Allie's feet were still bound, she'd be the slower of the two to reach the gun. And the gun was what mattered. The gun was a road block, a way to hold the other person in place. If she was the one holding the gun she could reason with Stacie, make her see sense. She could stop the fire, save the cabin, save them both.

'Come . . . on . . .' The knots were tight and stubborn. Allie's frozen touch struggled to navigate a way through the fibres. Snow danced into the room. It swirled in the air and then softly came to rest upon the petrol-slicked floorboards, the intricate shape of each flake bleeding into the viscous fluid. 'There.' One foot was free. Allie panted with relief and then turned towards her left side.

How long would it take Stacie to douse the upstairs of the cabin in petrol? Would she splash it over Gail and Emily as she had done with Allie? Pushing thoughts of her friends' burning corpses out of her mind, Allie slowed her breathing to try and stop the constant shaking of her hands. A single knot stood between her and freedom. Thankfully she was still wearing her hiking boots. Once this last rope had been untangled, she could get up. She could leave.

Her bones felt brittle. The marrow within them turned to ice. Clenching her teeth together Allie tugged at the rope, forced her fingers to work. The tension around her ankle eased and her restraint dropped limply to the ground. There wasn't time to rejoice. Straightening, she staggered forward, moving away from the chair. Every muscle was screaming at her, suddenly ablaze.

With a grunt Allie awkwardly approached the table. Each step was laboured, clumsy. It seemed like her entire body had forgotten how to function properly. She tried to shake out the stiffness of the cold as she drew closer to the gun. The blood began to flow around her legs and arms a little more easily, but her fingers were still locked and useless. Allie extended her hands towards the butt of the shotgun. Her flexed fingers grazed its surface but couldn't unlock them, couldn't get a secure hold around it. 'Shit.' Allie kept scratching at the gun in frustration, trying to make a more solid connection with it. She could just tuck it under her arm and run, but that was too risky – a single misfire and she'd go up in flames. She was going to have to leave the gun. Reluctantly drawing back from the table, Allie shifted her focus in the direction of the door. She was hurrying towards it, her body clenching in preparation for the cold that was about to slap against her. Then she saw the gloves. A bright pink pair laid out on the kitchen counter. Allie hastily grabbed them.

A shriek from upstairs. Allie froze, heart a jackhammer in her chest. Was it Stacie? Emily? The walls of the cabin creaked and moaned but there were no further cries. Had Allie imagined it? She knew she was wasting time deliberating. She had to leave. She pressed down on the door handle with both hands.

The wind roared at Allie in greeting. It folded around her in a freezing embrace, trying to penetrate her coat. Gasping against its powerful hold she fumbled to thrust her hands into the pink gloves. All the while she kept staggering forward, head bowed against the falling snow.

White. There was so much white it was blinding. And now, without the cloak of darkness, it shone brilliant and bright, stinging at her eyes. It was on the ground, in the air, weighing down tree branches. Allie moved as fast as she could. Her previous footsteps had been filled in, reclaimed by the storm. It swept around her, ever more furious.

Where was she even going? Allie darted towards a nearby tree and leaned against it. She tried to clench her hands, but her fingers remained rigid and useless. Down. She needed to get down. Reaching the little house with the green door was her best hope for survival, but she'd tried to get there previously and failed. Diana was still out there, laid in twisted repose and broken upon a ledge. Allie filled her chest with icy air and stepped away from the tree, tugging up the hood of her coat to protect her head. Her petrol-soaked hair was already frozen and brittle. Glancing back, she peered up at the cabin as it started to become obscured by all the densely falling snow. It did not erupt like some great volcano. Red pillars of flames hadn't yet burst forth through its roof. There was still time. The fire had yet to be lit, which meant that Stacie was still inside, perhaps still dousing the upper level. Allie trudged forward through the snow, determined not to waste another second of her escape.

Fifty

'You can talk to me, you know.' Gail was beside Emily on the bench in Emily's garden, beneath the willow tree. At eighteen, Gail felt wise beyond her years. It was why she had taken it upon herself to check in on each of her friends ahead of their starting university, to make sure they'd each completed their UCAS forms, that they were all in agreement about where they were going to go.

'We're stronger together,' she told them all, 'you know like the twig thing, where one snaps so easily but bundle a load together and they're not snapping, they're staying just as they are. That's us. Together . . . together we can face anything.' Ultimately it was for Allie, little lost Allie who'd never been quite the same since that day on the bridge. But each of her friends gave her pause for concern. So, on her way home from work she'd pulled her rusted Fiat Panda into Emily's large driveway and asked to come in for a chat.

'I submitted my UCAS form last week.' Emily was looking at her hands, at her hot-pink nails which looked freshly painted.

'I know, I never need to worry about you being on top of things.' Gail gave her an affectionate nudge with her shoulder. She was still wearing her green supermarket uniform which seemed almost fluorescent against the autumnal twilight of the garden.

'It's Diana you need to worry about.' Emily raised a hand to twist some of her golden hair around her finger. 'She's been so distracted lately, since she started seeing that guy from that band.'

'The drummer?'

Emily nodded. 'That's the one.'

Her grand house was watching over them, windows glowing golden in the dwindling light.

Gail inhaled and decided to try, as she infrequently did during opportunities such as these when she and Emily were alone, to ask the questions she herself had failed to answer. 'And how are you, Em?'

'Good, I'm good,' the answer always came with a sunny smile.

'Really?'

'Really?' Emily turned to her, corners of her blue eyes crinkling. 'Why?'

'I just . . .' Gail squared her shoulders, reminding herself how important she was to the group, how they needed her maternal guidance. If she didn't ask Emily, then who would? The others . . . something had changed in them all after that summer two years ago. Now, at seventeen, preparing to leave for college they were a world away from the girls they had been in school. They'd each withdrawn, even Emily, and Gail refused to let any of them get to a place where they could no longer be reached. 'I want you to know you can always talk to me.'

'Right, okay. Sure.' Emily was still eyeing her with confused suspicion. 'Thanks.'

'If you ever wanted to talk about how you're feeling, what's going on with you, or where you went that summer.'

Gail felt Emily stiffen beside her. Emboldened by the ensuing silence she carried on. 'I just want you to know that if you need to talk about where you went, what happened. It's been just over two years now and perhaps that's enough time that we can start to, you know, talk. Heal. You can tell me what happened, Em, I mean there's no pressure—'

'A convent,' Emily snapped tightly. 'I told you all that I went to—'

'You don't seriously think we believe that do you?' Gail gently queried.

Emily sank low on the bench, visibly crestfallen. Cheeks blushing, her lower lip began to tremble. 'Please' – her voice was as low as her posture – 'it was a convent and—'

'I'm here,' Gail implored her, springing off the bench and crouching before her blonde friend, a hand resting on each of Emily's slumped shoulders. 'I've always been here. You can talk, you can tell me the truth, Em.'

Emily's eyes were an infinite ocean of woe when she looked up at Gail. 'I'm fine, truly. Please don't ask me about that summer again.'

'We should think about uni as a new chapter in our lives, a way to move on from the past. We don't need to keep holding on to things. Em—'

'Allie nearly died that summer,' she barrelled over Gail's words. 'She could barely walk for months. Months, Gail. I don't want to dwell on me. She's the one who is still hurting from it all.'

'Emily—'

'You need to move on from that summer. I know I have.'

'Have you?' Gail frowned up at her from her perch on the floor, amid the amber and russet leaves that carpeted the lawn.

'I have to,' Emily stated stoically. She reached up and gave Gail's hands still resting on her shoulders a squeeze. 'And I need you to stop asking about it. If uni is truly going to be a new start for us, the past has to stay there, in the past. If you want to be a good friend to me, stop asking. Please.'

Gail nodded, hating that she knew she was losing. But the white flag of friendship had been raised. Whatever the five were to one another, they were friends first. Conceding, Gail forced a smile. 'Okay, I won't ask again. But I need you to help me pin Diana down for long enough to finish her UCAS form.'

'Deal.'

Fifty-One

Allie felt numb. The feeling radiated out from more than just the base of her spine. It had taken her nose, crept up her fingers and stolen each of her toes one by one. She relied on muscle memory alone to carry her through the snow. Her head throbbed. She felt like a deep chasm was opening up behind her eyes into which all her conscious thoughts were falling. Picking her way through the trees she moved further away from the cabin, further away from danger. But an old saying her late aunt favoured chirped in her ear like an incessant cricket.

Out of the frying pan and into the fire.

Only there was no fire out on the mountainside. Just ice.

Allie scrambled towards the next tree. She knew she was too tired to do this. Where she wasn't numb, she burned from over-exertion. Despite the snow in the air, her mouth felt paper-dry. Tilting her head towards the sky, she stuck out her tongue and let some snowflakes settle on it. They tasted of ice. Not water. And deep in her mind, a memory stirred. A memory telling her that this was wrong, better to be thirsty. She snapped her mouth closed and straightened.

'Sea water and snow,' Gail had said. 'Both will fail to hydrate you. The salt in sea water will be dehydrating and the cold of the snow will only further lower your core temperature. Avoid both.'

She'd reeled off her advice during one of her survival guide presentations to her friends. Allie always did her best to listen, though she doubted how much of the information actually sunk in. But this piece had stuck. So no more snow. She drew her chapped lips into a tight line and used what little of her energy remained to surge forwards until she reached a nearby tree. Gazing longingly at its trunk, she considered how glorious it would feel to rest for a while, even just a minute. But she didn't have the luxury of time. She had to get down the mountain and fast.

'I knew you'd come.' Allie smiled as the door to her little hospital room closed behind her friend. It was half past three on a Tuesday, and as reliable as the tide, Gail had turned up, still dressed in her neatly ironed school uniform, hair pulled back in a severe ponytail.

'As if I'd let you down,' Gail replied with a grin. She approached the bed and hauled several textbooks out of her navy backpack and slapped them down on the plastic tray table set up before Allie. 'History, science, maths,' her tall friend explained. 'I also need to grab you a copy of Othello *at some point but that wouldn't fit in my bag.'*

'No, that's . . .' Allie glanced at the spines of the stack of books. Thinking about practising algebra or learning key dates from the First World War felt surreal given her present location, but she knew that Gail was being more than just pragmatic, she was being helpful. In her mind, the broken girl in the hospital bed would soon be back on her feet and attending school once more and when that happened, she wouldn't want to have fallen behind her peers in her studies. 'I really appreciate you bringing those,' Allie concluded earnestly.

'No problem.' Gail sat down in the single chair in the room and primly crossed her legs at the ankles, leaning forward with attentive expectation. 'So how are you feeling?'

'Oh, you know . . .' Allie tried to sound flippant as she gestured to her surroundings. In truth, she felt broken, isolated and afraid. But those were sides of herself she wouldn't show to the friends who were good enough to turn up and spend time with her. Her visitors deserved to see Allie at her sparkly best, at least as much of it as she could muster. 'I'm doing okay. The doctors say that every day I'm improving.'

'Good, that's great.' The enthusiasm in Gail's voice was almost contagious. 'See, I told you that you'd be back at school in no time. Maybe I'll be able to put you on the netball team before Christmas.'

A laugh erupted from Allie. It made her stitches sting, but she endured the pain for the brief release of merriment. 'Ha. You wouldn't have put me on the team before my accident, I highly doubt there's a place for me now.'

'Ah, but you've shown great tenacity in here.'

'Hmm.' Allie sagged against her pillows and glanced out the window at the darkening sky. Autumn had arrived quickly that year, killing off summer in a burning glory of auburn and copper. 'And how are things with you?'

'Oh, you know me, always busy,' Gail replied briskly. 'But, you know, never too busy to come and see you,' she added with a diplomatic air.

'And Diana?' Allie wondered nervously. She knew that with Gail she could ask the questions she didn't dare broach with Stacie who took such enquiries to heart, as though she suddenly weren't providing enough companionship.

Gail drew her hands into a tight basket in her lap. 'She's . . . she's Diana.' Her shoulders dropped as she sighed. 'A law unto herself. You know how she can be. I keep urging her to come and visit.'

'But she doesn't.'

'No,' Gail agreed, the corners of her mouth drooping in sadness, 'she doesn't.'

'And Emily?'

There was a quick shake of the head and Allie began to feel despondent. 'She's still not at school.'

'Where is she?' There was desperation in the question. How could someone just disappear? Emily wasn't at school, wasn't at home, so where exactly was she?

'Truly, I don't know.' Gail began to tap her foot against the linoleum floor. 'I'm sure she'll resurface in time.'

'I miss her.'

'Me too.'

'I'm so glad you keep coming.'

This allowed some warmth to return to Gail's gaze and she smiled softly. 'I'm glad too. I'll always keep coming, Allie Bear. How about we go over some of the homework for this week? Might help to take your mind off things.'

'You're always looking out for me,' Allie noted with tenderness as Gail lifted herself out of the chair and came round to the side of the bed, drawing back the cover on the textbook on the top of the pile she'd brought with her.

'Of course . . .' Gail lifted the book towards her chest and scanned the text on the first page. 'That's what friends are for, Allie. Now, can you tell me what event triggered the start of the First World War?'

Fifty-Two

'Allie!'

Her name carried on the wind. It bounced off the neighbouring trees before finding its way to her ears. Allie froze. Her legs were planted apart, mid-step. Tilting her head towards the path she had just trodden, she strained to listen for another sound. Maybe she was dreaming. Maybe the cold had started to numb vital parts of her mind so that she was now free to hallucinate. What next? Would her body start to burn within her many layers? Would she feverishly remove her coat? Her gloves? Was this the start of hypothermia felt like?

'Allie!'

She instantly recognised the cadence of Stacie's voice, the lilt in her tone. Her knees buckled and Allie sunk low to the ground like an animal being hunted. She had two choices. She could either run or hide. Her heart beat so furiously it made her chest ache. But every beat reminded her that she was alive, that it wasn't all over yet. She could still get help. Could still reach the green door.

'Don't bother running, Allie. There's just you and me out here. Come back to the cabin before you freeze to death.'

Stacie's voice carried so easily through the snow, aided by the wind which blew down the mountainside. She sounded far away but Allie knew better than to trust her own senses, that they could be deceiving her. Glancing back, she saw her own footprints dug deep into the snow, a trail of breadcrumbs leading directly to her.

Allie seethed between her frozen teeth as she leaned forward and tried to get her mangled hands to smooth over her nearest set of prints. But what was the point? Each time she moved forward she'd leave fresh footprints in the snow. To spend time erasing every step she took would slow her down dramatically. Which meant that if Stacie didn't get to her then the cold would.

'I can't let you get off this mountain.' A threat. Bold and clear it rang out through the weakening storm. Trees shook as though quaking fearfully. Allie hurried onwards. The storm was definitely moving on. Since leaving the cabin she'd noticed that the snowfall was less intense. She was slowly starting to be able to see further ahead. Though the snow was lessening, the bite in the air remained just as sharp. Icy teeth continually gnawed at Allie as she pulled her feet through the snow. Stacie had been in the cabin the whole time, staying nice and warm. Her body would be more rested, more resilient. And her steps would probably be much faster as a result.

'Come . . . on,' Allie grunted at herself as she forced her leaden legs to maintain a swift motion. Death was on her heels and she was determined to outrun it.

The new year was three weeks old. Allie was finally home, swaddled in bandages, but free from the hospital. She sat on the mauve sofa in her living room, crutches leaned up close by. A fire was crackling in the hearth, bathing the large room in golden light. The warmth eased some of the aches which permanently resided in Allie's battered bones.

'So you're back?' She looked across at her visitor, a pale blonde who kept her hands pressed against her knees as she sat straight-backed in the nearby armchair.

'I'm back,' Emily agreed breathily. 'And you're walking.'

'Almost.' Allie found a loose thread in her towelling dressing gown and began to pull at it. She needed a distraction. It felt strangely alien to see Emily again after such a prolonged absence. She kept snatching glances at her friend, searching her porcelain skin for some clue about where she'd been all these months.

'I only came home yesterday,' Emily explained, speaking with forced politeness. It was as though she were addressing a stranger. 'I came here as soon as I was permitted.'

Permitted.

Allie wanted to scream the word back at her. Since when had they needed permission to come and see one another? They were best friends, weren't they?

'Look.' Emily drew in a fluttery breath and paled despite the crackling of the nearby fire. 'Allie, I've been gone a long time. I know that. And I can't . . . I . . .' She began to pick at the tips of her fingers, at nails that weren't polished their usual shade of sugary pink.

'Something happened,' Gail had stated ominously one afternoon in the hospital. 'With Emily, something bad happened, I just know it. When she does return, show her kindness.'

'But—' She held up a hand to silence Allie's rebuttal.

'Be the bigger person,' Gail had urged. 'Always, Allie, try to be the bigger person.'

Emily was fidgeting in the armchair, squirming as though tethered beneath invisible chains which dug deep into her skin. Allie knew the body language of torment when she saw it.

At that moment it didn't matter where Emily had been, what mattered was that she'd returned, that they could be the Fierce Five once again.

'I'm glad you're back,' she told her nervous guest. 'Truly. I missed you.'

'And I missed you, Allie Bear.' It took just three strides for Emily to cross the space between them. She hugged Allie tight, too tight really, crushing her arms closely against her shoulders, her chest. But Allie didn't complain. She breathed in the vanilla perfume, the strawberry shampoo, the smells which always clung to Emily. 'I won't leave you again.' The promise was released as a whisper. 'I'm here for you, Allie.'

'It's okay,' Allie assured her, wincing as her bones sang in protest at her friend's proximity. And at that moment, it was okay. Whatever had transpired to take Emily away that previous year it hadn't been enough to steal her permanently from the group and that was what mattered. Now things could go back to normal, they could all be whole again. Happy even.

Fifty-Three

If Allie made it to the base of the mountain, what then? Would she stumble up to the green door and paw against it with her frozen hands? When it finally opened what would she even say?

They're all dead and the only one left is trying to kill me.

How was she supposed to tell a stranger something she didn't quite believe herself?

It was the second day of Gail's birthday weekend. The cabin should be filled with the scent of cooked bacon as the girls slowly woke up, nursing hangovers but still smiling as they washed their breakfast down with mimosas. Come the afternoon there would be board games. They all loved Monopoly and Cluedo and things always tended to get quite competitive. As they laughed and joked together Allie would forget about Lucas, about her hollow flat and the numbness in her spine. She'd just laugh and smile, basking in the glow of being surrounded by her four best friends.

A cold wind slapped across her face. It smarted against her cheeks, causing Allie to grit her teeth as her eyes watered. Around her there were trees and the ground was starting to steeply decline. If Allie kept going, she could lead Stacie down to the spot where Diana fell. Maybe, if Stacie saw the ledge, the blood upon the snow and ice, she'd realise it had all been a terrible accident and cease with her accusations. Would that be enough to stop her? Or would she look down and just see someone who had fallen, someone who could have been pushed? Allie was no killer but was her plea of innocence going to be enough to stop Stacie's malicious intention to silence her final friend, to preserve their secrets in an ashen grave atop the mountain?

Venturing out to the ledge was too risky. If the snow at the edge of the mountain gave way either of them could easily fall and join Diana. And there was no guarantee that Stacie would even believe her, could be reasoned with. Allie began to take long, sideways steps to the left, seeking a new path. No one else was going to die. No matter what happened during her descent of the mountain, Allie was resolute that both she and Stacie would make it out alive.

A sharp wind punched her in the gut, knocking the breath from her lungs. With a gasp, Allie resumed her focus. She'd been walking sideways for a while now, her legs burning beneath her. The steep incline had fallen away and now the mountainside rolled away from her in a gentle slope. Her face stung. At least the parts that weren't numb. Stiffly, she changed her path so that she was now going down.

Stacie's voice occasionally carried to her on the wind.

'Allie, stop!'

'Come back! Please!'

'You can't leave!'

Were they threats or pleas? Allie didn't dare wait around to find out. She had to keep moving. The sloping mountainside was kinder on her legs than the higher area near the cabin had been. The snow covering the ground was also shallower. Instead of almost reaching her knees it was barely scraping the top of her hiking boots. Flakes continued to skitter down from grey clouds but they felt lacklustre compared to the intense blizzard which had preceded them.

With careful, methodical steps, Allie moved further down the mountain, buoyed by the hope that this new route would lead her to salvation.

Fifty-Four

Officer: Were you afraid?

POI: Of the storm?

Officer: Of your friends?

POI: Not the whole time.

Officer: But some of the time?

POI: Some of the time, yes. Definitely.

Officer: You were alone at this point.

POI: That's right.

Officer: And you were afraid?

POI: No, I wasn't afraid. I was terrified.

Fifty-Five

'Diana!'

A new name carried on the frigid air. Allie's stomach clenched with grief as she heard it. Her fallen friend was still on a ledge somewhere, wearing a blanket of snow. Allie had intended to go back, to take ropes and pickaxes and claim her.

'Diana!'

Allie kept walking, knowing that no matter how much Stacie shouted their friend's name no response would echo up the mountain towards her. Diana was now just as silent as the others.

'I'm going to get out of here,' Allie muttered stiffly as she kept trudging through the snow. She wished she had a clearer idea of where she was going, had taken the time to memorise the map of the mountain. 'I'm going to get home.' Allie felt like Dorothy, wishing for the impossible. 'Home. I'm going home.'

Even her hollow flat now seemed warm and inviting in her memory. She could handle the empty bed, the black hole by her new sofa. She could handle all of it. She just wanted to go home, to feel warm again, to be given a chance to mourn her friends. But the mountain was a tomb, one she feared she would never escape from.

'I'm going home, I'm going home.' Allie was so lost to her mantra that she failed to notice the snow disappear underfoot.

Her feet slid out from under her, the spikes on her hiking boots no longer keeping her secure. 'Argh.' Spreading her arms, Allie instinctively leaned forward and righted herself at the moment she was about to topple over. 'Shit.'

Ice. All around her. A ribbon of translucent perfection that twisted away further down the mountain. The river. She'd found the river.

'Ah!' Glee swelled within Allie, but it was only temporary. Her boots were slipping and sliding across the smooth surface of the river making her movements jerky and ill-balanced. 'Come . . . on.' It took great force to keep herself upright, her steps becoming smaller in an effort not to fall.

'If you reach the river, you're going the right way.' That's what Gail had said. Allie needed to be on the river, to follow it down and finally pound her frozen fists against the green door. But on the ice progress was slow-going. Allie looked towards the snowy banks. They were so densely filled with compacted snow, so ready to take her weight with ease.

Out on the ice, she was vulnerable. She could fall and break something vital. Or the ice beneath her could start to crack, slowly shattering its perfect veneer until its icy waters were free once again.

Allie tried to scramble towards the banks of the river. Her boots skidded over the ice, the spikes now more of a hindrance than a help. 'Home.' Urging herself on she kept manically moving her legs, trying to glide over to more forgiving terrain.

'Diana!'

Stacie's distant cries threaded their way through the trees, ghostly and chilling. She was still calling for the fallen, still hoping for a reply. But it was the strength in the call which made frozen fingers gather around Allie's heart and squeeze. Stacie was getting closer, her voice becoming clearer, louder.

Abandoning the riverbank, Allie scurried forward across the flat ice. As girls, whenever they went ice skating Stacie would linger at the edges of the rink, preferring to chat to boys rather than try to execute a well-timed turn.

'It's because she can't do it,' Diana would scoff. 'That's why she stays at the edge, to avoid falling flat on her face in front of everyone.'

To Allie, skating came easy. She was small with a low centre of gravity. She was able to stay on her feet and glide about with little effort. Despite their height, Emily and Gail had no issues with skating either. Like a pair of graceful swans, they manoeuvred around the ice, caring more about perfecting their movements than all the admiring glances they were attracting. Diana would fall. But each time she did she just got straight back up. It was only Stacie who remained at the railing, unwilling to even attempt it.

It was an old thread, undoubtedly frayed thin by time but it was all Allie had and so she clung to it, wrapped it around her wrists and used it to pull herself along. If Stacie feared the ice then she hopefully wouldn't follow her out onto the frozen river. Keeping distance between them was crucial, especially considering the shotgun in her friend's possession.

The ice shifted. Hairline fractures cracked along the surface in Allie's wake. She didn't turn to look at them, couldn't face seeing the veins of exertion sweeping across the river. It was barely holding her weight. It just needed to support her a little longer. Soon she'd be at the base of the mountain. Soon she'd be back home.

★

'I'd like to propose a toast to the happy couple.' Allie smiled nervously at the assembled wedding guests as she clutched a champagne flute in her hands, her bridesmaid dress already starting to itch against her skin. She focused on the rising bubbles in the glass instead of the sea of faces which had all turned towards her with open and expectant gazes. Her head ached. Her golden hair had been twisted up into a high chignon bun and while it looked pretty, it was heavy. Five hours had passed since the hairdresser painstakingly piled her hair atop her head and they were only just concluding the wedding breakfast. It was going to be a long day.

In the centre of the top table, Stacie giggled sweetly, clutching her new husband's arm with tight desperation, her long nails digging into the fabric of his tailored suit. Her hair was a waterfall of fire down her back, pricked with diamantés. In her glittering white princess dress, she looked elegant, glamorous. A sparkling mass of carefully quaffed perfection. But it was strange to see her looking so . . . bridal.

'Stacie is the first of us all to get married.' Allie gestured to the three other bridesmaids who flanked the newlyweds, all dressed in the same rose-hued gowns.

'Which means we are beyond thrilled for her,' Gail cut in. She was also standing, also holding her glass of champagne in her hands. 'If a little new at this.'

The Fierce Five were all on their feet. Bar one. Stacie twinkled like a star, her cheeks flushed with a radiant glow as she absorbed all of the adoring attention in the vast marquee.

'We've known Stacie since forever.' Diana gave a knowing grin and then looked across at Emily, passing an invisible baton along the ranks as they all shared the burden of the speech.

'It's normally traditional for the best man to give a speech . . .' Emily's voice was shrill with nerves. Holding her glass, she scratched along the back of her hand with her long nails. 'But Stacie wanted all of her best girls to stand up and say something.'

'Which we were delighted to do.' Speaking duties were back with Allie. She watched a bubble pop atop her champagne. 'Stacie is our best friend.'

'But we're not here to tell cheeky tales . . .' Diana raised an eyebrow which made some of the gathered guests snicker.

'Our secrets stay between us.' Gail's tone was more formal, more sincere.

'We're here to toast our best friend.' Emily stopped scratching to straighten her arm and raise her glass high. 'To wish her and Jim the very best as they start their married life together. To Stacie and Jim.'

The toast was repeated back at the bridesmaids with force. Allie drank down her champagne, feeling the bubbles pop.

'I wasn't sure this day would come.' The wedding breakfast was over and Jim was grinning like a guy whose favourite football team had just lifted an insanely large trophy. He had one arm around his new wife, hugging her tightly to his side. He was modestly handsome in a navy suit, a blond trimmed beard shadowing his jawline. 'You guys are thick as thieves . . .' With his free hand he gestured at the bridesmaids. 'I doubted if I'd ever be able to prise her away from you.'

'You'll never take me away from my girls,' Stacie said, playfully needling his side. Her blue eyes shone brightly between the thick sets of false lashes she'd carefully applied that morning. 'Not completely.'

'We're more than happy to share her with you.' Gail was a master at social situations like this. She oozed grace from every pore. Emily was the same. When her nerves about public speaking weren't eating at her she could relax and shine like the star she was. She never walked into a room, she glided. Gail and Emily were the cornerstones of the group, raising the others up when they failed to meet expectations.

Diana and Allie lacked that natural grace. Diana's scowl had hardened over the years and now she loathed having her picture taken, being constantly told to smile. She'd point out that she hadn't forgotten how, didn't need reminding, she just didn't want to smile.

'You're going to need to smile today, Diana, it's my day and I won't let you ruin it,' Stacie had snapped when they'd all gathered in her bridal suite for pre-ceremony shots.

'I like pictures of me to be on my terms,' Diana replied through gritted teeth as she forced herself to smile sweetly for the photographer and popped out her hip, hand atop it, as per his instructions, the force of the expression shown in the strain across her forehead. 'These are posed. They look unnatural.'

'They are wedding pictures.' Stacie's cheeks were reddening. Between clicks of the camera she looked sharply at Diana, her pallor almost matching her hair. 'They are meant to be posed.'

'I could take some more candid shots,' the photographer offered kindly.

'No.' With a click of her fingers Stacie dismissed the comment and rigidly stepped into her next position. She looked down at her bouquet of pink lilies, her friends gathered around her, also smiling in admiration at the floral display. 'I want my pictures to look posed and happy. Like a spread in OK! magazine. Got it?'

'Got it.' The photographer nodded and the camera clicked.

Allie was always nervous at large social gatherings. A marathon of self-defeating thoughts ran in a continual loop in her mind.

Was she stooping?

In her clingy pink dress could people see the scars on her back?

Would a day spent in heels make her spine ache?

'I'll be right back.' Jim planted a kiss on his wife's lips and drifted off to chat to some other guests.

'This has been the best day,' Stacie gushed to her friends, her blue eyes still bright.

'We're just glad you enjoyed it.' Gail placed a hand on the bride's shoulder and squeezed.

'And now you're Jim's problem, not ours,' Diana laughed.

'Ha, true.' Stacie looked at her bridesmaids in turn, no doubt checking their floor-length gowns for creases or blemishes. She lingered on Allie, a fold appearing between her eyebrows. 'Red?'

Allie blinked. 'What?'

'Red nails, Allie.' Stacie was looking fixedly at her hands, the fold deepening. 'I thought we talked about this. The theme for the day is pink. Everyone else managed it.'

'Oh, crap.' Allie closed her hands into fists, trying to hide the offending nails. The previous day they'd all been for manicures and like a moth to a flame when asked what shade of polish she'd like Allie had pointed to the bottle full of bright red paint. It was her favourite colour. It was blood, it was danger. It was defiance. All characteristics she yearned to embody. 'Stace, I didn't think, I just—'

'You were there at the salon.' Gail turned her entire body towards the bride, becoming a human wall between her and Allie. 'You should have spoken up if you didn't want her to paint them red.'

'Am I supposed to be babysitting you all?' Stacie demanded, appalled. 'Sticking to a colour scheme is a pretty simple request which I thought you'd all be able to follow.'

Stacie massaged her forehead and the fold disappeared. 'I've just been so stressed about today. I shouldn't be snapping at you guys.'

Gail pulled Allie back towards the group as they folded together for an embrace. A tangle of arms and taffeta. Allie breathed in the various perfumes, the hairspray and closed her eyes. She could almost pretend that they were girls again, that this was just another day in an endless summer. But as they drew apart she felt it, the space between them. It lingered in the gaps they had freshly created and didn't leave.

Fifty-Six

She took careful, deliberate steps. Allie had been ravaged by the storm. It had stolen all warmth from her body and what parts of her weren't numb tingled with an enduring sting. She slid her boots across the ice. Looking down she saw the delicate patterns which had been forged into it during the freezing process. Each time she moved forward her entire body tensed with fearful expectation, wondering how fast she could move before the ice beneath her suddenly gave way.

Was Stacie still pursuing her or had she given up the chase? Was she still intent on burning down the cabin and everything in it? Destroying their secrets?

'Don't think,' Allie told herself. 'Just keep going.' To think would be her undoing. She couldn't allow herself to imagine her friends' faces, to let the horror of what had happened sink into her bones. She needed to keep gliding, to keep her steps light. Because all too easily the ice could break and she'd be plunged into freezing darkness, a darkness from which she'd never escape.

The cracking. It was a sound Allie had heard before. Bone on bone as she lay face down on a stiff metal bed as a chiropractor worked to unknot her spine in a fight to keep the sensation at its base.

The cracking was soft yet constant. It accompanied Allie's every step. Focusing on the snowy landscape ahead she didn't look down, didn't want to see the damage being done to the delicate ice by her progress.

'Allie! Stop! Please stop!'

Allie felt her heart clench with panic. Stacie was calling her. She had been found. Speeding up as much as she dared Allie continued down the river, across the fragile ice.

'Just stop!' came the plea from behind her.

No. Keep going. Don't turn round.

'Allie!'

Popping sounds joined the cracking. Splinters were being freshly forged in the ice, reaching out towards the shoreline like large fissures. How much longer would it hold?

She kept going, tried to listen only to the sound of her own shallow breaths.

'Allie!'

Her name again, dragged across the icy river to her on a bitter breeze. Allie thought of the gun in Stacie's hands, imagined it taking aim at her exposed body as she scurried away in plain sight. One squeeze of the trigger and she'd fall, paint the ice red with her own blood. With a gasp she ceased moving and carefully turned, willing her mind to be playing tricks on her and conjuring phantom voices. But the threat was real. Stacie was perhaps twenty metres away, but she had joined her out on the river, out on the ice.

But she's scared of the ice.

The irrational thought burned bright in her mind. The Stacie Allie knew would never have ventured out onto the river, never have risked a fall and a broken ankle or worse. But this Stacie, with her red hair blowing out behind her, was not her Stacie. This version held a gun. This version had taken Emily's insulin, had shot Gail. Allie blinked, felt how stiff her eyelashes had become, and reminded herself that her friend was still in there somewhere. She had to be. All could not truly be lost.

'Stace, don't do this. Let's both get off this bloody mountain in one piece, okay?' Allie had to shout to let her words travel back up the river, back towards the solitary figure standing nervously on the ice in the distance like an untethered shadow. The gun was still in Stacie's grasp but it hung down, no longer aimed like a deadly arrow.

'You can't leave. You'll talk. I know you will!'

'Stace, I won't.' It was hard to speak. Each time Allie opened her mouth the cold eagerly invaded her, seeping down her throat like icy poison. 'We'll say we don't know what happened at the cabin. We'll say—'

'You killed Diana.' There was fire in the accusation. Despite the cold, Allie felt it singe her cheeks as it reached her. 'Bet you regret ever saving her that day out on the road.'

'No!' The truth burst freely from Allie's lips. She regretted nothing about that day. She reacted at the moment, truly believing her friend was in danger. But even then, the girls were keeping secrets from one another. If she'd known about Ollie, about what he'd done to Emily, would Allie have reacted differently? Keeping secrets – over the last twenty years it was a skill all the girls had learned to perfect.

'You can't leave this mountain.' Slowly, deliberately, Stacie raised the shotgun. Her arms were stiff and strong. Not even a slight tremor fluttered through her stance. 'We're going to go back to the cabin. Together. And together we'll watch it burn.'

The stench of petrol still clung to Allie's clothes. There was no way that Stacie expected her to just be a spectator to her grand bonfire. She intended her friend to burn, to silence the final secret that existed between the now fractured Fierce Five.

'Stacie . . .' Allie was lifting up her hands in submission.

'Allie Bear, please, I'm not asking.' The distance between them was too great to tell if the tremor in Stacie's voice was a result of tears falling down her ice-blasted face.

Run.

The impulse shot through Allie like an electric current. She needed to run. What was the range on the shotgun? Fifty metres? Less? Allie had no idea. And the distance between them was currently about twenty metres. Maybe twenty-five. If Allie ran and Stacie took the shot, there was every chance she'd miss.

And every chance she wouldn't.

Allie swallowed, tasting copper. Was the petrol she'd ingested polluting her system? There wasn't time to worry about it.

Run.

All of her muscles tightened. Even her spine tingled. Fight or flight. And this was definitely a time for flight.

Allie turned and ran. Cracks and pops snapped at her heels, stalking her down the river. In her spiked hiking boots, it was difficult to get any sort of traction, any sort of speed, but she did her best. With her arms spread like wings in case she fell, Allie sprinted down the river like a large-footed bird trying desperately to take flight.

The ice kept splintering. It popped and hissed as it buckled beneath the pressure of her weight. The green door had to be close now. Allie just needed to outrun Stacie's gun to reach it.

'You think I can't make the shot? I can!' Stacie's words were a taunt. A taunt that Allie fought to ignore. She just needed to keep running, to stay on her feet long enough to reach the end of the river, the base of the mountain. 'Please, Allie, just stop running. Come back, we can talk things through.'

Pop.

Crack.

The ice was communicating with her. Every strained sound was a plea for her to remove herself, to scramble away from the glistening surface before it shattered like a mirror.

'Come on.' Allie's legs darted beneath her, slipping one way and then another, but somehow she kept her momentum going forwards. In her mind's eye she saw Gail, lifeless against the bedroom floor of the cabin, a gaping hole in her chest. A hole which Stacie had put there. One shot. That's all it had taken to bring down the Wonder Woman of the group. It would surely take much less to end Allie. Weak little Allie with her battered spine.

'I mean it, Allie. Stop or I'll shoot!'

Allie believed her. Stacie had always been a woman of her word. If she shot now where would the bullet land? In Allie's back? Her legs? Her head? When the end came Allie hoped it would be quick. Better to fall beneath a bullet here than to burn to death at the cabin. The petrol remained a putrid reminder of what fate beheld her back up the mountain. All because of some lies. Lies that had snowballed over time.

'I never wanted this, Allie.' There was something genuinely repentant in Stacie's voice, but still, Allie wouldn't stop. Not again. She had snapped the umbilical cord of friendship when she'd started to run. Now she was truly alone. It was her against the mountain. Against the ice. Against Stacie. 'I didn't intend to hurt anyone. Not Emily. Not Gail. Not you.'

A lifetime of friendship. All those years had been worn away to nothing in a matter of hours. Allie had only ever known a world that contained her four best friends. Every step she had taken had been in their wake. School, college, university. Where her friends went, she followed. But if she managed to reach the end of the river there would be no one left to follow. No one to turn to. At some point, a battle line had been drawn and everyone had taken sides. Allie had failed to even notice that a war was raging between them all; she'd been too busy trying quite literally to find her feet.

And now she was running. On ice. In hiking boots. Her parents, her surgical consultant, they'd all be stunned to see her, but equally overjoyed. Allie had defied the odds, had learned to walk again. To run. But the numbness in her spine and the gun aimed at her back told her that she'd never be free from her past. There was always an anchor, one hand holding her beneath the water so that she spent her life on the brink of drowning.

'This was never meant to be about you.'

Stacie sounded far enough away that Allie's confidence grew. She ran faster. Biting down on her own thoughts to give her the strength she needed to keep going.

It's always been about me.

She kept running, kept slipping across the ice erratically in her frantic desire to reach the end of the river.

It's always been about all of us.

The Fierce Five had been a never-ending circle. It was hard to discern where one of the girls ended and another began, their lives were so intricately interwoven. But now everything was falling apart. Allie felt the frayed threads of her lifelong friendships unravelling and dragging behind her, sweeping across the ice like a moth-eaten cape.

She dared to twist to glance behind, down the length of the polished, frozen river. Distantly she saw a figure, a hazy shadow on the horizon, a halo of red hair billowing behind her. Stacie. Allie kept running, but stared for several seconds, trying to focus on the gun in Stacie's hands, aimed in her direction. Was it swaying in the wind? Or was that Allie's angle of perception deceiving her? Stacie seemed to have stopped running, fixed to the centre of the river, the gun dipping between her chest and knees. Was she giving in to exhaustion or the cold? Allie snapped her gaze forwards, knowing there wasn't the time to ponder why haste had left her purser.

She kept running. Kept scrambling across the ice. Allie imagined finding the green door at the base of the mountain and thrashing her frozen hands against it. Help was close. Was within reach. She just needed to keep moving. Needed to remain ahead of Stacie. Ahead of the gun. Just a bit further and—

A shot.

It tore through the air, shattering the snow-muffled silence of the mountain. With a gasp, Allie threw herself forward, against the mercy of the ice. Arms splayed, cheek pressed against the frozen river she waited. Tight, tense breaths stained the blue ice with mist. Allie waited to feel the warmth of her own blood pulsing out of her, seeping into her clothes. Where had the bullet pierced her flesh? She waited and she felt nothing, only the frigid embrace of the surrounding cold air. Did that mean . . .

She launched herself into an upright position before the thought had even fully formed in her mind. Her hands desperately reached for the base of her spine, the one point on her body that could conceal a deadly shot from her. Twisting her head back and forth she surveyed the ice, looking for the inky stain of crimson. But there was no blood. Just hairline fractures creeping along the river.

There had been a shot. Allie had definitely heard it; still felt it ringing in her ears, in her bones. It took several attempts, but she managed to climb back to her feet. The snow had ceased falling and even the wind was just a whisper. Pressing her hands against her arms, her chest, she double-checked that yes, she was still very much alive, not bleeding out upon the frozen river. She wasn't hallucinating. The burn on her cheek from the caress of the ice told her she was awake, told her that this was all very real. But then where had the sound come from? Had Stacie taken a shot and missed?

Looking back towards the mountain, the river was empty, the ice smooth and clear. There was no lone figure. Stacie was gone. A hole opened deep within Allie, trying to swallow her up with its familiar feeling. Stacie's sudden absence opened a latch on a memory.

Emily fainting in class.

Diana hanging off the bridge.

Danger.

The word became a siren in Allie's mind. Stacie was in danger. Feral instincts took over. Allie tried to sprint back up the river, but her hiking boots made her clumsy and slow.

'Dammit.' With a cry of despair she stopped, stooped down and flung off her gloves. Her fingers were still stiff as they awkwardly plucked at the laces of her boots. But Allie wouldn't give up. She needed them off. Needed speed. Allie was panting as she fought with her boots, determined not to lose another friend that day. Finally, the laces gave way and she hauled off the boots and tossed them aside where they landed near her gloves. Then she ran back up the river, across the weakened ice.

Fifty-Seven

'Stacie!'

Allie's footsteps whispered across the ice. She was faster without her boots, but not markedly so. Twice she was brought to her knees by the slick surface beneath her. Quickly she scrambled back to her feet and kept running. Up ahead she saw the hole that Stacie must have disappeared through, then the dwindling fire of splayed hair bobbing up and down in it.

The ice had split. A cragged canyon had opened up between its smooth surfaces, revealing the glossy black water below. Allie lunged forward as she reached its edge, throwing herself onto her stomach and plunging both hands into the water. It felt like reaching into a pit of needles. Every sharp end found her skin and pricked at her. The pain travelled up to her shoulders. Allie gritted her teeth and fought against it.

'Stacie.' She reached for the figure of her friend. Her frozen fingers feebly felt their way through the water. 'Stace, I'm here, let me pull you out.'

For a moment Stacie broke through the surface, her skin blue. Her eyes were wide with fear as she spluttered out a desperate breath and then she plunged back beneath the inky water just as suddenly as she'd appeared.

'Stacie!' Allie could feel her friend slipping away. Keeping her hands in the water she twisted upon the ice, surveying her surroundings. If only there was a nearby branch she could use or—

'Al—' Stacie resurfaced, dark water choking her words. 'Allie.'

She looked like a ghost. Her red hair turning as black as the river around her. There was ice in her eyes as she stared at her friend. 'My—'

The water reclaimed her with frightening force.

'No!' Allie squealed, moving as close to the edge as she dared. Her arms were now completely submerged, the prick of the needles making their way along her neck, her back. 'Stacie, just grab on to me, I can pull you out!'

'Something—' Like a frantic fish caught on a line Stacie flailed as she fought to be free. 'My ankle.' She kept sinking beneath the glossy sheen of the waterline. 'It's caught.'

'Okay.' Allie widened her legs, anchoring herself. Her fingers were now completely numb but still, she commanded them to reach out, to flex and twist until they had Stacie within their grasp. 'I'm going to pull you free. Okay? Just hold on to me. You got it? Don't let go.'

Allie's fingers knotted around the soaked fabric of Stacie's coat. The cold within the water slithered up her arms like desperate serpents, hungrily trying to devour her entire body. If only she wasn't so cold. If only she had more sensation within her hands, her arms. But everything was quickly growing numb.

'Stacie!'

Her friend was beneath the water, held down by her ankle. Her pale face shone like the moon within its dark depths. Stacie's long hair fanned out around her, flame-laced tendrils reaching for the surface.

'I've got you.' Allie tightened her grip as much as she could and pulled. She strained so hard she could feel her muscles threatening to snap. But no matter how much force she exerted, whatever was within the water, wrapped around Stacie's ankle, was stronger than she was. 'No!' Refusing to back down from the fight Allie scooted closer to the edge of the hole, letting the water reach up to her chin. 'Stace, I've got you, hold on,' she stated firmly as the freezing touch of the river slid between her teeth and iced her tongue.

'No!' A scream ripped out of Allie. She smacked her arms around in the water, connecting with nothing. 'No! No! No!' Her hands swirled in the icy depths but found no figure to grasp on to. 'Come back, I'm still here! Come back!' Stacie had slipped away from her reach, had plunged so deep into the frozen river that Allie could no longer follow.

'No!' Withdrawing from the hole Allie smashed her fists against the ice. She didn't care how fragile it was. If the river wanted to claim her too, then let it. 'Stacie!' Her friend's name was a ravaged cry on her lips. 'Stacie, come back! You can't go! You can't leave me!'

Kneeling at the edge of the ice, Allie looked down at the smooth black surface of the water, at her own ghostly reflection which rippled upon it. She looked utterly broken. And utterly alone.

'I wonder if I ever really knew you.' Lucas studied Allie as though she were an object in a museum as he stood over her, his back against the fireplace. 'I mean . . .' With a sigh, he thrust his free hand deep into his jeans pocket. His other hand clutched a bottle of beer, his fourth of the night. 'I thought I knew you. I thought I knew everything about you. I even read your damn book twice.'

Allie didn't flinch. She remained perfectly composed, knees neatly pressed together, hands folded in her lap as she sat on the sofa and looked up at her husband and reacted to the news that he intended to leave her.

'You're so guarded, Allie. So closed off. You're supposed to be my wife for God's sake and yet' – he gestured at her head with his half-empty bottle of beer – 'I never know what's going on in there. You never let me in. And to think that you kept such a secret from me.'

'Lucas, it's not healthy to know everything about someone.'

'Of course, it is!' he raged, cheeks reddening. 'There aren't supposed to be secrets between a husband and wife,' he groaned in frustration. 'But you're so bloody full of them. Of secrets. Secrets that affect our fucking life! I used to love how mysterious you were. But, Allie, you have to let me in. Do you trust anyone? Because if you don't trust me then who do you trust?'

'I . . .' Allie felt herself faltering. 'My friends. I trust my friends.'

'You mean the ones you never see?' Lucas replied cruelly.

'I see them.' She felt instantly ashamed of the lie. But the first part was true. She did trust her friends. 'Just because we don't see one another all the time doesn't mean we're not close,' she continued.

'Bullshit,' Lucas snapped. 'You and I, we share a bed, Allie. That's . . . it doesn't get closer than that. You're telling me you trust your absent friends over me?'

'I've known them all my life,' Allie responded plainly.

'You're not fifteen anymore, Allie. You guys . . . you've got partners, families, to consider. Your loyalties can't lie with each other first and foremost. At least they shouldn't.'

'Lucas, they're my best friends.'

'So they know it all do they?' He gestured again at her head, his expression manic. 'They know what goes on in that head of yours? They get to be privy to all your little secrets? Even though you never bloody see them? What are they, clairvoyant?'

Allie smiled curtly but said nothing. She was done talking. Slowly she got up and walked over to the front door, grabbing her parka which was hanging up on the wall beside it. As she shrugged it on Lucas stormed after her.

'Where the hell are you going?'

'Out. To clear my head.'

'Allie, we're not done here.' His breath reeked of beer and pain.

'Yes, we are.' Her response was simple, stoic, as she pushed him aside and pulled open the door to their flat.

'So you're just going to spend your life only letting your friends get close? Only letting your friends inside your head? What kind of life is that for a grown woman?'

Allie kept walking, head held high as she approached the stainless-steel doors of the lift.

'You're delusional, Allie!' Lucas yelled before slamming the door closed, not waiting for a response. Allie's confident smile swiftly died on her lips.

As she repeatedly pressed the call button for the lift she blinked rapidly to stave off tears.

Fifty-Eight

Numb from more than just the cold, Allie gradually withdrew from the hole in the ice, leaving her haunted reflection rippling upon its glassy surface. She staggered across the river, making for its snow-laden banks. There was no longer any need to follow it down towards the green door. Who was left to save?

It had stopped snowing, but the clouds overhead remained plump with the threat of more to come. Allie had to remind herself how to walk.

One foot.

Then the other.

She didn't slip or fall. Even the ice didn't want her now. It granted her safe passage to the snow-covered ground that bordered it and there Allie dropped as though she were falling onto a sumptuous bed. She dropped onto her back, arms outstretched, and stared wide-eyed at the dense sky which had softened from a steel grey to an off-white. She wanted to feel the snow on her face, to lie there until it buried her, until the mountain claimed her along with her friends.

Exhaustion fought with fear. Allie ignored them both as she pulled in deep, heavy breaths, tasting the sense of dread that lingered in the air. The snow was cold but welcoming against Allie's back. She was so dreadfully tired. It felt like the last of her own life force had slipped away with Stacie, down into the frigid depths of the frozen river.

There was no birdsong. No rustle of leaves as the wind whispered through them. The mountain was silent, all sounds muffled by the thick coating of snow. All Allie could hear were her own harried breaths. Somehow her organs were still functioning, still remembering how to breathe even though her world had just ended. Why wasn't her body reacting appropriately? She should be beside the hole in the ice, crippled over in pain. Instead, she was sprawled out on the ground, arms wide as though she were about to make a snow angel.

Something in the distance caught Allie's attention. A sound. Soft at first, like murmured conversation heard through a wall. But gradually it grew louder, clearer. The whir of an engine, the shredding of long blades ripping through the air in a ceaseless rotation. A helicopter.

Allie forced herself to sit up as she craned her neck to stare towards the sky. She didn't know whether to thrust her arms up and down to grab the pilot's attention or to lie back and hope that she was camouflaged by the snow and the trees.

The helicopter came into view. A mechanical bird soaring uneasily above the treetops. Allie took a deep breath. Help had finally arrived. Had someone spotted the flares? Had Gail managed to fix the generator? Allie was too exhausted to care. Closing her eyes, she let the darkness overwhelm her.

'Do you ever think what life would be like, if you hadn't pulled her back that day? If you'd kept both hands on the railing?' Lucas asked in the thick gloom of night.

Allie retreated from the window of her flat, where she'd been looking out at the glittering lights of the city. She saw Lucas's silhouette sitting in their bed, turned towards her, but it was too dark to read his expression.

'Sorry,' she muttered as she climbed beneath the thin sheets, her speech still thick with sleep. 'I didn't mean to wake you.'

'It's okay.' He put his hands on her shoulders. He was so warm, like being caressed by fire. Allie shifted beyond his reach, drawing the sheets up to her chin. 'So many nights I wake up to find you over by the window, staring out, one hand on your back.'

'Like I said, I didn't mean to wake you.'

'Allie.' Lucas crossed the centre of the bed so that he could look down at her, his voice soft. 'I'm not judging you, baby. I'm just worried. You stand at the window, looking haunted, massaging your back. That's why I asked. I mean, if you'd not pushed Diana aside that day you never would have ended up in hospital. You wouldn't have gone through all the crap that you did.'

'But Diana would have,' Allie replied bluntly.

'She made the choice to put her life at risk,' Lucas pressed, keeping his words soft and gentle yet probing. 'She could have kept holding on. She chose to let go. Your heroics cost you an awful lot, Allie. A price most people wouldn't be willing to pay.'

'Are you saying I shouldn't have saved my friend?' There was fire in the question as Allie's eyes fully opened, all thoughts of sleep promptly abandoned.

'I'm saying.' Lucas raised a hand to massage his neck, remaining close to her. 'You paid an awfully high price to save her life. I mean you almost lost the ability to walk. Do you ever wonder how things would be if you'd not pulled her back that day?'

'No.'

'No?'

'What good would that kind of thinking do? You can't change the past.'

'That's awfully pragmatic of you, Allie. I mean, it's only human to wonder what might have—'

'It wasn't my ability to walk that I lost that day. That could be reclaimed, eventually. It was something more than that. Something that I was always going to lose anyway.'

'And what was that?'

Allie hesitated. 'My innocence.'

'Allie . . .' She felt Lucas's hand on her cheek, his breath against her face. He sounded like his heart was breaking. 'Sweetheart, I don't like you dwelling on this. It worries me. You did a brave thing and I'm not trying to take that away from you.' He kissed her. A brush against her lips and then he was gone.

Closing her eyes, Allie sighed. This wasn't a path she wanted to go down. She'd already said too much. She was tired, her guard was lowered. At the window she'd stand and watch the twinkle of the streetlights, gaze at the honey glow of homes still lit up, wondering what made people choose to burn the midnight oil. It was a game she used to play as a girl, only her old bedroom offered a much less interesting view. Every home on her street would be plunged into darkness after eleven p.m. on a school night.

The city never slept. It always hummed with activity, always throbbed with life. Allie found that comforting.

At fifteen everything had changed for her. More than losing her ability to walk, her ability to one day have children, she lost her ability to believe in infinity. Life suddenly had limits. A beginning and an inevitable end. But she'd saved Diana and that was worth it. Better to lose her childish innocence than to lose Diana. She'd have been forced to grow up eventually anyway. It was a price she'd pay over and over if it meant keeping her friends forever. That had been the promise made around campfires and at sleepovers as they sat snuggled in brightly coloured sleeping bags like little neon worms.

'Best friends forever.'

Love. Loyalty. These feelings didn't have an expiry date like innocence did.

Tilting her head, Allie found Lucas's mouth and kissed him hard. He wrapped his arms around her in response, drawing their bodies together. She was done talking. Done feeling. She regretted nothing. She'd saved her best friend and she felt safe in the certainty that she'd made the right decision.

Fifty-Nine

POI: There's nothing else I'm going to say.

Officer: At the cabin, we have one gunshot victim. Two bodies were found out on the mountain. One individual is still missing. At the cabin there was the gunshot victim, and then there was yourself, comatose. So where is Stacie?

POI: I believe she fell through the ice.

Officer: When she was chasing Allie? Or when Allie was chasing her?

POI: How am I supposed to be able to answer that?

Officer: The on-site response team checked the crack in the ice. There's no sign of Stacie. When her body does show up will we get any surprises?

POI: Have you had any yet? Diana fell, you found her. I've not lied to you once. Where is Allie?

Officer: She's still in hospital in a critical condition, so she's not been able to do much talking.

POI: Well I've told you all I can. You can't hold me here forever.

Officer: You've not been overly forthcoming with the truth, Emily. Who shot Gail?

POI: As I said – I've told you all that I can. I only heard the second shot, I didn't see who fired the gun. Please, I'm still weak, I need to rest.

Officer: When Allie is finally well enough to make an official statement will her version of events corroborate with your own?

POI: Yes.

Officer: Because you'll both lie?

POI: Are you calling me a liar?

Officer: I'm asking if you've been completely truthful.

POI: And I'm telling you that yes, to the best of my abilities I have been.

Officer: Why doesn't that sound like confirmation?

POI: A traumatised mind is a tricky thing, Officer Fields. Memories can surface without warning at a later date.

Officer: So you're withholding something?

POI: I've told you all I know.

Officer: And Allie?

POI: I'm sure she'll talk once she's up to it.

Officer: Do you want her to get better?

POI: Of course. Why wouldn't I? She's my best friend.

Officer: Two of your friends are dead. One is missing and presumed to have also died. What if Allie is to blame?

POI: She might think that I'm to blame.

Officer: But you say you're not.

POI: Can I go now? You've got my statement.

Officer: What happens when Allie talks? Will we finally learn the truth about what happened up on that mountain? What happened to your friends?

POI: Those are all questions for my lawyer.

Officer: Emily—

POI: I have told you everything I can.

Officer: Tell me, do you regret meeting your friends at the cabin? Do you wish you hadn't gone?

POI: You've asked that before. You should know by now that regrets are like pin drops. Alone, they are silent, but get enough of them dropping at once and it can be deafening.

Officer: So you've a lot of regrets?

POI: Don't you?

Officer: Do you regret making it off that mountain?

POI: I think that might just be your stupidest question yet.

Officer: Two people died. One is missing. I'm going to get to the bottom of this.

POI: I don't care what you find, Officer Fields. You can't change anything.

Officer: Meaning?

POI: Meaning we're done here.

Sixty

Light. So much light it was blinding. It seared against her eyes as she slowly opened them.

'What the . . .' Gradually the brightness began to recede and Allie noted the tiles in the ceiling, the medicinal odour in the air.

'Allie . . .' Pressure against her hand. And a voice, a familiar voice. 'Allie, are you okay, I've been so worried about you.'

With great effort, she shifted her neck to peer down at her hand. Thin fingers were clasped over her own and a tube was connected to the back of her hand. Adjusting her gaze, she saw another tube ending in the smooth underside of her elbow and the starched fabric of hospital bedding which was tucked tightly around her bed.

Her body.

Allie's chin dipped to her chest and she saw the NHS logo emblazoned on the gown she was wearing. Where were her clothes? What was happening?

'You're awake again, good, let's get this on you.' A new voice, one Allie didn't recognise, was speaking on the opposite side of her bed. Then she was being held forwards and a clear mask was being adjusted over her face. It hissed at her, making her skin hot. 'Just breathe through this for a while, okay?'

'O-kay.' Her throat was beyond raw and her tongue was swollen and useless in her mouth. She felt like she'd spent the last twelve hours licking a brick wall. She was in the hospital, that much she could make out. But why? It was agonising to twist back in the direction of the voice she knew. Every fibre of her body ached as though a freight train had struck her while she slept.

'Allie . . .' The fingers tightened around her own and it was a strangely reassuring sensation.

'Emily?' Allie looked at her blonde friend who appeared pale even in the yellow light of the hospital room. Her mouth was drooped with sorrow and in her eyes there was something, an inescapable agony that Allie could already feel seeping into the space around them. 'Where? What?' The hissing of the mask tried to drown out her questions.

Where am I?

What happened?

Emily had questions of her own. 'What do you remember? Allie, do you remember being at the cabin? Do you remember going down the mountain?'

The cabin. The mountain.

Recognition glowed within Allie and then dimmed. She did remember being at the cabin, flying up to meet her friends, to celebrate Gail's thirty-fifth birthday. There had been music. And snow. Lots of snow. But they had all been there. So why was she now lying in a hospital bed?

Diana lying broken on a precipice.

Gail bathed in a pool of her own blood.

Stacie slipping away beneath the ice.

A trio of terrible events skipped through her mind like an old film reel. Allie started to whimper.

'They found you on the mountainside, passed out,' Emily explained, raising her voice to be heard over the hiss of the oxygen mask. 'When they brought you in you were suffering from severe hypothermia.'

337

Now that Allie thought about it, she could feel a warm sensation snaking up her arm via her wrist. Clearly whatever was being fed to her intravenously had been heated to help her body fight off the penetrating clutch of the cold.

Allie looked beyond Emily, towards the foot of her bed where she should have expected to find three more faces. Gail, Diana and Stacie, they were meant to be there too, each keeping a vigil at a corner. Only the room was empty. Even the nurse had left. There was only Emily at her bedside.

'Do you remember what happened?' Emily pressed. Her voice sounded off, even over the hiss of the oxygen mask Allie could hear the twinge in it, the ache. 'The police are asking questions and—'

'You're . . .' She drank deeply from the mask. 'You're okay?'

The journey down the mountain had all been for Emily, to ensure her survival. And now here she was. And she was real, wasn't she? Allie wasn't caught in some obscure purgatory as she lingered between life and death?

Emily's face softened into a tentative smile. 'I'm okay, Allie.' Her blue eyes began to sparkle with tears. 'Thanks to you someone saw the flares and sent help. They found me at the cabin just in time.'

'Stacie—'

'They say she's gone. She's not at the cabin and they can't find her out on the mountain. They believe she fell through the ice on the river.'

Allie could feel that her face was swollen, lips reluctant to allow speech. But she had so many questions burning through her, raising her temperature more than the IV pumping directly into her veins ever could.

'And Gail?'

'Let's not talk about it all now, okay? The main thing is that you're all right; you're going to pull through. Your mum and dad are on their way up here. And I think they've contacted Lucas too. Everything is going to be all right, Allie.'

Lucas too.

Was he still listed as her next of kin? On a seemingly endless list of things to do after a break-up had she forgotten to detach herself from him in more official capacities?

'No, I . . .' Allie fought to speak.

Because things weren't all right. Clearly. 'The others,' Allie pressed, looking again to the vacant spots around her bed. 'They can't be gone.'

It was too much. Allie felt the universe widening around her, making her feel small and vulnerable. And abandoned.

Emily squeezed her hand tighter. 'I'm here.' There was a strong insistence to her voice. She kept holding on, refusing to let go. 'And I'm not going anywhere, Allie Bear, you hear me? I'm going to do right by you this time.'

The hissing. The beeping. A concert of mechanical sounds was being conducted around Allie's head. Had she somehow slipped through some sort of worm hole and returned to being fifteen? The powerlessness, the alienation, it all felt the same. Only her legs . . .

Allie shifted to crane her neck as she wiggled her toes. They were hidden beneath her blanket but she saw the fabric shift, felt the stirring of movement in her nerves. She was still whole. Her relief sounded like a sob as it caught in her throat.

'I won't leave you,' Emily insisted.

'How can they all be gone?'

'I don't know. One minute I was in the cabin feeling like shit and then I was waking up here in hospital, like you.'

'The police?' Allie croaked, struggling to resist the urge to close her eyes and drift back into darkness. She badly needed to sleep, to rest.

'They'll have questions for you.'

Allie nodded.

Questions like *Who shot Gail* and *Where is Stacie?*

Stacie had insisted it wasn't her, just as Allie had insisted she hadn't pushed Diana. But they'd both had strong motivations to hurt the others.

'I'm here, Allie. Just rest.' Emily was gripping her hand hard. Too hard. Allie winced as the pressure of the needles within her veins intensified.

'Em . . .' The drugs in her system were blurring her vision, slowing her thoughts. Sleep. It was wrapping velvety gloves around her ankles and pulling her down. 'Em, I—'

'Rest, Allie. I'm here.' Emily's hand abruptly lifted, leaving Allie's pulsing in pain, 'I'll be right by your side. I'm not going anywhere. It's just you and me now.'

A single tear dropped down Allie's burned cheek. She thought of the five little girls pushed towards one another during their first day at play school, how they'd linked their squidgy hands together and made giggled introductions.

'I'm Stacie.'

'I'm Diana.'

'I'm Gail.'

'I'm Emily.'

And always last, always shy, 'I'm Allie.'

'Let's be best friends!' Stacie had smiled. The suggestion had been unanimously accepted as a group of equally nervous mothers looked on, relieved that their precious little ones had found some sort of acceptance with their peers.

'I like your hair,' Allie had whispered to Stacie. 'It's like fire.' Glancing around the circle she saw that she liked the blue of Emily's eyes, the firmness of Diana's stare and the strength in Gail's shoulders. Five little points on the same star.

'It was the lie.' The mattress shifted as Lucas joined her at the foot of the bed. 'Allie, I need you to know that.'

Her hands were on her knees and her back was straight, too straight. It ached to keep her posture so pristine.

'Allie?' She could feel Lucas's gaze on her — it had always held such heat. But she couldn't turn her head to look at him. How could she? The nearby wardrobe stood depleted of half of its contents. A single black suitcase was propped up by the front door. He was leaving. This was goodbye. 'Allie?' His tone sharpened as a hand reached and grabbed her own. But their flesh had barely touched when he was quickly withdrawing again. Allie understood. There was an ocean between them rather than just a few inches of a Laura Ashley duvet cover.

'You're all packed?'

'Seriously? That's all you have to say to me? Am I all packed?'

Allie began to hunch forward, studying her nails with interest. The red polish she'd applied the previous afternoon had already chipped. 'Look, Lucas . . .'

'I mean how . . .' Springs sighed as he stood up and moved to stand directly in front of her. Still, she wouldn't look at him. 'How could you lie to me about something like that?'

'I didn't . . . I—'

'Allie, you can't have children. You've known that since you were fifteen, yet you waited until we'd been married for three whole months before telling me. Why? Why not trust me with that sooner? Christ, Allie, I'm your husband.'

'But that will soon be past tense, won't it?'

'Did you ever even want this?' Lucas cupped her chin with a warm hand and forced her to look up. His eyes glistened in the early afternoon light but there were no crinkles in the corners. 'I *thought we were in love, Allie. You were my world. And yet . . .'* He dropped his hand so suddenly that Allie felt a sweep of air across her neck. It made her shiver. *'All along your friends knew. Why couldn't you trust me like you trusted them? Allie, I'd have understood!'*

'Then why leave?' With her head released Allie resumed staring at her nails. She heard the petulance in her voice.

'The lie, Allie! How many times do I have to explain that it is because you lied to me! Over and over! You let me concoct this fairy tale in my mind about the family we'd never have. And I don't even care about that. I care that you never felt able to tell me the truth. That says so much.'

The most recent chip, when had it occurred? Was it when she was at the Tesco Express that morning filling her basket with food she knew she wasn't going to eat?

'You know what I thought when I first met you?' The floorboards winced as Lucas began pacing back and forth along the length of their little bedroom. *'I thought, "Wow, what a strong, accomplished woman." I read your book, Allie, and I was blown away. You'd been through so much. You were a survivor. And now . . .'* He returned to her side on the bed but kept a tentative distance. Allie permitted herself to glance at him out of the corner of her eye. *'I think you never got over what happened that day. I think in your mind you're still that broken girl.'* There were tears on Lucas's cheeks, catching the light and carrying it down to his chin. *'I think a part of you is forever trapped out there on that bridge.'*

'N-no.' Her throat was sandpaper. Lucas was wrong. Of course he was. Allie was resilient, a fighter. She had the book and the scars to prove it. *'Lucas . . .'* Her fingertips grazed his sleeve as he stood up for the final time.

'You did this, Allie. Not me.' Bowing, he planted a single kiss on her forehead and then he was leaving, opening and closing

doors as he made his way out of their shared flat. Allie listened to the squeak of his suitcase wheels as he hauled his luggage out into the hallway. And then, straining, she could just make out the chime of the lift as it parted its doors for him.

Her nails were blood red. Allie stretched out her fingers, noting all the chips, the cracks. If she closed her eyes she could still smell the cocoa butter of the suntan lotion, could still taste the sweetness of the 99 upon her lips. She welcomed the silence which followed Lucas's departure.

Sixty-One

The hotel room felt stark – the cream walls too bare, the white sheets on the bed too crisp. Allie stood by the window, chin dipped against her chest as she watched flurries of snowflakes spiral together in a dizzying dance before they floated to the car park below. The sky was a grey slab ominously threatening more snow, more ice. Even with the heating in the room cranked right up Allie felt the lingering cold from the mountainside against her skin like a second layer she'd never be able to peel off.

'You should come and sit,' Emily urged from her position, genteelly perched at the end of the bed. Her blonde hair was swept back in a loose bun and the thick grey jumper she wore hung off her delicate frame. 'Really, Allie, you need to be resting.'

'I . . .' A restless energy snaked along Allie's veins, infecting her entire system. 'I can't.' Turning back towards the room she faced her friend who somehow managed to appear poised, elegant. She was like Allie's mother, always calm and composed in a crisis. In contrast, Allie had not dressed for two days straight, still clad in her crumpled pyjamas and the thick towelling robe provided by the hotel. She was dwarfed within its white fabric but didn't care. Engulfing herself in it like a cloak made her feel safe, protected. Her hair was greasily matted to her head. Lucas was due to arrive the following morning and she was committed to showering before he did. Until then she could languish in her lethargy for a few more hours. 'Seriously, Em, go and be with Adam and the twins. Don't worry about me.'

Emily sent a pinched smile in Allie's direction. 'We leave tomorrow and you've been mostly sleeping since we checked in to the hotel, but I think we should talk, don't you? While it's just the two of us.'

Allie hugged her arms against her chest. She was relieved that her charade was working, that Emily thought she'd been sleeping. In reality, she'd been lying upon her hotel bed and staring at the ceiling until her eyes ached and became bloodshot. But she couldn't close them. To close them was to let in not just the darkness, but the awful memories of what had happened, of what had become of her friends.

'The police are going to want to speak to us both again before we leave,' Emily continued.

'But we've told them everything.' There was no ignoring the exhaustion in her bones. Allie shuffled several steps towards the bed and lowered herself down beside Emily. Their company together still felt so incomplete, like a pair of bookends now defunct since they had nothing to hold up. 'You said . . .' Raising a hand, Allie massaged her temple. A permanent headache had taken up residence behind her eyes. 'You said you remember hearing what happened between Stacie and Gail.'

'Uh huh.' Emily nodded briskly. 'It feels like it was a dream but obviously it wasn't. They were arguing, Stacie kept insisting that she'd made a mistake, that something was an accident and then the gun went off. Twice, maybe.'

Allie nodded sombrely in agreement. She'd been present for the second devastating shot that had been fired.

'Stacie's mistake.' Allie paused to gnaw on the inside of her cheek. This was why she'd been avoiding her surviving friend for the last few days. She'd learned so much at the cabin, all of it painful. To breathe life back into such revelations now felt foolish – their wounds needed time to heal before being ripped open anew. But burying secrets and feelings is what had led them to this Scottish Premier Inn, to this bleak moment where five had become two. 'You remember her admitting to stealing your meds?'

'I remember.' Emily's eyes didn't cloud over as Allie expected them to.

'And she said . . .' Drawing in a breath, Allie stopped running from her concerns, attempted to learn from what had transpired between them all. 'She said you guys talked. About that summer.'

There was no need to be more specific, the sudden clenching of Emily's jaw told her that.

'We did, yes.'

Allie didn't think her heart could break anymore but the organ surprised her by splitting again, pumping furiously within her chest despite all the damage it kept enduring. Pressing a hand to her chest she forced herself to keep speaking, to keep excavating the truth from the past.

'At that party at Ashley Smith's house, something happened. Something with Oliver Henderson.'

Inhaling sharply, Emily looked up to the ceiling, blinking. Her blue eyes shone like the ice on the river which had taken Stacie. Allie suddenly felt sick. This was all too soon, she was still too weak to go wandering down memory lane. She should stop now, push the subject no further.

'Stacie already knew it all. I think she'd known for some time. She mentioned some investigator she'd slept with.' With a shake of icy blonde hair Emily sighed and continued,

'I guess it was building up in her. Resentment, anger. I don't know. It was why she took my insulin.' Another sigh, tighter than the first. 'Still, I gave her what she so badly wanted: a torrid trip into our past. I told Stacie how Ollie raped me at the party. How there had been a baby.' Emily's voice became so soft it was barely a whisper. She kept her eyes trained to the ceiling, long fingers clenched together as she held her hands in a tense basket in her lap.

'Em, I . . .' Allie had a thousand responses stored up inside her.

You should have told me.

It's okay.

I'm here for you.

Instead, she opted for a cold slice of the truth. 'You never told us. Any of us.'

'How could I?' Emily's lips quivered. 'Stacie adored Oliver, she'd never have believed me. And I mean . . .' With a sigh, she dipped her head and unclasped her hands. 'My parents were so terrified of the truth coming out. Of my reputation being damaged. It was all they cared about. They sent me away, made me a dirty little secret.'

'Em.' Allie hugged her, drawing them close together. She could smell the sweetness of the twins in Emily's hair, the lingering cloud of Adam's cologne on her jumper. 'I'm sorry, I'm so, so sorry. If I'd known, if only—'

'I don't want them to find Stacie,' Emily whispered fearfully into her shoulder.

'What?'

'I want her to have truly disappeared beneath the ice.'

'You've every right to be angry at her and—'

'Allie, they *can't* find her.' There was a sudden urgency to Emily's words.

'They'll surely search the river and—'

'I need her to be gone.'

Allie eased back and regarded her friend before carefully asking, 'And if she isn't?'

'We're done with ifs, Allie.' Emily straightened and slid out of the embrace. 'And we're done with lies. I should have spoken up, I know that now. So much damage bled out from that day and now . . .' Raising a pink nail to her lips she began to nibble on it. Allie knew what she was going to say.

And now it's too late.

The damage from their silence was done. Stacie, Gail and Diana had paid the ultimate price for all the secrets the Fierce Five had so diligently kept from one another.

'They can't find her,' Emily muttered, still gnawing on her fingernail.

'But they might,' Allie countered. 'What's so wrong with that?'

'I don't want them to find Stacie in case she didn't drown.'

Allie frowned, confused. 'She fell through the ice. If she didn't drown, then it was . . . hypothermia.'

'Or blood loss,' Emily said, head bowed.

'Blood loss?' Allie echoed. 'I don't—'

'Upstairs, back at the cabin, I kept sliding in and out of consciousness. I heard you downstairs with her, arguing. The petrol . . .' Emily reached for Allie's hands and clasped them tightly within her own, her touch cold. 'Earlier, she'd trodden on a mirror, kicked it under the bed. I . . . Christ, it was worse than childbirth getting off that bed, fumbling for it, grabbing a shard and climbing back in, tucking it up under the duvet. I . . . she wanted to kill us, Allie. I knew that. She'd finally gone over the edge and there was no bringing her back. When she came up to me with the petrol can . . .' Emily paused and squeezed her eyes closed as her grip on Allie tightened.

A shriek.

Allie had heard it, back at the cabin, when she was at the door. But she'd barely paused to give it credence, considering it a trick of the wind or nothing at all. When instead . . .

'She came up to me, petrol can raised and I . . . I used everything I had left. I thought of Adam, the twins and I . . . I pushed that piece of mirror so deep into her side that she cried like a mouse in a trap. She looked at me, at the mirror I was holding. And she told me I was going to burn. She poured petrol down my throat and I can . . .' Emily coughed awkwardly. 'I can still taste it. But I had to do it, Allie.' She opened her eyes and gazed up imploringly at her last friend. 'I had to try and stop her somehow. Slow her down at least. One of us had to live.'

'No . . . I.' Allie breathed in deep. 'I understand.' And she did.

'She still loved him.' Emily's blue eyes glittered darkly.

'What?'

'Ollie.' Emily's porcelain cheeks filled with blood when she said his name. 'After all that he did, she still loved him. I saw it in her eyes when she told me about my insulin.'

'Look, let's not think on that, let's—'

'When I found that shard of mirror, I knew that if I saw her again I'd plunge it so deep into her that it would pierce something vital.'

'To protect yourself, right.' Allie nodded tightly. 'And to help save me. Em, I get it.'

'Only I wish I'd done more. I wish I'd had the energy to slash her throat and then watch her crumple to the floor, gasping like a fish as she drowned in her own blood.'

Allie felt cold. 'You should be resting,' she declared hastily. 'We both should.'

'If they find her body,' Emily fretted, suddenly reaching for Allie's arm and gripping so tight that her nails pierced the skin, 'and they find out what I did, I'll lose Adam, the twins. Allie, I'll lose everything!'

'No,' Allie assured her firmly, 'you won't.'

She recalled the way Stacie had wobbled out on the ice, one hand clamped to her side. If the wound hadn't weakened her might she have reached Allie quicker? Might she have been strong enough to fire one final, deadly shot? 'I won't let anything happen to you, Em. You saved me. Stacie is gone, the river has carried her away. And if they do find her, it was self-defence.'

'And if they don't believe me' – Emily's whole body trembled – 'what then, Allie? I need to think about the twins, about Adam and—'

'I'll say I stabbed her.' Allie released the words almost as an instinct, overcome with the desire to protect a friend. A desire she'd never been able to suppress.

'Allie, no, I couldn't—'

'I don't have everything to lose,' Allie consoled her softly, reaching out to stroke Emily's golden hair. 'You have everything, Em. A loving husband, two beautiful girls. Your life is perfect.'

A delicate smile pulled on Emily's pink lips as she relinquished her grip on Allie's arm. 'I knew you'd understand, Allie Bear. I know I can trust you to protect me, just like you tried to save Diana that day on the bridge.'

Allie smiled uncertainly. 'I mean, of course, Ems. I'd always protect you.'

'You're such a good friend,' Emily gushed. 'I'm so lucky to have you. Like you said, I have everything and you have nothing, and you respect that.' Allie was engulfed by vanilla-scented blonde hair as Emily embraced her tightly, her bun pressing against Allie's mouth. 'Now . . .' As they parted, Emily dipped her hand into her pocket and pulled out her phone. 'Just so we're clear . . .' her attention was briefly diverted away from Allie '. . . if they find Stacie and it transpires that she has actually bled out, what will you say?'

'I'll . . .' Allie swallowed nervously. 'I'll say that I stabbed Stacie, back at the cabin, just before I got away.'

'After she tied you up?' Emily prompted.

'Yes,' Allie confirmed. 'After she tied me up. I managed to stab her in the side which bought me some time to get out of the cabin and run down the mountain, get a head start on her.'

Emily tapped her phone and then leaned over and planted a single kiss on Allie's cheek. 'That's all I needed, Allie Bear.' She wriggled the phone in her hand, smiling widely. 'Just a little insurance, not that you'd ever go back on your word. You're far too noble for that.'

'Wait, I—' Blood was rushing to Allie's cheeks, her temples. What had just happened?

The pressure on the mattress was shifting, Emily was getting up, making for the door. 'You just rest now, okay?' She threw the instruction over her shoulder. 'You've been through quite an ordeal.' The door clicked shut and Allie looked about her hotel room, shrinking within her dressing gown.

I'll lose Adam, the twins. Allie, I'll lose everything.

Allie looked at her empty bed, then at her bare fingers which she cradled in her lap, almost choking on the nothingness of it all.

Sixty-Two

Inconclusive. That was the final verdict from the police report. Allie had held the phone and listened to her father relay the finer details of it all as though in a dream.

'It's all going to be okay, Allie,' he reassured her over and over. 'Everything you and Emily said adds up. Gail's injuries were typical of a shot from a shotgun at close range and Diana had very evidently suffered a fatal fall. And Stacie . . .'

Raindrops tapped against a nearby window like brittle fingers. Allie turned to face the greyness of the city, to see rivers running in gutters.

Stacie was gone.

The lack of a body gave way to wild and fanciful dreams. Sometimes Allie would be hurrying to catch the tube and see the flash of red hair in the crowd and her heart would batter desperately against her ribs as her palms grew slick, wondering if her friend had somehow returned to the city. It was impossible, she knew that, but still, her hope refused to die.

In reality, Stacie would have been carried by the river out to sea once the ice thawed. There was probably nothing left of her. The funerals had been hard. First Diana's and then Gail's, before finally, Stacie's, where an empty casket was burned as her mother wept into a faded handkerchief.

Allie wondered what her heart looked like these days. If you could pull apart her chest and peer at it would it appear as ragged and beaten as it felt?

'It's time to put all this behind you.' Her father was still talking; he'd stopped being her lawyer several sentences ago and was now back in parent mode. 'Why don't you move back up here, with us? It must be so lonely in that flat and—'

'I'm fine, Dad. Really.' It didn't feel as much of a lie anymore. The air in her flat smelt sweet, inviting. There were flowers in the kitchen, red roses gathered in a vase of mottled black glass. They'd arrived two mornings ago with a note from Lucas –

I'd say hang in there, but I know you already will be, because you're tough. L xxx

They weren't reuniting or anything like that. He wasn't what bound her to the city. A tentative friendship had developed between them since the incident at the cabin and Allie was grateful for it. In a week Lucas would leave London for Los Angeles and she only wished him well, felt no desire for him to stay.

The truth was that she could never return home, not now. They existed on every street, in the park, at the cinema, the shopping centre, beneath every lamppost. The ghosts of her lost friends, Allie felt that was where they'd linger now. If she went home, she'd only see them everywhere, feel the immensity of her loss all around her. It was easier to get lost in a city, to place yourself within a crowd and try to blend in.

But then she'd see a flash of red hair and feel on the brink of coming undone.

'Allie, are you okay? Has your mother called?' Her father's voice became rapid with worry.

'Dad, I'm fine. And I appreciate the update about the investigation.'

'Allie, sweetheart, I'm—'

'I wish I could chat more but I'm going out.'

'Oh?' This silenced him. Allie could imagine her father cocking his head in surprise and scratching thoughtfully at his chin with his free hand. 'Well that's . . . that's good.'

'Uh huh. So bye, Dad. Speak soon.' She was about to hang up. 'Love you.' Lately, it was how she ended all her personal calls, too many times she'd almost uttered the same parting words to her agent. And there had been multiple calls to her of late. Allie pressed the red cancel button on her mobile and drifted through her flat, towards the window, pressing a palm against the glass and looking out at the umbrellas which flooded the street below as people hurried through the rain.

She wasn't going out. That had been a lie, but one she felt was necessary. Better her father think she was out enjoying herself than spending another night home alone. But being alone was a good thing. As Allie had told her agent that very afternoon:

'I know what book I'm going to write next.'

Epilogue

'The mountain.' The reporter didn't bother to hide the irritation in her voice. Not that Stephanie cared. 'What do you think happened up on the mountain?'

Outside the supermarket, people were stopping to gawk at the news cameras and the smartly dressed reporter. They leaned over their trollies, all thoughts of shopping briefly abandoned.

Stephanie smiled. She was the star of her very own show. This must have been how it felt for them every day. For the Fabulous Five. Wherever they went heads turned, everyone desperate to catch a glimpse of them.

'Early reports indicate a sole survivor,' the reporter carried on. Her voice was tight and flat. There was no compassion, no sparkle in her eyes. To her, the five were just names on a list. A news story. A byline in tomorrow's paper. The reporter couldn't know. She hadn't seen them, hadn't lived alongside them as Stephanie had.

'I heard she'll write a book,' Stephanie repeated the shred of gossip which had been passed along the line at the post office that morning. It had been worth returning the dress which made her calves look overly chunky just to hear what everyone was saying.

'A book?' Only the reporter's lips moved. The rest of her face remained eerily still, as though she were moulded from plastic not skin.

'Allie.' It felt good to say her name. To remember the bright smile she reserved for those she considered kind. A smile which she had flashed in Stephanie's direction once or twice. 'People are saying that she's going to write a book about what happened.'

'Yes.' The reporter gave a serious nod. 'I've heard that too. What do you think the book will be about?'

'What happened of course. Up on the mountain.' And Stephanie would be first in line to buy a copy come publication day. Hardback edition, naturally. She'd get it signed too. Would a flicker of recognition dance across Allie's pretty face when she looked up and saw Stephanie standing there all plump cheeks and smiles? It hadn't when Stephanie got her copy of *Wilted Rose* signed but it mattered not. It had been manic in Waterstones that day, Allie had ignored her for fear of showing favouritism. Allie was smart like that, always thinking ahead.

'But will it be about what *really* happened?' The reporter leaned in, bringing her cloud of perfume with her.

'Yes.' Stephanie felt her face going up in flames. She didn't like the way the reporter laced her questions with doubt. The police had their evidence and Allie had the truth. The two would of course add up. How could anyone suspect otherwise? 'Allie's book will be the truth. It will be about what really happened up there.'

'Well then.' The reporter was pulling back from her, twisting so that she was looking directly into the camera. 'I guess come publication day we'd all better go out and buy it if we want to learn what really happened on that mountain.' There was a hint of mockery in her voice but Stephanie didn't care. No one was going to tarnish her Fabulous Five. Her golden girls. And with the release of a new book about them, she knew that they were going to live on forever, just as they should.

Eighteen Months Later

Allie leaned back in her leather chair. The glow from the projection behind her illuminated her feet, painting her brand-new moccasins, which were still too tight around her heel, a deep shade of red. The rich crimson was bleeding out from the image of her new book cover which was not only broadcast against the bare brickwork of the wall but adorned around the room on flyers and standees. It was release day. A day Allie had spent the previous year working towards, forcing herself to relive some of the worst moments of her life and for what – a book?

She could almost hear Diana seething in her ear that it was all a waste of time, a pointless charade. But this was Allie's truth to tell and she intended to do just that.

Pulling in a breath, Allie looked out at the eager faces before her. She could smell the flowers from the hotel lobby. Roses. Red. Their velvety petals looked to have been dipped in blood. Not for the first time, Allie wasn't completely convinced by the cover image her publisher had eventually settled on – a single rose resting atop several droplets of blood – fearing it didn't reflect the true meaning of her latest book. It was both sinister and beautiful.

'How much of what is within the book is true?'

A man in dark jeans with curly hair in the front row had his hand raised. The question-and-answer portion of the evening had commenced. Allie let her eyes fall closed for a moment as she drew on her agent's advice:

'You don't have to answer anything you're not comfortable with, but people will want something.'

'They'll want the truth,' Allie had challenged.

'And you gave them that.' Her agent tapped the hardback cover of the new tome. 'Right?'

'Well . . .' Allie clasped her hands in her lap, crossed her legs at the base of her chair and kept her spine as straight as she could, just as she'd been taught. She wanted to appear professional. Respectable. This was her book launch after all. She looked the reporter square in the eyes. They were dark and shrewd. Like Gail's. She felt her resolve start to crumble so she clenched her hands together even tighter.

'Emily has always refused to comment,' he continued, his words soaked in the earnest endeavour for the truth. 'She will neither confirm nor deny the contents of your book.'

'It is Emily's prerogative not to comment. I know she doesn't welcome all the media attention and just wants to spend time with her twins.'

'But how much of the book is true?' the curly-haired man persisted. Around him other people were raising their hands while staring at her with wide, curious eyes. It was all anyone wanted to know. How much of it all was true. The man briefly released Allie from his gaze to check his notebook. 'That day on the bridge, is that where it all started?'

Allie cleared her throat. It was so easy to journey back there, back to the bridge, with the sun on her back and the smell of melted tarmac in her lungs.

'The truth?' she asked and the man nodded eagerly. 'That day on the bridge. That was where it all ended.'

Bernard Morris

Since its release just over two years ago, the popular novel, *WE ARE ALL LIARS* has been shrouded in controversy. Almost as soon as the book appeared in stores, social media was rife with the speculation that this novel was more than just a work of fiction, that it was in fact based on real events and real people.

Today a Crown Court judge has thrown out the case brought against author Allie Ontario. Four of her school friends accused Miss Ontario of libel – stating that while the foundations of her story were based in truth, her characterisations of them were false and defamatory.

'The book explored issues within our past which were both private and painful,' stated Gail Denton. 'We felt as though we were left with no other recourse than to bring a libel case against Allie for how she has used our shared history for personal gain and with the intention of causing additional damage to our lives.'

'More than our pride has been dented,' added Emily Ashburn. 'The very real revelations in Allie's book have had very real implications in our lives.'

Part of the libel case dealt with how Mrs Ashburn was now going through divorce proceedings, which she claimed were directly caused by the contents of Miss Ontario's novel.

However, Judge George Horton felt that there was no intent to cause harm since *We're All Liars* has always been represented as a work of fiction.

Miss Ontario was not present at the hearing, but she did release a statement for the press in which she stressed that her book was fictional and also her intention to reach out to those who brought the initial suit against her.

'*WE ARE ALL LIARS* is just a story; if some individuals feel that they have been misrepresented then that is unfortunate, but not deliberate. I'd like to see my friends again in the future to convey this sentiment to them in person.'

In light of these latest developments, the already popular novel is set to enjoy a flurry of media attention and additional sales. Miss Ontario wasn't available for further comment at the time of going to press.

Allie,

I don't care if this letter finds you well, I just care that this letter finds you.

Your first book annoyed us all, for sure. But we believed you when you said it was what you needed to do in order to move on, to heal. Then comes your second book and this time around you destroyed us, some of us quite literally. And this time you didn't even bother to change the names of everyone involved. I guess you wanted to avoid any ambiguity, make it clear what you truly thought of us all.

If I was to ever see you again, I'd tell you to your face how hurt and angry I am. But I don't see you. Ever. You've become a ghost ever since you declined the invitation to Gail's thirty-fifth birthday weekend. You just disappeared from our lives and as we sat and wondered why you had gone, you were busy writing this book, hammering the final nail in the coffin of our friendship. And to think that you had the audacity to write about how we felt, from our perspectives. How Stacie felt over losing Ollie, how Emily felt when she gave away her baby. These are intimate, private moments, Allie. These are our lives, not something you can use and pervert the truth for your own sick gain.

Do you want me to say I'm sorry? Because I'm not. As I told you after Wilted Rose, *I always had a grip on the railing of that bridge. I'm glad you at least acknowledged some truth in this new book of yours. Your accident was on you, it always was. And maybe I was at fault for not visiting you in hospital, but, Allie, I was fifteen, I was still a child. You can't keep judging me for past mistakes.*

I saw on the news that you're using crutches now, so I assume your back is getting much worse, as you always feared it would. I won't say I'm sorry about this turn of events. I'm indifferent to your suffering.

But I hope that writing this book has at least given you some closure. Are we all as dead to you now as we are in the story? I'm a bigger person than you – I can send this letter and trample down the earth on the grave of what we once were while also stopping to place flowers. I'm not a monster, none of us are. We're good people who deserved better from someone we trusted, someone we once loved. I wish you the best of luck for your future, Allie, because if you keep clinging to the past like you do, you're going to need it.

Regards,
Diana Bishop

Acknowledgements

This book has been on quite a journey so I feel like there are a number of people I need to thank for sticking with me through it. My awesome agent, Emily Glenister, thank you for your unwavering support. And for sending team at Orion – not only do you create fantastic covers for me, you give the best editorial advice and make tough things, like structural edits, so much fun. Lucy Frederick – I know I talked about Disney too much but appreciate you listening and always being so kind. And, Rhea Kurien, this book is just the beginning for us which is so exciting. I can't wait to see where we go next.

Of all the books I have written, this is the most personal. People who know me will see the parallels between myself and Allie. And so I have to thank Dr Townson and Mr Cheetham for putting me back together all those years ago when I was so utterly broken.

My friends – unlike the Fierce Five our struggles have only brought us all closer during the years. Thank you for always being there. For picking me up when I fell down and for showing me what true friendship looks like.

Mum and Dad – thank you for always encouraging me to dream. Long ago I told you I wanted to become a writer and you have only ever supported me.

Sam – sometimes thank you isn't enough. You know what you do. You keep me together.

Rollo – still my favourite writing buddy. You're older now, smellier, but just as loyal and lovable.

And my little Rose. Each night after bath time I disappear into these other worlds, my books. But coming back to you, being by your side, is always the best part of my day.

Finally, last but most certainly not least – all the readers. I cannot tell you how amazing it is to be tagged in a review online, or see an awesome picture of my book on Instagram. To know that someone has read and enjoyed my book is simply the most wonderful feeling. Thank you for taking the time to read it. I hope to keep entertaining you for a long time to come.

Carys

xoxo